INVERSIONS

IAIN M. BANKS

INVERSIONS

POCKET BOOKS

New York London Toronto Sydney Singapore

POCKET BOOKS, a division of Simon & Schuster Inc.
1230 Avenue of the Americas, New York, NY 10020

Copyright © 1998 by Iain M. Banks

First published in Great Britain in 1998 by Orbit

Library of Congress Cataloging-in-Publication Data

Banks, Iain.
  Inversions / Iain M. Banks.
    p. cm.
  ISBN 1-4165-8378-5 ISBN 978-1-4165-8378-3
  I. Title.

PR6052.A485 I58 2000
823'.914—dc21   99-051901

First Pocket Books hardcover printing February 2000

10 9 8 7 6 5 4 3 2 1

POCKET and colophon are registered trademarks of Simon & Schuster Inc.

Designed by Jaime Putorti

Printed in the U.S.A.

BP/✄

FOR MICHELLE

PROLOGUE

The only sin is selfishness. So said the good Doctor. When she first expressed this opinion I was young enough initially to be puzzled and then to be impressed at what I took to be her profundity.

It was only later, in my middle-age, when she was long gone from us, that I began to suspect that the opposite is just as true. Arguably there is a sense in which selfishness is the only true virtue, and therefore that—as opposites are given to cancelling each other out—selfishness is finally neutral, indeed valueless, outside a supporting moral context. In later years still—my maturity, if you will, or my old age, if you wish—I have with some reluctance again come to respect the Doctor's point of view, and to agree with her, tentatively at least, that selfishness is the root of most evil, if not all.

Of course I always knew what she meant. That it is when we put our own interests before those of others that we are most likely to do wrong, and that there is a commonality of guilt whether the crime is that of a child stealing coins from his mother's purse or an Emperor ordering genocide. With either act, and all those in between, we say: Our gratification matters more to us than whatever distress or anguish may be caused to you and yours by our actions. In other words, that our desire outranks your suffering.

My middle-years objection was that only by acting on our desires, by attempting to bring about what pleases us because it feels agreeable, are we able to create wealth, comfort, happiness and what the good Doctor would have termed in that vague, generalising way of hers "progress."

Eventually, though, I came to admit to myself that, while my objection might be true, it is insufficiently all-embracing to cancel out the Doctor's assertion entirely, and that while it may sometimes be a virtue, selfishness by its nature is more often a sin, or a direct cause of sin.

We never like to think of ourselves as being wrong, just misunderstood. We never like to think that we are sinning, merely that we are making hard decisions, and acting upon them. Providence is the name of the mystical, divinely inhuman Court before which we wish our actions to be judged, and which we hope will agree with us in our estimation both of our own worth and the culpability or otherwise of our behaviour.

I suspect the good Doctor (you see, I judge her too in naming her so) did not believe in Providence. I was never entirely sure what she did believe in, though I was always quite convinced that she believed in something. Perhaps, despite all she said about selfishness, she believed in herself and nothing else. Perhaps she believed in this Progress that she talked about, or perhaps in some strange way, as a foreigner, she believed in us, in the people she lived with and cared for, in a way that we did not believe in ourselves.

Did she leave us better off or not? I think, undeniably, better. Did she do this through selfishness or selflessness? I believe that in the end it does not matter in the least, except as it might have affected her own peace of mind. That was another thing she taught me. That you are what you do. To Providence—or Progress or the Future or before any other sort of judgment apart from our own conscience—what we have done, not what we have thought, is the result we are judged by.

So, the following is the collected chronicle of our deeds. One part of my tale is presented as something I can vouch for, for I was there. As to the other part, I cannot confirm its veracity. I stumbled across its original version by sheer chance, long after the events described in it had taken place, and while I believe it forms an interesting counterpoint to the story in which I was involved, I present it more as an artistic flourish than as a judgment born of intense study and reflection. Nevertheless, I believe the two tales belong together, and carry more weight united than they could separately. It was, I think there is no doubt, a crucial time. Geographically the crux was divided, but—after all—much was, then. Division was the only order.

I have tried in what I have written here not to judge, yet I confess that I hope the Reader—a sort of partial Providence, perhaps—will do just that, and not think badly of us. I freely admit that a specific of my motive (especially in amending and adding to my earlier self's chronicle, as well as in refining the language and grammar of my co-teller) is to try to make sure that the Reader will not think ill of *me*, and of course that is a selfish desire. Yet still I would hope that such selfishness might lead to good, for the simple reason that otherwise this chronicle might not exist.

Again, the Reader must decide whether that would have been the more fortunate outcome, or not.

Enough. A young and rather earnest man wishes to address us:

1
THE DOCTOR

Master, it was in the evening of the third day of the southern planting season that the questioner's assistant came for the Doctor to take her to the hidden chamber, where the chief torturer awaited.

I was sitting in the living room of the Doctor's apartments using a pestle and mortar to grind some ingredients for one of the Doctor's potions. Concentrating on this, it took me a moment or two fully to collect my wits when I heard the loud and aggressive knocking at the door, and I upset a small censer on my way to the door. This was the cause both of the delay in opening the door and any curses which Unoure, the questioner's assistant, may have heard. These swear-words were not directed at him, neither was I asleep or even remotely groggy, as I trust my good Master will believe, no matter what the fellow Unoure—a shifty and unreliable person, by all accounts—may say.

The Doctor was in her study, as was usual at that time in the evening. I entered the Doctor's workshop, where she keeps the two great cabinets containing the powders, creams, ointments, draughts and various instruments that are the stock of her trade as well as the pair of tables which support a variety of burners, stoves, retorts and flasks. Occasionally she treats patients in here too, when it becomes her surgery. While the unpleasant-smelling Unoure waited in the living room, wiping his nose on his already filthy sleeve and peering round with the look of one choosing what to steal, I went through the workshop and tapped at the door to the study which also serves as her bedroom.

"Oelph?" the Doctor asked.

"Yes, mistress."

"Come in."

I heard the quiet thud of a heavy book being closed, and smiled to myself.

The Doctor's study was dark and smelled of the sweet istra flower whose leaves she habitually burned in roof-hung censers. I felt my way through the gloom. Of course I know the arrangement of the Doctor's study intimately—better than she might imagine, thanks to the inspired foresight and judicious cunning of my Master—but the Doctor is prone to leaving chairs, stools and shelf-steps lying where one might walk, and accordingly I had to feel my way across the room to where a small candle flame indicated her presence, sitting at her desk in front of a heavily curtained window. She sat upright in her chair, stretching her back and rubbing her eyes. The hand-thick, fore-arm-square bulk of her journal lay on the desk in front of her. The great book was closed and locked, but even in that cave-darkness I noticed that the little chain on the hasp was swinging to and fro. A pen stood in the ink well, whose cap was open. The Doctor yawned and adjusted the fine chain round her neck which holds the key for the journal.

My Master knows from my many previous reports that I believe the Doctor may be writing an account of her experiences here in Haspide to the people of her homeland in Drezen.

The Doctor obviously wishes to keep her writings secret. However, sometimes she forgets that I am in the room, usually when she has set me the task of tracking down some reference in one of the books in her extravagantly endowed library and I have been silently doing so for some time. From the little that I have been able to glimpse of her writings on such occasions I have determined that when she writes in her journal she does not always use Haspidian or Imperial—though there are passages in both—but sometimes uses an alphabet I have never seen before.

I believe my Master has thought of taking steps to check with other natives of Drezen regarding whether, in such instances, the Doctor writes in Drezeni or not, and to this end I am attempting to commit to memory as much as I can of the Doctor's relevant journal writings whenever I can. On this occasion, however, I was unable to gain a view of the pages she had surely been working on.

It is still my wish to be able to serve my Master better in this regard and I would respectfully again submit that the temporary removal of her journal would allow a skilled locksmith to open the journal without damaging it and a better copy of her secret writings to be taken, so allowing the matter to be settled. This could easily be done when the Doctor is elsewhere in the palace or better still elsewhere in the city, or even when she is taking one of her frequent baths, which tend to be prolonged (it was during one of her baths that I procured for my Master one of the Doctor's scalpels from her medicine bag, which has now been delivered. I would add that I was careful to do this immediately after a visit to the Poor Hospital, so that someone there would be suspected). However, I do of course bow to my Master's superior judgment in this regard.

The Doctor frowned at me. "You're shaking," she said. And indeed I was, for the sudden appearance of the torturer's assistant had been undeniably unsettling. The Doctor glanced past me towards the door to the surgery, which I had left open so that Unoure might be able to hear our voices and so perhaps be dissuaded from any mischief he might be contemplating. "Who's that?" she asked.

"Who's what, mistress?" I asked, watching her close the cap of the ink well.

"I heard somebody cough."

"Oh, that is Unoure, the questioner's assistant, mistress. He's come to fetch you."

"To go where?"

"To the hidden chamber. Master Nolieti has sent for you."

She looked at me without speaking for a moment. "The chief torturer," she said evenly, and nodded. "Am I in trouble, Oelph?" she asked, laying one arm across the thick hide cover of her journal, as if looking to provide, or gain, protection.

"Oh no," I told her. "You're to bring your bag. And medicines." I glanced round at the door to the surgery, edged with light from the living room. A cough came from that direction, a cough that sounded like the sort of cough one makes when one wants to remind somebody that one is waiting impatiently. "I think it's urgent," I whispered.

"Hmm. Do you think chief torturer Nolieti has a cold?" the Doctor asked, rising from her chair and pulling on her long jacket, which had been hanging on the back of the seat.

I helped her on with her black jacket. "No, mistress, I think there is probably somebody being put to the question who is, umm, unwell."

"I see," she said, stamping her feet into her boots and then straightening. I was struck again by the Doctor's physical presence, as I often am. She is tall for a woman, though not exceptionally so, and while for a female she is broad at the shoulder I have seen fish-wives and net-women who look more powerful. No, what seems most singular about her, I think, is her carriage, the way she comports herself.

I have been afforded tantalising half-glimpses of her—after one of her many baths—in a thin shift with the light behind her, stepping in a coil of powdered, scented air from one room to another, her arms raised to secure a towel about her long, damp red hair, and I have watched her during grand court occasions when she has worn a formal gown and danced as lightly and delicately—and with as demure an expression—as any expensively tutored season-maiden, and I freely confess that I have found myself drawn to her in a physical sense just as any man (youthful or not) might be to a woman of such healthy and generous good looks. Yet at the same time there is something about her deportment which I—and I suspect most other males—find off-

putting, and even slightly threatening. A certain immodest forthright-
ness in her bearing is the cause of this, perhaps, plus the suspicion that
while she pays flawless lip service to the facts of life which dictate the
accepted and patent preeminence of the male, she does so with a sort of
unwarranted humour, producing in us males the unsettlingly contrary
feeling that she is indulging us.

The Doctor leaned over the desk and opened the curtains and the
shutters to the mid-eve Seigen glow. In the faint wash of light from the
windows I noticed the small plate of biscuits and cheese at the edge of
the Doctor's desk, on the far side of the journal. Her old, battered dagger lay also on the plate, its dull edges smeared with grease.

She picked up the knife, licked its blade and then, after smacking
her lips as she gave it a final wipe on her kerchief, slipped the dagger
into the top of her right boot. "Come on," she said, "mustn't keep the
chief torturer waiting."

"Is this really necessary?" the Doctor asked, looking at the blindfold
held in questioner's assistant Unoure's grubby hands. He wore a long
butcher's apron of blood-stained hide over his filthy shirt and loose,
greasy-looking trousers. The black blindfold had been produced from a
long pocket in the leather apron.

Unoure grinned, displaying a miscellany of diseased, discoloured
teeth and dark gaps where teeth ought to have been. The Doctor
winced. Her own teeth are so even that the first time I saw them I naturally assumed they were a particularly fine false set.

"Rules," Unoure said, looking at the Doctor's chest. She drew her
long jacket closed across her shirt. "You're a foreigner," he told her.

The Doctor sighed, glancing at me.

"A foreigner," I told Unoure forcibly, "who holds the King's life in
her hands almost every day."

"Doesn't matter," the fellow said, shrugging. He sniffed and went to
wipe his nose with the blindfold, then looked at the expression on the
Doctor's face and changed his mind, using his sleeve again instead.
"That's the orders. Got to hurry," he said, glancing at the doors.

We were at the entrance to the palace's lower levels. The corridor
behind us led off from the little-used passageway beyond the west-wing

kitchens and the wine cellars. It was quite dark. A narrow circular light-well overhead cast a dusty sheen of slatey light over us and the tall, rusted metal doors, while a couple of candles burned dimly further down the corridor.

"Very well," the Doctor said. She leaned over a little and made a show of inspecting the blindfold and Unoure's hands. "But I'm not wearing that, and you're not tying it." She turned to me and pulled a fresh kerchief from a pocket in her coat. "Here," she said.

"But—" Unoure said, then jumped as a bell clanged somewhere beyond the flaking brown doors. He turned away, stuffing the blindfold into his apron, cursing.

I tied the scented kerchief across the Doctor's eyes while Unoure unlocked the doors. I carried the Doctor's bag with one hand and with my other hand led her into the corridor beyond the doors and down the many twisting steps and further doors and passageways to the hidden chamber where Master Nolieti waited. Halfway there, the bell rang again from somewhere ahead of us, and I felt the Doctor jump, and her hand become damp. I confess my own nerves were not entirely settled.

We entered the hidden chamber from a low doorway we each had to stoop under (I placed my hand on the Doctor's head to lower her head. Her hair felt sleek and smooth). The place smelled of something sharp and noxious, and of burned flesh. My breathing seemed to be quite beyond my control, the odours forcing their way into my nostrils and down into my lungs.

The tall, wide space was lit by a motley collection of ancient oil lamps which threw a sickly blue-green glow over a variety of vats, tubs, tables and other instruments and containers—some in human shape—none of which I cared to inspect too closely, though all of them attracted my wide-open eyes like suns attract flowers. Additional light came from a tall brazier positioned underneath a hanging cylindrical chimney. The brazier stood by a chair made from hoops of iron which entirely enclosed a pale, thin and naked man, who appeared to be unconscious. The entire frame of this chair had been swivelled over on an outer cradle so that the man appeared caught in the act of performing a forward somersault, resting on his knees in mid-air, his back parallel with the grid of a broad light-well grille above.

The chief torturer Nolieti stood between this apparatus and a broad workbench covered with various metal bowls, jars and bottles and a collection of instruments that might have originated in the workplaces of a mason, a carpenter, a butcher and a surgeon. Nolieti was shaking his broad, scarred grey head. His rough and sinewy hands were on his hips and his glare was fastened on the withered form of the encaged man. Below the metal contraption enclosing the unfortunate fellow stood a broad square tray of stone with a drain hole at one corner. Dark fluid like blood had splattered there. Long white shapes in the darkness might have been teeth.

Nolieti turned round when he heard us approach. "About fucking time," he spat, fixing his stare on first me, then the Doctor and then Unoure (who, I noticed, as the Doctor stuffed her kerchief back into a pocket in her jacket, was making a show of folding the black blindfold he had been told to use on her).

"My fault," the Doctor said in a matter-of-fact manner, stepping past Nolieti. She bent down at the man's rear. She grimaced, nose wrinkling, then came to the side of the apparatus and with one hand on the iron hoops of the frame-chair brought it squeaking and complaining round until the man was in a more conventional sitting position. The fellow looked in a terrible state. His face was grey, his skin was burned in places, and his mouth and jaw had collapsed. Little rivulets of blood had dried under each of his ears. The Doctor put her hand through the iron hoops and tried to open one of the man's eyes. He made a terrible, low groaning sound. There was a sort of sucking, tearing noise and the man gave a plaintive moan like a kind of distant scream before settling into a ragged, rhythmic, bubbling noise that might have been breathing. The Doctor bent forward to peer into the man's face and I heard her give a small gasp.

Nolieti snorted. "Looking for these?" he asked the Doctor, and flourished a small bowl at her.

The Doctor barely glanced at the bowl, but smiled thinly at the torturer. She rotated the iron chair to its previous position and went back to look at the caged man's rear. She pulled away some blood-soaked rags and gave another grimace. I thanked the gods that he was pointing away from me and prayed that whatever the Doctor might have to do would not require my assistance.

"What seems to be the problem?" the Doctor asked Nolieti, who seemed momentarily nonplussed.

"Well," the chief torturer said after a pause. "He won't stop bleeding out his arse, will he?"

The Doctor nodded. "You must have let your pokers get too cold," she said casually, squatting and opening her bag and laying it by the side of the stone drain-tray.

Nolieti went to the Doctor's side and bent down over her. "How it happened isn't any of your fucking business, woman," he said into her ear. "Your business is to get this fucker well enough to be questioned so he can tell us what the King needs to know."

"*Does* the King know?" the Doctor asked, looking up, an expression of innocent interest on her face. "Did he order this? Does he even know of the existence of this unfortunate? Or was it guard commander Adlain who thought the Kingdom would fall unless this poor devil suffered?"

Nolieti stood up. "None of that is your business," he said sullenly. "Just do your job and get out." He bent down again and stuck his mouth by her ear. "And never you mind the King or the guard commander. *I'm* king down here, and I say you'd best attend to your own business and leave me to mine."

"But it is my business," the Doctor said evenly, ignoring the threatening bulk of the man poised over her. "If I know what was done to him, and how it was done, I might be better able to treat him."

"Oh, I could *show* you, Doctor," the chief torturer said, looking up at his assistant and winking. "And we have special treats we save just for the ladies, don't we, Unoure?"

"Well, we haven't time to flirt," the Doctor said with a steely smile. "Just tell me what you did to this poor wretch."

Nolieti's eyes narrowed. He stood up and withdrew a poker from the brazier in a cloud of sparks. Its yellow-glowing tip was broad, like the blade of a small flat spade. "Latterly, we did him with this," Nolieti said with a smile, his face lit by the soft yellow-orange glow.

The Doctor looked at the poker, then at the torturer. She squatted and touched something at the encaged man's rear.

"Was he bleeding badly?" she asked.

"Like a man pissing," the chief torturer said, winking at his assistant again. Unoure quickly nodded and laughed.

"Better leave this in, then," the Doctor muttered. She rose. "I'm sure it's good you enjoy your job so, chief torturer," she said. "However, I think you've killed this one."

"You're the doctor, you heal him!" Nolieti said, stepping back towards her, brandishing the orange-red poker. I do not think he intended to threaten the Doctor, but I saw her right hand begin to drop towards the boot where her old dagger was sheathed.

She looked up at the torturer, past the glowing metal rod. "I'll give him something that might revive him, but he may well have given you all he ever will. Don't blame me if he dies."

"Oh, but I will," Nolieti said quietly, thrusting the poker back into the brazier. Cinders splashed to the flag stones. "You make sure he lives, woman. You make sure he's fit to talk or the King'll hear you couldn't do your job."

"The King will hear anyway, no doubt," the Doctor said, smiling at me. I smiled nervously back. "And guard commander Adlain, too," she added, "perhaps from me." She swung the man in the cage-chair back upright and opened a vial in her bag, wiped a wooden spatula round the inside of the vial and then, opening the bloody mess that was the man's mouth, applied some of the ointment to his gums. He moaned again.

The Doctor stood watching him for a moment, then stepped to the brazier and put the spatula into it. The wood flamed and spluttered. She looked at her hands, then at Nolieti. "Do you have any water down here? I mean clean water."

The chief torturer nodded at Unoure, who disappeared into the shadows for a while before bringing a bowl which the Doctor washed her hands in. She was wiping them clean on the kerchief which had been her blindfold when the man in the chair cage gave a terrible screech of agony, shook violently for a few moments, then stiffened suddenly and finally went limp. The Doctor stepped towards him and went to put her hand to his neck but she was knocked aside by Nolieti, who gave an angry, anguished shout of his own and reached through the iron hoops to place his finger on the pulse-point on the neck which the Doctor has taught me is the best place to test the beat of a man's vitality.

The chief torturer stood there, quivering, while his assistant gazed on with an expression of apprehension and terror. The Doctor's look was one of grimly contemptuous amusement. Then Nolieti spun round and stabbed a finger at her. "You!" he hissed at her. "You killed him. You didn't want him to live!"

The Doctor looked unconcerned, and continued drying her hands (though it seemed to me that they were both already dry, and shaking). "I am sworn to save life, chief torturer, not to take it," she said reasonably. "I leave that to others."

"What was in that stuff?" the chief torturer said, quickly squatting to wrench open the Doctor's bag. He pulled out the open vial she had taken the ointment from and brandished it in her face. "This. What is it?"

"A stimulant," she said, and dipped a finger into the vial, displaying a small fold of the soft brown gel on her finger tip so that it glinted in the light of the brazier. "Would you like to try it?" She moved the finger towards Nolieti's mouth.

The chief torturer grabbed her hand in one of his and forced the finger back, towards her own lips. "No. You do it. Do what you did to him."

The Doctor shook her hand free of Nolieti's and calmly put her finger to her mouth, spreading the brown paste along her top gum. "The taste is bitter-sweet," she said in the same tone she uses when she is teaching me. "The effects last between two and three bells and usually have no side effects, though in a body seriously weakened and in shock, fits are likely and death is a remote possibility." She licked her finger. "Children in particular suffer severe side effects with almost no restorative function and it is never recommended for them. The gel is made from the berries of a biennial plant which grows on isolated peninsulae on islands in the very north of Drezen. It is quite precious, and more usually applied in a solution, in which form, too, it is most stable and long-lasting. I have used it to treat the King on occasion and he regards it as one of my more efficacious prescriptions. There is not much left now and I would have preferred not to waste it on either those who are going to die anyway, or on myself, but you did insist. I am sure the King will not mind." (I have to report, Master, that as far as I am aware, the Doctor has never used this particular gel—of which she has several jars—on the King, and I am not sure she had ever used it to treat any patient.) The Doctor closed her mouth and I could see her wipe her tongue round her top gum. Then she smiled. "Are you sure you won't try some?"

Nolieti said nothing for a moment, his broad, dark face moving as though he was chewing on his tongue.

"Get this Drezen witch out of here," he said eventually to Unoure, and then turned away to stamp on the brazier's foot-bellows. The brazier hissed and glowed yellow, showering sparks up into its sooty chimney. Nolieti glanced at the dead man in the cage-chair. "Then take this bastard to the acid bath," he barked.

We were at the door when the chief torturer, still working the foot-bellows with a regular, thrusting stroke, called out, "Doctor?"

She turned to look at him as Unoure opened the door and fished the black blindfold from his apron. "Yes, chief torturer?" she said.

He looked round at us, smiling as he continued to fire the brazier. "You'll be here again, Drezen woman," he said softly to her. His eyes glittered in the yellow brazier light. "And next time you won't be able to walk out."

The Doctor held his gaze for a good while, until she looked down and shrugged. "Or you will appear in my surgery," she told him, looking up. "And may be assured of my best attention."

The chief torturer turned away and spat into the brazier, his foot stamping on the bellows and breathing life into that instrument of death as we were ushered out of the low door by the assistant Unoure.

Two hundred heartbeats later we were met at the tall iron doors which led into the rest of the palace by a footman of the royal chamber.

"It's my back again, Vosill," the King said, turning onto his front on the wide, canopied bed while the Doctor rolled up first her own sleeves and then the King's tunic top and shift. And we were in the principal bed-chamber of King Quience's private apartments, deep within the inner-most quadrangle of Efernze, the winter palace of Haspide, capital of Haspidus!

This has become such a regular haunt of mine, indeed such a regular place of work, that I confess I am inclined to forget that I am honoured indeed to be present. When I stop to consider the matter though, I think, Great Gods, I—an orphan of a disgraced family—am in the presence of our beloved King! And regularly, and intimately!

At such moments, Master, I thank you in my soul with all the vigour that is mine to command, for I know that it was only your kindness, wisdom and compassion that put me in such an exalted position and entrusted me with such an important mission. Be assured that I shall continue to try with all my might to be worthy of that trust, and fulfil that task.

Wiester, the King's chamberlain, had let us into the apartments. "Will that be all, sir?" he asked, bending and hunching over as well as his ample frame would allow.

"Yes. That's all for now. Go."

The Doctor sat on the side of the King's bed and kneaded his shoulders and back with her strong, capable fingers. She had me hold a small jar of rich-smelling unguent which she dipped her fingers into every now and again, spreading the ointment across the King's broad, hairy back and working it into his pale gold skin with her fingers and palms.

As I sat there, with the Doctor's medicine bag open at my side, I noticed that the jar of brown gel which she had used to treat the wretch in the hidden chamber was still lying opened on one of the bag's ingeniously fashioned internal shelves. I went to stick my own finger into the jar. The Doctor saw what I was doing and quickly took hold of my hand and pulled it away from the jar and said quietly, "I wouldn't, Oelph, if I were you. Just put the top back on carefully."

"What's that, Vosill?" the King asked.

"Nothing, sir," the Doctor said, replacing her hands on the King's back and leaning forward on to him.

"Ouch," the King said.

"Mostly muscular tension," the Doctor said softly, flicking her head so that her hair, which had partly fallen across her face, was sent spilling back over her shoulder.

"My father never had to suffer so," the King said morosely into his gold-threaded pillow, his voice made deeper by the thickness and weight of fabric and feathers.

The Doctor smiled quickly at me. "What, sir," she said. "You mean he never had to suffer my clumsy ministrations?"

"No," the King said, groaning. "You know what I mean, Vosill. This back. He never had to suffer this back. Or my leg cramps, or my headaches, or my constipation, or any of these aches and pains." He was silent a moment as the Doctor pushed and pressed at his skin. "Father never had to suffer anything. He never—"

"—had a day's illness in his life," the Doctor said, in chorus with the King.

The King laughed. The Doctor smiled at me again. I held the jar of ointment, inexpressibly happy for just that moment, until the King sighed and said, "Ah, such sweet torture, Vosill."

Whereupon the Doctor paused in her rocking, kneading motion, and a look of bitterness, even contempt, passed briefly over her face.

2
THE BODYGUARD

This is the story of the man known as DeWar, who was principal bodyguard to General UrLeyn, Prime Protector of the Tassasen Protectorate, for the years 1218 to 1221, Imperial. Most of my tale takes place in the palace of Vorifyr, in Crough, the ancient capital city of Tassasen, during that fateful year of 1221.

I have chosen to tell the story after the fashion of the Jeritic fabulists, that is in the form of a Closed Chronicle, in which—if one is inclined to believe such information of consequence—one has to guess the identity of the person telling the tale. My motive in doing so is to present the reader with a chance to choose whether to believe or disbelieve what I have to say about the events of that time—the broad facts

of which are of course well known, even notorious, throughout the
civilised world—purely on the evidence of whether the story "rings
true" for them or not, and without the prejudice which might result
from knowing the identity of the narrator closing the mind of the
reader to the truth I wish to present.

And it is time the truth was finally told. I have read, I think, all
the various accounts of what happened in Tassasen during that
momentous time, and the most significant difference between those
reports seems to be the degree to which they depart most outra-
geously from what actually happened. There was one travesty of
a version in particular which determined me to tell the true story
of the time. It took the form of a play and claimed to tell my own
tale, yet its ending could scarcely have been wider of the mark. The
reader need only accept that I am who I am for its nonsensicality to
be obvious.

I say this is DeWar's story, and yet I freely admit that it is not the
whole of his story. It is only part, and arguably only a small part, measured solely in years. There was a part before, too, but history allows
only the haziest notion of what that earlier past was like.

So, this is the truth as I experienced it, or as it was told to me by
those I trusted.

Truth, I have learned, differs for everybody. Just as no two people
ever see a rainbow in exactly the same place—and yet both most certainly see it, while the person seemingly standing right underneath it
does not see it at all—so truth is a question of where one stands, and
the direction one is looking in at the time.

Of course, the reader may choose to differ from me in this belief,
and is welcome to do so.

"DeWar? Is that you?" The Prime Protector, First General and Grand
Aedile of the Protectorate of Tassasen, General UrLeyn, shaded his eyes
from the glare of a fan-shaped plaster-and-gem window above the
hall's polished jet floor. It was mid-day, with Xamis and Seigen both
shining brightly in a clear sky outside.

"Sir," DeWar said, stepping from the shadows at the edge of the
room, where the maps were kept in a great wooden lattice. He bowed to

the Protector and set a map on the table in front of him. "I think this is the map you might need."

DeWar: a tall, muscular man in early middle-age, dark-haired, dark-skinned and dark-browed, with deep, hooded eyes and a watchful, brooding look about him that quite suited his profession, which he once described as assassinating assassins. He seemed both relaxed and yet tensed, like an animal perpetually hunkered back ready to pounce, yet perfectly capable of remaining in that coiled position for as long as it might take for its prey to come into range and let drop its guard.

He was dressed, as ever, in black. His boots, hose, tunic and short jacket were all as dark as an eclipse-night. A narrow, sheathed sword hung from his right hip, a long dagger from his left.

"You fetch maps for my generals now, DeWar?" UrLeyn asked, amused. The General of generals of Tassasen, the commoner who commanded nobles, was a relatively small man who by dint of the bustling, busy force of his character made almost everybody feel that they were no taller than he. His hair was brindled, grey and thinning but his eyes were bright. People generally called his gaze "piercing." He was dressed in the trousers and long jacket he had made the fashion amongst many of his fellow generals and large sections of the Tassaseni trading classes.

"When my general sends me away from him, sir, yes," DeWar replied. "I try to do whatever I can to help. And such actions help prevent me dwelling on the risks my lord might be exposing himself to when he has me leave his side." DeWar tossed the map on to the table, where it unrolled.

"The borders . . . Ladenscion," UrLeyn breathed, patting the soft surface of the old map, then looking up at DeWar with a mischievous expression. "My dear DeWar, the greatest danger I expose myself to on such occasions is probably a dose of something unpleasant from some lass newly brought in, or possibly a slap for suggesting something my more demure concubines find excessively rude." The General grinned, hitching up the belt round his modest pot-belly. "Or a scratched back or bitten ear, if I'm lucky, eh?"

"The General puts us younger men to shame in many ways," DeWar murmured, smoothing out the parchment map. "But it is not unknown for assassins to have less respect for the privacy of a great leader's harem than, say, his chief bodyguard."

"An assassin prepared to risk the wrath of my dear concubines would almost deserve to succeed," UrLeyn said, eyes twinkling as he pulled at his short grey moustache. "Providence knows their affection is rough enough at times." He reached out and tapped the younger man's elbow with one bunched fist. "Eh?"

"Indeed, sir. Still, I think the General could—"

"Ah! The rest of the gang," UrLeyn said, clapping his hands as the double doors at the far end of the hall opened to admit a number of men—all clad similarly to the General—and a surrounding flock of aides in military uniforms, frock-coated clerks and assorted other helpers. "YetAmidous!" the Protector cried, walking quickly forward to greet the big, rough-faced man leading the group, shaking his hand and clapping his back. He greeted all of the other noble generals by name, then caught sight of his brother. "RuLeuin! Back from the Thrown Isles! Is all well?" He wrapped his arms round the taller, thicker-set man, who smiled slowly as he nodded and said, "Yes, sir." Then the Protector saw his son and bent down to lift him into his arms. "And Lattens! My favourite boy! You finished your studies!"

"Yes, Father!" the boy said. He was dressed like a little soldier, and flourished a wooden sword.

"Good! You can come and help us decide what to do about our rebellious barons in the marches!"

"Just for a while, brother," RuLeuin said. "This is a treat. His tutor needs him back on the bell."

"Ample time for Lattens to make all the difference to our plans," UrLeyn said, sitting the child on the map table.

Clerks and scribes scuttled over to the great wooden map lattice on one wall, fighting to be first. "Never mind!" the General called after them. "Here's the map!" he shouted, as his brother and fellow generals clustered round the great table. "Somebody already . . ." the General began, looking round the table for DeWar, then shaking his head and returning his attention to the map.

Behind him, hidden from the Protector by the taller men gathered about him but never more than a sword length away, his chief bodyguard stood, arms casually crossed, hands resting on the pommels of his most obvious weapons, unnoticed and almost unseen, gaze sweeping the surrounding crowd.

"Once there was a great Emperor who was much feared throughout what was then all the known world, save for the outer wastelands which nobody with any sense bothered about and where only savages lived. The Emperor had no equals and no rivals. His own realm covered the better part of the world and all the kings of all the rest of the world bowed down before him and offered him generous tribute. His power was absolute and he had come to fear nothing except death, which comes eventually for all men, even Emperors.

"He determined to try and cheat death too by building a monumental palace so great, so magnificent, so spell-bindingly sumptuous that Death itself—which was believed to come for those of royal birth in the shape of a great fiery bird visible only to the dying—would be tempted to stay in the great monument and dwell there and not return to the depths of the sky with the Emperor clutched in its talons of flame.

"Accordingly the Emperor caused a great monumental palace to be built on an island in the centre of a great circular lake on the edge of the plains and the ocean, some way from his capital city. The palace was fashioned in the shape of a mighty conical tower half a hundred storeys tall. It was filled with every imaginable luxury and treasure the empire and kingdoms could provide, all secured deep within the furthest reaches of the monument, where they would be hidden from the common thief yet visible to the fiery bird when it came for the Emperor.

"There too were placed magical statues of all the Emperor's favourites, wives and concubines, all guaranteed by his holiest holy men to come alive when the Emperor died and the great bird of fire came to take him.

"The chief architect of the palace was a man called Munnosh who was renowned throughout the world as the greatest builder there had ever been, and it was his skill and cunning that made the whole great project possible. For this reason the Emperor showered Munnosh with riches, favours and concubines. But Munnosh was ten years younger than the Emperor, and as the Emperor grew old and the great monument neared completion, he knew that Munnosh would outlive him, and might speak, or be made to speak of how and where the great cache of riches had been placed within the palace, once the Emperor had died and was living there with the great bird of fire and the magically alive statues. Munnosh might even have time to complete a still greater monument for the next King who ascended to the Imperial throne and became Emperor.

"With this in mind, the Emperor waited until the great mausoleum was all but finished and then had Munnosh lured to the very deepest level of the vast edifice, and while the architect waited in a small chamber deep underground for what he had been promised would be a great surprise, he was walled in by the Imperial guards, who closed off all that part of the lowest level.

"The Emperor had his courtiers tell Munnosh's family that the architect had been killed when a great block of stone fell on him while he was inspecting the building, and they grieved loudly and terribly.

"But the Emperor had misjudged the cunning and wariness of the architect, who had long suspected something just like this might happen. Accordingly, he had had constructed a hidden passage from the lowest cellars of the great monumental palace to the outside. When Munnosh realised he had been immured, he uncovered the hidden passage and made his way to the ground above, where he waited until the night and then stole away on one of the workers' boats, gliding across the circular lake.

"When he returned to his home his wife, who thought she was a widow, and his children, who thought they were without a father, at first thought he was a ghost, and shrank from him in fear. Eventually he persuaded them that he was alive, and that they should accompany him into exile, away from the Empire. The whole family made their escape to a distant Kingdom where the King had need of a great builder to oversee the construction of fortifications to keep out the savages of the wastelands, and where everybody either did not know who this great architect was, or pretended not to for the sake of the fortifications and the safety of the Kingdom.

"However, the Emperor heard that a great architect was at work in this distant Kingdom, and, through various rumours and reports, came to suspect that this master builder was indeed Munnosh. The Emperor, who was by now very frail and elderly and near death, ordered the secret opening-up of the great mausoleum's lower levels. This was done, and of course Munnosh was not there, and the secret passageway was discovered.

"The Emperor ordered the King to send his master builder to the Imperial capital. The King at first refused, asking for more time because the fortifications were not ready yet and the savages of the wasteland were proving more tenacious and better organised than had been anticipated, but the Emperor, still nearer to death now, insisted, and eventually the King gave in and with great reluctance sent the architect Munnosh to the capital. The architect's family treated his departure as they had the false news that he had been killed, those many years ago.

"The Emperor at this time was so close to dying that he spent almost all his time in the great death-defying palace Munnosh had constructed for him, and it was there that Munnosh was taken.

"When the Emperor saw Munnosh, and knew that it was his old chief architect, he cried out, 'Munnosh, treacherous Munnosh! Why did you desert me and your greatest creation?'

" 'Because you had me walled up within it and left to die, my Emperor,' Munnosh replied.

" 'It was done only to assure the safety of your Emperor and to preserve your own good name,' the old tyrant told Munnosh. 'You ought to have accepted what was done and let your family mourn you decently and in peace. Instead you led them into benighted exile and only ensured that now they will have to mourn you a second time.'

"When the Emperor said this, Munnosh fell to his knees and began to weep and to plead for forgiveness from the Emperor. The Emperor held out one thin, shaking hand and smiled and said, 'But that need not concern you, because I have sent my finest assassins to seek out your wife and your children and your grandchildren, to kill them all before they can learn of your disgrace and death.'

"At this Munnosh, who had concealed a mason's stone chisel beneath his robes, leapt forward and tried to strike the Emperor down, aiming the chisel straight at the old man's throat.

"Instead Munnosh was struck down, before his blow could fall, by the Emperor's chief bodyguard, who never left his master's side. The man who had once been Imperial chief architect landed dead at his Emperor's feet, head severed by a single terrible blow from the bodyguard's sword.

"But the chief bodyguard was so full of shame that Munnosh had come so close to the Emperor with a weapon, and also so appalled at the cruelty which the Emperor intended to visit on the innocent family of the architect—which was but the grain that breaks the bridge, for he had witnessed a lifetime's cruelty from the old tyrant—that he killed the Emperor and then himself, with another two swinging blows from his mighty sword, before anybody else could move to stop him.

"The Emperor got his wish then, dying within the great palatial mausoleum he had built. Whether he succeeded in cheating death or not we cannot know, but it is unlikely, as the Empire fell apart very soon after his death and the vast monument he caused to be constructed at such crippling expense to his empire was looted utterly within the year and fell quickly into disrepair, so that now it is used only as a ready source of dressed stone for the city of Haspide, which was founded a few centuries later on the same island, in what is now called Crater Lake, in the Kingdom of Haspidus."

"What a sad tale! But what happened to the family of Munnosh?" asked the lady Perrund. The lady Perrund had once been the first concubine of the Protector. She remained a prized partner of the General's household and one whom he was still known to visit on occasion.

The bodyguard DeWar shrugged. "We don't know," he told her. "The Empire fell, the Kings fought amongst themselves, the barbarians invaded from all sides, fire fell from the sky and a dark age resulted that lasted many hundreds of years. Little historical detail survived the fall of the lesser kingdoms."

"But we may hope that the assassins heard their Emperor was dead and so did not carry out their mission, may we not? Or that they were caught up in the chaos of the Empire's collapse and had to look to their own safety. Would that not be likely?"

DeWar looked into the eyes of the lady Perrund and smiled. "Perfectly possible, my lady."

"Good," she said, crossing one arm across the other and settling back to lean over the game board again. "That is what I shall choose to believe, then. Now we can restart our game. It was my move, I believe."

DeWar smiled as he watched Perrund put one clenched fist to her mouth. Her gaze, beneath long fair lashes, flicked this way and that across the game board, coming to rest on pieces for a few moments, then sweeping away again.

She wore the long, plain red day-gown of the senior ladies of the court, one of the few fashions the Protectorate had inherited from the earlier Kingdom, which the Protector and his fellow generals had overthrown in the war of succession. It was a given within the court that Perrund's seniority was founded more upon the intensity of her earlier service to the Protector UrLeyn than on her physical age, a reputation—that of most favoured concubine to a man who had not yet chosen a wife—she was still fiercely proud of.

There was another reason for her promotion to such seniority, and the mark of that was the second badge she wore, the sling—also red—that supported her withered left arm.

Perrund, anybody in the court would tell you, had given more of herself in the service of her beloved General than any other of his women, sacrificing the use of a limb to protect him from an assassin's blade and indeed very nearly losing her life altogether, for the same cut that had severed muscles and tendons and broken bone had opened an artery as well, and she had come close to bleeding to death even as UrLeyn had been hurried away from the mêlée by his guards and the assassin had been overpowered and disarmed.

The withered arm was her only blemish, even if it was a terrible one. Otherwise she was as tall and fair as any fairy-tale princess, and the younger women of the harem, who saw her naked in the baths, inspected her golden-brown skin in vain for the more obvious signs of encroaching age. Her face was broad—too broad, she thought, and so framed it carefully in her long blond hair to make it look slimmer when she did not wear a head-dress, and chose head-dresses which performed the same function when she was to be seen in public. Her nose was slim and her mouth at first plain until she smiled, which she often did.

Her pupils were gold flecked with blue and her eyes were large and open and somehow innocent. They could quickly look hurt at insults and when she was told tales of cruelty and pain, but such expressions were like summer storms—over quickly and immediately replaced by a prevailing, temperate brightness. She seemed to take an almost child-ish delight in life in general which was never far from being embodied in the sparkle of those eyes, and people who thought they knew about such things said they believed she was the only person in the court whose force of gaze could match that of the Protector himself.

"There," she said composedly, moving a piece across the board into DeWar's territory and then sitting back. Her good hand massaged the withered one, which lay in the red sling, motionless and unresponsing. DeWar thought it looked like the hand of a sickly child, it was so pale and thin and the skin so nearly translucent. He knew that she still expe-rienced pain from the disabled limb, three years after the initial injury, and that she did not always realise when her good hand stroked and kneaded the sick one, as it did now. He saw this without looking at it, his gaze held by hers as she leaned further back into the couch's cushions, which were as plump, red and numerous as berries on a winter bush.

They sat in the visiting chamber of the outer harem, where on spe-cial occasions close relatives of the concubines were sometimes allowed to visit them. DeWar, once again waiting on UrLeyn while the General spent a while with the harem's most recent young recruits, had for some time been granted the singular dispensation of being allowed to enter the visiting chamber whenever the Protector was in the harem. This meant that DeWar was a little closer to UrLeyn than the General would ideally have preferred his chief bodyguard to be dur-ing such interludes, and much further away than DeWar felt comfort-able with.

DeWar knew the sort of jokes that circulated the Court about him. It was said that his dream was to be so close to his master at all times that he could wipe the General's backside in the toilet and his prick in the harem-alcove. Another was that he secretly desired to be a woman, so that when the General wanted sex he need look no further than his faithful bodyguard, and no other bodily contact need be risked.

Whether Stike, the harem's chief eunuch, had heard that particu-

lar rumour was moot. Certainly he watched the bodyguard with what
appeared to be great and professional suspicion. The chief eunuch sat
massively in his pulpit at one end of the long chamber, which was lit
from above by three procelain light-domes. The chamber's walls were
entirely covered with thickly pendulous swathes of ornately woven
brocade, while further loops and bowls of fabric hung suspended from
the roof spaces between the domes, ruffling in the breeze from the ceiling louvres. The chief eunuch Stike was dressed in great folds of white
and his vast waist was girdled with the gold and silver key-chains of his
office. He occasionally spared a glance for the few other veiled girls who
had chosen the visiting chamber for their giggled conversations and
petulant games of card and board, but he concentrated on the only
man in the room and his game with the damaged concubine Perrund.

DeWar studied the board. "Ah-ha," he said. His Emperor piece was
threatened, or certainly would be in another move or two. Perrund
gave a dainty snort, and DeWar looked up to see his opponent's good
hand held up flat against her mouth, painted finger-nails golden
against her lips and an expression of innocence in her wide eyes.

"What?" she asked.

"You know what," he said, smiling. "You're after my Emperor."

"DeWar," she said, tutting. "You mean I'm after your Protector."

"Hmm," he said, putting his elbows on his knees and his chin on
his bunched fists. Officially the Emperor was called the Protector piece
now, after the dissolution of the old Empire and fall of the last King of
Tassasen. New sets of the game of "Monarch's Dispute" sold in
Tassasen these days came in boxes which, to those who could read,
proclaimed the game they contained to be "Leader's Dispute," and held
revised pieces: a Protector instead of an Emperor, Generals in place of
Kings, Colonels instead of Dukes, and Captains where before there had
been Barons. Many people, either fearful of the new regime or simply
wishing to show their allegiance to it, had thrown out their old sets of
the game along with their portraits of the King. It seemed that only in
the Palace of Vorifyr itself were people more relaxed.

DeWar lost himself studying the position of the pieces for a few
moments. Then he heard Perrund make another noise, and looked up
again to see her shaking her head at him, eyes glittering.

Now it was his turn to say, "What?"

"Oh, DeWar," she said. "I have heard people in the Court say you are the most cunning person they know in it, and thank Providence that you are so devoted to the General, because if you were a man of independent ambition they would fear you."

DeWar shrugged. "Really? I suppose I ought to feel flattered, but—"

"And yet you are so easy to play at Dispute," Perrund said, laughing.

"Am I?"

"Yes, and for the most obvious reason. You do too much to protect your Protector piece. You sacrifice everything to keep it free from threat." She nodded at the board. "Look. You are thinking about blocking my Mounted piece with your eastern General, leaving it open to my Tower after we've exchanged Caravels on the left flank. Well, aren't you?"

DeWar frowned deeply, staring at the board. He felt his face flush. He looked up again at those golden, mocking eyes. "Yes. So I am transparent, is that it?"

"You are predictable," Perrund told him softly. "Your obsession with the Emperor—with the Protector—is a weakness. Lose the Protector and one of the Generals takes its place. You treat it as though its loss would be the end of the game. I was wondering . . . Did you ever play 'A Kingdom Unjustly Divided' before you learned 'Monarch's Dispute'?" she asked. "Do you know of it?" she added, surprised, when he looked blank. "In that game the loss of either King does indeed signify the end of the game."

"I've heard of it," DeWar said defensively, picking up his Protector piece and turning it over in his hands. "I confess I haven't played it properly, but—"

Perrund clapped her good hand on her thigh, attracting the frowning stare of the watchful eunuch. "I knew it!" she said, laughing and rocking forward on the couch. "You protect the Protector because you can't help it. You know it's not really the game but it would hurt you to do otherwise because you are so much the bodyguard!"

DeWar put the Protector piece back down on the board and drew himself up on the small stool he sat upon, uncrossing his legs and adjusting the positions of his sword and his dagger. "It's not that," he said, pausing to study the board again briefly. "It's not that. It's just . . . my style. The way I choose to play the game."

"Oh, DeWar," Perrund said with an unladylike snort. "What nonsense! That is not style, it's fault! If you play like that it's like fighting with one hand tied behind your back . . ." She looked down ruefully at the arm in the red sling. "Or one hand wasted," she added, then held up her good hand to him as he went to protest. "Now just you never mind that. Attend to my point. You cannot stop being a bodyguard even when playing a silly game to pass the time with an old concubine while your master dallies with a younger one. You must admit it and be proud—secretly or not, it's equal to me—or I shall be quite thoroughly upset. Now, speak and tell me I'm right."

DeWar sat back, holding both hands out wide in a gesture of defeat. "My lady," he said, "it is just as you say."

Perrund laughed. "Don't give in so easily. Argue."

"I can't. You're right. I am only glad that you think my obsession might be commendable. But it is just as you say. My job is my life, and I am never off-duty. And I never will be until I am dismissed, I fail in my job, or—Providence consign such an eventuality to the distant future—the Protector dies a natural death."

Perrund looked down at the board. "In a ripe old age, as you say," she agreed before looking up at him again. "And do you still feel you're missing something which might prevent such a natural end?"

DeWar looked awkward. He picked up the Protector piece again and, as though addressing it, in a low voice said, "His life is in more danger than anybody here seems to think. Certainly it is in more danger than he appears to believe." He looked up at the lady Perrund, a small, hesitant smile on his face. "Or am I being too obsessive again?"

"I don't know," Perrund said, sitting closer and dropping her voice too, "why you seem so sure that people want him dead."

"Of course people want him dead," DeWar said. "He had the courage to commit regicide, the temerity to create a new way of governing. The Kings and Dukes who opposed the Protector from the start found him a more skilled politician and far better field commander than they'd expected. With great skill and a little luck he prevailed, and the acclamation of the newly enfranchised in Tassasen has made it difficult for anybody else in the old Kingdom or indeed anywhere in the old Empire to oppose him directly."

"There must be a 'but' or an 'however' about to make its appearance here," Perrund said. "I can tell it."

"Indeed. *But* there are those who have greeted UrLeyn's coming to power with every possible expression of enthusiasm and who have gone out of their way to support him in most public ways, yet who secretly know that their own existence—or at the very least their own supremacy—is threatened by his continued rule. They are the ones I'm worried about, and they must have made their plans for our Protector. The first few attempts at assassination failed, but not by much. And only your bravery stopped the most determined of them, lady," DeWar said.

Perrund looked away, and her good hand went to touch the withered one. "Yes," she said. "I did tell your predecessor that as I had stepped in to perform his job he ought to do the decent thing and attempt to fulfil mine one day, but he just laughed."

DeWar smiled. "Commander ZeSpiole tells that story himself, still."

"Hmm. Well, perhaps as Commander of the Palace Guard, ZeSpiole does such a good job keeping would-be assassins away from the palace that none ever achieve the sort of proximity that might call for your services."

"Perhaps, but either way they will be back," DeWar said quietly. "I almost wish they had been back by now. The absence of conventional assassins makes me all the more convinced there is some very special assassin here, just waiting for the right time to strike."

Perrund looked troubled, even sad, the man thought. "But come, DeWar," she said, "is this not too gloomily contrary? Perhaps there are no attempts on the Protector's life because no one of moment any longer wishes him dead. Why assume the most depressing explanation? Can you never be, if not relaxed, then content?"

DeWar took a deep breath and then released it. He replaced the Protector piece. "These are not times when people in my profession can relax."

"They say the old days were always better. Do you think so, DeWar?"

"No, lady, I do not." He gazed into her eyes. "I think a lot of nonsense is talked about the old days."

"But, DeWar, they were days of legends, days of heroes!" Perrund said, her expression indicating she was not being entirely serious. "Everything was better, everybody says so!"

"Some of us prefer history to legends, lady," DeWar said heavily, "and sometimes everybody can be wrong."

"Can they?"

"Indeed. Once everybody thought the world was flat."

"Many still do," Perrund said, raising one brow. "Few peasants want to think they might fall out of their fields, and a lot of us who know the truth find it hard to accept."

"Nevertheless, it is the case." DeWar smiled. "It can be proved."

Perrund smiled too. "With sticks in the ground?"

"And shadows, and mathematics."

Perrund gave a quick, sideways nod. It was a mannerism that seemed to acknowledge and dismiss at the same time. "What a very certain, if rather dismal world you seem to live in, DeWar."

"It is the same world that everyone inhabits, if they but knew, my lady. It's just that only some of us have our eyes open."

Perrund drew in a breath. "Oh! Well, those of us still stumbling around with our eyes tightly shut had best be grateful to people like you then, I should think."

"I'd have thought that you at least, my lady, would have no need of a sighted guide."

"I am just a crippled, ill-educated concubine, DeWar. A poor orphan who might have met a terrible fate if I had not caught the eye of the Protector." She made her withered arm move by flexing her left shoulder towards him. "Sadly I later caught a blow as well as a glance, but I am as glad of one as the other." She paused and DeWar drew a breath to speak, but then she nodded down at the board and said, "Are you going to move, or not?"

DeWar sighed and gestured at the board. "Is there any point, if I am so deficient an adversary?"

"You must play, and play to win even if you know you will probably lose," Perrund told him. "Otherwise you should not have agreed to begin the game in the first place."

"You changed the nature of the game when you informed me of my weakness."

"Ah no, the game was always the same, DeWar," Perrund said, sitting suddenly forward, her eyes seeming to flash as she added with a degree of relish, "I merely opened your eyes to it."

DeWar laughed. "Indeed you did, my lady." He sat forward and went to move his Protector piece, then sat back again and with a despairing gesture said, "No. I concede, my lady. You have won."

There was some commotion amongst the group of concubines nearest to the doors which led into the rest of the harem. In his high pulpit, the chief eunuch Stike wobbled to his feet and bowed to the small figure bustling into the long chamber.

"DeWar!" The Protector UrLeyn called, hauling his jacket on over his shoulders as he strode towards them. "And Perrund! My dear! My darling!"

Perrund stood suddenly, and DeWar watched her face come alive again, the eyes widening, her expression softening and her face blossoming into the most dazzling smile as UrLeyn approached. DeWar stood too, the faintest of hurt expressions vanishing from his face, to be replaced by a relieved smile and a look of professional seriousness.

3
THE DOCTOR

Master, you asked to know most particularly of any sorties which the Doctor made outside the Palace of Efernze. What I am about to relate took place the afternoon following our summons to the hidden chamber and our encounter with the chief torturer Nolieti.

A storm raged above the city, making of the sky a darkly boiling mass. Fissures of lightning split that gloom with an eye-blinding brightness, as though they were the concentrated blues of the everyday sky fighting to prise the blackness of the clouds apart and shine upon the ground again, however briefly. The westerly waters of Crater Lake leapt against the city's ancient harbour walls and surged amongst the deserted outer docks. It made even the ships within the sheltered inner quays roll and shift uneasily, their hulls compressing the cane fenders to make them creak and crack in protest, while their tall masts swung across the black sky like a forest of disputing metronomes.

The wind whistled through the streets of the city as we made our way out of the Blister Gate and headed across Market Square towards the Warren. An empty stall had been blown over in the square and its sack roof flapped and tore in the gusts, clapping against the cobblestones like a trapped wrestler slapping the ground as he begs for mercy.

The rain came in blustery torrents, stinging and cold. The Doctor handed me her heavy medicine bag as she wrapped and buttoned her cloak more tightly about her. I still believe that this—along with her jacket and coat—should be purple, as she is a physician. However, when she had first arrived two years earlier the doctors of the city had let it be known that they would take a dim view of her pretending to this badge of their rank, and the Doctor herself had seemed indifferent in the matter, and so as a rule she wore mostly dark and black clothes (though sometimes, in a certain light, in some of the garments she paid to have made by one of the court tailors, I thought one could just catch a hint of purple in the weave).

The wretch who had brought us out into this awfulness limped on ahead, glancing back at us every now and again as if to make sure we were still there. How I wished we were not. If ever there was a day for curling up by a roaring fire with a cup of mulled wine and a Heroic Romance, this was it. Come to that, a hard bench, a tepid cup of leaf and one of the Doctor's recommended medical texts would have seemed like bliss to me, compared to this.

"Filthy weather, eh, Oelph?"

"Yes, mistress."

They do say the weather has been much more violent since the fall of the Empire, which is either Providence punishing those who helped overthrow it, or an Imperial ghost exacting revenge from beyond the grave.

The cur who had lured us into this absurd mission was a hobble-legged child from the Barrows. The palace guards hadn't even let her into the outer bastion. It had been sheer bad luck that some fool of a servant, bringing the guards a note of instruction, had overheard the brat's preposterous pleadings and taken sympathy on her, coming to find the Doctor in her workshop—mortar and pestling her pungently arcane ingredients with my help—and report that her services were requested. By some bastard from the slums! I could not believe it when she agreed. Couldn't she hear the storm groaning round the lanterns in the roof above? Hadn't she noticed I'd had to light all our lamps in the room? Was she deaf to the gurgle of drain water in the walls?

We were on our way to see some destitute breed who were distantly related to the servants of the Mifelis, the chiefs of the trader clan the Doctor had worked for when she had first come to Haspide. The King's personal physician was about to pay a call in a storm, not on anyone noble, likely to be ennobled or indeed even respectable, but on a family of slack-witted all-runt ne'er-do-wells, a tribe of contagiously flea'd happen-ills so fundamentally useless they were not even servants but merely the hangers-on of servants, itinerant leeches on the body of the city and the land.

Coinless and hopeless, to be short about it, and even the Doctor might have had the sense to refuse but for the fact that she had, bizarrely, heard of this sickly urchin. "She has a voice from another world," she'd told me as she'd swirled on her cloak, as though this was all the explanation required.

"Please hurry, mistress!" wailed the whelp who'd come to summon us. Her accent was thick and her voice made irksome by her disease-dark snaggle teeth.

"Don't tell the Doctor what to do, you worthless piece of shit!" I told her, trying to be helpful. The lame brute ducked and hobbled away in front, across the glistening cobbles of the square.

"Oelph! Kindly keep a civil tongue in your head," the Doctor told me, grabbing her medicine bag back from me.

"But mistress!" I protested. At least, though, the Doctor had waited until our limping guide was out of earshot before chastising me.

She screwed up her eyes against the lashing rain and raised her voice above the howl of the wind. "Do you think we can get a cab?"

I laughed, then turned the offending noise into a cough. I made a show of looking around as we approached the lower edge of the

Square, where the lame child had disappeared down a narrow street. I could just make out a few scavenging people scattered along the eastern side of the Square, flapping back and forth in their rags as they collected the half-rotted leaves and rain-sodden husks which had been blown there from the centre of the Square, where the vegetable market had been. Not another soul to be seen. Certainly not a cabbie, rickshaw puller or chair carrier. They had more sense than to be out in weather like this. "I think not, mistress," I said.

"Oh dear," the Doctor said, and seemed to hesitate. For one wonderful moment I thought she might see sense and return us both back to the warmth and comfort of her apartments, but it was not to be. "Oh well," she said, holding the top of her cloak closed at her neck, settling her hat more firmly on her gathered-up hair and putting her head down to hurry onwards. "Never mind. Come on, Oelph."

Cold water was creeping down my neck. "Coming, mistress."

The day had passed reasonably well until then. The Doctor had bathed, spent more time writing in her journal, then we had visited the spice market and nearby bazaars while the storm was still just a dark brew on the western horizon. She had met with some merchants and other doctors at the house of a banker to talk about starting a school for doctors (I was consigned to the kitchen with the servants and so heard nothing of consequence and little of sense), then we walked smartly back up to the palace while the sky clouded over and the first few rain squalls swept in over from the outer docks. I fondly and quite mistakenly congratulated myself for escaping back to the comfort and warmth of the palace before the storm set in.

A note on the door to the Doctor's rooms informed us that the King desired to see her and so it was off towards his private apartments as soon as we'd put down our bags full of spices, berries, roots and earths. A servant intercepted us in the Long Corridor with news that the King had been wounded in a practice duel and—hearts in our mouths—we made quickly for the game halls.

"Sire, a leech! We have the finest! The rare Emperor leech, from Brotechen!"

"Nonsense! A burn-glass veining is what is required, followed by an emetic!"

"A simple letting will suffice. Your majesty, if I may—"

"No! Get away from me, you wittering purple rogues! Away and become bankers the lot of you—admit what you really love! Where's Vosill? Vosill!" the King cried up the broad stairs as he started up them, left hand clutched round his right upper arm. We were just starting down.

The King had been injured in a duelling round and it seemed as if every other doctor of repute in the city must have been in the duelling chamber that day, for they were clustered round the King and the two men at his side like purple-coated chasers round a beast at bay. Their own masters followed at their heels, holding duelling swords and half-masks, with one large, grey-faced individual isolated near the rear presumably being the one who'd cut the King.

Guard Commander Adlain was to one side of the King, Duke Walen on the other. Adlain, I will record only for posterity, is a man the nobility and grace of whose features and carriage are matched only by our good King, though the Guard Commander's appearance is swarthy where King Quience's is fair—a faithful, loyal shadow ever at the side of our splendid ruler. But what monarch could wish for a more glorious shadow!

Duke Walen is a short, stooped man with leathery skin and small, deeply recessed eyes which are slightly crossed.

"Sir, are you sure you won't let my physician tend to that wound?" Walen said in his high, grating voice, while Adlain shooed away a couple of the harrying doctors. "Look," the Duke cried, "it's dripping! The royal blood! Oh, my word! Physician! Physician! Really, my lord, this doctor fellow is quite the best. Let me just—"

"No!" the King bellowed. "I want Vosill! Where is she?"

"The lady would appear to have more pressing engagements," Adlain said, not unreasonably. "Lucky it's just a scratch, eh, my lord?" Then he looked up the steps to see the Doctor and myself descending. His expression became a smile.

"Vo—!" the King roared, head down as he bounded up the curve of steps, briefly leaving both Walen and Adlain behind.

"Here, sir," the Doctor said, stepping down to meet him.

"Vosill! Where in the name of all the skies of hell have you been?"

"I—"

"Never mind that! Let's to my chambers. You." (And the King addressed me!) "See if you can hold off this pack of blood-sucking scavengers. Here's my duelling sword." The King handed me his own sword! "You have full permission to use it on anyone who looks remotely like a physician. Doctor?"

"After you, sir."

"Yes *of course* after me, Vosill. I am the King, dammit!"

It has always struck me how well our glorious King resembles the portraits one sees displayed of him in paintings and in the profiles which grace our coins. I was fortunate enough to have the opportunity to study those magnificent features that mid-Xamis, in the King's private apartments, while the Doctor treated the duelling wound and the King stood, clad in a long gown with one sleeve rolled up, in silhouette against the luminous expanse of an ancient plaster window, face raised and jaw set, as the Doctor worked at his out-held arm.

What a noble visage! What a regal demeanour! A mane of majestically curling blond hair, a brow of intelligence and stern wisdom, clear, flashing eyes the colour of the summer sky, a sharply defined, heroic nose, a broad, gracefully cultured mouth and a proud, brave chin, all set on the frame both strong and lithe which would be the envy of an athlete in his prime (and the King is in his most magnificent middle-age, when most men have started to go to fat). They do say that King Quience is excelled in his appearance and physique only by his late father, Drasine (whom they are already calling Drasine the Great, I am happy to report. And rightly so).

"Oh, sir! Oh dear! Oh my goodness! Oh, help! Oh, what a calamity! Oh!"

"Leave us, Wiester," the King said, sighing.

"Sir! Yes, sir. Immediately, sir." The fat chamberlain, still alternately waving and kneading his hands, left the apartments, muttering and moaning.

"I thought you had armour to stop this sort of thing happening, sir," the Doctor said. She wiped the last of the blood away with a swab which she then handed to me for disposal. I handed her the alcohol in exchange. She soaked another swab and applied it to the gash on the King's bicep. The wound was a couple of fingers long and a couple of pinches deep.

"Ouch!"

"I'm sorry, sir."

"Aow! *Aow!* Are you sure this isn't some quackery of your own, Vosill?"

"The alcohol kills the ill humours which can infect a wound," the doctor said frostily. "Sir."

"As does, you claim, mouldy bread," the King snorted.

"It has that effect."

"And sugar."

"That too, sir, in an emergency."

"Sugar," the King said, shaking his head.

"Don't you, sir?"

"What?"

"Have armour?"

"Of course we have armour, you imbecile—Aow! Of course we have armour, but you don't wear it in the *duelling chamber.* In the name of Providence, if you were going to wear armour you might as well not duel at all!"

"But I thought it was a *practice,* sir. For real fighting."

"Well, of course it's a *practice,* Vosill. If it wasn't a practice the fellow who cut me wouldn't have stopped and damn near fainted, he'd have leapt in for the kill, if it was that sort of duel. Anyway, yes, it was a practice." The King shook his magnificent head and stamped one foot. "*Damn* me, Vosill, you ask the most stupid questions."

"I beg your pardon, sir."

"It's only a scratch, anyway." The King looked around, then gestured at a footman standing by the main doors, who quickly went to a table and drew his majesty a glass of wine.

"How much less than a scratch is an insect bite," the Doctor said. "And yet people die from those, sir."

"They do?" the King said, accepting the wine goblet.

"So I've been taught. A poisonous humour transmitted from the insect to the bloodstream."

"Hmm," the King said, looking sceptical. He glanced at the wound. "Still just a scratch. Adlain wasn't very impressed." He drank.

"I imagine it would take a great deal to impress Guard Commander Adlain," the Doctor said, though not I think unkindly.

The King gave a small smile. "You don't like Adlain, do you, Vosill?"

The Doctor flexed her brows. "I don't regard him as a friend, sir, but equally I don't regard him as an enemy, either. We both seek to serve you in our appointed ways according to the skills at our command."

The King's eyes narrowed as he considered this. "Spoken like a politician, Vosill," he said quietly. "Expressed like a courtier."

"I shall take that as a compliment, sir."

He watched her clean out the wound for a while. "Still, perhaps you ought to be wary of him, eh?"

The Doctor looked up. I believe she might have been surprised. "If your majesty says so."

"And Duke Walen," the King said with a grunt. "Your ears should burn when he talks about women being doctors, or for that matter women being anything other than whores, wives and mothers."

"Indeed, sir," the Doctor said through gritted teeth. She looked to me to ask for something, then saw that I already held the appropriate jar in my hand. I was rewarded with a smile and a nod of appreciation. I took the alcohol-soaked swab and dropped it in the rubbish bag.

"What's that?" the King said, brows furrowed in suspicion.

"It's an ointment, sir."

"I can *see* it's an ointment, Vosill. What does it—Oh."

"As you feel, sir, it dulls the pain. Also it fights the particles of ill humour which infest the air, and aids the healing process."

"Is that like the stuff you put on my leg that time, on the abscess?"

"It is, sir. What an excellent memory your majesty has. That was the first time I treated you, I believe."

The King caught sight of his reflection in one of the great mirrors which adorned his private resting chambers and drew himself up straighter. He looked at the footman by the door, who came over and took the wine goblet from him, then the King lifted up his chin and pushed his hand through his hair, shaking his head so that his locks, which had been flattened by the sweat under his duelling half-mask, fell bouncing free again.

"That's right," he said, inspecting his noble outline in the looking glass. "I was in a poor state, from what I can recall. All the saw-bones thought I was going to die."

"I was very glad your majesty sent for me," the Doctor said quietly, binding the wound.

"It was an abscess that killed my father, you know," the King told the Doctor.

"So I have heard, sir." She smiled up at him. "But it did not kill you."

The King smiled and looked ahead. "No. Indeed." Then he grimaced. "But then he did not suffer from my twisted guts, or my aching back, or my other aches."

"He is not recorded as mentioning such things, sir," the Doctor said, rolling the dressing round and round the King's mightily muscled arm.

He looked at her sharply. "Are you suggesting I'm a whiner, Doctor?"

Vosill looked up, surprised. "Why, no, sir. You bear your many unfortunate ills with great fortitude." She kept on unwinding the bandage. (The Doctor has bandages specially made for her by the court tailor, and insists upon the cleanliness of the conditions of their manufacture. Even so, before she will use them she boils them in already-boiled water which she has treated with the bleaching powder she also has specially made for her, by the palace apothecary.) "Indeed your majesty is to be extolled for his willingness to talk of his ailments," the Doctor told him. "Some people—taking stoicism, manly pride or simple reticence beyond its fit limit—suffer in silence until they are at death's door, and then promptly pass over that threshold, when a word, a single complaint at a much earlier stage in their illness would have let a doctor diagnose the problem, treat it and cause them to live. Pain, or even just discomfort, is like the warning sent by a frontier guard, sir. You are free to choose to ignore it, but you should not be unduly surprised if you are subsequently over-run by invaders."

The King gave a small laugh and looked on the Doctor with a tolerant, kindly expression. "Your cautionary military metaphor is duly appreciated, Doctor."

"Thank you, sir." The Doctor adjusted the bandage so that it would sit properly on the King's arm. "There was a note on my door which said you wanted to see me, sir. I assume whatever that was about must have predated your fencing injury."

"Oh," the King said. "Yes." He put one hand up to the back of his neck. "My neck. That stiffness again. You might look at it later."

"Of course, sir."

The King sighed, and I could not help noticing that his stance altered, so that he was less upright, less regal, even. "Father had the constitution of a haul. They say he once took on a yoke and pulled one of the poor beasts backwards through a paddy."

"I heard it was a calf, sir."

"So? A haul *calf* weighs more than most men," the King said sharply. "And besides, were you there, Doctor?"

"I was not, sir."

"No. You weren't." The King stared into the distance, a look of sadness on his face. "But, you're right, I think it was a calf." He sighed again. "The old stories talk of the kings of old lifting hauls—*adult* hauls, Doctor—lifting hauls above their heads and then throwing them at their enemies. Ziphygr of Anlios ripped a wild ertheter in half with his bare hands, Scolf the Strong tore off the head of the monster Gruissens with one hand, Mimarstis the Sompolian—"

"Might these not be simply legends, sir?"

The King stopped talking and looked straight ahead for a moment (I confess I froze), then he turned as far round towards the Doctor as he could with the bandage still being wound. "Doctor Vosill," he said quietly.

"Sir?"

"You do not interrupt the King."

"Did I interrupt you, sir?"

"You did. Do you know nothing?"

"App—"

"Do they teach you naught in this archipelago anarchy of yours?

Do they instil no manners whatsoever in their children and their women? Are you so degenerate and impolite that you have no conception of how to behave towards your betters?"

The Doctor looked hesitantly at the King.

"You may answer," he told her.

"The archipelagic republic of Drezen is notorious for its ill manners, sir," the Doctor said, with every appearance of meekness. "I am ashamed to report that I am considered one of the polite ones. I do apologise."

"My father would have had you flogged, Vosill. And that was *if* he'd decided to take pity on you as a foreigner and therefore unused to our ways."

"I am grateful that in your sympathy and understanding you surpass your noble father, sir. I will try never to interrupt you again."

"Good." The King resumed his proud stance. The Doctor kept on winding the last of the bandage. "Manners were better in the old days too," the King said.

"I'm sure they were," the Doctor said. "Sir."

"The old gods walked amongst our ancestors. The times were heroic. Great deeds could still be done. We had not fallen from our strength then. The men were greater and braver and stronger. And the women were more fair and more graceful."

"I'm sure it was just as you say, sir."

"Everything was better then."

"Just so, sir," the Doctor said, tearing the end of the bandage lengthwise.

"Everything just gets . . . worse," the King said with another sigh.

"Hmm," the Doctor said, securing the dressing with a knot. "There, sir, is that better?"

The King flexed his arm and shoulder, inspected his bulging arm, then rolled the gown's sleeve down over the wound. "How long till I can fence again?"

"You can fence tomorrow, gently. Pain will let you know when to stop, sir."

"Good," the King said, and clapped the Doctor on the shoulder. She had to take a step to one side, but looked pleasantly surprised. I thought

I saw a blush on her face. "Well done, Vosill." He looked her up and down. "Shame you're not a man. You could learn to fence too, hmm?"

"Indeed, sir." The Doctor nodded to me and we started to put away the instruments of her profession.

The sick brat's family lived in a pair of filthy, stinking rooms at the top of a cramped and rickety tenement in the Barrows, above a street the storm had turned into a rushing brown sewer.

The concierge was not worthy of the name. She was a fat drunken harridan, a repulsively odoured toll-taker who demanded coin from the Doctor on the pretext that our coming in from the street with such filth on our feet and hose would mean she'd be put to extra work removing it. Judging from the state of the hallway—or as much of it as could be made out in the one-lamp gloom—the city fathers might as well charge her for bringing the muck of its interior out on to the streets of the city, but the Doctor just tutted and dug into her purse. The harridan then demanded and got more coin for letting the crippled child up the stairs with us. I knew better than to attempt to say anything on the Doctor's behalf, and so had to content myself with glaring at the obese nag in the most threatening way I could.

The way up the narrow, creaking, alarmingly pitched staircase led us through a variety of stenches. I experienced in turn sewage, animal ordure, unwashed human bodies, rotting food and some foul form of cooking. This medley was accompanied by an orchestration of noises: the buffeting screech of the wind outside, the wail of babies crying from what seemed like most of the rooms, the shouts, curses, screams and thuds of an argument behind one half-splintered door and the woeful-sounding lowing of beasts shackled in the courtyard.

Raggedly dressed children ran up and down the stairs in front of us, squealing and grunting like animals. People crowded on to the cramped and ill-lit landings on each level to watch us pass and make remarks about the fineness of the Doctor's cloak and the contents of her big dark bag. I kept a handkerchief to my mouth all the way up the stairs, and wished I had soaked it in perfume more recently than I had.

Achieved by a final flight of stairs even more fragile-looking and shaky than those we had encountered on the way up, the top floor of this cess-pile was, I swear, swaying in the wind. Certainly I felt dizzy and sick.

The two cramped, crowded rooms we found ourselves in were probably unbearably hot in the summer and cold in the winter. The wind howled through two small windows in the first chamber. They had probably never had any plaster in them, just a frame with material for blinds and perhaps some shutter-planks. The shutters were long gone, probably burned for winter fuel, and the ragged flaps which were all that remained of the blinds did little to keep out the gale's blast, letting wind and rain billow in.

In this room ten or more people, from babes-in-arms to shrunken ancients, huddled on the floor and a single pallet bed. Their hollow eyes watched as we were ushered quickly towards the room beyond by the crippled waif who'd brought us to this midden-rack. We entered this next chamber by pushing through a tattered fabric door-covering. Behind us, the people muttered to each other with a harsh, lisping sound that might have been a native dialect or a foreign language.

This room was darker, its shutters just as absent as in the room before but its windows covered with the bellying forms of coats or jackets pinned across the frames. Rain had collected in the sodden fabric of the garments before flowing in little rivulets from their bottom edges down the stained plaster of the walls to the floor, where it had pooled and spread.

The floor was curiously sloped and ridged. We were in one of those extra storeys that are added to already cheaply built tenements by builders, landlords and residents who value economy above safety. There was a slow groaning noise from the walls and a sharp cracking, snapping noise from overhead. Water leaked from the sagging ceiling in a handful of places, dripping to the grimy, straw-covered floor.

A thick-set, wild-haired woman in a gruesomely filthy dress greeted the Doctor with much wailing and crying and hoarse, foreign-sounding words and led her through a press of dark, foul-smelling bodies to a low bed set against the far end of the room beneath a bowed wall whose lathe showed through straw-hung lumps of plaster. Something scuttled away along the wall and disappeared into a long crack near the ceiling.

"How long has she been like this?" I heard the Doctor ask, kneeling by the lamp-lit bed and opening her bag. I edged forward, to see a thin girl dressed in rags lying on the bed, her face grey, her thin dark hair plastered to her forehead, her eyes bulging behind her tremulous, flickering eyelids while her breath came in quick, shallow gasps. Her whole body shook and quivered on the bed and her head twitched and her neck muscles spasmed continually.

"Oh, I don't know!" wailed the woman in the dirty gown who had greeted the Doctor. Under the unwashed scent she smelled of something sickly sweet. She sat down heavily on a torn straw cushion by the bed, making it bulge. She elbowed a few of the other people around her out of the way and put her head in her hands while the Doctor felt the sick child's forehead and pulled one of her eyelids open. "All day, maybe, Doctor. I don't know."

"Three days," said a slight child standing near the head of the bed, her arms clamped round the thin frame of the crippled one who'd brought us here.

The Doctor looked at her. "You're . . . ?"

"Anowir," the girl replied. She nodded at the slightly older girl on the bed. "Zea is my sister."

"Oh no, not three days, not my poor dear girl!" the woman on the straw cushion said, rocking back and forth and shaking her head without looking up. "No, no, no."

"We wanted to send for you before now," Anowir said, looking from the wild-haired woman to the stricken face of the crippled girl she was holding and who was holding her, "but—"

"Oh no, no, no," the fat woman wailed from behind her hands. Some of the children whispered to each other, in the same tongue we'd heard in the outer room. The thick-set woman ran her grubby fingers through her unkempt hair.

"Anowir," the Doctor said in a kindly fashion to the girl holding the crippled child, "can you and some of your brothers and sisters go down to the docks as fast as you can and find an ice merchant? Fetch some ice. It doesn't have to be in first-quality blocks, crushed is fine, in fact it's best. Here." The Doctor reached into her purse and counted out some coins. "How many want to go?" she asked, looking round the host of mostly young, tearful faces.

Quickly a number was settled on and she gave them a coin each. This struck me as far too much for ice at this point in the season, but the Doctor is unworldly in these matters. "You may keep any change," she told the suddenly eager-looking children, "but you must each bring all you can carry. Apart from anything else," she said, smiling, "it'll help weigh you down in that gale outside and stop you blowing away. Now, go!"

The room suddenly emptied and only the sick child on the bed, the fat woman on the cushion—whom I took to be the invalid's mother—and the Doctor and I were left. Some of the people in the outer room came to peer through the tattered door-cloth, but the Doctor told them to keep away.

Then she turned to the wild-haired woman. "You must tell me the truth, Mrs. Elund," she said. She nodded to me to open her bag while she pulled the sick child further up the bed and then had me bunch the straw mattress up underneath her back and head. As I knelt to this, I could feel the heat coming off the girl's fevered skin. "Has she been like this for three days?"

"Three, two, four . . . who knows!" wailed the wild-haired woman. "All I know is my precious daughter is dying! She's going to die! Oh, Doctor, help her! Help us all, for no one else will!" The thick-set woman suddenly threw herself, with some awkwardness, off the cushion and on to the floor, burying her head in the folds of the Doctor's cloak even as the Doctor was unfastening the garment and trying to free herself from it.

"I'll do what I can, Mrs. Elund," the Doctor said, and then looked at me as she let the cloak fall off her shoulders and the girl on the bed started to splutter and cough. "Oelph, we'll need that cushion, too."

Mrs. Elund sat up and looked round. "That's mine!" she cried as I gathered up the burst cushion and stuffed it behind the sick girl's head while the Doctor held her upright. "Where am I to sit? I've given up my bed for her already!"

"You must find somewhere else," the Doctor told her. She reached down and pulled up the girl's thin dress. I looked away as she examined the child's mid-parts, which appeared inflamed.

The Doctor bent closer, rearranging the child's legs and taking some instrument from her bag. After a while she put the girl's legs back together and pulled the patient's dress and skirts back down. She busied herself with the child's eyes and mouth and nose, and held her wrist for a while, eyes closed. There was silence in the room save for the noises of the storm and the occasional sniffle from Mrs. Elund, who had settled on the floor with the Doctor's cape wrapped half around her. I had the distinct impression the Doctor was trying to control a desire to shout and scream.

"The money for the song school," the Doctor said tersely. "If I went to the school now, do you think they would tell me it had been spent there on Zea's lessons?"

"Oh, Doctor, we're a poor family!" the wild-haired woman said, putting her face in her hands again. "I can't watch what they all do! I can't keep watch on what she does with the money I give her! She does what she wants to do, that one, I tell you! Oh, save her, Doctor! Please save her!"

The Doctor shifted her position where she knelt and reached in under the bed. She pulled out a couple of fat clays, one stoppered, one not. She sniffed the empty clay and shook the stoppered one. It sloshed. Mrs. Elund looked up, her eyes wide. She swallowed. I caught a whiff from the clay. The smell was the same as that on Mrs. Elund's breath. The Doctor looked at the other woman over the top of the empty clay. "How long has Zea known men, Mrs. Elund?" the Doctor asked, replacing the clays under the bed.

"Known men!" the wild-haired woman screeched, sitting upright. "She—"

"And on this bed, too, I'd think," the Doctor said, pulling up the girl's dress to look at the bed's covers again. "That's where she's picked up the infection. Somebody's been too rough with her. She's too young." She looked at Mrs. Elund with an expression I can only say I was devoutly glad was not directed at me. Mrs. Elund's jaw worked and her eyes went wide. I thought she was about to speak, then the Doctor said, "I understood what the children said when they left, Mrs. Elund. They thought Zea might be pregnant, and they mentioned the sea captain and the two bad men. Or did I misunderstand something?"

Mrs. Elund opened her mouth, then she went limp and her eyes closed and she said, "Oooh . . ." and fell in what looked like a dead faint to the floor, folding herself on to the Doctor's cloak.

The Doctor ignored Mrs. Elund and busied herself at her bag for a moment before bringing out a jar of ointment and a small wooden spatula. She drew on a pair of the rike's bladder gloves she'd had the Palace hide-tailor make for her and pulled the girl's dress up once more. I looked away again.

The Doctor used various of her precious ointments and fluids on the sick child, telling me as she did so what effect each ought to have, how this one alleviated the effects of high temperature on the brain, how this one would fight the infection at its source, how this one would do the same job from inside the girl's body, and how this one would give her strength and act as a general tonic when she recovered. The Doctor had me remove her cloak from underneath Mrs. Elund and then hold the cloak out of a window in the other room, waiting—with arms that became increasingly sore—until it was saturated with water before bringing it back inside and placing its dark, sopping folds over the child, whose clothes, save for a single tatty shift, the Doctor had removed. The girl continued to shake and twitch, and seemed no better than when we had arrived.

When Mrs. Elund made the noises that indicated she was coming back from her faint, the Doctor ordered her to find a fire, a kettle and some clean water to boil. Mrs. Elund seemed to resent this, but left without too many curses muttered under her breath.

"She's burning up," the Doctor whispered to herself, one graceful, long-fingered hand on the child's forehead. It occurred to me then, for the first time, that the girl might die. "Oelph," the Doctor said, looking at me with worry in her eyes. "Would you see if you can find the children? Hurry them up. She needs that ice."

"Yes, mistress," I said wearily, and made for the stairs and their mixture of sights, sounds and smells. I had just been starting to think that parts of me were drying off.

I exited into the loud darkness of the storm. Xamis had set by now and poor Seigen, somewhere beyond the clouds, seemed to have no more power to penetrate them than an oil lamp. The rain-lashed streets were deserted and gloomy, full of deep shadows and buffeting squalls that threatened to bowl me over into the gurgling open sewer overflowing at the centre of each thoroughfare. I headed downhill under the darkly threatening bulk of the over-hanging buildings, in what I imagined must be the direction of the docks, hoping that I could find my way back and starting to wish that I'd taken one of the people in the outer room as a guide.

I think sometimes the Doctor forgets that I am not a native of Haspide. Certainly I have lived here longer than she, for she only arrived a little over two years ago, but I was born in the city of Derla, far to the south, and passed the majority of my childhood in the province of Ormin. Even since I came to Haspide most of the time I have spent here has been not in the city itself but in the Palace, or in the summer palace in the Yvenage hills, or on the road to it or on the way back from it.

I wondered if the Doctor had really sent me out to look for the children or whether there was some arcane or secret treatment she intended to carry out which she did not want me to witness. They say all doctors are secretive—I have heard that one medical clan in Oartch kept the invention of birthing forceps secret for the best part of two generations—but I had thought Doctor Vosill was different. Perhaps she was. Perhaps she really did think I'd be able to make the ice she'd requested arrive quicker, though it seemed to me there was little I could really do. A cannon boomed out over the city, marking the end of one watch and the start of another. The sound was muffled by the storm and seemed almost like part of it. I buttoned my coat up as far as I could. While I was doing this the wind whipped my hat off my head and sent it tumbling down the street until it fetched up in the street's central drain. I ran after it and lifted it out of the stinking stream, wrinkling my nose in disgust at the smell. I rinsed it as best I could under an overflowing drain, wrung it out and sniffed at it, then threw it away.

I found the docks after a while, by which time I was thoroughly soaked again. I hunted in vain for an ice warehouse, and was told in no uncertain terms, by the odd sea-faring and trading types I discovered in a few small ramshackle offices and a couple of crowded, smoke-stuffed taverns, that I was in the wrong place to find ice warehouses. This was the salt-fish market. I was able to confirm this when I slipped on some fish guts lying rotting under a wind-ruffled puddle and was nearly pitched into the troubled, tossing waters of the dock alongside. I could have got wetter as a result of such a fall, but unlike the Doctor I cannot swim. Eventually I found myself being forced—by a tall stone wall which started sheer on a wind-whipped quay and extended off into the distance—to walk back uphill into the maze of tenements.

The children had beaten me to it. I arrived back at the accursed building, ignored the frightful threats of the foul-smelling harridan at the door, dragged myself up the steps past the smells and through the cacophony of sounds, following a trail of dark water spots to the top floor, where the ice had been delivered and the girl packed in it, still covered in the Doctor's cloak and now again surrounded by her siblings and friends.

The ice arrived too late. We had arrived too late, perhaps by a day or so. The Doctor struggled through into the night, trying everything she could think of, but the girl slipped away from her in a blazing fever the ice could not alleviate, and sometime around when the storm started to abate, in the midnight of Xamis, while Seigen still struggled to pierce the tattering dark shrouds of the storm clouds and the voices of the singers were carried away and lost on the quickness of the wind, the child died.

4

THE BODYGUARD

L et me search him, General."

"We can't search him, DeWar, he's an ambassador."

"ZeSpiole is right, DeWar. We can't treat him as though he's some peasant supplicant."

"Of course not, DeWar," said BiLeth, who was the Protector's advisor on most matters foreign. He was a tall, thin, imperious man with long, scant hair and a short, considerable temper. He did his best to look down his very thin nose at the taller DeWar. "What sort of ruffians do you want us to appear?"

"The ambassador certainly comes with all the usual diplomatic accoutrements," UrLeyn said, striding onwards along the terrace.

"From one of the Sea Companies, sir," DeWar protested. "They're hardly an Imperial delegation of old. They have the clothes and the jewels and the chains of office, but do any of them match?"

"Match?" UrLeyn said, mystified.

"I think," ZeSpiole said, "the chief bodyguard means that all their finery is stolen."

"Ha!" BiLeth said, with a shake of his head.

"Aye, and recently, too," DeWar said.

"Nevertheless," UrLeyn said. "In fact, all the more so because of that."

"Sir?"

"All the more so?"

BiLeth looked confused for a moment, then nodded wisely.

General UrLeyn came to a sudden stop on the white and black tiles of the terrace. DeWar seemed to stop in the same instant, ZeSpiole and BiLeth a moment later. Those following them along the terrace between the private quarters and the formal court chambers—generals, aides, scribes and clerks, the usual attenders—bumped into each other with a muffled clattering of armour, swords and writing boards as they drew to a stop behind.

"The Sea Companies may be all the more important now that the old Empire is in tatters, my friends," General UrLeyn said, turning in the sunlight to address the tall, balding figure of BiLeth, the still taller and shadow-dark bodyguard and the smaller, older man in the uniform of the palace guard. ZeSpiole—a thin, wizened man with deeply lined eyes—had been DeWar's predecessor as chief bodyguard. Now instead of being charged with the immediate protection of UrLeyn's person he was in command of the palace guard and therefore with the security of the whole palace. "The Sea Companies' knowledge," UrLeyn said, "their skills, their ships, their cannons . . . they have all become more important. The collapse of the Empire has brought us a surfeit of those who call themselves Emperors . . ."

"At least three, brother!" RuLeuin called.

"Precisely," UrLeyn said, smiling. "Three Emperors, a lot of happy Kings, or at least Kings who are happier than they were under the old Empire, and indeed a few more people calling themselves Kings who would not have dared to do so under the old regime."

"Not to mention one for whom the title King would be an insult, indeed a demotion, sir!" YetAmidous said, appearing at the General's shoulder.

UrLeyn clapped the taller man's back. "You see, DeWar, even my good friend General YetAmidous rightly numbers me with those who have benefited from the demise of the old order and reminds me that it was neither my cunning and guile nor exemplary generalship which led me to the exalted position I now hold," UrLeyn said, his eyes twinkling.

"General!" YetAmidous said, his broad, furrowed, rather doughy-looking face taking on a hurt expression. "I meant to imply no such thing!"

The Grand Aedile UrLeyn laughed and clapped his friend on the shoulder again. "I know, Yet, don't worry. But you take the point, DeWar?" he said, turning to him again, yet raising his voice to make it clear he was addressing all the rest of those present, not just his chief bodyguard. "We have been able," UrLeyn told them, "to take more control of our own affairs because we do not have the threat of Imperial interference hanging over us. The great forts are deserted, the drafts are returned home or have become aimless bands of brigands, the fleets were sunk vying with one another or left rotting, deserted. A few of the ships had commanders who could hold them together with respect rather than fear, and some of those ships are now part of the Sea Companies. The older Companies have found a new power now that the Empire's ships no longer harry them. With that power they have a new responsibility, a new station in life. They have become the protectors, not the raptors, the guards, not the raiders."

UrLeyn looked round all the people in the group, standing blinking on the terrace of black and white tiles under the fierce glare of Xamis and Seigen at their mid.

BiLeth nodded even more wisely than before. "Indeed, sir. I have often—"

"The Empire was the parent," UrLeyn went on, "and the Kingdoms—and the Sea Companies, to a lesser degree—were the children. We were left to play amongst ourselves for much of the time, unless we made too much noise, or broke something, whereupon the adults would come and punish us. Now the father and the mother are dead, the degenerate relatives dispute the will, but it is too late, and the children have grown to young adulthood, left the nursery and taken over the house. Indeed, we have quit the tree-house to occupy the whole estate, gentlemen, and we must not show too much disrespect to those who used to play with their boats in the pond." He smiled. "The least we can do is treat their ambassadors as we would wish ours to be treated." He clapped BiLeth on the shoulder, making the taller man waver. "Don't you think?"

"Absolutely, sir," BiLeth said, with a scornful look at DeWar.

"There you are," UrLeyn said. He turned on his heel. "Come." He paced away.

DeWar was still at his side, a piece of blackness moving across the tiles. ZeSpiole had to walk fast to catch up. BiLeth took longer strides. "Delay the meeting, sir," DeWar said. "Let it be held in less formal circumstances. Invite the ambassador to meet you . . . in the baths, say, then—"

"In the *baths*, DeWar," the General scoffed.

"How ridiculous!" BiLeth said.

ZeSpiole just chuckled.

"I have seen this ambassador, sir," DeWar told the General as the doors were opened for them and they entered the coolness of the great hall, where half a hundred courtiers, officials and military men were waiting, scattered about its plain stone floor. "He does not fill me with confidence, sir," DeWar said quietly, quickly looking round. "In fact he fills me with suspicion. Especially as he has requested a private meeting."

They stopped near the doors. The General nodded to a small alcove set into the thickness of the wall where there was just enough room for two to sit. "Excuse us, BiLeth, Commander ZeSpiole," he said. ZeSpiole looked discomfited, but nodded. BiLeth drew back a little as though profoundly insulted, but then bowed gravely. UrLeyn and DeWar sat in the alcove. The General held up one hand to prevent the people approaching them from coming too close. ZeSpiole held out his arms, keeping people back.

"What do you find suspicious, DeWar?" he asked softly.

"He is like no ambassador I've ever seen. He doesn't have the look of one."

UrLeyn laughed quietly. "What, is he dressed in sea-boots and a storm cape? Are there barnacles on his heels and seabird-shit on his cap? Really, DeWar . . ."

"I mean his face, his expression, his eyes, his whole bearing. I have seen hundreds of ambassadors, sir, and they are as various as you might expect, and more. They are unctuous, open-seeming, blustering, resigned, modest, nervous, severe . . . every type. But they all seem to care, sir, they all seem to have some sort of common interest in their office and function. This one . . ." DeWar shook his head.

UrLeyn put his hand on the other man's shoulder. "This one just feels wrong to you, is that right?"

"I confess you put it no better than I, sir."

UrLeyn laughed. "As I said, DeWar, we live in a time when values and roles and people are changing. You do not expect me to behave as other rulers have behaved, do you?"

"No, sir, I do not."

"Just so we cannot expect every functionary of every new power to conform to expectations formed in the days of the old Empire."

"I understand that, sir. I hope I am already taking that into account. What I am talking about is simply a feeling. But it is, if I may term it so, a professional feeling. And it is partly for those, sir, that you employ me." DeWar searched his leader's eyes to see if he was convinced, if he had succeeded in transmitting any of the apprehension he felt. But the Protector's eyes still twinkled, amused more than concerned. DeWar shifted uncomfortably on the stone bench. "Sir," he said, leaning closer, his expression pained. "I was told the other day, by someone whose opinion I know you value, that I am incapable of being other than a bodyguard, that my every waking moment, even when I am meant to be relaxing, is spent thinking of how better to keep you from harm." He took a deep breath. "My point is that if I live only to shield you from danger and think of nothing else even when I might, how much more must I attend to my anxieties when I am at the very core of my duty, as now?"

UrLeyn regarded him for a moment. "You ask me to trust your mistrust," he said quietly.

"Now the Protector does put it better than I could have."

UrLeyn smiled. "And why would any of the Sea Companies wish me dead in the first place?"

DeWar dropped his voice still further. "Because you are thinking of building a Navy, sir."

"Am I?" UrLeyn asked with seeming surprise.

"Aren't you, sir?"

"Why would anyone think that?"

"You turned over some of the Royal Forests to the people, and then recently introduced the condition that some of the older trees might be thinned."

"They're dangerous."

"They are healthy, sir, and of the age and shape for ships' timbers. Then there is the Mariners' Refuge in Tyrsk, a naval college in the making, and—"

"Enough. Have I been so indiscreet? Are the Sea Companies' spies so numerous and so perceptive?"

"And you have held talks with Haspidus and Xinkspar about enlisting, I'd imagine, the wealth of one and the skills of the other in the formation of such a Navy."

UrLeyn looked troubled now. "You know about this? You must eavesdrop from a great distance, DeWar."

"I hear nothing that you would not expect me to hear through simple proximity, sir. What I hear, without searching them out, are rumours. People are not stupid and functionaries have their specialities, sir, their areas of expertise. When an ex-admiral comes to call, one may guess it is not to discuss breeding better pack animals for crossing the Breathless Plains."

"Hmm," UrLeyn said, looking out at the people gathered around them but not seeing them. He nodded. "You can draw the blinds in a brothel, but people still know what you're doing."

"Exactly, sir."

UrLeyn slapped his knee and made to stand. DeWar was on his feet first. "Very well, DeWar, to humour you, we'll meet in the painted chamber. And we'll make the meeting more private even than he has asked for, just me and him. You may eavesdrop. Are you mollified?"

"Sir."

* * *

Fleet Captain Oestrile, ambassador of the Kep's Haven Sea Company, dressed in an ornate rendition of a nautical uniform, with long turned-over boots of blue hide, trousers of grey pike-fish skin and a thick, high-collared frock coat of aquamarine edged with gold—all topped by a tricorn hat embellished with angel-bird feathers—strode slowly into the painted chamber in the palace of Vorifyr.

The ambassador walked down a narrow carpet of gold thread which ended at a small stool set a couple of strides from the front of the only other article of furniture which the gleaming wooden floor supported, namely a small dais topped by a plain chair on which sat the Prime Protector, First General and Grand Aedile of the Protectorate of Tassasen, General UrLeyn.

The ambassador took off his hat and executed a small bow to the Protector, who motioned the ambassador to the stool. The ambassador looked at the low stool for a moment, then unbuttoned a couple of buttons at the lower edge of his coat and sat carefully, laying his extravagantly feathered hat to one side. He had no obvious weapons, not even a ceremonial sword, though around his neck was a belt supporting a stout cylinder of polished hide, with a buttoned cap at one end and finished with inscribed gold filigree. The ambassador looked round the walls of the chamber.

The walls were painted in a series of panels depicting the various parts of the old Kingdom of Tassasen: a forest full of game, a dark and towering castle, a bustling city square, a harem, a pattern of fields sectioning a flood plain, and so on. If the subjects were relatively mundane, the artwork was almost definitively so. People who had heard of the painted chamber—which was rarely opened and even more rarely used—and who expected something special, were invariably disappointed. The paintings were, it was generally agreed, rather dull and unexceptional.

"Ambassador Oestrile," the Protector said. He was dressed in his usual style of the long jacket and trousers he had made the fashion. The old Tassasen chain of state, with the crown removed, was his only concession to formality.

"Sire," the fellow said.

UrLeyn thought he saw in the ambassador's manner a little of what DeWar had meant. There was a sort of empty gleam in the young man's gaze. An expression which included such open eyes and such a wide smile in such a young, shiningly smooth face ought not to be quite as disquieting as it somehow contrived to be. The fellow was of average build, his hair was short and dark, though red-powdered after some fashion UrLeyn did not recognise. He sported fine whiskers for one so young. Young. Perhaps that was part of it, thought UrLeyn. Ambassadors tended to be older and fatter. Well, he should not talk of changing times and changing roles and then be himself surprised.

"Your journey?" UrLeyn asked. "I trust it was unexciting?"

"Unexciting?" the young fellow said, seemingly confused. "How so?"

"I meant safe," the Protector said. "Your journey was safe?"

The fellow looked relieved for a moment. "Ah," he said, smiling broadly and nodding. "Yes. Safe. Our journey was safe. Very safe." He smiled again.

UrLeyn began to wonder if the young fellow was entirely right in the head. Perhaps he was young for an ambassador because he was some doting father's favourite son, and the father was blind to the fact the lad was soft in the brain. He didn't speak Imperial very well, either, but UrLeyn had heard a few strange accents from those who were of the nautical powers.

"Well, Ambassador," he said, holding his hands out to each side. "You asked for an audience."

The young man's eyes went wider still. "Yes. An audience." He slowly took the belt from round his neck and then looked down at the polished hide cylinder in his lap. "First of all, sir," he said, "I have a gift for you. From the Fleet Captain Vritten." He looked up expectantly at UrLeyn.

"I confess I have not heard of Fleet Captain Vritten, but continue."

The young fellow cleared his throat. He wiped sweat from his brow. Perhaps, UrLeyn thought, he has a fever. It is a little warm in here, but insufficiently so to make a man sweat like that. The Sea Companies spend much of their time in the tropics so it cannot be that he is unused to heat, sea breezes or not.

The captain undid the buttoned end of the cylinder and withdrew another cylinder, also clad in gold-inscribed hide, though its ends appeared to be gold, or brass, and one end was tapered by a series of shining metal rings. "What I have here, sir," the ambassador said, looking down at the cylinder, which he now held in both hands, "is a seeing-piece. An optiscope, or telescope as such instruments are also known."

"Yes," UrLeyn said. "I have heard of such things. Naharajast, the last Imperial mathematician, claimed to have used one directed at the skies to make his predictions concerning the fire-rocks which appeared in the year of the Empire's fall. Last year an inventor—or someone who claimed to be an inventor—came to our palace and showed us one. I had a look through it myself. It was interesting. The view was cloudy, but it was undeniably closer."

The young ambassador seemed not to hear. "The telescope is a fascinating device . . . a *most* fascinating device, sir, and this one is a particularly fine example." He pulled the device apart so that it clicked out to three or so times its compacted length, then held it up to one eye, looking at UrLeyn, then round the painted panels of the room. UrLeyn formed the impression he was hearing a memorised script. "Hmm," the young ambassador said, nodding his head. "Extraordinary. Would you care to try it, sir?" He stood and held out the instrument to the Protector, who motioned the ambassador to approach. Clutching the hide instrument's protective cylinder awkwardly in his other hand, the captain stepped forward, offering the eye-piece end of the device to UrLeyn, who leant forward in his chair and duly took hold of it. The ambassador let go of the thicker end of the instrument. It began to fall to the floor.

"Oh, heavy, isn't it?" UrLeyn said, quickly bringing his other hand round to save the device. He had almost to jump out of the chair to keep his balance, going down on one knee towards the young captain, who took a single step back.

Ambassador Oestrile's hand suddenly held a long, thin dagger which he swept up and then brought swinging down. UrLeyn saw this even as his knee hit the dais and he finally caught the seeing-piece. With his hands full, still off-balance and kneeling beneath the other man, UrLeyn knew instantly that there was nothing he could do to parry the blow.

The crossbow bolt slammed into Ambassador Oestrile's head an instant after glancing off the high collar of his coat. The bolt lodged in his skull just above his left ear, most of its length protruding. If either man had had the time and inclination to look, they would have seen that a small hole had appeared in the painting of the bustling city square. Oestrile staggered back still clutching the dagger, his feet slipping on the polished wooden floor. UrLeyn let himself fall back against the chair, putting both hands to the eye-piece end of the telescope. He started to swing it back behind him, thinking to use it as a club.

Ambassador Oestrile gave a roaring bellow of pain and rage, put one hand to the crossbow bolt and gripped it, shaking his head, then suddenly threw himself forward again at UrLeyn, dagger first.

With a resounding crash DeWar burst through the thin plaster panel depicting the city square. A wave of dust rolled out across the gleaming floor and plaster shards scattered everywhere as DeWar, sword already drawn, thrust the blade straight at the ambassador's midriff. The blade broke. DeWar's momentum carried him onwards so that he side-charged into the ambassador. Still roaring, the ambassador was toppled to the floor with a thud, waving his dagger. DeWar threw away the broken sword, spun to one side and drew his own dagger.

UrLeyn had dropped the heavy telescope and stood. He drew a small knife from his jacket and took shelter behind the tall chair. Oestrile reared to his feet, the crossbow bolt still in his skull. His boots struggled to find purchase on the polished wooden floor as he stumbled towards the Protector. DeWar, bare footed, was on him before he'd taken half a step, coming quickly up behind him, putting one hand over his face and pulling his head back with fingers stuck into the man's nostrils and one eye. Ambassador Oestrile screamed as DeWar sliced his dagger across the man's exposed throat. Blood sprayed and bubbled as the scream was drowned.

Oestrile crashed to his knees, finally dropped the dagger, then fell sideways, neck spurting blood on to the gleaming floor.

"Sir?" DeWar asked UrLeyn breathlessly, still half watching the body twitching on the floor. Sounds of a commotion came from outside the chamber's doors. Thuds sounded. "Sir! Protector! General!" a dozen voices babbled.

"I'm fine! Stop breaking the damn door down!" UrLeyn shouted. The commotion became a little less intense. He looked at where the painted plaster scene of the busy city square had been. In the little cupboard-sized room which had been revealed behind there was a stout wooden post with a crossbow fastened to it. UrLeyn looked back at DeWar, and put his own small knife back in its pocket sheath. "No damage done, thank you, DeWar. And you?"

"I am uninjured too, sir. Sorry I had to kill him." He looked down at the body, which gave out one final bubbling sigh and then seemed to collapse in on itself a little. The pool of blood on the floor was deep and dark and still spreading viscously. DeWar knelt, keeping his dagger at what was left of the man's throat as he felt for a pulse.

"Never mind," the Protector said. "Took some killing, too, did you not think?" He gave an almost girlish chuckle.

"I think some of his strength and his bravery came from a potion or some such drug-brew, sir."

"Hmm," UrLeyn said, then looked to the doors. "Will you shut up!" he yelled. "I'm perfectly all right, but this piece of shit tried to kill me! Palace guard?"

"Aye, sir! Five present!" shouted a muffled voice.

"Get Commander ZeSpiole. Tell him to find the rest of the diplomatic mission and arrest them. Clear everybody away from those doors, then enter. Nobody but the palace guards are allowed in here until I say so. Got all that?"

"Sir!" The commotion intensified for a while, then began to subside again until there was almost no noise in the painted chamber.

DeWar had unbuttoned the failed assassin's coat. "Chain mail," he said, fingering the coat's lining. He tapped the garment's collar. "And metal." He gripped the shaft of the crossbow bolt, strained, then stood and put one bare foot on Ambassador Oestrile's head, eventually pulling the bolt free with a delicate crunching noise. "No wonder it was deflected."

UrLeyn stepped to the side of the dais. "Where did the dagger come from? I didn't see."

DeWar crossed to the tall chair, leaving bloody footprints. He lifted first the telescope and then the hide cylinder it had been transported within. He peered into the case. "There's some sort of clip at the bottom." He inspected the telescope. "There is no glass at the large end. The dagger must have nested inside the device when it was inside the case."

"Sir?" a voice came from the door.

"What?" UrLeyn shouted.

"Guard Sergeant HieLiris and three others here, sir."

"Come in," UrLeyn told them. The guards entered, looking warily about. All looked surprised at the hole where the city painting had been. "You have not seen that," the Protector told them. They nodded. DeWar stood cleaning his dagger on a piece of cloth. UrLeyn stepped forward and kicked the dead man in the shoulder, sending him flopping on to his back.

"Take this away," he told the guards. Two of them sheathed their swords and took one end of the body each.

"Better take a limb each, lads," DeWar told them. "That coat's heavy."

"See to the clear-up, will you, DeWar?" asked UrLeyn.

"I should be at your side, sir. If this is a determined attack there might be two assassins, the second waiting for us to relax when we think the attack has failed."

UrLeyn drew himself up and took a deep breath. "Don't worry about me. I'm going off to lie down now," he said.

DeWar frowned. "Are you sure you're all right, sir?"

"Oh, I'm fine, DeWar," the Protector said, following the trail of blood as the guards carried the body to the doors. "I'm going off to lie down on top of somebody very young and plump and firm." He grinned back at DeWar from the doors. "Proximity to death does this to me," he announced. He laughed, looking down at the trail of blood, then at the black pool of it by the dais. "I should have been an undertaker."

5

THE DOCTOR

Master, it was now about the time of year when the Court works itself into the most excited and febrile state as everyone prepares for the Circuition and the move to the Summer Palace. The Doctor was busy with her preparations just as everybody else was busy with theirs, though of course in her case there might have been expected to be an added excitement given that this would be her first Circuition. I did all that I could to help her, though I was constrained in this for a while by a slight fever which kept me in my bed for a few days.

I confess I hid the symptoms of my illness for as long as I could, feeling that the Doctor would think me weak, and also because I had heard from the apprentices of other doctors that however kindly and pleasant

their masters might be with their paying patients, when their own
devoted helpers took poorly they were, to a man (which naturally they
all were), notoriously brusque and unsympathetic.

Doctor Vosill was, however, a very agreeable and understanding
doctor to me while I was ill, and tended to my needs as though she were
my mother (which I do not think she is quite old enough to be).

I would not record anything beyond my brief infirmity, and might
even have skipped over it entirely, save to explain to my Master why
there was a gap in my reports, but for the following, which struck me as
possibly shedding some light on the Doctor's mysterious past before she
appeared in the city two years ago.

I was, I freely confess, in a strange state at the height of my sickness, devoid of appetite, sweating freely and falling into a state of semi-
unconsciousness. Whenever I closed my eyes I was convinced I was
seeing odd and vexatious shapes and figures who tormented me with
their manic and incomprehensible shiftings and cavortings.

My greatest fear, as may be imagined, was that I might say something that would reveal to the Doctor the fact that I had been charged
with reporting on her actions. Of course, given that she is obviously a
good and trustworthy person from all that I have seen and reported so far
(and so evidently devoted to our good King), it may be that no ultimate
damage would result from such a revelation, but however that may be I
will of course heed my Master's wishes and keep my mission a secret.

Be assured then, Master, that no word or hint of that assignment
was transmitted by me, and the Doctor remains none the wiser regarding these reports. Still, while that most precious confidence remained
locked well within myself, other of my normal inhibitions and self-
constraints had slackened off due to the influence of the fever, and I
found myself on my bed in my cell one day, while the Doctor—who had
just returned from treating the King (he had a bad neck around this
time, I think)—was washing my much-sweated upper body.

"You are too good to me, Doctor. A nurse should do this."

"A nurse will do this if I am called away to the King again."

"Our dear King! How I love him!" I cried (which was sincere, if a little embarrassing).

"As do we all, Oelph," the Doctor said, squeezing water from a cloth over my chest and—with what seemed like a thoughtful look—rubbing my skin clean. She was crouched at the side of my bed, which is a very low one due to the constraints of space within my cell.

I looked into the Doctor's face, which seemed sad just then, I thought. "Don't fear, Doctor. You will keep him well! He worries that his father was the stronger man and he died young, but you'll keep him well, won't you?"

"What? Yes, yes, of course."

"Oh! You weren't worried about me, were you?" (And I confess my heart gave a little leap within my hot and breathless chest, for what young man would not be taken with the idea of a good and handsome woman, especially one tending so intimately to his bodily needs as at that point, worrying about and caring for him?) "Don't worry," I said, putting out a hand. "I'm not going to die." She looked uncertain, so I added, "Am I?"

"No, Oelph," she said, and smiled kindly. "No, you're not going to die. You're young and strong and I'll look after you. Another half-day and you should start to come round again." She looked down at the hand I had extended to her, which I now realised was on her knee. I gulped.

"Ah, this old dagger of yours," I said, not so fevered that I could not feel embarrassed. I tapped the old knife's pommel where it protruded from the top of the Doctor's boot, near where my hand had rested. "It has, ah, always fascinated me. What sort of knife is it? Have you ever had to use it? I dare say it cannot be a surgical tool. It looks too dull. Or is it some ceremonial token? What—?"

The Doctor smiled and put one hand over my lips, quieting me. She reached down and pulled the dagger from its sheath in her boot, handing it to me. "Here," she said. I took its battered-looking length in my hands. "I'd tell you to be careful," she said, still smiling, "but there's little point."

"Nor much in the way of edge," I said, running one sweaty thumb along it.

The Doctor laughed loudly. "Why, Oelph, a joke," she said, clapping me gently on the shoulder. "And one that works in many a language too. You must be getting better." Her eyes looked bright.

I felt suddenly shy. "You have looked after me so well, mistress . . ." I was not sure what else to say, and so I studied the dagger. It was a heavy old thing, about a hand and a half long and made of old steel which had become minutely pitted with small rusty holes. The blade was slightly

bent and the tip had been broken off and rounded with time. There were
a few nicks on each blade-edge, which truly were so dull one would have
to saw away with some force to cut anything much more robust than a
jellyfish. The tusk grip was pitted too, though on a larger scale. Around
the pommel and in a trio of lines down the length of the grip down to the
stop there were a few semiprecious stones each no bigger than a crop
grain, and many holes where it appeared similar stones had once rested.
The top of the pommel was formed by a large dark smoky stone which,
when I held it up to the light, I could just see through. Round the pommel's bottom rim what I mistook at first for some wavy carving was really
a line of little pits which had lost all but one of the small pale stones.

I ran a finger down them. "You should have this repaired, mistress," I told her. "The palace armourer would oblige, I'm sure, for the
stones do not look expensive and the workmanship is not of the first
order. Let me take it down to the armoury when I am well. I know the
deputy armourer's assistant. It would be no trouble. It would please me
to do something for you."

"There is no need," the Doctor said. "I like it well enough just as it
is. It has sentimental value. I carry it as a keepsake."

"From whom, mistress?" (The fever! Normally I would not have
been so bold!)

"An old friend," she said easily, mopping off my chest and then
putting the cloths aside and sitting back on the floor.

"From Drezen?"

"From Drezen," she nodded. "Given to me the day I set sail."

"It was new then?"

She shook her head. "It was old then." The thin light of a Seigen
sunset shone through a cracked-open window and reflected redly on
her netted, gathered hair. "A family heirloom."

"They do not take very good care of their heirlooms if they let them
fall into such disrepair, mistress. There must be more holes than stones."

She smiled. "The stones that are missing were used to good effect.
Some bought protection in uncultured places where a person travelling
alone is seen more as prey than as guest, and others paid my way on
some of the sea passages that brought me here."

"They do not look very valuable."

"They are more highly prized elsewhere, perhaps. But the knife, or what it carried, kept me safe and it kept me moving. I have never had to use it—well, I have had to brandish it and wave it around a bit—but I have never had to use it to hurt anyone. And as you say, that is just as well for me, for it is quite the dullest knife I have seen since I arrived here."

"Quite so, mistress. It would not do to have the dullest dagger in the Palace. All the others are so very sharp."

She looked at me (and I can only say, she looked at me *sharply*, for that was a piercing gaze). She gently took the dagger from me and rubbed a thumb down one blade. "I think perhaps I will have you take it to the armoury, though only to have an edge put on it."

"They might re-point it too, mistress. A dagger is for stabbing."

"Indeed." She put it back in its sheath.

"Oh, mistress!" I cried, suddenly full of fear. "I'm sorry!"

"For what, Oelph?" she said, her beautiful face, so concerned, suddenly close to mine.

"For—for talking to you like this. For asking you personal questions. I am only your servant, your apprentice. This is not seemly."

"Oh, Oelph," she said, smiling, her voice soft, her breath cool on my cheek. "We can ignore seemliness, at least in private, don't you think?"

"May we, mistress?" (And I confess my heart, fevered though it was, leapt at these words, wildly expecting what I knew I could not expect.)

"I think so, Oelph," she said, and took my hand in hers and squeezed it gently. "You may ask me whatever you like. I can always say no, and I am not the type to take offence easily. I would like us to be friends, not just Doctor and apprentice." She tilted her head, a quizzical, amused expression on her face. "Is that all right with you?"

"Oh, yes, mistress!"

"Good. We'll—" Then the Doctor cocked her head again, listening to something. "There's the door," she said, rising. "Excuse me."

She returned holding her bag. "The King," she said. Her expression, it seemed to me, was half-regretful, half-radiant. "Apparently his toes are sore." She smiled. "Will you be all right by yourself, Oelph?"

"Yes, mistress."

"I'll be back as soon as I can. Then maybe we'll see if you're ready for something to eat."

* * *

It was a five-day later, I think, that the Doctor was called to the Slave Master Tunch. His house was an imposing one in the Merchants' Quarter, overlooking the Grand Canal. Its tall, raised front doors sat imposingly above the sweeping double staircase leading from the street, but we were not able to enter that way. Instead our hired seat was directed to a small quay a few streets away, where we transferred to a little cabin-punt which took us, shutters closed, down a side canal and round to the rear of the building and a small dock hidden from the public waters.

"What *is* all this about?" the Doctor asked me as the punt's shutters were opened by the boatman and the vessel bumped against the dark timbers of a pier. It was well into summer yet still the place seemed chilly and smelled of dankness and decay.

"Mistress?" I said, fastening a spiced kerchief round my mouth and nose.

"This secrecy."

"I—"

"And why are you doing that?" she asked, obviously annoyed, as a servant helped the boatman secure the punt.

"What, this, mistress?" I asked, pointing to the kerchief.

"Yes," she said standing up and rocking our small craft.

"It is to combat the evil humours, mistress."

"Oelph, I have told you before that infectious agents are transmitted in breath or bodily fluids, even if they are insect body fluids," she said. "A bad smell by itself will not make you ill. Thank you." The servant accepted her bag and laid it carefully on the small dock. I did not reply. No doctor knows everything and it is better to be safe than sorry. "Anyway," she said, "I am still unclear why all this secrecy is required."

"I think the Slave Master does not want his own doctor to know of your visit," I told her as I clambered on to the dock. "They are brothers."

"If this Slaver is so close to death, why isn't his doctor at his side?" the Doctor said. "Come to that, why isn't he there as his brother?" The servant held out a hand to help the Doctor out of the boat. "Thank you," she said again. (She is always thanking servants. I think the menials of Drezen must be a surly lot. Or just spoiled.)

"I don't know, mistress," I confessed.

"The Master's brother is in Trosila, ma'am," the servant said (which just goes to show what happens when you start speaking to servants).

"Is he?" the Doctor said.

The servant opened a small door leading to the rear of the house. "Yes, ma'am," he said, looking nervously at the boatman. "He has gone in person to seek some rare earth which is said to help the condition the Master is suffering from."

"I see," the Doctor said. We entered the house. A female servant met us. She wore a severe black dress and had a forbidding face. Indeed her expression was so bleak my first thought was that Slave Master Tunch had died. However, she gave the tiniest of nods to the Doctor and in a precise, clipped voice said, "Mistress Vosill?"

"That's me."

She nodded at me. "And this?"

"My apprentice, Oelph."

"Very good. Follow me."

The Doctor looked round as we started up some bare wooden stairs, a conspiratorial look on her face. I was caught in the act of directing a most harsh stare at the black back of the woman leading us, but the Doctor just smiled and winked.

The servant who had talked to the Doctor locked the dock door and disappeared through another which I guessed led to the servants' floor.

The passageway was steep and narrow and unlit save for a slit window every storey, where the wooden steps twisted to double back on themselves. There was a narrow door at each floor, too. It crossed my mind that perhaps these confined quarters were for children, for the Slaver Tunch was well known for specialising in child slaves.

We came to the second landing. "How long has Slaver Tunch—?" the Doctor began.

"Please do not talk on these stairs," the strict-looking woman told her. "Others may hear."

The Doctor said nothing, but turned back to look at me again, her eyes wide and the corners of her mouth turned down.

We were led into the rest of the house at the third storey. The corridor we found ourselves in was broad and plush. Paintings adorned the walls, and facing us were wall-high glass windows letting in the sight of

the tops of the grand houses on the far side of the canal and the sky
and clouds beyond. A series of tall, wide doors opened off the corridor.
We were ushered towards the tallest and widest.

The woman put her hand on the door's handle. "The servant," she
said. "On the dock."

"Yes?" said the Doctor.

"He talked to you?"

The Doctor looked into the woman's eyes for a moment. "I asked
him a question," she said (this is one of the few times I have ever heard
the Doctor directly lie).

"I thought so," the woman said, opening the door for us. We
stepped into a large, dark room lit only by candles and lanterns. The
floor underfoot felt warm and furry. At first I thought I'd stepped on a
hound. There was a perfume of great sweetness in the room and I
thought I detected the scent of various herbs known to have a healing
or tonic effect. I tried to detect a smell of sickness or corruption, but
could not. A huge canopied bed sat in the middle of the room. It held a
large man attended by three people: two servants and a well-dressed
lady. They looked round as we entered and light flooded into the room.
The light started to wane behind us as the severe-looking woman
closed the doors from outside.

The Doctor turned round and said through the narrowing gap,
"The servant—"

"Will be punished," the woman said with a wintry smile.

The doors thudded shut. The Doctor breathed deeply and then
turned to the candle-lit scene in the centre of the room.

"You are the woman doctor?" the lady asked, approaching us.

"My name is Vosill," the Doctor told her. "Lady Tunch?"

The woman nodded. "Can you help my husband?"

"I don't know, ma'am." The Doctor looked round the shadowy, half-
hidden spaces of the room, as if trying to guess its extent. "It would help
if I could see him. Is there a reason for the curtains being drawn?"

"Oh. We were told the darkness would reduce the swellings."

"Let's take a look, shall we?" the Doctor said. We crossed to the bed.
Walking on the thick floor covering was an odd, disconcerting experience, like walking on the deck of a pitching ship.

The Slave Master Tunch had, by repute, always been a huge man. He was bigger now. He lay on the bed, breathing quickly and shallowly, his skin grey and blotched. His eyes were closed. "He seems to sleep almost all the time," the lady told us. She was a thin little thing, scarcely more than a child, with a pinched, pale face and hands that were forever kneading each other. One of the two servants was mopping her husband's brow. The other was fussing at the bottom of the bed, tucking in bed clothes. "He was soiled, just earlier," the lady explained.

"Did you keep the stool?" the Doctor asked.

"No!" the lady said, shocked. "We have no need to. The house has a water closet."

The Doctor took the place of the servant mopping the man's brow. She looked into his eyes, she looked in his mouth and then she pulled back the coverings over the huge bulge of his body before pulling up his shirt. I think the only fatter people I have seen have been eunuchs. Master Tunch was not just fat (though goodness knows, there is nothing wrong with being fat!), he bulged. Oddly. I saw this myself, even before the Doctor pointed this out.

She turned to the lady. "I need more light," she told her. "Would you have the curtains opened?"

The lady hesitated, then nodded to the servants.

Light washed into the great room. It was even more splendid than I had imagined. All the furniture was covered in gold leaf. Cloth of gold hung from the bed's great frame. It was drawn up into a great sphincter shape in the centre of the ceiling and even formed the curtains themselves. Paintings and mirrors covered every wall and pieces of sculpture—mostly nymphs and a few of the old, wanton goddesses—stood on the floor or sat upon the tables, desks and sideboards, where a veritable profusion of what looked like human skulls covered in gold leaf were scattered. The carpets were a soft and lustrous blue-black, and were, I guessed, zuleon fur, from the far south. They were so thick I wasn't surprised that walking on them had been unsettling.

Slave Master Tunch looked no better in the light of day than he had by candle glow. His flesh was everywhere puffy and discoloured and his body seemed a strange shape, even for one so large. He moaned and one fat hand came fluttering up like a doughy bird. His wife took it and held it to her cheek one-handed. There was an awkwardness about the way she tried to use both hands that mystified me at the time.

The Doctor pressed and prodded the giant frame in a variety of places. The man groaned and whimpered but uttered no intelligible word.

"When did he start to bloat like this?" she asked.

"About a year past, I think," the lady said. The Doctor looked at her quizzically. The lady looked bashful. "We were only married a half-year ago," the Slaver's wife said. The Doctor was looking at her oddly, but then she smiled.

"Was there much pain at the start?"

"The Housemistress has told me that his last wife said it was about Harvest when he began to get the pains, and then his . . ." She patted her own waist. "His girth began to become greater."

The Doctor kept prodding the great body. "Did he become ill tempered?"

The lady smiled a small, hesitant smile. "Oh, I think he was always . . . he was never one to suffer fools gladly." She started to hug herself, then winced with pain before she could cross her arms, settling instead for massaging her upper left arm with her right hand.

"Is your arm sore?" the Doctor asked her.

The lady stepped back, eyes wide. "No!" she exclaimed, still clutching her arm. "No. There's nothing wrong with it. It's fine."

The Doctor pulled the man's night dress back down and drew the covers over him. "Well, there's nothing I can do for him. Best let him sleep."

"Sleep?" the lady wailed. "All day, like an animal?"

"I'm sorry," the Doctor said. "I should have said best let him remain unconscious."

"Is there nothing you can do for him?"

"Not really," the Doctor said. "The illness is so advanced that he is hardly even feeling the pain now. It's unlikely he'll come round again. I can write you a prescription for something to give him if he does, but I imagine his brother has already dealt with that."

The lady nodded. She was staring at the great form that was her husband, one fist at her mouth, her teeth biting on her knuckle. "He's going to die!"

"Almost certainly. I'm sorry."

The lady shook her head. Eventually she tore her gaze away from the bed. "Should I have called you earlier? If I had, would that—?"

"It would have made no difference," the Doctor told her. "There is nothing any doctor could have done for him. Some diseases are not treatable." She looked down—with a cold expression, it seemed to me—at the body lying panting on the great bed. "Happily some are also not transmissible." She looked up at the lady. "You need have no fear on that point." She glanced round at the servants as she said this.

"How much do I owe you?" the wife asked.

"Whatever you think fit," the Doctor said. "I have been able to do nothing. Perhaps you feel I deserve nothing."

"No. No, not at all. Please." The lady went to a bureau near the bed and took out a small plain purse. She handed it to the Doctor.

"You really should have that arm seen to," the Doctor said softly, while studying the other woman's face, and her mouth, most closely. "It might mean—"

"No," the lady said quickly, looking away and then walking off to the nearest of the tall windows. "I am perfectly well, Doctor. Perfectly. Thank you for coming. Good day."

We sat in the hired chair on the way back, wobbling and weaving through the crowds of Land Street, heading for the Palace. I was folding away my spiced kerchief. The Doctor smiled sadly. She had been in a thoughtful, even morose mood all the way back (we had left the same way we had arrived, via the private dock). "Still worried about ill humours, Oelph?"

"It is how I was raised, mistress, and it seems like a sensible precaution."

She sighed heavily and looked out at the people. "Ill humours," she said, and seemed to be talking more to herself than to me.

"Those ill humours you talked about from insects, mistress . . ." I began, recalling something that my master had communicated to me.

"Hmm?"

"Can they be extracted from the insects and used? I mean, might some assassin, say, be able to have made a concentrate of such insects and administer the potion to a victim?" I tried to look innocent.

The Doctor had a look about her I thought I recognised. Usually it meant that she was about to launch into some extremely long and involved explanation concerning how some aspect of medicine worked, and how all the assumptions that I might have held about the subject were completely wrong. On this occasion, though, she seemed to fall back from the brink of such a lecture, and looked away and just said, "No."

There was silence between us for a while. During that time I listened to the braided canes of the chair as they creaked and cracked around us.

"What was wrong with the lady Tunch's arm, mistress?" I asked eventually.

The Doctor sighed. "It had been broken, I think, and then set badly," she said.

"But any saw-smith can set a bone, mistress!"

"It was probably a radial fracture. Those are always more difficult." She looked out at the milling people all walking, bargaining, arguing and yelling on the street. "But yes, a rich man's wife . . . especially one with a doctor in the family . . ." She looked round slowly at me. "You would think such a person would receive the best of attention, wouldn't you? Instead of, it would seem, none."

"But . . ." I began, then started to understand. "Ah."

"Ah, indeed," the Doctor said.

We both watched the people for a while, as our quartet of hired men carried the chair through them, uphill towards the Palace. The Doctor sighed after a while and said, "Her jaw had been broken not long ago, too. It hadn't been treated, either." Then she took the purse mistress Tunch had given her out of her coat and said something that wasn't really like her at all. "Look, here's a drinking house. Let's go for a drink." She looked at me closely. "Do you drink, Oelph?"

"I don't, that is, I'm not really, well, I have but not—"

She held a hand up out of the side of the chair. One of the rear men shouted to those in front and we drew to an orderly halt right outside the door of the inn.

"Come on," she said, slapping me on the knee, "I'll teach you."

6

THE BODYGUARD

The concubine lady Perrund, attended at a discreet distance by a eunuch of the harem guard, took her daily constitutional as usual a little after breakfast. Her route that day took her to one of the higher towers on the east wing where she knew she could gain access to the roof. It was a fine, clear day and the view could be particularly fine, looking out over the palace grounds to the spires and domes of the city of Crough, the plains beyond, and the hills in the deep distance.

"Why, DeWar!"

The chief bodyguard DeWar sat in a large, sheet-covered chair that was one of twenty or so pieces of furniture which had been stored in the tower room. His eyes were closed, his chin was resting on his chest. His head jerked up, he looked around and blinked. The concubine Perrund sat in a seat beside him, her red gown bright against the dark blue of the sheet. The white-clad eunuch guard stood by the door.

DeWar cleared his throat. "Ah, Perrund," he said. He drew himself up in the chair and straightened his black tunic. "How are you?"

"Pleased to see you, DeWar, though surprised," she told him, smiling. "You looked as though you were slumbering. I thought of all people the Protector's chief bodyguard would be the least likely to need sleep during the day."

DeWar glanced round at the eunuch guard. "The Protector has given me the Xamis-morning off," he said. "There's a formal breakfast for the Xinkspar delegation. There are guards everywhere. He thinks I am surplus."

"You think otherwise."

"He is surrounded by men with weapons. Just because they're our guards doesn't mean there isn't a threat. Naturally I think I ought to be there but he will not be told." DeWar rubbed his eyes.

"So you became unconscious out of pique?"

"Did I look asleep?" DeWar asked innocently. "I was only thinking."

"And very fast a-thought you looked. What did you conclude?"

"That I must not answer so many questions."

"A fine decision. People do pry so."

"And you?"

"Oh, I rarely think. There are so many people who think—or think they think—better than I. It would be presumptuous."

"I meant what brings you here? Is this your morning walk?"

"Yes. I like to take the air from the roof."

"I must remember not to position myself here next time I want to think."

"I vary my route, DeWar. There is no certain escape in any public part of the palace. The only safe place might be within your own chambers."

"I shall try to remember."

"Good. I trust you are happy now?"

"Happy? Why would that be?"

"There has been an attempt on the Protector's life. I understood you were there."

"Ah, that."

"Aye, that."

"Yes. I was there."

"So, are you happy now? The last time we talked you expressed dismay that there had been so few assassins recently, taking this as incontrovertible proof that we must be entirely surrounded by them."

DeWar smiled ruefully. "Ah yes. Then, no, I am no happier, my lady."

"I thought not." The lady Perrund rose to go. DeWar stood as she did. "I understand the Protector visits us in the harem later today," she said. "Will you be joining us then?"

"I imagine so."

"Good. I'll leave you to your thinking." The lady Perrund smiled, then made for the door which led to the roof, followed by the eunuch guard.

DeWar watched her and the guard go, then stretched and yawned.

The palace concubine Yalde was a favourite of General YetAmidous and was often called to his home in the palace grounds. The girl could not speak, though she appeared to have a tongue and everything else required for speech, and understood Imperial well enough and the local language of Tassaseni a very little. She had been a slave. Perhaps there was something that had happened to her during that time which had addled whatever part of her brains would normally have granted her the power of speech. Still, she could whimper and moan and shout when she was being pleasured, as the General never tired of telling his friends.

Yalde sat on the same vast couch as the General, in the principal receiving room of his house, feeding him finger fruits from a crystal bowl while he played with her long black hair, twisting and untwisting it in one large hand. It was night, a bell or so after a small banquet YetAmidous had thrown. The men still wore their dining robes. Present with YetAmidous were RuLeuin, UrLeyn's brother, BreDelle, the Protector's physician, Guard Commander ZeSpiole, the Generals Duke Simalg and Duke Ralboute and a few aides and court juniors.

"No, there are paper screens or something," said RuLeuin. "He must have burst through those."

"It was the ceiling, I tell you. Think. It would be the best place. Hint of danger, and—whumpf! Straight down. Why, you could just drop a cannon ball on whoever was causing the trouble. Quite easy, really. A fool could do it."

"Nonsense. The walls."

"ZeSpiole should know," YetAmidous said, interrupting RuLeuin and Simalg. "ZeSpiole? What do you have to say?"

"I wasn't there," ZeSpiole said, waving a goblet around. "And the painted chamber was never used while I was chief bodyguard."

"Still, you must know of it," YetAmidous said.

"Of course I know of it," ZeSpiole said. He stopped waving his goblet round long enough for a passing servant to fill it with wine. "Lots of people *know* of it, but no one goes in there."

"So how did DeWar surprise the Sea Company assassin?" Simalg asked. Simalg was a Duke with vast lands in the east, but had been one of the first of the old noble families to declare for UrLeyn during the war of succession. He was a thin, ever-languorous-looking man with long straight brown hair. "The ceiling, was it not. ZeSpiole? Do tell me I'm right."

"The walls," RuLeuin said. "Through a painting, a portrait in which the eyes had been cut out!"

"I can't say."

"But you must!" Simalg protested.

"It's a secret."

"Is it?"

"It is."

"There we are," YetAmidous said to the others. "It is a secret."

"Does the Protector say so, or his smug saviour?" Ralboute asked. A stout but muscled man, Duke Ralboute had been another early convert to UrLeyn's cause.

"You mean DeWar?" ZeSpiole asked.

"Does he not seem smug to you?" Ralboute asked, and drank from his goblet.

"Yes, smug," Doctor BreDelle said. "And too clever by half. Or even more."

"And hard to pin down," Ralboute added, pulling his dining

robe more loosely over his huge frame and brushing some crumbs away.

"Try lying on him," Simalg suggested.

"I'll lie on you," Ralboute told the other noble.

"I think not."

"Do you think DeWar would lie with the Protector?" YetAmidous asked. "Do we think he really is a lover of men? Or are these only rumours?"

"You never see him inside the harem," RuLeuin said.

"Would he be allowed?" BreDelle asked. The court physician was only allowed to make professional calls to the harem, when its own female nurse could not cope.

"Chief bodyguard?" ZeSpiole said. "Yes. He could pick amongst the household concubines. The ones dressed in blue."

"Ah," YetAmidous said, and stroked under the chin of the dark-haired girl at his side. "The household girls. One level beneath my little Yalde."

"I think DeWar does not make use of that particular privilege," Ralboute said.

"They say he keeps the company of the concubine Perrund," RuLeuin said.

"The one with the wasted arm." YetAmidous nodded.

"I have heard that too," BreDelle agreed.

"One of UrLeyn's own?" Simalg looked aghast. "You don't mean that he has her? Providence! The Protector would make sure he could stay in the harem as long as he liked—as a eunuch."

"I cannot imagine that DeWar is that foolish or so intemperate," BreDelle said. "It could only be courtly love."

"Or they could be plotting something, could they not?" Simalg suggested.

"I hear he visits a house in the city, though not often," RuLeuin said.

"A house with girls?" YetAmidous asked. "Not boys?"

"Girls," RuLeuin confirmed.

"I think I'd ask for double fare, if I were a girl who had to accommodate that fellow," Simalg said. "He has a sour smell about him. Have you never noticed?"

"You may have a nose for these things," said Doctor BreDelle.

"Perhaps DeWar has a special dispensation from the Protector," Ralboute suggested. "A secret one which lets him bed Perrund."

"She's crippled!" YetAmidous said.

"Yet still, I think, beautiful," Simalg said.

"And it must be said that some people have been known to find infirmity attractive," Doctor BreDelle added.

"Cleaving the regal lady Perrund. A privilege you enjoyed, ZeSpiole?" Ralboute asked the older man.

"Sadly not," ZeSpiole said. "And I do not think DeWar does either. I suspect theirs is a meeting of minds, not bodies."

"Too clever by twice," Simalg muttered, beckoning more wine.

"What privileges do you most miss from the post DeWar now has?" Ralboute asked, looking down as he peeled a piece of fruit. He shooed away a servant who offered to do this for him.

"I miss being near the Protector every day, but little else. It is an unnerving job. A young man's job. My present post is quite exciting enough without having to deal with murderous ambassadors."

"Oh, come, ZeSpiole," Ralboute said, sucking at his fruit and then spitting out a mush of seeds into a waste bowl before sucking again and swallowing. He wiped his lips. "You must resent DeWar, mustn't you? He usurped you."

ZeSpiole was silent for a moment. "Usurpation can be the right course, sometimes, Duke, don't you think?" He looked round the others. "We all of us usurped the old King. It needed to be done."

"Absolutely," said YetAmidous.

"Of course," RuLeuin agreed.

"Mmmm!" BreDelle nodded, mouth full of a sweetmeat.

Ralboute nodded. Simalg gave a sigh. "Our Protector did the usurping," he said. "The rest of us helped."

"And proud to do so," YetAmidous said, slapping the edge of his couch.

"So you don't resent the fellow at all?" Ralboute asked ZeSpiole. "You are a child of Providence indeed." He shook his head and used his fingers to break the flesh of another fruit.

"I no more resent him than you ought to resent the Protector," ZeSpiole said.

Ralboute was stopped in his eating. "Why should I resent UrLeyn?" he asked. "I honour UrLeyn and what he has done."

"Including putting us here in the palace," Simalg said. "We might have still been juniors, out of favour. We owe the Grand Aedile as much as any trader who pins his voting document—what do you call it? Franchisement. His Franchisement high on his wall."

"Just so," ZeSpiole said. "And yet if anything was to happen to the Protector—"

"Providence forbid!" YetAmidous said.

"—might not a Duke such as you—a person of high birth under the old regime yet who had also been a faithful general under the Protector's new order—be just the sort of person the people might turn to, as successor?"

"Or there's the boy," Simalg said, yawning.

"This talk's uncomfortable," RuLeuin said.

"No," ZeSpiole said, looking at RuLeuin. "We must be able to talk of such things. Those who wish Tassasen and UrLeyn ill most certainly will not shrink from such talk. *You* need to think of such things, RuLeuin. You are the Protector's brother. People might turn to you if he was taken from us."

RuLeuin shook his head. "No," he said. "I have risen so considerably on his cloak-tails. People already think I have climbed too far." He glanced over at Ralboute, who looked back with wide, expressionless eyes.

"Oh yes," Simalg said, waving a hand, "we Dukes are frightfully against such accidents of birth."

"Where's that housemaster?" YetAmidous said. "Yalde, be a dear and go and fetch the musicians back, would you? All this talk is making my head ache. We need music and songs!"

"Here!"

"There! There he is!"

"Quick! Catch him! Catch him! Quickly!"

"Aah!"

"Too late!"

"I win I win I win!"

"You win again! What cunningness in one so young!" Perrund picked the boy up with her good arm and swung him on to the seat beside her. Lattens, UrLeyn's son, squirmed as he was tickled then yelped and dived under a fold in the concubine's gown and tried to hide there as DeWar, who had run most of the length of the visiting chamber of the outer harem in a vain attempt to head Lattens off, arrived panting and growling.

"Where's that child?" he demanded gruffly.

"Child? Why, what child could that be?" the lady Perrund asked, hand at her throat, her blue-flecked eyes wide.

"Ach, never mind. I'll just have to sit down here to get my breath back after chasing the young scamp." There was a giggle as DeWar sat down right beside the boy, whose hose and shoes stuck out from the woman's robe. "What's this? Here are that rascal's shoes. And look!" DeWar grabbed Lattens' ankle. There was a muffled shriek. "And his leg! I'll bet the rest is attached! Yes! Here he is!" Perrund pulled away the fold of her gown to let DeWar tickle the boy, then brought a cushion from another part of the couch and put it under the boy's bottom. DeWar plonked him there. "Do you know what happens to boys who win at hide-and-seek?" DeWar asked. Lattens, wide-eyed, shook his head and made to suck his thumb. Perrund gently stopped him from doing this. "They get," DeWar growled, coming very close to the child, "sweets!"

Perrund handed him the box of crystallised fruits. Lattens squealed with delight and rubbed his hands together, staring into the box and trying to decide which to have first. Eventually he grabbed a small handful.

Huesse, another red-gowned concubine, sat heavily down on a couch across from Perrund and DeWar. She too had been involved in the game of hide-and-seek. Huesse was Lattens' aunt. Her sister had died giving birth to Lattens towards the start of the war of succession. Huesse was a plumply supple woman with unruly fair ringleted hair.

"And have you had your lessons for today, Lattens?" Perrund asked.

"Yes," the boy said. He was small made, like his father, though he had the red-tinged golden hair of his mother and his aunt.

"And what did you learn today?"

"More things about equal triangles, and some history, about things which have happened."

"I see," Perrund said, settling the boy's collar back down and patting his hair flat again.

"There was this man called Narajist," the boy said, licking his fingers free of sugar dust.

"Naharajast," DeWar said. Perrund motioned him quiet.

"Who looked in a tube at the sky and told the Emperor . . ." Lattens screwed up his eyes and peered up at the three glowing plaster domes lighting the chamber. "Poeslied—"

"Puiside," DeWar muttered. Perrund frowned severely and tutted.

"—there were big fiery rocks up there and Watch Out!" The boy stood and shouted the last two words, then sat down again and leant over the box of sweets, one finger to his lips. "And the Emperor didn't and the rocks killed him dead."

"Well, it's a little simplified," DeWar began.

"What a sad story!" Perrund said, now ruffling the boy's hair. "The poor old Emperor!"

"Yes," the boy shrugged. "But daddy came along and made everything all right again."

The three adults looked at each other and laughed. "Indeed he did," Perrund said, taking away the box of sweets and hiding it behind her. "Tassasen is powerful again, isn't it?"

"Mm-hmm," Lattens said, trying to squirm behind Perrund in pursuit of the box of sweets.

"I think it might be time for a story," Perrund said, and pulled the boy back to a sitting position. "DeWar?"

DeWar sat and thought for a moment. "Well," he said, "it's not much of a story, but it is a story of sorts."

"Then tell it."

"It is suitable for the boy?" Huesse asked.

"I shall make it so." DeWar sat forward and shifted his sword and dagger. "Once upon a time there was a magical land where every man was a king, every woman a queen, each boy a prince and all girls princesses. In this land there were no hungry people and no crippled people."

"Were there any poor people?" asked Lattens.

"That depends what you mean. In a way no, because they could all have any amount of riches they wanted, but in a way yes, for there were people who chose to have nothing. Their hearts' desire was to be free from owning anything, and they usually preferred to stay in the desert or in the mountains or the forests, living in caves or trees or just wandering around. Some lived in the great cities, where they too just roved about. But wherever they chose to wander, the decision was always theirs."

"Were they holy people?" Lattens asked.

"Well, in a way, maybe."

"Were they all handsome and beautiful, too?" Huesse asked.

"Again, that depends what you mean by beautiful," DeWar said apologetically. Perrund sighed with exasperation. "Some people see a sort of beauty in ugliness," DeWar said. "And if everybody is beautiful there is something singular in being ugly, or just plain. But, generally, yes, everybody was as beautiful as they wanted to be."

"So many ifs and buts," Perrund said. "This sounds a very equivocal land."

"In a way," DeWar smiled. Perrund hit him with a cushion. "Sometimes," DeWar continued, "as people in the land brought more of it under cultivation—"

"What was the name of the land?" Lattens interrupted.

"Oh . . . Lavishia, of course. Anyway, sometimes the citizens of Lavishia would discover whole groups of people who lived a bit like the wanderers, that is, like the poor—or holy—people in their own land, but who did not have the choice of living like that. Such people lived like that because they had to. These were people who hadn't had the advantages in life the people of Lavishia were used to. In fact, dealing with such people soon became the biggest problem the people of Lavishia had."

"What? They had no war, famine, pestilence, taxes?" Perrund asked.

"None. And no real likelihood of the last three."

"I feel my credulity being stretched," Perrund muttered.

"So in Lavishia everybody was happy?" Huesse asked.

"As happy as they could be," DeWar said. "People still managed to make their own unhappinesses, as people always do."

Perrund nodded. "Now it begins to sound plausible."

"In this land there lived two friends, a boy and a girl who were cousins and who had grown up together. They thought they were adults but really they were still just children. They were the best of friends but they disagreed on many things. One of the most important things they disagreed about was what to do when Lavishia chanced upon one of these tribes of poor people. Was it better to leave them alone or was it better to try and make life better for them? Even if you decided it was the right thing to do to make life better for them, which way did you do this? Did you say, Come and join us and be like us? Did you say, Give up all your own ways of doing things, the gods that you worship, the beliefs you hold most dear, the traditions that make you who you are? Or do you say, We have decided you should stay roughly as you are and we will treat you like children and give you toys that might make your life better? Indeed, who even decided what was better?"

Lattens was shifting and wriggling on the couch. Perrund was trying to keep him still. "Were there really not any wars?" the child asked.

"Yes," Perrund said, looking concernedly at DeWar. "This may all be a little abstract for a child of Lattens' age."

DeWar smiled sadly. "Well, there were some very small wars very far away, but to be brief, the two friends decided that they would put their arguments to a test. They had another friend, a lady, who . . . very much liked both of the friends, and who was very clever and very beautiful and who had a favour which she was prepared to grant either of them." DeWar looked at Perrund and Huesse.

"*Either* of them?" Perrund asked with a small smile. Huesse looked at the floor.

"She was broad-minded," DeWar said, and cleared his throat. "Anyway, it was agreed that the two cousins would present their arguments to her and whoever lost the argument had to leave and let the favour be granted to the other one alone."

"Did this third friend know about the cousins' amusing agreement?" Perrund inquired.

"Names! What are the names?" Lattens demanded.

"Yes, what are they called?" Huesse said.

"The girl was called Sechroom and the boy's name was Hiliti. Their beautiful friend was called Leleeril." DeWar looked at Perrund. "And no, she did not know about the agreement."

"Tut," Perrund pronounced.

"So, the three met in a hunting lodge in the high, high mountains—"

"As high as the Breathless Plains?" Lattens asked.

"Not so high, but steeper, with very sharp peaks. Now—"

"And which cousin believed in what?" Perrund asked.

"Hmm? Oh, Sechroom believed that one should always interfere, or try to help, while Hiliti thought it best to leave people be," DeWar said. "Anyway, they had good food and fine wine and they laughed and told each other stories and jokes and the two friends Sechroom and Hiliti explained their different ideas to Leleeril and asked which she thought was right. She tried to say that they were both right in their own ways, and that sometimes one was right and one wrong and sometimes the other way round . . . but eventually Sechroom and Hiliti said Leleeril had to choose one or the other, and she chose Hiliti, and poor Sechroom had to leave the hunting lodge."

"What was it Leeril was going to give Hiliti?" Lattens asked.

"Something sweet," DeWar said, and, magician-like, produced a crystallised fruit from his pocket. He presented the sweet to the delighted boy, who bit happily into it.

"What happened?" Huesse asked.

"Leleeril found out that her favours had been subject to a bet and she was hurt. She went away for a while—"

"Did she *have* to go away?" Perrund asked. "You know, the way girls in polite society sometimes have to, while nature takes its course?"

"No, she just wanted to be somewhere else, away from everybody she knew."

"What, without her parents?" Huesse asked sceptically.

"Without anybody. Then Sechroom and Hiliti realised that perhaps Leleeril had felt more for one of them than they had imagined and that they had done a bad thing."

"There are three Emperors now," Lattens said suddenly, munching on his sugary fruit. "I know their names." Perrund shushed him.

"Leleeril came back," DeWar told them, "but she had made new friends where she had been, and she had changed while she had been away, and so went away again, to stay. As far as is known she lived happily ever after. Sechroom became a soldier-missionary in the Lavishian army, to help fight in the very small, very far-away wars."

"A female soldier?" asked Huesse.

"Of a sort," DeWar said. "Perhaps more missionary, or even spy, than soldier."

Perrund shrugged. "The balnimes of Quarreck are said all to be warrior women."

DeWar sat back, smiling.

"Oh," Huesse said, looking disappointed. "Is that all?" she asked.

"That's all for now." DeWar shrugged.

"You mean there's more?" Perrund said. "You'd better tell us. The suspense might be too much to bear."

"Perhaps I'll tell you more some other time."

"What about Hiliti?" Huesse asked. "What became of him after his cousin left?"

DeWar just smiled.

"Very well then," Perrund chided him. "Be mysterious."

"Where is Lavishia?" Lattens asked. "I know geography."

"Far away," DeWar told the boy.

"Far away across the sea?"

"Far away, over the sea."

"Further than Tyrsk?"

"Much further."

"Further than the Thrown Isles?"

"Oh, a lot further than that."

"Further than . . . Drizen?"

"Even further than Drezen. In the land of make-believe."

"And are the mountains sugar hills?" Lattens asked.

"All of them. And the lakes are fruit juice. And all the game animals grow on trees, ready cooked. And other trees grow their own treehouses, and catapults and bows and arrows grow on them like fruits."

"And I suppose the rivers run with wine?" Huesse asked.

"Yes, and the houses and the buildings and the bridges are made of diamond and gold and everything precious."

"I've got a pet eltar," Lattens told DeWar. "It's called Wintle. Want to see it?"

"Certainly."

"It's in the garden, in a cage. I'll fetch it. Come on, let's go," Lattens said to Huesse, pulling her on to her feet.

"Probably time he had his run round the garden anyway," Huesse said. "I shall be back soon, with the unruly Wintle."

DeWar and Perrund watched the woman and the child leave the chamber under the watchful eyes of a white-clad eunuch in the high pulpit.

"Now then, Mr. DeWar," Perrund said. "You have delayed long enough. You must tell me all about this ambassador assassin you foiled."

DeWar told her as much as he felt he could about what had happened. He left out the details of exactly how he had been able to respond so promptly to the assassin's attack, and Perrund was too polite to press him further.

"What of the delegation that came with the Sea Company's ambassador?"

DeWar looked troubled. "I think they knew nothing of what he intended. One of them did, maybe. He had charge of the drugs the assassin had taken, but the rest were ignorant. Naive innocents who thought this was a great adventure."

"Were they sorely questioned?" Perrund asked quietly.

DeWar nodded. He looked down at the floor. "Only their heads are going back. I'm told at the end they were glad to lose them."

Perrund put her hand briefly on the man's arm, then drew it away again, glancing at the eunuch in the pulpit. "The blame lies with their masters who sent them to their deaths, not with you. They would not have suffered less if their plan had succeeded."

"I know that," DeWar said, smiling as best he could. "Perhaps it might be called professional lack of empathy. My training is to kill or disable as quickly as possible, not as slowly."

"So are you really not content?" Perrund asked. "There has been an attempt, and a serious one at that. Do you not feel this disproves your theory that there is someone here at court?"

"Perhaps," DeWar said awkwardly.

Perrund smiled. "You are not really appeased by this at all, are you?"

"No," DeWar admitted. He looked away. "Well, yes, a little, but more because I think I have decided you are right. I will worry whatever happens and always put the worst construction on it. I am unable not to worry. Worrying is my natural state."

"So you should not worry about worrying so much," Perrund suggested, a smile playing about her lips.

"That is more or less it. Otherwise one might never stop."

"Most pragmatic." Perrund leant forward and put her chin in her hand. "What was the point of your story about Sechroom, Hiliti and Leleeril?"

DeWar looked awkward. "I don't really know," he confessed. "I heard the story in another language. It doesn't survive the translation very well, and . . . there was more than just the language that needed translation. Some of the ideas and . . . ways that people do things and behave required alteration to make sense, too."

"Well then, you were mostly successful. Did your story really happen?"

"Yes. It really happened," DeWar said, then sat back and laughed, shaking his head. "No, I'm jesting with you. How could it happen? Search the latest globes, scour the newest maps, sail to the ends of the world. You will not find Lavishia, I swear."

"Oh," Perrund said, disappointed. "So you are not from Lavishia?"

"How can one be from a place that does not exist?"

"But you are from . . . Mottelocci, wasn't it?"

"Mottelocci indeed." DeWar frowned. "I don't recall ever telling you that."

"There are mountains there, aren't there? It is one of the . . . what are they called, now? The Half-Hiddens. Yes. The Half-Hidden Kingdoms. Unreachable half the year. But a small paradise, they say."

"Half a paradise. In spring and summer and autumn it is beautiful. In winter it is terrible."

"Three seasons from four would be sufficient to please most people."

"Not when the fourth season lasts longer than the other three put together."

"Did something like your story happen there?"

"Perhaps."

"Were you one of the people?"

"Maybe."

"Sometimes," Perrund said, sitting back with a look of exasperation on her face, "I can quite understand why rulers employ torturers."

"Oh, I can always understand," DeWar said softly. "Just not . . ." He seemed to catch himself, then sat upright, pulling his tunic tighter down. He looked up at the vague shadows cast on the softly glowing bowl of the light dome overhead. "Perhaps we have time for a game of something. What do you say?"

Perrund remained looking at him for a moment, then sighed and also drew herself upright. "I say we had better play 'Monarch's Dispute.' It is the one game you might be suited for. Though there are also," she said, waving to a servant at a distant door, " 'Liar's Dice' and 'Secret Keep.' "

DeWar sat back on the couch, watching Perrund as she watched the servant approach. "And 'Subterfuge,' " she added, "and 'Blaggard's Boast' and 'Whiff of Truth' and 'Travesty' and 'The Gentleman Misinformant' and . . ."

7
THE DOCTOR

My master has a plan for your mistress. A little surprise."

"I'll bet!"

"More like a big one! Eh?"

"So would mine."

There were various other comments and whistles from round the table, though nothing, in retrospect, that seemed much like wit.

"What do you mean?" I asked.

Feulecharo, apprentice to Duke Walen, just winked. He was a stocky fellow, with wild brown hair that resisted all attempts to control it save those employing shears. He was polishing a pair of boots while the rest of us tucked into our evening meal, in a tent on the Prospect

Plain, one day into the 455th Circuition. On this first rest stop it was traditional for the senior pages and apprentices to dine together. Feulecharo had been allowed to join us by his master, but he was being punished for one of his regular misdemeanours with extra work, hence the boots, and a set of rustily ancient ceremonial armour he was supposed to polish before we set off the next day.

"What sort of plan?" I insisted. "What can the Duke want with the Doctor?"

"Let's just say he's suspicious," Feulecharo said, tapping his nose with a polishing brush.

"Of what?"

"My master is suspicious, too," Unoure said, breaking a piece of bread in half and smearing some gravy round his plate.

"How very true," drawled Epline, page to Guard Commander Adlain.

"Well, he is," Unoure insisted sullenly.

"Still testing out his new ideas on you, is he, Unoure?" one of the other pages called. He turned to the others. "We saw Unoure in the baths once—"

"Aye, it would be the once!"

"What year was that?"

"We did," continued the page, "and you should see the lad's scars! I tell you, Nolieti is a perfect beast to him!"

"He teaches me everything!" Unoure said, standing up, his eyes bright with tears.

"Shut up, Unoure," Jollisce said. "Don't let this rabble bait you so." Slight but elegantly fair, and older than most of us, Jollisce was page to Duke Ormin, who was the Doctor's employer after the Mifeli trading family and before the King commandeered her services. Unoure sat down again, muttering under his breath. "What plans, Feulecharo?" Jollisce asked.

"Never mind," Feulecharo said. He started whistling and began to pay uncharacteristically close attention to the boots he was polishing, and soon started to talk to them, as though trying to persuade them to clean themselves.

"That boy is intolerable," Jollisce said, and took up a pitcher of the watered wine which was the strongest drink we were allowed.

A little after supper, Jollisce and I wandered along one edge of the camp. Hills stretched ahead of us and on both sides. Behind us, past the lip of the Prospect Plain, Xamis was still slowly setting in a fiery riot of colour, somewhere far beyond the near-circle of Crater Lake, falling over the round edge of sea.

Clouds, caught half in Xamis's dying light and half in the late morning glare of Seigen, were lit with gold on one side, and red, ochre, vermilion, orange, scarlet . . . a wide wilderness of colours. We walked amongst the settling animals as each was quieted. Some—the hauls, mostly—had a bag over their heads. The better mounts had elegant eye-muffs while the best had their own travelling stables and lesser beasts merely warranted a blindfold made of whatever rag came to hand. One by one they folded themselves to the ground and prepared to sleep. Jollisce and I walked among them, Jollisce smoking a long pipe. He was my oldest and best friend, from the time when I had briefly been in the service of the Duke before being sent to Haspide.

"Probably it's nothing," he said. "Feulecharo likes to listen to himself talk, and he likes to pretend he knows something everybody else doesn't. I wouldn't worry about it, but if you think you ought to report it to your mistress, then of course you must do so."

"Hmm," I said. I recall (looking back on that earlier self from this more mature vantage point) that I was not sure what to do. Duke Walen was a powerful man, and a schemer. He was not the sort of man somebody like the Doctor could afford to have as an enemy, and yet I had to think of my own, real Master, as well as my Mistress. Should I tell neither of them? Or one—if so, which? Or both?

"Listen," Jollisce said, stopping and turning to me (and it seemed to me he'd waited until there was nobody else around before he divulged this last piece of intelligence). "If it's any help, I have heard that Walen might have sent somebody to Equatorial Cuskery."

"Cuskery?"

"Yes, do you know of it?"

"Sort of. It's a port, isn't it?"

"Port, city-state, Sea Company sanctuary, lair of sea monsters if you believe some people . . . but the point is, it's about the furthest north people come in any numbers from the Southern lands, and they supposedly have quite a number of embassies and legations there."

"Yes?"

"Well, apparently one of Duke Walen's men has been sent to Cuskery to look for somebody from Drezen."

"From Drezen!" I said, then lowered my voice as Jollisce frowned and looked about us, over the sleeping bodies of the great animals. "But . . . why?"

"I can't imagine," Jollisce said.

"How long does it take to get to Cuskery?"

"It takes nearly a year to get there. The journey is somewhat quicker coming back, they say." He shrugged. "The winds."

"That's a long way to send somebody," I said, wondering.

"I know," Jollisce said. He sucked on his pipe. "My man assumed it was some trade thing. You know, people are always expecting to make their fortunes from spices or potions or new fruits or something, if they can get stuff past the Sea Companies and avoid the storms, but, well, my master came by some information that indicated Walen's fellow was looking for just one person."

"Oh."

"Hmm." Jollisce stood and faced the Xamis-set, his face made ruddy by the glow of flame-coloured cloud in the west. "Good sunset," he said, drawing deep on his pipe.

"Very," I agreed, not really looking.

"Best ones were just around the time the Empire fell, of course. Didn't you think?"

"Hmm? Oh yes, naturally."

"Providence's recompense for the sky falling in on us," Jollisce mused, frowning into the bowl of his pipe.

"Hmm. Yes." Who to tell? I thought. Who to tell . . .

Master, the Doctor attended the King in his tent each day during the Circuition from Haspide to Yvenir because our monarch was afflicted with an aching back.

The Doctor sat on the side of the bed King Quience lay upon. "If it's really that sore, sir, you should rest it," she told him.

"Rest?" the King said, turning over on to his front. "How can I rest? This is the Circuition, you idiot. If I rest so does everybody else, and then by the time we get to the Summer Palace it'll be time to come back again."

"Well," the Doctor said, pulling the King's shift up out of his riding breeches to expose his broad, muscled back. "You might lie on your back in a carriage, sir."

"That would hurt too," he said into his pillow.

"It might hurt a little, sir, but it would quickly become better. Sitting on a mount will only make it worse."

"Those carts, they sway all over the place and the wheels bang down into holes and ruts. These roads are much worse than they were last year, I'm sure. Wiester?"

"Sir?" the fat chamberlain said, quickly stepping out of the shadows to the King's side.

"Have somebody find out whose responsibility this bit of road is. Are the appropriate taxes being collected? If they are, are they being spent on it and if not where are they going?"

"At once, sir." Wiester bustled off, leaving the tent.

"You can't trust Dukes to levy taxes properly, Vosill," the King sighed. "At any rate, you can't trust their tax collectors. They have too damn much authority. Far too many tax collectors have bought themselves baronies for my liking."

"Indeed, sir," the Doctor said.

"Yes. I've been thinking I might set up some sort of more . . . town- or city-sized, umm . . ."

"Authority, sir?"

"Yes. Yes, authority. A council of responsible citizens. Perhaps just to oversee the roads and city walls and so on, at first. Things they might care about more than Dukes, who only bother about their own houses and how much game is in their parks."

"I'm sure that's a very good idea, sir."

"Yes, I'm sure it is too." The King looked round at the Doctor. "You have them, don't you?"

"Councils, sir?"

"Yes. I'm sure you've mentioned them. Probably comparing our own backward arrangements unfavourably, I don't doubt."

"Would I do that, sir?"

"Oh, I think you would, Vosill."

"Our arrangements do seem to produce comfortable roads, I would certainly claim that."

"But then," the King said glumly, "if I take power from the barons, they'll get upset."

"Well, make them all arch-Dukes, sir, or give them some other awards."

The King thought about this. "What other awards?"

"I don't know, sir. You might invent some."

"Yes, I might," the King said. "But then, if I go giving power to the peasants or the tradespeople and so on, they'll only want more."

The Doctor continued to massage the King's back. "We do say that prevention is better than cure, sir," she told him. "The time to look after the body is before there is anything wrong with it. The time to rest is before you feel too tired to do anything else, and the time to eat is before hunger consumes you."

The King frowned as the Doctor's hands moved over his body. "How I wish it was all so easy," he said with a sigh. "I think the body must be a simple thing in comparison to a state if it can be maintained on the basis of such platitudes."

The Doctor, I thought, looked a little hurt by this. "Then I am glad that my concern is for the health of your body, sir, not that of your country."

"I *am* my country," the King said sternly, though with an expression which belied his tone.

"Then be glad, sir, that your kingdom is in a better state than its king, who will not lie in a carriage like a sensible monarch would."

"Don't treat me like a child, Vosill!" the King said loudly, twisting round towards her. "Ow!" he said, grimacing, and collapsed back again. "What you don't realise, Vosill," he said, through gritted teeth, "being a woman, I suppose, is that in a carriage you have less room for manoeuvre. They take up the whole road, you see? A man on a mount, why, he can negotiate his way around all the irregularities on the road surface."

"I see, sir. Nevertheless, it is a fact that you are spending the whole day in the saddle, bouncing up and down and compressing the small pads between your vertebrae and forcing them into the nerve. That's what is making your spine hurt. Lying in a carriage, almost no matter how much it shakes and bounces, will certainly be better for you."

"Look, Vosill," the King said in an exasperated tone, levering himself up on one elbow and looking round at the Doctor. "How do you think it would look if the King took to a pleasuring couch and lay amongst the perfumed pillows of a ladies' carriage like some porcelain-arsed concubine? What sort of monarch could do that? Eh? Don't be ridiculous." He lay carefully back on his front again.

"I take it your father never did such a thing, sir."

"No, he . . ." the King began, then looked suspiciously back at the Doctor before continuing. "No, he didn't. Of course not. He rode. And I will ride. I shall ride and make my back sore because that's what's expected of me. You shall make my back better because that's what's expected of you. Now, do your job, Doctor, and stop this damned prattling. Providence preserve me from the wittering of women! Aow! Will you be careful!"

"I have to find out where it hurts, sir."

"Well, you've found it! Now do what you're supposed to do, which is make it *stop* hurting. Wiester? Wiester!"

Another servant came forward. "He's just stepped out, sir."

"Music," the King said. "I want music. Fetch the musicians."

"Sir." The servant turned to go.

The King snapped his fingers, bringing the servant back.

"Sir?"

"And wine."

"Sir."

"What a beautiful sunset, don't you think, Oelph?"

"Yes, mistress. Providence's recompense for the sky falling in upon us," I said, recalling Jollisce's phrase (I was sure it was one he'd heard from somebody else anyway).

"I suppose it's something," the Doctor agreed.

We were sitting on the broad front bench of the covered wagon which had become our home. I had been counting. I had slept in the carriage for eleven of the last sixteen days (the other five I had been billeted with the other senior pages and apprentices in buildings in one of the towns we had camped within) and I would probably sleep in it again for another seven days out of the next ten, until we reached the city of Lep-Skatacheis, where we would stop for half a moon. Thereafter the wagon would be my home for eighteen days out of twenty-one until we reached Yvenage. Perhaps nineteen out of twenty-two if we encountered difficulties on the hill roads and were delayed.

The Doctor looked away from the sunset, gazing up the road, which was lined with tall trees standing in sandy earth on both sides. An orange-brown haze hung in the air above the swaying tops of the grander carriages ahead. "Are we nearly there yet?"

"Very nearly, mistress. This is the longest day's travel on either leg. The scouts should be in sight of the camp ground and the forward party ought to have the tents erected and the field kitchens set up. It is a long draw, but they say the way to look at it is as saving a day."

Ahead of us on the road were the grand carriages and covered wagons of the royal household. Immediately in front of us were two hauls, their broad shoulders and rumps swaying from side to side. The Doctor had refused a driver. She wanted to take the whip herself (though she used it little). This meant that we had to feed and care for the beasts ourselves each evening. I did not appreciate this, though my fellow pages and apprentices certainly did. So far the Doctor had taken on a much higher proportion of this menial work than I'd expected, but I resented doing any of it at all, and found it hard to believe that she could not see she was exposing both of us to ridicule by taking on such a degrading task.

She was looking at the sunset again. The light caught the edge of her cheek, outlining it in a colour like that of red gold. Her hair, falling loose across her shoulders, was glossily radiant with highlights like spun ruby.

"Were you still in Drezen when the rocks fell from the sky, mistress?"

"Hmm? Oh. Yes. I didn't leave until about two years later." She seemed lost in thought, and her expression suddenly melancholy.

"Did you come by way of Cuskery, by any chance, mistress?"

"Why, yes, Oelph, I did," the Doctor said, her expression lightening as she turned to me. "You've heard of it?"

"Vaguely," I said. My mouth had gone quite dry while I wondered whether to say anything about what I had heard from Walen's page and Jollisce. "Umm, is it far from there to here?"

"The voyage is a good half a year," the Doctor said, nodding. She smiled up at the sky. "A very hot place, lush and steamy and full of ruined temples and various odd animals that have the run of the place because they are held to be sacred by some ancient sect or another. The air is saturated with the smell of spices, and when I was there there was a full night, when Xamis and Seigen had both long set, almost together, and Gidulph, Jairly and Foy were in the day sky, and Iparine was eclipsed by the world itself and for a bell or so there was only the starlight to shine on the sea and the city, and the animals all howled into the darkness and the waves I could hear from my room sounded very loud, though it was not really dark, just silver. People stood in the streets, very quiet, looking at the stars, as though relieved to find their existence was not a myth. I wasn't in the street just then, I was . . . I'd met a terribly nice Sea Company captain that day. Very handsome," she said, and sighed.

In that instant she was like a young girl (and I a jealous youth).

"Did your ship go straight from there to here?"

"Oh no, there were four voyages after Cuskery: to Alyle on the Sea Company barquentine *Face of Jairly,*" she said, and smiled broadly, staring ahead. "Then from there to Fuollah on a trireme, of all things . . . a Farossi vessel, ex-Imperial navy, then overland to Osk, and from there to Illerne by an argosy out of Xinkspar, finally to Haspide on a galliot of the Mifeli clan traders."

"It all sounds most romantic, mistress."

She gave what looked like a sad smile. "It was not without its privations and indignities on occasion," she said, tapping at the top of her boot, "and once or twice this old dagger was drawn, but yes, looking back, it was. Very romantic." She took a deep breath and let it out, then swivelled and looked up into the skies, shading her eyes from Seigen.

"Jairly has not yet risen, mistress," I said quietly, and was surprised at the coldness I felt. She looked at me oddly.

Some sense returned to me. No matter that since my fever in the palace, when she had said that we ought to be friends, she was still my mistress and I was still her servant as well as her apprentice. And as well as a mistress, I had a Master. Probably nothing I could find out from the Doctor would be new to him, for he had many sources, but I could not be sure, and so I supposed I had an obligation to him to find out all I could from her, in case some small piece of it might prove useful.

"Was that—I mean taking the Mifeli clan ship from Illerne to Haspide—how you came to be employed by the Mifelis?"

"No, that was just coincidence. I helped around the seamen's infirmary for a while after I first landed before one of the younger Mifelis needed treatment on a home-bound ship—it had signalled ahead to the Sentry Isles. The Mifelis' own doctor then suffered terribly from seasickness and would not go out on the cutter to meet the galleon. I was recommended to Prelis Mifeli by the infirmary's head surgeon, so I went instead. The boy lived, the ship came in and I was made the Mifeli head-family doctor right there on the docks. Old man Mifeli doesn't waste time making decisions."

"And their old doctor?"

"Pensioned off." She shrugged.

I watched the rear end of the two hauls for a while. One of them shat copiously. The steaming shit disappeared under our wagon, but not before wreathing us in its vapours.

"Dear me, what an awful smell," the Doctor said. I bit my tongue. This was one of the reasons that people who were in a position to do so usually kept as much distance between themselves and beasts of burden as they could.

"Mistress, may I ask you a question?"

She hesitated for a moment. "You have been asking me various questions already, Oelph," she said, and graced me with a sly, amused look. "I take it you mean may you ask me a question that may be impertinent?"

"Umm . . ."

"Ask away, young Oelph. I can always pretend I didn't hear you."

"I was just wondering, mistress," I said, feeling most awkward, and very warm all of a sudden, "why you left Drezen?"

"Ah," she said, and taking up the whip waggled it over the yokes of the two hauls, barely tickling their necks with the end of it. She looked briefly at me. "Partly the urge to have an adventure, Oelph. Just the desire to go somewhere nobody I knew had been before. And partly . . . partly to get away, to forget somebody." She smiled brightly, dazzlingly at me for a moment before looking away up the road again. "I had an unhappy love affair, Oelph. And I am stubborn. And proud. Having made up my mind to leave and having announced that I would travel to the other ends of the world, I could not—I would not—back down. And so I hurt myself twice, once by falling for the wrong person, and then a second time by being too obstinate—even in a more temperate mood—to retreat from a commitment made in a fury of injured pride."

"Was this the person who gave you the dagger, mistress?" I asked, already hating and envying the man.

"No," she said, with a sort of snorting laugh which I thought was most unladylike. "I had been wounded by him quite enough without carrying such a token of his." She gazed down at the dagger, sheathed as usual in the top of her right boot. "The dagger was a gift from . . . the state. Some of the decoration on the dagger was given to me by another friend. One I used to have terrible arguments with. A double-edged gift."

"What was it you argued about, mistress?"

"Lots of things, or lots of aspects of the same thing. Whether the might beyond might had a right to impose its values on others." She looked at my puzzled expression and laughed. "We argued about here, for one thing."

"Here, mistress?" I asked, looking around.

"About—" She seemed to catch herself, then said, "About Haspide, the Empire. About this whole other hemisphere." She shrugged. "I won't bore you with the details. In the end I left and he stayed, though I did hear later that he too sailed away, some time after I did."

"Do you regret coming here now, mistress?"

"No," she said, smiling. "For most of the voyage to Cuskery I did . . . but the equator signalled a change, as they say it often does, and since then, no. I still miss my family and friends, but I am not sorry now that I made the decision."

"Do you think you will ever go back, mistress?"

"I have no idea, Oelph." Her expression was troubled and hopeful at once. Then she produced another smile for me. "I am the doctor to the King, after all. I would consider that I have not done my job properly if he would *let* me leave. I may be forced to look after him until he's an old man, or until he grows displeased with me because I grow whiskers on my lips and my hair thins on my head and my breath smells, and he has my head chopped off because I interrupt him once too often. Then you might have to become his doctor."

"Oh, mistress," was all I could say.

"I don't know, Oelph," she confided in me. "I'm not so sure about making plans. I'll wait and see which way fate takes me. If Providence, or whatever we wish to call it, has me stay, then I'll stay. If it somehow calls me back to Drezen, I'll go." She dipped her head towards me and with what she probably thought was a conspiratorial look said, "Who knows, my destiny might lead me back through Equatorial Cuskery. I might get to see my handsome Sea Company captain again." She winked at me.

"Was the land of Drezen much affected by the rocks from the sky, mistress?" I asked.

She did not seem to heed my tone, which I had worried might seem excessively frosty. "More than here in Haspidus," she said. "But much less than the Inlands of the Empire. One city on a far northern island was washed almost entirely away by a wave, killing ten or more thousand people, and some ships were lost, and of course the crop yields all over were down for a couple of growing seasons, so the farmers moaned, but then the farmers always do. No, we escaped relatively lightly."

"Do you think it was the work of the gods, mistress? There are those who say that Providence was punishing us for something, or perhaps just punishing the Empire. Others hold that it was the work of the old gods, and that they are coming back. What do you think?"

"I think it could be any of those things, Oelph," the Doctor said thoughtfully. "Though there are some people in Drezen—philosophers—who have a much more bleak explanation, mind you."

"Which is what, mistress?"

"That such things happen for no reason at all."

"No reason?"

"No reason beyond the workings of pure chance."

I thought about this. "Do they not think that there is good and bad? And that one deserves to be emulated and the other not, but rather punished?"

"A very small number would say that there are no such entities. Most agree there are, but that they only exist in our minds. The world itself, without us, does not recognise such things, just because they are not things, they are ideas, and the world contained no ideas until people came along."

"So they believe that Man was not created with the world?"

"That's right. Or at least not people with wits."

"Are they then Seigenists? Do they believe that the Lesser Sun created us?"

"Some would say it did. They would claim that people were once no more than animals and that we too used to fall asleep promptly when Xamis set, and rise when it rose. Some believe that all we are is light, that the light of Xamis holds the world together like an idea, like a hugely complicated dream, and the light of Seigen is the very expression of us as thinking beings."

I tried to comprehend this curious concept, and was just starting to decide that it was not so different from normal beliefs when the Doctor asked suddenly, "What do you believe in, Oelph?"

Her face, turned to me, was the colour of the soft, tawny dusk. Seigen-light caught fallen wisps of her half-curled red hair.

"What? Why, what all other civil people believe, mistress," I said, before thinking that perhaps she, coming from Drezen where they obviously had some odd ideas, might believe something quite different. "That is to say, what people hereabouts, that is in Haspidus . . ."

"Yes, but what do you personally believe?"

I frowned at her, an expression such a graceful, gentle face did not deserve to have directed at it. Did the Doctor really imagine that everybody went around believing different things? One believed what one was told to believe, what it made sense to believe. Unless one was a foreigner, of course, or a philosopher. "I believe in Providence, mistress."

"But when you say Providence, do you really mean god?"

"No, mistress. I don't believe in any of the old gods. No one does any more. No one of sense, at any rate. Providence is the rule of laws, mistress," I said.

I was trying not to insult her by sounding as though I was talking to a child. I had experienced aspects of the Doctor's naïveté before, and ascribed it to simple ignorance of the manner in which matters were organised in what was to her a foreign land, but even after the best part of a year it appeared there were still subjects that each of us assumed we viewed in a mutual light and from a similar perspective which in fact we saw quite differently. "The laws of Nature determine the ordering of the physical world and the laws of Man determine the ordering of society, mistress."

"Hmm," she said, with an expression that might have been simply thoughtful or tinged with scepticism.

"One set of laws grows out of the other as do plants from the common clay," I added, remembering something I'd been taught in Natural Philosophy (my determined and strenuous endeavours to take in absolutely nothing of what I had regarded as entirely the most irrelevant part of my schooling had patently not met with total success).

"Which is not so dissimilar to the light of Xamis ordering the major part of the world, and that of Seigen illuminating the human," she mused, staring towards the sunset again.

"I suppose not, mistress," I agreed, struggling to follow.

"Ha," she said. "All very interesting."

"Yes, mistress," I said, dutifully.

Adlain: Duke Walen. A pleasure, as ever. Welcome to my humble tent. Please.

Walen: Adlain.

   A: Some wine? What about food? Have you eaten?

   W: A glass, thank you.

A: Wine. I'll take some too. Thank you, Epline. So, you are well?

W: Well enough. You?

A: Fine.

W: I wonder, could you . . . ?

A: What, Epline? Yes, of course. Epline, would you . . . ? I'll call . . . Now then, Walen? . . . There is nobody else here.

W: Hmm. Very well. This doctor. Vosill.

A: Still her, eh, dear Duke? This is becoming an obsession. Do you really find her that interesting? Perhaps you ought to tell her. She may prefer older men.

W: Mocking the wisdom that comes with age is a fit sport only for those who expect never to attain much of it themselves, Adlain. You know the substance of my complaint.

A: I regret I don't, Duke.

W: But you have told me of your own doubts. Did you not have her writing checked in case it was a code or something similar?

A: I thought about it. I decided not to, directly.

W: Well, perhaps you should, directly. She is a witch. Or a spy. One of the two.

A: I see. And what strange old gods or other demons do you think she serves? Or which master?

W: I do not know. We will not know, unless we put her to the question.

A: Ah-ha. Would you like to see that happen?

W: I know it is unlikely while she retains the King's favour, though that might not last forever. In any event, there are ways. She might simply disappear and be questioned . . . informally, as it were.

A: Nolieti?

W: I have . . . not discussed this with him as such, but I have already ascertained most reliably that he would be more than happy to oblige. He suspects strongly that she released through death one of those he was questioning.

A: Yes, he mentioned that to me.

W: Did you think to do anything?

A: I told him he should be more careful.

W: Hmm. At any rate, she might be discovered in such a manner, though that would be somewhat risky, and she would have to be killed thereafter anyway. Working to force her from the King's favour might take longer and could, pressing the matter as one may have to, entail risks which were hardly less than those attached to the former course of action.

A: Obviously you have given the matter considerable thought.

W: Of course. But if she was to be taken, without the King's knowledge, the help of the guard commander might be crucial.

A: It might, mightn't it?

W: So? Would you help?

A: In what way?

W: Provide the men, perhaps?

A: I think not. We might have one lot of the palace guard fighting their fellows, and that would never do.

W: Well then, otherwise?

A: Otherwise?

W: Damn it, man! You know what I must mean!

A: Blind eyes? Gaps in rosters? That sort of thing?

W: Yes, that.

A: Sins of omission rather than commission.

W: Expressed however you wish. It is the acts, or lack of them I would know about.

A: Then, perhaps.

W: No more? Merely, "perhaps"?

A: Were you thinking of doing this in close proximity to the present, dear Duke?

W: Perhaps.

A: Ha. Now, you see, unless you—

W: I don't mean today, or tomorrow. I am looking for an understanding that should it become necessary, such a plan might be put into effect with as little delay as possible.

A: Then, if I was convinced of the urgency of the cause, it might.

W: Good. That is better. At last. Providence, you are the most—

A: But I would have to believe that the safety of the monarch was threatened. Doctor Vosill is a personal appointee of the King. To move against her might be seen as moving against our beloved Quience himself. His health is in her hands, perhaps as much as it is in mine. I do my modest best to keep at bay assassins and others who might wish the King ill, while she combats the illnesses that come from within.

W: Yes, yes, I know. She is close. He depends on her. It is already too late to act before her influence achieves its zenith. We might only work to hasten the descent. But by then it might be too late.

A: You think that she means to kill the King? Or influence him? Or does she merely spy, reporting to another power?

W: Her brief might include all of those, depending.

A: Or none.

W: You seem less concerned in this than I imagined, Adlain. She has come from the ends of the world, entered the city barely two years ago, doctored to one merchant and one noble—both briefly—and then suddenly she's closer to our King than anybody else! Providence, a wife would spend less time with him!

A: Yes. One might wonder whether she performs any of the more intimate duties of a wife.

W: Hmm. I think not. To bed one's physician is unusual,

but that only arises from the unnaturalness of having a woman claiming to be a doctor in the first place. But, no, I have seen no sign. Why, do you know?

A: I merely wondered if you knew.

W: Hmm.

A: Of course, she does seem to be a rather good doctor. At the very least she has done the King no obvious harm, and that in my experience is far more than one might reasonably expect from a court physician. Perhaps we should leave her alone for now, while we have nothing more definite than your suspicions, however reliable they have proved in the past.

W: We might. Will you have her watched?

A: Well, no more than at present.

W: Hmm. And besides, I have another investment in the truth or otherwise of her story that may yet yield her.

A: You do? How so?

W: I shall not trouble you with the details, but I have my doubts concerning certain of her claims and hope presently to bring before the King one who can discredit her and show her to have borne false witness to him. It is a long-term investment but it should bear interest during our time at the Summer Palace or, if not, then shortly thereafter.

A: I see. Well, we must hope that you do not lose your capital. Can you tell me what form it takes?

W: Oh, it is the coin of man. And land, and tongue. But I must hold mine. I'll say no more.

A: I think I shall have more wine. Will you join me?

W: Thank you, no. I have other matters to attend to.

A: Allow me . . .

W: Thank you. Ah. My old bones . . . at least I am able to ride, though next year I may take carriage. I thank Providence the way back is easier. And that we are not far from Lep now.

A: I'm sure in the hunt you can out-jump men half your
      age, Duke.
W: I am sure I cannot, but your flattery is still gratifying.
      Good day.
A: Good day, Duke . . . Epline!

All this I copied—with a few deletions to make the narrative less
tedious—from the part of the Doctor's journal written in Imperial. I
never did show it to my Master.

Could she have overheard all this? It seems inconceivable. The
guard commander Adlain had his own physician and I'm sure he never
once called upon the Doctor's services. What would she have been
doing anywhere near his tent?

Could they have been lovers and she was hiding under some bed
covers all the time? That seems no more likely. I was with her almost all
of the time, every single day. Also, she confided in me, sincerely, I am
convinced. She simply did not like Adlain. Indeed she felt threatened by
him. How could she suddenly have tumbled into bed with a man she
feared, never giving the remotest sign before that she desired to, or
afterwards that she had? I know that illicit lovers can be ingenious in
the extreme and suddenly find within themselves reserves of guile and
the ability to act that even they did not until then know they possessed,
but to imagine the Doctor and the guard commander in such a sexual
conspiracy is surely to draw the bow one notch too far.

Was Epline the source? Did she have some sort of hold over him? I
do not know. They seemed not really to know each other, but who can
tell? They may have been lovers, but the same unlikeliness attaches to
that liaison as does to that of her and Adlain.

I cannot think who else could have heard all of this. It did occur to
me that she might have made it all up, that what she wrote here consti-
tuted her darkest imaginings regarding what others in the Court might
be planning for her, yet somehow that too does not feel right either. In
the end I am left with something that I am certain reflects a genuine
conversation, but with no clear idea how the Doctor came by it.

But there we are. Some things never do make perfect sense. There
must be some explanation, and it is perhaps a little like the Doctrine of

the Perfect Partner. We must be content to know that she exists, somewhere in the world, and try not to care overmuch that we will probably
never meet her.

We arrived without incident at the city of Lep-Skatacheis.

On the morning after we arrived the Doctor and I went to the
King's chambers before the business of the day was due to start. As
usual on such occasions, the King's business—and much of the
Court's—comprised of hearing certain legal disputes which had been
deemed too complicated or too important for the city authorities and
the Marshal to decide upon. According to my experience, gained during the three previous years I had travelled this way, such sitting in
judgment was not a function of his responsibilities the King relished.

The King's chambers were on a corner of the City-Marshal's
palace, overlooking the reflecting terraces of the pools which led down
towards the distant river. Swifts and darts played in the warm air outside, wheeling and tumbling beyond the cool stone of the balcony
balustrades. The chamberlain Wiester let us in, fussing as usual.

"Oh. Are you on time? Was there the bell? Or a cannon? I did not
hear the bell. Did you?"

"A few moments ago," the Doctor told him, following him across
the reception room to the King's dressing chamber.

"Providence!" he said, and opened the doors.

"Ah, the good Doctor Vosill!" the King exclaimed. He was standing
on a small stool in the centre of the great dressing chamber, being
dressed in his ceremonial judicial robes by four servants. One wall of
plaster windows, south facing, flooded the room with soft, creamy
light. Duke Ormin stood nearby, tall and slightly stooped and dressed in
judicial robes. "How are you today?" the King asked.

"I am well, your majesty."

"A very good morning to you, Doctor Vosill," Duke Ormin said,
smiling. Duke Ormin was ten or so years older than the King. He was a
lanky-legged sort of a fellow with a very broad head and a surprisingly
large torso which always looked, to me at least, stuffed, as though he
had a couple of pillows forced up his shirt. An odd-looking fellow, then,
but most civil and kind, as I knew myself, having been briefly in his

employ, though at a fairly menial level. The Doctor, too, had been retained by him, more recently, when she had been his personal physician before she had become the King's.

"Duke Ormin," the Doctor said, bowing.

"Ah!" the King said. "And I was favoured with a 'your majesty'! Usually I am lucky to escape with a 'sir'."

"I beg the King's pardon," the Doctor said, bowing now to him.

"Granted," Quience said, putting back his head and letting a couple of servants gather his blond curls together and pin a skull cap in place. "I am obviously in a magnanimous mood this morning. Wiester?"

"Sire?"

"Inform the good lord judges I shall be joining that I am in such a good mood they will have to be certain to be at their most sourly pitiless in court this morning to provide a balance for my irrepressible leniency. Take heed, Ormin."

Duke Ormin beamed, his eyes almost disappearing as his face screwed up in a grin.

Wiester hesitated, then started to make for the door. "At once, sire."

"Wiester."

"Sire?"

"I was joking."

"Ah. Ha ha." The chamberlain laughed.

The Doctor put her bag down on a seat near the door.

"Yes, Doctor?" the King asked.

The Doctor blinked. "You asked me to attend you this morning, sir."

"Did I?" The King looked mystified.

"Yes, last night." (This was true.)

"Oh, so I did." The King looked surprised as his arms were raised and a sleeveless black robe edged in some shiningly white fur was placed over his shoulders and fastened. He flexed, shifting his weight from stockinged foot to stockinged foot, clenching his fists, executing a sort of rolling motion with his shoulders and his head and then declaring, "You see, Ormin? I am becoming quite forgetful in my old age."

"Why now, sir, you have barely left your youth," the Duke told him. "If you go calling yourself old as though by royal decree, what must we think who are significantly older than you and yet who still fondly harbour the belief that we are not yet old? Have mercy, please."

"Very well," the King agreed, with a roll of the hand. "I declare myself young again. And well," he added, with a renewed look of surprise as he glanced at the Doctor and me. "Why, I seem to be quite bereft of any aches and pains for you to treat this morning, Doctor."

"Oh." The Doctor shrugged. "Well, that's good news," she said, picking up her bag and turning for the door. "I'll bid you good day then, sir."

"Ah!" the King said suddenly. We each turned again.

"Sir?"

The King looked most thoughtful for a moment, then shook his head. "No, Doctor, I can think of nothing with which to detain you. You may go. I shall call you when I need you next."

"Of course, sir."

Wiester opened the doors for us.

"Doctor?" the King said as we were in the doorway. "Duke Ormin and I go hunting this afternoon. I usually fall off my mount or get torn up by a barb bush, so I may well have something for you to treat later."

Duke Ormin laughed politely and shook his head.

"I shall start to prepare the relevant potions now," the Doctor said. "Your majesty."

"Providence, twice."

8

THE BODYGUARD

Am I so trusted now?

"Or I am. Probably because I am regarded as being beyond the interest of any but the most desperate of men. Or because the General does not intend to visit me again and so—"

"Careful!"

DeWar grabbed at Perrund's arm just as she was about to step from the street-side into the path of a ten-team of mounts hauling a war carriage. He pulled her back towards him as first the panting, sweat-lathered team and then the great swaying bulk of the cannon-wagon itself raced past, shaking the cobblestones beneath their feet. A smell of sweat and oil rolled over them. He felt her draw away from it all, press-

ing her back against his chest. Behind him, the stone counter of a
butcher's shop dug into his back. The noise of the wagon's man-high
wheels resounded between the cracked, uneven walls of the two- and
three-storey buildings leaning over the street.

On top of the huge black gun carriage a bombardier uniformed in
the colours of Duke Ralboute stood lashing wildly at the mounts. The
wagon was followed by two smaller carriages full of men and wooden
cases. These in turn were trailed by a ragged pack of shouting children.
The wagons thundered through the open gates set within the inner
city's walls and disappeared from view. People on the street who had
shrunk back from the speeding vehicles flowed back into the thoroughfare again, muttering and shaking their heads.

DeWar let Perrund go and she turned to him. He realised with a
flush of embarrassment that in his instinctive reaction to the danger he
had taken hold of her by the withered arm. The memory of its touch,
through the sleeve of her gown, the sling and the fold of her cloak,
seemed imprinted in the bones of his hand as something thin, fragile
and childlike.

"I'm sorry," he said, blurting the words.

She was still very close to him. She stepped away, smiling uncertainly. The hood of her cloak had fallen, revealing her lace-veiled face
and her golden hair, which was gathered inside a black net. She drew
the hood back up. "Oh, DeWar," she chided. "You save somebody's life
and then you apologise. You really are—oh, I don't know," she said,
readjusting the hood. DeWar had time to be surprised. He had never
known the lady Perrund lost for words. The hood she was struggling
with fell back again, caught by a gust of wind. "Damn thing," she said,
taking hold of it with her good arm and pulling it back once more. He
had started to put his hand up, to help her with the hood, but now had
to let his hand fall back. "There," she said. "That's better. Here. I'll take
your arm. Now, let us walk."

DeWar checked the street and then they crossed it, carefully avoiding the small piles of animal dung. A warm wind blew up between the
buildings, lifting whirls of straw from the cobblestones. Perrund held
DeWar's arm with her good hand, her forearm laid lightly on his. In
DeWar's other hand he held a cane basket she had asked him to carry

for her when they'd left the palace. "Obviously I am not fit to be let out by myself," she told him. "I have spent far too long in rooms and court-yards, and on terraces and lawns. Everywhere, in fact, where there is no traffic any larger or more threatening than a eunuch with an urgently needed tray of scented waters."

"I didn't hurt you, did I?" DeWar asked, glancing at her.

"No, but if you had I think I might still count it better than being mangled beneath the iron wheels of a piece of siege artillery proceed-ing at a charge. Where do you think they are going in such a hurry?"

"Well, they won't go anywhere very far at that rate. The mounts already looked half exhausted and that was before they'd left the city. I imagine that was a show for the locals. But they will be heading for Ladenscion eventually, I imagine."

"Is the war begun, then?"

"What war, my lady?"

"The war against the troublesome barons of Ladenscion, DeWar. I am not an idiot."

DeWar sighed and looked around, checking that nobody in the street was paying them too close attention. "It is not officially begun yet," he said, putting his lips close to the hood of her cloak—she turned towards him and he smelled her perfume, sweet and musky—"but I think one might safely say it is inevitable."

"How far away is Ladenscion?" she asked. They ducked under dis-plays of fruit hanging outside a grocer's.

"About twenty days' ride to the border hills."

"Will the Protector have to go himself?"

"I really couldn't say."

"DeWar," she said softly, with what sounded like disappointment.

He sighed and looked around again. "I shouldn't think so," he said. "He has much to do here, and there are more than enough generals for the job. It . . . it shouldn't take too long."

"You sound unconvinced."

"Do I?" They stopped at a side street to let a small herd of hauls pass, heading for the auction grounds. "I seem to be in a minority of one in thinking the war . . . suspicious."

"Suspicious?" Perrund sounded amused.

"The barons' complaints and their stubbornness, their refusal to negotiate, seem disproportionate."

"You think they're inviting war for its own sake?"

"Yes. Well, not just for its own sake. Only a madman would do that. But for some further reason than the desire to assert their independence from Tassasen."

"But what else could their motive be?"

"It is not their motive that troubles me."

"Then whose?"

"Someone behind them."

"They are being encouraged to make war?"

"It feels so to me, but I am just a bodyguard. The Protector is cloistered with his generals now and believes he needs neither my presence nor my opinion."

"And I am grateful for your company. But I had formed the impression the Protector valued your counsel."

"It is most valued when it most closely accords with his own view."

"DeWar, you are not jealous, are you?" She stopped and turned to him. He looked into her face, shaded and half hidden by the hood of the cloak and the thin veil. Her skin seemed to glow in that darkness like a hoard of gold at the back of a cave.

"Maybe I am," he admitted, with a bashful grin. "Or perhaps I am once again exercising my duties in areas which are inappropriate."

"As in our game."

"As in our game."

They turned together and walked on. She took his arm again. "Well then, who do you think might be behind the vexatious barons?"

"Kizitz, Breistler, Velfasse. Any one or combination of our three claimant Emperors. Kizitz will make mischief wherever he can. Breistler has a claim to part of Ladenscion itself and might seek to offer his forces as compromise occupants to keep the barons' and our armies apart. Velfasse has his eye on our eastern provinces. Drawing our forces to the west might be a feint. Faross would like the Thrown Isles back, and may have a similar strategy. Then there's Haspidus."

"Haspidus?" she said. "I thought King Quience supported UrLeyn."

"It may suit him to be seen to support UrLeyn for now. But

Haspidus lies behind—beyond—Ladenscion. It would be easier for Quience to provide the barons with matériel than anybody else."

"And you think Quience opposes the Protector out of Regal principle? Because UrLeyn dared to kill a king?"

"Quience knew the old king. He and Beddun were as close to being friends as two kings can be, so there might be something of the personal in his animosity. But even without that, Quience is no fool, and he has no pressing problems to occupy him at the moment. He has the luxury of time to think long, and the brains to know that UrLeyn's example cannot go unopposed for ever if he wishes to pass on the crown to his heirs."

"But Quience has no children yet, does he?"

"None that are regarded as mattering, and he has yet to decide who to marry, but even if he was concerned only for his own reign, he might still want to see the Protectorate fail."

"Dear me. I had no idea we were quite so surrounded by enemies."

"I'm afraid we are, my lady."

"Ah. Here we are."

The old stone-built building across the crowded street from them was the paupers' hospital. It was here Perrund had wanted to come with her basket of foods and medicines. "My old home," she said, staring over the heads of the people. A small troop of colourfully dressed soldiers appeared round a corner and came marching down the street, attended by a boy drummer at their head, tearful women to each side and capering children behind. Everybody turned to look except Perrund. Her gaze remained fixed on the worn, stained stones of the old hospital across the street.

DeWar looked this way and that. "Have you been back since?" he asked.

"No. But I have kept in touch. I have sent them some little things in the past. I thought it would be amusing to deliver them myself this time. Oh. What are those?" The troop of soldiers was passing in front of them. The soldiers wore bright red and yellow uniforms and polished metal hats. Each carried a long wood-mounted metal tube slung slanted across their shoulders and waving in the air above their gleaming helmets.

"Musketeers, my lady," DeWar told her. "And that is Duke Simalg's banner at their head."

"Ah. These are the musket guns. I have heard about them."

DeWar watched the troop pass with a troubled, distracted look. "UrLeyn won't have them in the palace," he said eventually. "They can be useful on the battlefield."

The sound of the beating drum faded. The street filled again with its ordinary commerce. A gap opened in the traffic of carts and carriages between them and the hospital, and DeWar thought they would take advantage of it, but Perrund lingered on the pavement, her hand clutching at his forearm while she stared at the ornate and time-stained stonework of the ancient building.

DeWar cleared his throat. "Will there be anybody there from when you were?"

"The present matron was a nurse when I was here. It's her I've corresponded with." Still she did not move.

"Were you here long?"

"Only ten days or so. It was only five years ago, but it seems much longer." She kept staring at the building.

DeWar was not sure what to say. "It must have been a difficult time."

From what he had succeeded in teasing from her over the past few years, DeWar knew that Perrund had been brought here suffering from a terrible fever. She and eight of her sisters, brothers and cousins had been refugees from the war of succession during which UrLeyn had taken control of Tassasen following the fall of the Empire. Travelling from the southlands where the fighting had been worst, they had made for Crough, along with a large part of the rest of the population of Tassasen's south. The family had been traders in a market town, but most of them had been killed by the King's forces when they had taken the town from UrLeyn's troops. The General's men had retaken it, with UrLeyn at their head, but by then Perrund and her few remaining relatives were on the road for the capital.

They had all contracted some form of plague on the journey and only a hefty bribe had got them through the city gates at all. The least sick of them had driven their wagon to one of the old royal parks where refugees could camp and the last of their money had paid for a doctor and medicines. Most of them had died then. Perrund had been found a place in the paupers' hospital. She had come close to death but then recovered. When she had gone in search of the rest of her family her quest had ended at the lime pits beyond the city walls where people had been buried hundreds at a time.

She had thought of killing herself then, but was afraid to, and besides considered that as Providence had seen fit to have her recover from the plague, perhaps she was not meant to die quite yet. There was, anyway, a general feeling that the worst of times might be over. The war had ended, the plague had all but disappeared and order had returned to Crough and was returning to the rest of Tassasen.

Perrund had helped out at the hospital, sleeping on the floor of one of the great open wards where people wept and shouted and moaned throughout the day and night. She had begged for food in the street and she had turned down many an offer that would have let her buy food and comfort with her sex, but then a eunuch of the palace harem—UrLeyn's, now that the old King was dead—had visited the hospital. The doctor who had found Perrund a place in the hospital had told a friend at court that she was a great beauty, and—once she had been persuaded to clean her face and put on a dress—the eunuch had thought her suitable.

So she was recruited to the languid opulence of the harem, and became a frequent choice of the Protector. What would have seemed like a restrictive kind of luxury, even a sort of well-furnished prison to the young woman she had been a year earlier, when she and her family were living together and peaceably in their prosperous little market town, she saw instead, after the war and everything that had come with it, as a blessed sanctuary.

Then had come the day when UrLeyn and various of his court favourites, including some of his concubines, were to be painted by a famous artist. The artist brought with him a new assistant who turned out to have a mission of rather more serious intent than simply helping to fix UrLeyn's and the others' likenesses in paint, and only Perrund throwing herself between his knife and UrLeyn had saved the Protector's life.

"Shall we?" DeWar asked, when Perrund still had not moved from the pavement.

She looked at him as though she had forgotten he was there, then she smiled from the depths of the hood. "Yes," she said. "Yes, let's."

She held his arm tightly as they crossed the street.

"Tell me more about Lavishia."

"Where? Oh, Lavishia. Let me think. Well now, in Lavishia everybody is able to fly."

"Like birds?" Lattens asked.

"Just like birds," DeWar confirmed. "They can leap from cliffs and tall buildings—of which there are a great many in Lavishia—or they can just run along the street and jump into the air and soar away up into the sky."

"Do they have wings?"

"They do have wings but they are invisible wings."

"Can they fly to the suns?"

"Not on their own. To fly to the suns they have to use ships. Ships with invisible sails."

"Don't they burn in the heat of the suns?"

"Not the sails, they're invisible and the heat goes straight through them. But the wooden hulls scorch and blacken and burst into flame if they go too close, of course."

"How far is it to the suns?"

"I don't know, but people say that they are different distances away, and some clever people claim that they are both very far away indeed."

"These would be the same clever people called mathematicians who tell us the world is a ball, and not flat," Perrund said.

"They would," DeWar confirmed.

A travelling troupe of shadow players had come to court. They had set up in the palace's theatre, whose plaster windows had shutters which could be closed against the light. They had stretched a white sheet very tightly across a wooden frame whose lower edge was just above head height. Below the frame hung a black cloth. The white screen was lit from behind by a single strong lamp set some distance back. Two men and two women manipulated the two-dimensional puppets and their accompanying shadow-scenery, using thin sticks to make the characters' limbs and bodies swivel. Effects like waterfalls and flames were achieved using thin strips of dark paper and bellows to make them flutter. Using a variety of voices, the players told ancient stories of kings and queens, heroes and villains, fidelity and betrayal and love and hate.

It was the interval now. DeWar had been round the back of the screen to make sure that the two guards he had stationed there were still awake, and they were. The shadow players had objected at first, but he had insisted the guards stay there. UrLeyn was sitting in the middle of the small auditorium, a perfect and stationary target for somebody behind the screen with a cross bow. UrLeyn, Perrund and everybody else who had heard about the two guards behind the screen thought DeWar was once again taking his duties far too seriously, but he could not have sat there and watched the show comfortably with nobody he trusted behind the screen. He had stationed guards by the window shutters too, with instructions to open them promptly if the lantern behind the screen went out.

These precautions taken, he had been able to watch the shadow players' performance—from the seat immediately behind UrLeyn—with a degree of equanimity, and when Lattens had clambered over the seat in front and come and sat on his lap demanding to know more about Lavishia he had felt sufficiently relaxed to be happy to oblige. Perrund, sitting one seat along from UrLeyn, had turned round to ask her question about mathematicians. She watched DeWar and Lattens with an amused, indulgent expression.

"Can they fly under the water, too?" Lattens asked. He wriggled off DeWar's lap and stood in front of him, an intent look on his face. He was dressed like a little soldier, with a wooden sword at his side in a decorated scabbard.

"They certainly can. They are very good at holding their breath and can do it for days at a time."

"And can they fly through mountains?"

"Only through tunnels, but they have lots of tunnels. Of course, some of the mountains are hollow. And others are full of treasure."

"Are there wizards and enchanted swords?"

"Yes, enchanted swords by the cistern-full, and lots of wizards. Though they tend to be a trifle arrogant."

"And are there giants and monsters?"

"Plenty of both, though they are all very nice giants and extremely helpful monsters."

"How boring," Perrund murmured, reaching out her good hand and patting down some of Lattens' more wayward curls.

UrLeyn turned round in his seat, eyes twinkling. He drank from a glass of wine, then said, "What's this, DeWar? Are you filling my boy's head with nonsense?"

"There would be a wonder," said BiLeth, from a couple of seats away. The tall foreign minister looked bored with the proceedings.

"I'm afraid I am, sir," DeWar admitted to UrLeyn, ignoring BiLeth. "I'm telling him about kind giants and pleasant monsters, when everybody knows that giants are cruel and monsters are terrifying."

"Preposterous," BiLeth said.

"What's that?" RuLeuin asked, also turning round. UrLeyn's brother sat beside him on the other side from Perrund. He was one of the few generals who had not been sent off to Ladenscion. "Monsters? We have seen monsters on the screen, haven't we, Lattens?"

"Which would you rather have, Lattens?" UrLeyn asked his son. "Good giants and monsters, or bad ones?"

"Bad ones!" Lattens shouted. He drew his wooden sword from its scabbard. "So I can cut their heads off!"

"That's the boy!" his father said.

"Indeed! Indeed!" BiLeth agreed.

UrLeyn shoved his wine goblet at RuLeuin and then reached over to pull Lattens up off his feet, depositing him in front of him and making to fence the child with a dagger still in its sheath. Lattens' face took on a look of great concentration. He fenced with his father, thrusting and parrying, feinting and dodging. The wooden sword clicked and clacked off the sheathed dagger. "Good!" his father said. "Very good!"

DeWar watched Commander ZeSpiole get up from his seat and shuffle sideways towards the aisle. DeWar excused himself and followed, meeting up with the other man in the privy beneath the theatre, where one of the shadow players and a couple of guards were also making use of the facility.

"Did you receive your report, Commander?" DeWar asked.

ZeSpiole looked up, surprised. "Report, DeWar?"

"About my and the lady Perrund's trip to her old hospital."

"Why should that occasion a report, DeWar?"

"I thought it might because one of your men followed us there from the palace."

"Really, who was that?"

"I don't know his name. But I recognised him. Shall I point him out the next time I see him? If he was not acting on your orders you may wish to ask him why he has taken to following people going about their honest and officially sanctioned business in the city."

ZeSpiole hesitated, then said, "That will not be necessary, thank you. I'm sure that any such report, supposing it had been made, would state only that yourself and the concubine concerned paid a perfectly innocent visit to the said institution and returned without incident."

"I'm sure it would, too."

DeWar returned to his seat. The shadow players announced they were ready to begin the second half of their show. Lattens had to be calmed down before it could be resumed. When it did, he squirmed in his seat between his father and Perrund for a while, but Perrund stroked his head and made quiet, shushing, soothing noises, and before too long the shadow players' stories started to reclaim the boy's interest.

He had the seizure about halfway through the second half, suddenly going rigid and starting to shake. DeWar noticed it first, and sat forward, about to say something, then Perrund turned, her face glowing in the screen light, shadows dancing across it, a frown forming there. "Lattens . . . ?" she said.

The boy made a strange, strangling sound and jerked, falling off his seat at the feet of his father, who looked startled and said, "What?"

Perrund left her seat and sank down by the boy.

DeWar stood up and turned to face the rear of the theatre. "Guards! The shutters! Now!"

The shutters creaked and light spilled down the banked rows of

seats. Startled faces peered out of the sudden light. People started looking round at the windows, muttering. The shadow players' screen had
gone white, the shadows disappearing. The man's voice telling the
background story halted, confused.

"Lattens!" UrLeyn said, as Perrund started to set the boy into a sitting position. Lattens' eyes were closed, his face grey and sheened with
sweat. "Lattens!" UrLeyn lifted his child up into his arms.

DeWar remained standing, his gaze flitting about the theatre.
Others were standing too, now. A bank of worried-looking faces were
arranged before him, all looking down at the Protector.

"Doctor!" DeWar shouted when he saw BreDelle. The portly doctor
stood blinking in the light.

9
THE DOCTOR

Master, I thought it right to include in my report mention of the events which took place in the Hidden Gardens on the day Duke Quettil presented Geographer Kuin's latest map of the world to the King.

We had arrived at the summer palace of Yvenir in the Yvenage Hills on schedule and were happily settled into the Doctor's quarters, in a round tower of the Lesser House. The view from our rooms took in the scattered houses and pavilions set within the wooded lower slopes of Palace Hill. These buildings gradually increased in number while the distances between them shrank until they merged against the ancient walls of Mizui city itself, which filled the flat bottom of the valley immediately beneath the palace. On the valley floor to either side of Mizui could be seen numerous farms, fields and water meadows, while behind these climbed gently forested hills, themselves surmounted by the round, snow-covered mountains in the distance.

The King had indeed fallen off his mount while hunting near Lep-Skatacheis (though it had been on the last day of our stop there, not the first) and had been hobbling round since then on a badly twisted ankle. The Doctor had strapped the ankle and done what she could, but the King's duties were such that he could not rest the limb as much as the Doctor wanted him to, and so it took a while to heal.

"You. Yes, more wine. No, not that stuff. That. Ah. Adlain. Come and sit by me."

"Majesty."

"Wine for the Guard Commander. Come on. You have to be quicker than that. A good servant acts to carry out a master's wishes even as the wish is still being formed. Isn't that so, Adlain?"

"I was about to say that myself, sir."

"I'm sure you were. What news?"

"Oh, mostly the woes of the world, sir. Hardly fit to be revealed in a fine place like this. It might spoil the view."

We were in the Hidden Gardens behind the Great Palace, almost at the summit of the hill. The red, creeper-covered garden walls hid all but the highest towers of the palace. The view from the little hanging valley which contained the gardens led the eye down to the distant plains, which were blue with distance and faded out into the light of the sky at the horizon.

"Any sign of Quettil?" the King asked. "He's supposed to be giving me something or other. All has to be arranged of course, being Quettil. Can't just happen. No doubt we're due to get the full pomp."

"The Duke Quettil is not one to murmur when a shout might attract more attention," Adlain agreed, taking off his hat and setting it on the long table. "But I understand the map he intends to present to you is a particularly fine one, and long in the making. I expect we shall all be most impressed."

Duke Quettil occupied the Duke's Palace within the grounds of Palace Hill. The Province and Dukedom of Quettil, of which the city of Mizui and the Yvenage Hills were but a modest part, was entirely his to command, and he was, by repute, not shy about imposing his authority. He and his retinue were due to enter the Hidden Gardens shortly after the mid-day bell to present the King with his new map.

"Adlain," the King said. "You know the new Duke Ulresile?"

"Duke Ulresile," Adlain said to the thin, sallow youth at the King's left side. "I was sorry to hear about your father."

"Thank you," the boy said. He was barely older than I, and less substantial, more wispy. The fine clothes he wore looked too big for him, and he appeared uncomfortable. He had, I thought, yet to take on the look of a powerful man.

"Duke Walen," Adlain said, bowing to the older man, who sat to the King's right.

"Adlain," Walen said. "You look as though the mountain air suits you."

"I have yet to find air that does not, thank you, Duke."

King Quience sat at a long table set within a shady pergola, attended by the Dukes Walen and Ulresile, a smattering of lesser nobility and various servants, including a pair of Palace serving girls who were identical twin sisters and to whom the King seemed to have taken a particular shine. Each had gold-green eyes, yellow-white tangles of hair and seemed to be almost but not entirely in control of tall, sinuous bodies that in places appeared to defy the law of gravity. Each was clothed in a cream-coloured dress edged with red piping and ruffled with lace, which, if not exactly what a rustic shepherdess might wear, was perhaps what a famously handsome and well-endowed actress might have worn if she was taking part in an expensively produced Romantic Play which featured rustic shepherdesses. One such creature might have caused a normal fellow's heart to melt into his boots. That there were two such beauties capable of occupying the same world at once seemed unfair. Especially as both seemed quite as taken with the King as he did with them.

I confess that I had been unable to take my eyes off the two golden-brown globes which bulged like swollen fawn moons at the lacy cream horizon of each girl's bodice. The sunlight poured down over those perfect orbs, highlighting the nearly invisibly fine down there, their voices tinkled like the fountains, their musky perfume filled the air, and the

King's very talk and tone taunted and teased with the implication of romance.

"Yes, those little red ones. Some of those. Mmm. Delicious. How one does enjoy those little red ones, eh?"

The two girls giggled.

"How's it looking, Vosill?" the King said, still smirking. "When can I start chasing these girls?" He made to lunge at the shepherdesses and tried to grab them, but they yelped and danced out of the way. "They keep getting away from me, dammit. When can I start hunting them properly?"

"Properly, sir? How would that be?" the Doctor asked.

The Doctor and I were there tending to the King's ankle. The Doctor changed the strapping on it every day. Sometimes she changed it twice a day if the King had been out riding or hunting. As well as the swelling from the sprain, there was a small cut on the ankle which was taking its time to heal, and the Doctor was scrupulous in keeping this cleaned and treated, nevertheless it still seemed to me that any common nurse or even chamber-servant could have performed this function. However, the King appeared to want the Doctor to do it each day herself, and she seemed quite happy to acquiesce. I cannot think of any other doctor who might have made an excuse not to treat the King, but she was quite capable of it.

"Why, properly in the sense of having a decent chance of catching them, Vosill," the King said, leaning forward towards the Doctor and using what is, I believe, called a stage whisper. The two shepherdesses laughed tinklingly.

"Decent, sir? How so?" the Doctor asked, and blinked, it seemed to me, more than the flower- and leaf-shaded sunlight called for.

"Vosill, stop asking these childish questions and tell me when I may run again."

"Oh, you may run now, sir. But it would be most painful, and your ankle would probably give way within a few dozen steps. But you most certainly can run."

"Aye, run but fall over," the King said, sitting back and reaching for his wine glass.

The Doctor glanced at the two shepherdesses. "Well," she said, "perhaps something soft would break your fall."

She sat at the King's feet with her back to Duke Walen, cross-legged. This odd and unladylike position was one she adopted often, seemingly without thinking, and which made her adoption of men's clothes, or at least some part of them, almost a necessity. For once, the Doctor had changed out of her long boots. She wore dark hose and soft pointed shoes of velvet. The King's feet rested on solid silver footstools topped with plump cushions, vividly dyed and patterned. The Doctor washed the King's feet as usual, inspected them and, on this occasion, carefully trimmed his toe-nails. I was left to sit on a small stool at her side, holding her bag open while she lost herself in this labour.

"Would you break my fall, my lovelies?" the King asked, sitting back in his chair.

The two girls dissolved into laughter again. (The Doctor, I think, muttered something about being most sure to if he landed on their heads.)

"They might break your heart, sir," Adlain observed, smiling.

"Indeed," Walen said. "With one to pull in each direction, a man might suffer terribly."

The two serving girls giggled and fed more little pieces of fruit to the King, who made to tickle them with a long feather from a fan-tailed tsigibern. Musicians played on a terrace behind us, fountains plashed melodiously, insects hummed but did not annoy us, the air was fresh and full of the scent of flowers and freshly tilled and watered earth, and the two servant girls bent and leant to pop fruits into the King's mouth, then squealed, jumped and jiggled when he lunged at them with his feather. I confess I was glad I did not have to pay too much attention to what the Doctor was doing.

"Do try to keep still, sir," she muttered as the King stabbed at the two girls with the tsigibern feather.

Chamberlain Wiester came panting up the path beneath the flowers and vines, his splendidly buckled shoes glinting in the sunlight and crunching on the semi-precious path stones. "Duke Quettil, your majesty," he announced. A blare of trumpets and a clash of cymbals sounded from the garden gates, followed by the roaring scream of what sounded like a fierce and angry animal. "And retinue," Wiester added.

Duke Quettil arrived with a bevy of maidens scattering scent-crushed petals in his path, a troupe of jugglers tossing glittering clubs back and forth across the path, a band of trumpeteers and cymbalists, a pride of chokered, growling galkes each with its own grim, oiled and muscled handler straining to keep his charge in order, a school of identically dressed clerks and retainers, a clutch of beefy-looking men clad only in loin cloths supporting what looked like a tall thin wardrobe on a bier, and a pair of tall, pitch-skinned Equatorials holding a tasselled parasol over the Duke himself, who was transported on a litter glittering with precious metals and cut stones by an octet of toweringly statuesque golden-skinned balnimes, each bald and naked save for a tiny cache-sex and accoutred with a huge long bow slung over their shoulder.

The Duke was dressed, as they say, fit to embarrass an Emperor. His robes were predominantly red and gold, and his ample frame displayed them to some effect as the balnimes lowered his litter, a step-stool was placed by his slippered feet and he stepped on to a gold-cloth carpet. Above his round, full, eyebrow-less face, his jewelled head-dress sparkled in the sun and his many-ringed fingers were heavy with gems as he made a sweeping if awkward bow to the King.

The trumpets and cymbals fell silent. The musicians on the terrace had given up trying to compete with the trumpeteers and cymbalists as soon as they'd entered, so we were left with the sounds of the garden itself, plus the galkes' growling.

"Duke Quettil," said the King. "An impromptu visit?"

Quettil smiled broadly.

The King laughed. "Good to see you, Duke. I think you know everybody here."

Quettil nodded to Walen and Ulresile, then to Adlain and a few others. He couldn't see the Doctor because she was on the far side of the table, still tending to the King's feet.

"Your majesty," Quettil said. "As a further token of our honour at being allowed to play host to you and your court here again for the summer, I wish to make a presentation." The oiled muscle-men brought the bier in front of where the King sat and set it down. They opened the richly carved and inlaid doors of the thin container to reveal a huge square map easily the height of a man. Set within the square was a circle, filled with the shapes of continents and islands and seas and embellished with monsters, drawings of cities and small figures of men and women in a huge variety of dress. "A map of the world, sir," Quettil said. "Prepared for you by the Master Geographer Kuin from the very latest intelligence purchased by your humble servant and passed on to him by the most brave and reliable captains of the four waters."

"Thank you, Duke." The King sat forward in his seat, peering at the map. "Does it show the site of Anlios of old?"

Quettil looked at one of his liveried servants, who stepped forward quickly and said, "Yes, your majesty. Here." He pointed.

"What of the lair of the monster Gruissens?"

"Believed to be here, your majesty, in the region of the Vanishing Isles."

"And Sompolia?"

"Ah, home of Mimarstis the Mighty," Quettil said.

"So people claim," the King said.

"Here, your majesty."

"And is Haspide still in the centre of the world?" the King asked.

"Ah," said the servant.

"In every sense but the physical, sir," Quettil said, looking a little discomfited. "I did ask Master Geographer Kuin for the most accurate map it might be possible to draw up with the latest and most trustworthy information, and he has chosen—one might almost say decreed—that the Equator must be the waist-band of the world for the purposes of accurate map-making. As Haspide lies some goodly distance from the Equator, it cannot therefore assume the—"

"Quettil, it doesn't matter," the King said airily, waving one hand. "I prefer accuracy to flattery. It is a most magnificent map and I thank you sincerely. It will sit in my throne room so that all may admire it, and I shall have more utilitarian copies drawn up for our sea captains. I think I have never seen a single object which contrives to be at once so decorous and yet so useful. Come and sit by me. Duke Walen, will you kindly make room for our visitor?"

Walen muttered that he would be glad to, and servants scraped his chair away from the King's, leaving room for the balnimes to swing

Quettil's litter round the table and set it by the King. The Duke resumed his seat. The balnimes smelled strongly of some animalistic musk. My head seemed to spin. They retreated to the rear of the terrace and squatted on their haunches, long bows aslant behind.

"And what is this?" Quettil said, looking down from his fabulous seat at the Doctor and myself.

"My physician," the King told him, smiling broadly at the Doctor.

"What, a foot-doctor?" Quettil asked "Is this some new fashion of Haspide I've not heard about?"

"No, a doctor for all the body, as any royal physician must be. As Tranius was to my father. And to me."

"Yes," Duke Quettil said, looking around. "Tranius. What of him?"

"He fell prey to shaking hands and blurred sight," the King told him. "He retired to his farm in Junde."

"Apparently the rural life suits him," Adlain added. "For by all accounts the old fellow has made a full recovery."

"Ormin recommended Doctor Vosill without reserve," Quience told the Duke, "save that for the loss of her services to himself and his family."

"But . . . a *woman?*" Quettil said, letting one of his servants taste his wine and then accepting the crystal. "You entrust more than one organ to a woman's care? You are a brave man indeed, sir."

The Doctor had sat back and twisted a little so that she had her back to the table. In this position she was able to face both the King and Quettil. She said nothing, though there was a small, tight smile on her face. I began to be alarmed. "Doctor Vosill has been invaluable this last year," the King said.

"What's that? Without value? Valueless?" Quettil said with a humourless smile, and reached out with one slippered foot to prod the Doctor in the elbow. She rocked back slightly and looked down at the place where the jewelled slipper had touched her. I felt my mouth become dry.

"Indeed without value because she is beyond value," Quience said smoothly. "I value my life above all else, and the good doctor here helps to preserve it. She is as good as part of me."

"Part of you?" Quettil scoffed. "But it is a man's part to be part of a woman, sir. You are, as ever, far too generous, my King."

"I have heard," Guard Commander Adlain said, "people say something of that nature. That the King's only fault is that he is too indulgent. In fact he is precisely as indulgent as he needs to be to discover those who would take advantage of his sense of fairness and his desire to be tolerant. Having so discovered them—"

"Yes, yes, Adlain," the Duke Quettil said, waving a hand towards the Guard Commander, who fell silent and looked down at the table. "I'm sure. But even so, to let a woman look after you . . . Your majesty, I am only thinking of the good of the Kingdom which you inherited from the man I was privileged to regard as my best friend, your good father. What would he have said?"

Quience's expression darkened for a moment. Then it brightened and said, "He might have let the lady speak for herself." The King folded his hands and looked down at the Doctor. "Doctor Vosill?"

"Sir?"

"I have been given a present by Duke Quettil. A map of the world. Would you care to admire it? Perhaps you can even give us your thoughts on it, as you have travelled over more of the globe than the rest of us."

The Doctor rose smoothly from her cross-legged sitting position to stand and swivel and look at the great map displayed on the far side of the table. She gazed at it for a moment then reversed her earlier motion, turning and folding herself down again and taking up a small pair of scissors. Before she applied them to the King's toe-nails, she looked at the Duke and said, "The representation is inaccurate, sir."

Duke Quettil looked down upon the Doctor and gave a small, high laugh. He glanced at the King and looked as though he was trying to control a sneer. "You think so, madam?" he said in an icy tone.

"I know so, sir," the Doctor said, busying herself at the quick of the King's left big toe and frowning mightily. "Oelph, the smaller scalpel . . . Oelph." I jumped, dug in her bag and handed her the tiny instrument with a shaking hand.

"What do you know of such matters, might I ask, madam?" the Duke Quettil asked, glancing at the King again.

"Perhaps the lady doctor is a Mistress Geographer," Adlain suggested.

"Perhaps she should be taught some manners," Duke Walen said testily.

"I have travelled round the world, Duke Quettil," the Doctor said, as though addressing the King's toe, "and seen the reality of much of what is shown, rather fancifully, on your map."

"Doctor Vosill," the King said, not unkindly. "It might be more polite if you were to stand and look at the Duke when you address him."

"Might it, sir?"

The King withdrew his foot from her hand as he sat forward and said sharply, "Yes, madam, it might."

The Doctor gave the King such a look I began to whimper, though I think I was able to turn the sound into a clearing of the throat. However, she paused, handed me back the small scalpel and stood smoothly again. She bowed to the King and then the Duke. "With your permission, sirs," she said, then took up the tsigibern feather which the King had left lying on the table. She dropped, ducking under the long table and appearing on the far side. She pointed at the lower part of the great map with the feather.

"There is no continent here, only ice. There are island groups here and here. The Northern Isles of Drezen are simply not as shown. They are more numerous, generally smaller, less regular and extend further to the north. Here, the westernmost Cape of Quarreck is shown twenty sails' or so too far to the east. Cuskery . . ." She tipped her head to one side, considering. "Is shown fairly accurately. Fuol is not here, it's here, though the whole continent of Morifeth is shown . . . slanted to the west here. Illerne is north of Chroe, not opposite it. These are the places I know of from personal knowledge. I have it on good authority that there is a great inland sea . . . here. As for the various monsters and other nonsenses—"

"Thank you, Doctor," the King said, and clapped his hands. "Your views have been most amusing, I'm sure. Duke Quettil has doubtless gained great insight from watching his splendid plan suffer such correction." The King turned to a grim-faced Quettil. "You must forgive the good doctor, my dear Duke. She is from Drezen, where their brains seem to suffer from being upside-down all the time. Obviously all is topsy-turvy there, and the women think it fit to tell their lords and masters what is what."

Quettil forced a smile. "Indeed, sir. I quite understand. Still, it was a most diverting display. I always held with your father that it was both unseemly and unnecessary that women be allowed on to a stage when castrati were so readily available, however I see that women's fanciful and imaginative nature may be put to good use when it comes to providing us with such humorous vignettes. I see now that such frivolity and such licence is indeed most welcome. As long as one does not take it too seriously, of course."

I was watching the Doctor closely and with great trepidation as the Duke spoke these words. Her expression, much to my relief, stayed calm and untroubled. "Do you think," the Duke asked the King, "that she holds similarly picturesque views regarding the location of the organs within the human body as she does the features of the globe?"

"We must ask her. Doctor," the King said. "Do you disagree with our best physicians and surgeons as you so obviously do with our most esteemed navigators and map-makers?"

"On location, no, sir."

"But from your tone," Adlain said, "you disagree on something. What would that be?"

"Function, sir," the Doctor told him. "But that is mostly to do with plumbing and so not perhaps of paramount interest."

"Tell me, woman," Duke Walen said. "Did you have to leave this land of Drezen to escape justice?"

The Doctor looked coldly at Duke Walen. "No, sir."

"Strange. I thought perhaps you might have tried the patience and forbearance of your masters there, too, and so have had to flee to escape their punishment."

"I was free to stay and free to leave, sir," the Doctor said evenly. "I chose to leave to travel the world and see how things are elsewhere."

"And found little you agree with, it would seem," Duke Quettil said. "I am surprised you have not returned to wherever it was you came from."

"I have found the favour of a good and just king, sir," the Doctor said, laying the feather back on the table where she had found it, then looking at the King as she put her hands behind her back and drew herself up. "I am privileged to be able to serve him as best I can for as long as it pleases him. I consider that worth all the hardships my journey entailed, and everything that I have found disagreeable since I left my home."

"The truth of it is that the Doctor is far too valuable to let go," the King assured Duke Quettil. "She is practically our prisoner, though we don't let her know that or she would at the very least go into the most awful huff, would you not, Doctor?"

The Doctor lowered her head with a look that might almost have been demure. "Your majesty might banish me to the ends of the world. I would still be the prisoner of his regard."

"Providence, it can be almost civil at times!" Quettil roared suddenly, slapping one hand on the table.

"She can even look handsome, in the right clothes and with her hair done properly," the King said, picking up the tsigibern feather again and twirling it in front of his face. "We shall have a ball or two while we are here, I dare say. The Doctor will put on her most feminine finery and amaze us all with daintiness and grace. Won't you, Vosill?"

"If it please the King," she said, though I noticed that her lips were tight.

"Something we can all look forward to," Duke Ulresile said suddenly, then appeared to blush and quickly busied himself with cutting a piece of fruit.

The other men looked at him, then all smiled and exchanged knowing looks. The Doctor looked at the young man who had just spoken. I thought I saw her eyes cross for a moment.

"Just so," the King said. "Wiester."

"Your majesty?"

"Music, I think."

"Certainly, sir." Wiester turned to the musicians on the terrace behind. Quettil dismissed most of his retinue. Ulresile concentrated on eating enough to feed both the departed galkes and the Doctor returned to the King's feet, rubbing fragrant oils into the harder parts of the skin. The King sent the two shepherdesses away.

"Adlain was about to give us some news, were you not, Adlain?"

"I thought we might wait until we were inside, sir."

The King looked round. "I see nobody we cannot trust."

Quettil was looking down at the Doctor, who looked up and said, "Shall I go, sir?"

"Have you finished?"

"No, sir."

"Then stay. Providence knows I have trusted you with my life often enough and Quettil and Walen probably don't think you have the memory or the wit to be an adequate spy, so assuming that we trust young . . ."

"Oelph, sir," the Doctor told the King. She smiled at me. "I have found him an honest and trustworthy apprentice."

". . . young Oelph here, I think we can talk with reasonable freedom. My Dukes and Guard Commander may choose to spare you their more spicy phrases, Doctor, or they may not, but I suspect you would not blush to hear them anyway. Adlain." The King turned to the Guard Commander.

"Very well, sir. There have been several reports that someone in a Sea Company delegation tried to assassinate the regicide UrLeyn, about twelve days ago."

"What?" the King exclaimed.

"I take it we must conclude that sadly this attempt did not succeed?" Walen said.

Adlain nodded. "The 'Protector' escaped unharmed."

"*What* Sea Company?" the King asked, eyes narrowed.

"One that probably does not really exist," Adlain said. "One that several of the others fashioned specifically to make the attempt. A single report has it that the members of the delegation died under torture without revealing anything except their own sad ignorance."

"This is due to all the talk of forming a navy," Walen said, looking at Quience. "It is foolishness, sir."

"Perhaps," the King agreed. "But foolishness we must appear to support for now." He looked at Adlain. "Contact all the ports. Send a message to each of the Companies that enjoy our favour to the effect that any further attempt on UrLeyn's life will meet with our most profound and practical displeasure."

"But sir!" Walen protested.

"UrLeyn continues to enjoy our support," the King said with a
smile. "We cannot be seen to oppose him, no matter how much his
demise may please us. The world is a changed place and too many people are watching Tassasen to see what happens there. We must trust to
Providence that the Regicidal regime fails of its own accord and so con-
vinces others of its wrongness. If we are seen to intervene to bring
about its downfall from without we shall only persuade the sceptical
that there must have been some threat—and therefore, by their way of
thinking, some merit—in the enterprise."

"But sir," Walen said, leaning forward and looking past Quettil so
that his old chin was almost on the table, "Providence does not always
behave as we have the right to expect. I have had too many opportunities to observe this in my life, sir. Even your dear father, a man without
peer in such matters, could be too prone to waiting for Providence to
accomplish with most painful slowness what a quick and even merci-
ful act could have achieved in a tenth of the time. Providence does not
move with the alacrity and dispatch one might expect or desire, sir.
Sometimes Providence needs to be given a nudge in the right direction." He looked defiantly round the others. "Aye, and a sharp nudge,
at that."

"I thought older men usually counselled patience," Adlain said.

"Only when that is what is required," Walen told him. "Now it is
not."

"Nevertheless," the King said with perfect equanimity. "What will
happen to General UrLeyn will happen. I have an interest in this that
you may guess at, my dear Duke Walen, but neither you nor anybody
else who holds my favour worth the having may anticipate it. Patience
can be a means of letting matters mature to a proper state for action,
not just a way of letting time slip away."

Walen looked at the King for a good few moments, then seemed to
accept what the King had said. "Forgive an old man for whom the furthest scope of patience may lie beyond that of his own grave, your
majesty."

"We must hope that will not be so, for I would not wish you such an
early death, dear Duke."

Walen looked reasonably mollified at this. Quettil patted his hand, which the older man seemed not so sure about. "The regicide has more to worry about than assassins, in any event," Duke Quettil said.

"Ah," the King said, sitting back with a contented look. "Our eastern problem."

"Rather say UrLeyn's western one, sir." Quettil smiled. "We have heard that he continues to send forces towards Ladenscion. Simalg and Ralboute, two of his best generals, are already in the city of Chaltoxern. They have issued an ultimatum to the barons that they must open the high passes and allow the Protectorate's forces free passage to the inner cities by Jairly's new moon, or suffer the consequences."

"And we have reason to believe that the barons' position might be more robust than UrLeyn believes," the King said, with a sly smile.

"Rather a lot of reasons," Quettil said. "In fact, about . . ." he began, but the King held up one hand and made a sort of half-patting, half-waving motion and partially closed his eyes. Quettil glanced round about us and gave a small slow nod.

"Duke Ormin, sir," chamberlain Wiester said. The stooped figure of the Duke Ormin came awkwardly up the path. He halted by the tall map case, smiling and bowing. "Sir. Ah, Duke Quettil."

"Ormin!" the King said (Quettil gave the most perfunctory of nods). "Good to see you. How is your wife?"

"Much better, sir. A slight fever, no more."

"Sure you don't want Vosill here to take a look at her?"

"Quite sure, sir," Ormin said, raising himself up on his feet to look over the table. "Ah, Doctor Vosill."

"Sir," the Doctor said to the Duke, bobbing briefly.

"Come and sit with us," the King said. He looked around. "Duke Walen, would you—no, no." Duke Walen's face had taken on the look of a man told a poisonous insect has just fallen into his riding boot. "You moved before, didn't you . . . Adlain, would you make room for the Duke?"

"With pleasure, sir."

"Ah, a most magnificent map," Duke Ormin said as he took his seat.

"Isn't it?" the King said.

"Sir? Your majesty?" the young man to Walen's right piped up.

"Duke Ulresile," the King said.

"Might I go to Ladenscion?" the young Duke asked. He appeared at last to be animated and even excited. When he had expressed his anticipation at seeing the Doctor dressed for a ball he had seemed only to make himself more callow. Now he appeared enthused, his expression passionate. "I and a few friends? We have all the military means and a good number of men. We would put ourselves under the authority of whatever baron you most trust and would gladly fight for the—"

"My good Ulresile," the King said. "Your enthusiasm does you no end of credit, but grateful though I am for the expression of such an ambition, its fulfilment would lead only to my fury and contempt."

"How so, sir?" the young Duke asked, blinking furiously, his face flushing.

"You sit here at my table, Duke Ulresile, you are known to enjoy my favour and to accept my advice and that of Quettil here. Then you go to fight the forces of one I have pledged to support and must, I repeat, be seen to support, at least for now."

"But—"

"You will find in any event, Ulresile," Duke Quettil said, glancing at Quience, "that the King prefers to rely on his paid generals rather than his nobles to command forces of any significance."

The King gave Quettil a controlled smile. "It was the custom of my dear father to trust major battles to those trained from an early age in war and nothing else. My nobles command their lands and their own leisure. They gather harems, improve their palaces, commission great works of art, manipulate the taxes that we all benefit from and oversee the improvement of land and the furbishment of cities. In the new world that exists about us now, that would appear to provide more than enough—indeed perhaps too much—for a man to think about without having to concern himself with the exigencies of war as well."

Duke Ormin gave a small laugh. "King Drasine used to say," he said, "that war is neither science nor art. It is a craft, with elements of both the scientific and the artistic about it, but a craft nevertheless, and best left to craftsmen trained to it."

"But sir!" Duke Ulresile protested.

The King held up one hand to him. "I have no doubt that you and your friends might carry many a battle, all on your own, and be easily the equal of any one of my waged generals, but in winning the day you might lose the year and even jeopardise the reign. Matters are in hand, Ulresile." The King smiled at the young Duke, though he could not see it because he was staring tight-lipped at the table. "However," the King continued, a tone of tolerant amusement in his voice that had Ulresile look up briefly, "by all means keep that fire stoked and your blade sharp. Your day will come in due time."

"Sir," Ulresile said, looking back at the table.

"Now," the King began, then became aware of some sort of commotion at the gates to the palace.

"Majesty . . ." Wiester said, frowning in the same direction and drawing himself up on tip-toes to see better.

"Wiester, what can you see?" the King asked.

"A servant, sir. Hurrying. Indeed, running."

At this point, both the Doctor and I looked round, under the table. And indeed, there was a plump youth in the uniform of the palace footmen, running up the path.

"I thought they were not allowed to run for fear of scattering the stones over the flower beds," the King said, shading his eyes against the sunlight's new slant.

"Indeed so, sir," Wiester said, and assumed his most stern and censorious expression as he stepped to the end of the table and walked purposefully down to meet the lad, who stopped before him and bent over to lean his hands on his knees while he panted, "Sir!"

"What, boy?" Wiester bellowed.

"Sir, there's been a murder, sir!"

"A murder?" Wiester said, taking a step back and seeming to shrink in on himself. The Guard Commander Adlain was on his feet instantly.

"What's this?" Quettil asked.

"What did he say?" Walen said.

"Where?" Adlain demanded from the youth.

"Sir, in the questioning chamber of Master Nolieti, sir."

Duke Quettil gave a small, high laugh. "Why, is that unusual?"

"Who is murdered, boy?" Adlain said, walking down the path towards the servant.

"Sir, Master Nolieti, sir."

10
THE BODYGUARD

"Once upon a time there was a land called Lavishia, and two cousins lived there, called Sechroom and Hiliti."

"I think you have already told this story, DeWar," Lattens said in a small, croaky voice.

"I know, but there is more to it. Some people's lives have more than one story. This is a different one."

"Oh."

"How are you feeling? Are you well enough to hear one of my stories? I know they are not very good."

"I am well enough, Mr. DeWar."

DeWar plumped the boy's cushions up and got him to drink a little water. He was in a small but luxurious room off the private apartments, near the harem so that concubines like Perrund and Huesse could come and sit with him, but close to his father's quarters and that of Doctor BreDelle, who had pronounced the boy prone to nervous exhaustion and pressure of blood on the brain, and was bleeding him twice a day. There had been no return of the fits the boy had suffered that first day, but he was recovering his strength only very slowly.

DeWar came to see the boy when he could, which was usually when Lattens' father was visiting the harem, as now.

"Well, if you are sure."

"I am. Please tell your story."

"Very well. One day the two friends were playing a game."

"What sort of a game?"

"A very complicated one. Fortunately we don't need to concern ourselves with the details of how the game is played. All that matters is that they were playing it and they came to disagree about the rules, because there were more than one set of rules regarding how the game should be played."

"That is strange."

"Yes, but it was just that sort of game. So they disagreed. What it boiled down to was that Sechroom said that—as in life in general—you should always do what seemed like the right thing to do at the time, while Hiliti said that sometimes you had to do what appeared to be the wrong thing at the time in order to do the right thing eventually. Do you see?"

"I'm not sure."

"Hmm. Let me see. I know. That little pet eltar of yours. What's it called?"

"What, Wintle?"

"Yes, Wintle. Remember when you brought it inside and it peed in a corner?"

"Yes," Lattens said.

"And we had to take it and rub its nose in its own mess so that it wouldn't do it again?"

"Yes."

"Well, that wasn't very nice for poor little Wintle, now was it?"

"No."

"Can you imagine if somebody did that to you when you were young, if you'd done a pee in the corner?"

"Eurgh!"

"But it was the right thing to do, because eventually Wintle will stop doing that when he's brought inside, and so he can be brought in and enjoy himself with us instead of having to stay in the cage in the garden all the time."

"Yes?"

"And that is the sort of thing that people mean when they talk about being cruel to be kind. Have you heard that phrase before?"

"Yes. My teacher says it often."

"Yes, I think it is a phrase adults say to children quite often. But that was what Sechroom and Hiliti disagreed about. Sechroom said that you should never be cruel to be kind. Sechroom thought there must always be another way of teaching people lessons, and that good people had a duty to try and find those ways, and then to use them. Hiliti thought this was silly, and that throughout history it had been proved that sometimes you did have to be cruel to be kind, whether what you were trying to teach was a little pet eltar or a whole people."

"A whole people?"

"You know. Like an Empire or a country. Like Tassasen. Everybody."

"Oh."

"So, one day after they had fallen out over this game, Hiliti decided that he would teach Sechroom a lesson. He and Sechroom had grown up playing tricks and pranks on each other and each had come to expect such behaviour from the other. This day, a short time after their disagreement over the game, Hiliti and Sechroom and two other friends rode on their great mounts to one of their favourite places, a—"

"Was this before or after the other story, when the lady Leeril gave Hiliti sweets?"

"This was afterwards. The four of them came to this place in the hills where there was a clearing and a tall waterfall and lots of fruit trees all around and lots of rocks—"

"Were any of the rocks sugar rocks?"

"Lots of them. In many different flavours, though Sechroom and Hiliti and their two friends had brought their own picnic. So they ate the picnic and they swam in the pool at the foot of the waterfall and they played some games of hide-and-seek and so on and then Hiliti said he had a special game he wanted to show Sechroom. Hiliti asked the other two friends to remain where they were by the side of the pool, while Hiliti and Sechroom climbed up the rocks until they were at the top of the waterfall, standing right beside where the waters fell over the edge.

"Now, Sechroom didn't know, but Hiliti had ridden up there the day before and hidden a wooden plank by the side of the waterfall.

"Hiliti brought this plank out of the bushes and said that Sechroom had to stand on the end of the plank, with the other end sticking out over the drop. Then Hiliti would walk out on to the plank, towards the end, but—and this was where Sechroom started to get a little frightened—Hiliti would put on a blindfold first, so that he couldn't see what he was doing. Sechroom would have to guide him, and the thing was to see how close to the end of the plank Sechroom would let him get. How much did they really trust each other? That was the question.

"Then, assuming that Hiliti didn't fall off the plank and tumble to his death on the rocks below, or, if he was lucky, miss the rocks but land in the pool, it would be Sechroom's turn, and she would have to do the same thing, with Hiliti standing on the end of the plank and telling Sechroom to go forward or stop. Sechroom wasn't very sure about any of this, but eventually agreed because she didn't want to seem lacking in trust. Anyway, Hiliti put the blindfold on, told Sechroom to adjust the length of the plank hanging over the drop until she was happy with it, then he stepped on to the plank and went shuffling and wobbling along towards the end, with his hands and arms out-stretched. Like this."

"Did he fall off?"

"No, he didn't. Sechroom told him to stop when he got right to the very end of the plank and Hiliti could feel the edge. Hiliti undid the blindfold and stood there, arms out, waving at the two girls sitting far below. They were cheering and waving. Hiliti turned carefully and went back to the safety of the cliff edge, and then it was Sechroom's turn.

"Sechroom put on the blindfold and heard Hiliti adjust the amount the plank stretched out over the drop. Then she stepped on to it, sliding her feet very slowly and carefully and keeping her arms out to each side just as Hiliti had done."

"Like this."

"Like that. Well, the plank went up and down and Sechroom felt very frightened. A breeze had started up and it blew against Sechroom and made her feel even more frightened, but she kept sliding her feet along towards the end of the plank, which by now was starting to seem very far away.

"Just as she got to the end, Hiliti told her to stop, and she did. Then she slowly put her hands to the back of her head and undid the blindfold."

"Like this."

"Like that. She waved down to the friends standing on the grass."

"Like this."

"Like that, then she turned round to walk back along the plank, just as Hiliti stepped off the plank and let it and Sechroom fall."

"No!"

"Yes! Now the plank didn't fall very far because Hiliti had tied a length of rope to the end, but Sechroom fell screaming into the pool at the foot of the waterfall and hit the water with a tremendous splash and disappeared. Their two friends dashed and splashed into the water to help, while Hiliti calmly drew the plank back up and then knelt on the side of the cliff, looking down, waiting for Sechroom to surface.

"But Sechroom did not surface. The two other friends swam around looking for her and diving down into the depths of the pool and searching amongst the rocks all jumbled at the sides of the pool but they could find no sign of Sechroom. Up on the cliff Hiliti was horrified at what he'd done. He had only meant to teach Sechroom a lesson, to show her that you could not trust anybody. He wanted to be cruel to be kind because he thought that Sechroom's ideas might be the death of her one day if she was not taught to be more careful, but now it looked like his—Hiliti's—ideas had been the death of his cousin and best friend, for much time had passed by then and Sechroom could not possibly have survived so long under water."

"Did Hiliti dive into the water too?"

"Yes! He dived into the pool and hit the water so hard that he knocked himself out, but the two other friends rescued him and brought him back to the grass by the side of the pool. They were still slapping his cheeks and trying to press water out of his lungs when Sechroom appeared from the water, her head and neck all bloody and stumbled up to see how her friend was."

"She was alive!"

"She had struck her head on an underwater rock when she'd fallen into the pool and had nearly drowned, but she'd been brought up to the surface behind the waterfall and floated along with the current until she'd wedged between some rocks. There she had recovered and had realised what Hiliti had been up to. She was angry with Hiliti and with the two other friends as well, because she thought—mistakenly—that they were in on the trick too, and so she hadn't shouted out when the two had swum nearby, and had ducked under the water so that they wouldn't see her. Only when she thought Hiliti had injured himself too did she swim and wade out of the pool."

"Did Sechroom forgive Hiliti?"

"Mostly, though the two were never quite so close friends again."

"But they were both all right?"

"Hiliti came to quickly and was mightily relieved to see his friend. Sechroom's head wound was not as bad as it looked, though to this day she bears a funny, triangular scar on her head where the rock hit, just here, above the left ear. Luckily her hair covers the scar."

"Hiliti was bad."

"Hiliti was trying to prove a point. People often behave badly when they are trying to prove a point. Of course, he claimed that he *had* proved it. He said that he had taught Sechroom exactly the lesson he had sought to teach her, and taught it so well that Sechroom put the results of that lesson into effect almost instantly, for what was Sechroom doing, hiding there amongst the rocks behind the waterfall, but trying to teach Hiliti a lesson?"

"Ah-ha."

"Ah-ha indeed."

"So Hiliti was right?"

"Sechroom would never agree to that. Sechroom held that her

head was damaged and her brains were addled at the time and that that proved *her* point, which had become that it was only damaged people with confused brains who ever saw the justice in trying to be cruel to be kind."

"Mmm." Lattens yawned. "That was a better story than the last one, but quite a difficult one."

"I think you must rest now. You have to get better, don't you?"

"Like Sechroom and Hiliti did."

"That's right. They got better." DeWar tucked the boy in as Lattens' eyes slowly closed. The boy reached out and felt for something. His hand closed on a square of worn, pale yellow material, which he gripped tightly in one small hand and brought up to hold by his cheek, settling his head further down into the pillow with a few small nestling movements.

DeWar got up and made for the door, nodding to the nurse sitting knitting by the window.

The General met his bodyguard in the visiting chamber of the outer harem. "Ah, DeWar," UrLeyn said, walking swiftly from the doors to the harem and settling his long jacket over his shoulders. "Did you see Lattens?"

"I did, sir," DeWar said, falling into step as they exited the harem. Two men of the palace guard who had been effectively tripling the guard on the harem entrance trailed them by a few steps. This additional escort for the Protector was DeWar's response to the increased danger he perceived UrLeyn to be in after the attack by the Sea Company ambassador and the start of the war in Ladenscion, which had begun a few days earlier.

"He was asleep when I looked in," UrLeyn said. "I'll see him later. How was he?"

"Still recovering. I think the doctor bleeds him too much."

"Now, DeWar, each to his own. BreDelle knows what he's doing. I dare say you would not appreciate him trying to teach you the finer points of sword-play."

"Indeed not, sir, but even so." DeWar looked awkward for a moment. "There is something I'd like to do, sir."

"Yes? What?"

"I'd like to have Lattens' food and drink tasted. Just to make sure that he is not being poisoned."

UrLeyn stopped and looked at his bodyguard. "Poisoned?"

"Purely as a precaution, sir. I'm sure he has some . . . normal illness, trivial enough. But just to be on the safe side. With your permission."

UrLeyn shrugged. "Very well, if you think it necessary. I dare say my tasters won't object to the odd extra bit of food." He set off again, striding quickly.

They exited the harem and set off up the steps to the rest of the palace two at a time until UrLeyn stopped about halfway up and then continued one step at a time. He rubbed his lower back. "Occasionally my body chooses to remind me of my true age," he said. He grinned and tapped DeWar on the elbow. "I believe I deprived you of your opponent, DeWar."

"My opponent, sir?"

"Your game-playing companion." He winked. "Perrund."

"Ah."

"I tell you, DeWar, these young things are all very well, but you realise they're still girls when you have a real woman." He put his hand to his back again. "Providence, though. She puts me through my paces, I tell you." He laughed and stretched his arms. "If ever I expire in the harem, DeWar, Perrund may be to blame, and yet no blame will attach."

"Yes, sir."

They approached the King's Chamber where UrLeyn had taken to holding his daily briefings on the war. A buzz of conversation could be heard from beyond the guarded double doors. UrLeyn turned to DeWar. "Right, DeWar. I shall be in here for the next couple of bells."

DeWar looked at the doors with a pained expression, as a small boy with no coin might look at a sweet shop counter. "I really do think I ought to be with you during these briefings, sir."

"Now, DeWar," UrLeyn said, taking hold of his elbow. "I shall be safe with my military men, and there will be a double guard on the doors here."

"Sir, leaders who have been assassinated have usually believed that they were safe until the instant before it happened."

"DeWar," UrLeyn said kindly. "I can trust all these men with my life. I have known almost all of them for most of it. Certainly I have known most of them for longer than I have known you. I can trust them."

"But, sir—"

"And you make some of them uncomfortable, DeWar," UrLeyn said, with a hint of impatience. "They think a bodyguard should not be so opinionated as you have been. And your mere presence suffices to unsettle some of them. They think there's an extra shadow in the room."

"I shall dress in motley, put on the uniform of a fool—"

"You will not," UrLeyn told him, and put his hand on the other man's shoulder. "I order you to amuse yourself as you see fit for the next two bells and then return here and resume your duties after my generals have told me how many more towns we've taken since yesterday." He clapped DeWar's shoulder. "Now be gone. And if I'm not here when you come back I shall have returned to the harem for another bout with your opponent." He grinned at the other man and squeezed his arm. "All this talk of war and victorious battles seems to put a young man's blood in my cock!"

He left DeWar standing there, staring at the tiled floor of the corridor while the doors opened and closed on the sound of talking men. The two palace guards joined their comrades on either side of the doors.

DeWar's jaw worked as though he was chewing on something, then he spun and walked quickly away.

The plasterer had almost finished the remedial work on the Painted Chamber. A final layer was drying and he was kneeling on his white-spotted sheet surveying his tools and buckets and trying to remember the correct order to put them away. This was a job normally done by his apprentice, but he had had to do it himself on this job because it was all so secret.

The chamber's door was unlocked and the black-clad figure of

DeWar, the Protector's bodyguard, walked in. The plasterer felt a chill go through him when he saw the look on the tall man's dark face. Providence, they didn't intend to kill him now he'd done his job, did they? He'd known it was secret—what he had plastered up was a hidden alcove for someone to spy on people, that was obvious—but could it be so secret they'd kill him afterwards to stop him from talking? He'd done jobs in the palace before. He was honest and he kept his mouth shut. They knew that. They knew him. One of the palace guards was his brother. He could be trusted. He wouldn't tell anyone about this. He'd swear to that on his children's lives. They couldn't kill him. Could they?

He shrank back as DeWar approached. The bodyguard's sword wagged from side to side in its black scabbard while the long dagger at his other hip bounced in its own dark sheath. The plasterer looked into the other man's face and saw only a blank, cold expression that was more terrifying than a look of pitiless fury or an assassin's lying smile. He tried to find his voice, but could not. He felt his bowels start to loosen.

DeWar hardly seemed to see him. He glanced down at him, then at the new plaster partition still drying between the other painted panels, like a blood-drained lifeless face between living ones, then he walked past, to the small dais. The plasterer, his mouth dry, swivelled round where he knelt to watch. The bodyguard clutched one arm of the small throne on the dais, then he went and stood before a panel on the far side of the room which showed a scene set within a harem, full of stylised images of languidly buxom ladies in revealing dresses all lounging around, playing games and sipping from tiny glasses.

The black figure stood there for a moment. When he spoke, the plasterer jumped.

"Is the panel finished?" he asked. His voice was loud and hollow-sounding in the bare room.

The plasterer swallowed, coughed dryly and eventually was able to croak, "Ye-ye-yes, yes, sir. Ready for the p-painter by tomorrow."

Still facing the painting of the harem, still with hollow-sounding voice, the bodyguard said, "Good." Then without warning, and with no back-swing, just a single startlingly sudden thrust, he rammed his right fist straight through the panel he was standing in front of.

On the other side of the chamber, the plasterer yelped.

DeWar stood there a moment longer, half his lower arm protruding from the harem painting. A few painted plaster pieces fell dryly to the floor as he slowly withdrew his arm again.

The plasterer trembled. He wanted to get up and run but he felt glued to the spot. He wanted to raise his arms to defend himself but they seemed pinned to his sides.

DeWar stood, looking down at his right forearm, slowly brushing the white plaster dust off the black material. Then he spun on his heel and walked quickly to the door, where he paused and looked back with a face that seemed now to have taken on an expression of inconsolable torment. He glanced at the panel he had just punctured. "You may find another panel which needs repair. It must have been broken earlier, must it not?"

The plasterer nodded vigorously. "Yes. Yes, oh yes, of course, sir. Oh yes, very very definitely. I noticed it myself earlier, sir. I'll attend to it immediately, sir."

The bodyguard looked at him for a moment. "Good. The guard will let you out."

Then he was gone, and the door closed and was locked.

11
THE DOCTOR

The Guard Commander of Yvenir palace held a scented kerchief to his nose. Before him was a stone slab fitted with iron manacles, leg-irons and hide straps. None of these was required to restrain the current occupant of the slab, for spread upon it lay the limp body of the King's chief torturer, Nolieti, naked save for a small cloth draped over his genitals. Beside Guard Commander Polchiek stood Ralinge, chief torturer to Duke Quettil, and a young, grey-faced and sweating scribe sent by Guard Commander Adlain, who had taken personal command of the hunting party seeking the apprentice Unoure. These three were faced on the other side of the slab by Doctor Vosill, her assistant (that is, myself) and Doctor Skelim, personal physician to Duke Quettil.

The questioning chamber underneath the palace of Yvenir was relatively small and low-ceilinged. It smelled of a variety of unpleasant things, including Nolieti himself. It was not that the body had started to decay—the murder had happened only a couple of hours ago—but from the dirt and grime visible on the otherwise pale skin of the dead chief torturer it was obvious that he had not been the most personally hygienic of men. Guard Commander Polchiek watched a flea crawl out from beneath the cloth over the man's groin and start to travel up the slack curve of his stomach.

"Look," Doctor Skelim said, pointing at the tiny black shape moving over the mottled grey skin of the corpse. "Somebody's leaving the sinking ship."

"Looking for warmth," Doctor Vosill said, reaching quickly out to the insect. It disappeared an instant before her hand got there, jumping away. Polchiek looked amused, and I too wondered at the Doctor's naïveté. What was that proverb about there being only so many ways to catch a flea? But then the Doctor's fingers snapped closed in mid air, she inspected what she had there, nipped their tips more tightly together and then brushed the remains off on her hip. She looked up at Polchiek, whose face wore a surprised expression. "It might have jumped on one of us," she said.

A light-well above the slab had been opened for what was—to judge from the amount of dust and debris that rained down upon the unfortunate scribe sent to do the opening by Doctor Vosill—the first time in a long time. A brace of floor-standing candelabra added their own light to the gruesome scene.

"May we proceed?" the Guard Commander of Yvenir asked in a rumbling voice. Polchiek was a big, tall man with a single great scar from grey hair line to chin. A fall while hunting the previous year had left him with a knee that could not bend. It was for this reason that Adlain and not he was in charge of the search for Unoure. "I have never enjoyed attending any sort of event down here."

"I don't imagine the subjects of those events did either," Doctor Vosill observed.

"Nor did they deserve to," Doctor Skelim said, one of his small hands playing nervously with his collar ruff as his gaze flicked round the barrel-vaulted walls and ceiling. "It is a cramped, oppressive sort of place, isn't it?" He glanced at the Guard Commander.

Polchiek nodded. "Nolieti used to complain that there was barely room to swing a whip," he said. The grey-faced scribe began to make notes in a small slate-book. The fine point of the chalk made a scratching, squeaking noise on the stone.

Skelim snorted. "Well, he will swing no more of those. Is there any word on Unoure, Guard Commander?"

"We know which way he went," Polchiek said. "The hunting party should pick him up before dark."

"Do you think he will be in one piece?" asked Doctor Vosill.

"Adlain is not unused to hunting in these woods, and my hounds are well trained. The youth may suffer a bite or two, but he'll be alive when he is delivered to Master Ralinge here," Polchiek said, glancing at the wide little barrel of a man standing at his side and staring with a sort of greedy fascination at the wound that had gone most of the way towards separating Nolieti's head from his shoulders. Ralinge looked slowly up at Polchiek when he heard his name mentioned, and smiled, showing a full set of teeth which he was proud to have removed from his victims and which he had used to replace his own diseased items. Polchiek made a rumbling, disapproving noise.

"Yes. Well, Unoure's fate is what concerns me here, gentlemen," Doctor Vosill said.

"Really, madam?" Polchiek said, keeping his kerchief at his mouth and nose. "What concern of yours is his fate?" He turned to Ralinge. "I believe his destiny now lies in the hands of those of us on this side of the table, Doctor. Or does the lad have a medical condition that may rob us of the chance to question him on the matter?"

"Unoure is unlikely to have been the murderer," the Doctor said.

Doctor Skelim made a derisory snorting noise. Polchiek looked up at the ceiling, which for him was not far away. Ralinge did not take his gaze off the wound.

"Really, Doctor?" Polchiek said, sounding bored. "And what brings you to that strange conclusion?"

"The man is dead," Skelim said angrily, waving one thin hand at the corpse. "Murdered in his own chamber. His assistant was seen running into the woods while the body was still oozing blood. His master used to beat him, and worse. Everybody knows that. Only a woman would not see the obvious in this."

"Oh, let the good lady doctor have her say," Polchiek said. "I for one am already quite fascinated."

"*Doctor*, indeed," muttered Skelim, looking away to one side.

The Doctor ignored her colleague and bent over to grip the ragged flaps of skin that had been Nolieti's neck. I found myself swallowing hard. "The wound was caused by a serrated instrument, probably a large knife," she said.

"Astonishing," Skelim said sarcastically.

"There was a single cut, from left to right," the Doctor said, teasing apart the flaps of skin near the corpse's left ear. I confess that her assistant was feeling a little queasy at this juncture, though—like the torturer Ralinge—I could not tear my gaze from the wound. "It severed all the major blood vessels, the larynx—"

"The what?" Skelim said.

"The larynx," the Doctor said patiently, pointing to the roughly slashed pipe inside Nolieti's neck. "The upper part of the wind-pipe."

"We call it the upper part of the wind-pipe here," Doctor Skelim told her with a sneer. "We have no need for foreign words. Quacks and the like tend to use them when they're trying to impress people with their spurious wisdom."

"But if we look deeper," the Doctor said, levering the corpse's head right back and lifting its shoulders partly off the surface of the slab. "Oelph. Would you put that block underneath the shoulders here?"

I picked a piece of wood shaped like a miniature executioner's block up off the floor and stuck it under the dead man's shoulders. I was feeling sick. "Hold his hair, would you, Oelph?" the Doctor said, forcing Nolieti's head back still further. There was a glutinous sucking noise as the wound opened further. I took hold of Nolieti's sparse brown hair and looked away as I pulled on it.

"Looking deeper," the Doctor repeated, seemingly quite unaffected as she bent close over the tangle of multi-coloured tissues and tubes that had been Nolieti's throat, "we can see that the murder weapon cut so deep it nicked the victim's upper spinal column, here, at the third cervical vertebra."

Doctor Skelim snorted derisively again, but from the corner of my eye I saw him leaning closer to the opened wound. A sudden retching sound came from the far side of the table as Guard Commander Adlain's scribe turned quickly away and doubled over by a drain, his slate-book clattering to the ground. I felt my own bile rising and tried to swallow it back.

"Here. Do you see? Lodged in the cartilage of the voice box. A splinter of the vertebra, deposited there as the weapon was withdrawn."

"Very interesting, I'm sure," Polchiek said. "What is your point?"

"The direction of the cut would indicate the murderer was right-handed. Almost certainly the right hand was used, in any event. The depth and penetration points to a person of considerable strength, and incidentally reinforces the likelihood that the murderer was using his favoured hand, for people are rarely able to apply so much power so accurately and so certainly with their non-favoured hand. Also the angle of the cut—the way the wound slopes upward relative to the victim's throat—implies that the murderer was a good head or so taller than the victim."

"Oh, Providence!" Doctor Skelim said loudly. "Why not rip out his innards and read them like the priests of old to find the murderer's name? I guarantee they will say 'Unoure' in any event, or whatever his name is."

Doctor Vosill turned to Skelim. "Don't you see? Unoure is shorter than Nolieti, and left-handed. I imagine he is of average strength, perhaps a little more, but he does not have the look of a particularly powerful man."

"Perhaps he was in a rage," Polchiek suggested. "People can gather an inhuman strength in certain circumstances. I have heard they do so particularly in a place like this."

"And Nolieti might have been kneeling down at the time," Doctor Skelim pointed out.

"Or Unoure was standing on a stool," Ralinge said in a voice that was surprisingly soft and sibilant. He smiled.

The Doctor glanced towards a nearby wall. "Nolieti was standing at that workbench when he was attacked from behind. Arterial blood sprayed the ceiling and venous blood fell directly on the bench itself. He was not kneeling."

The scribe completed his retching, picked up his fallen slate-book and stood again, returning to his place by the table with an apologetic look at Polchiek, who ignored him.

"Mistress?" I ventured.

"Yes, Oelph?"

"Might I let go his hair now?"

"Yes, of course, Oelph. I beg your pardon."

"What does it matter exactly how Unoure did it?" Doctor Skelim said. "He must have been here when it happened. He ran away after it had happened. Of course he did it." Doctor Skelim looked disgustedly at Doctor Vosill.

"The doors to the chamber were neither locked nor guarded," the Doctor pointed out. "Unoure may have been on any sort of errand and come back to find his master killed. As for—"

Doctor Skelim shook his head and held up one hand towards the Doctor. "These womanly fancies and this unhealthy attraction to mutilation may represent a form of sickness in the mind on your part, madam, but they have little to do with the business of apprehending the culprit and getting the truth out of him."

"The doctor is right," Polchiek told the Doctor. "It is clear that you know your way around a corpse, madam, but you must accept that I know mine around an act of villainy. Running is invariably a sign of guilt, I have found."

"Unoure may simply have been frightened," the Doctor said. "He did not appear to be possessed of a great amount of wit. He may simply have panicked, not thinking that running away was the most suspicious thing he could have done."

"Well, we shall shortly apprehend him," Polchiek said with an air of finality. "And Ralinge here will find out the truth."

When the Doctor spoke it was with a degree of venom I think all of us found surprising. "Will he, indeed," she said.

Ralinge smiled broadly at the Doctor. Polchiek's scarred face took on a look of some grimness. "Yes, madam, he will," he told her. He flapped one hand at the corpse still lying between us. "This has all been most diverting, I'm sure, but on the next occasion you wish to impress some of your betters with your macabre knowledge of human anatomy I would ask you not to include those of us with better things to do, and certainly not me. Good day."

Polchiek turned and left, ducking under the doorway and acknowledging the salute of a guard. The scribe who had been sick looked up hesitantly from his incomplete notes and appeared uncertain what to do next.

"I agree," Doctor Skelim said with a note of relish in his voice as he brought his small face up towards the Doctor's. "You might have bewitched our good King for now, madam, but you do not deceive me. If you have any regard for your own safety, you will request leave to depart from us as quickly as possible and return to whatever decadent regime raised you. Good day."

The grey-faced scribe hesitated again, watching the Doctor's impassive face as Skelim swept smartly out of the chamber, head held high. Then the scribe muttered something to the still smiling Ralinge, closed his slate-book with a snap and followed the small doctor.

"They don't like you," Duke Quettil's chief torturer said to the Doctor. His smile broadened still further. "I like you."

The Doctor looked across the slab at him for a few moments, then held up her hands and said, "Oelph. A wet towel, if you please."

I ran and fetched a pitcher of water from a bench, picked a towel from the Doctor's bag and soaked it, then watched her as she washed her hands, not taking her gaze off the small, round man across the slab from her. I handed her a dry towel. She dried her hands.

Ralinge kept on smiling. "You might think you hate what I am, lady doctor," he said softly. His voice sounded distorted by his grisly collection of teeth. "But I know how to give pleasure as well as pain."

The Doctor handed me the towel and said, "Let us go, Oelph." She nodded at Ralinge and then we walked towards the door.

"And pain can be pleasure, too," Ralinge called after us. I felt my scalp crawl and the urge to be sick returned. The Doctor did not react at all.

"It's just a cold, sir."

"Ha. Just a cold. I've known people die from colds."

"Indeed, sir, but you should not. How is your ankle today? Let's take a look at it, shall we?"

"I believe it is getting better. Will you change the dressing?"

"Of course. Oelph, would you . . . ?"

I took the dressing and a few instruments from the Doctor's bag and arranged them on a cloth on the King's huge bed. We were in the King's private chamber, the day after Nolieti's murder.

The King's apartments at Yvenir are arranged within a splendid domed cupola set high at the rear of the palace, upon what is the roof to the main part of the great building. The gold-leaf-covered dome is set back from the terraced edge of the roof and separated from it by a small formal garden. As the roof level is just above the height of the tallest trees on the ridge behind, marking the summit of the hills on this side of the valley, the view from the north-facing windows which bring light into the most spacious and airy apartments is of nothing but sky beyond the clipped geometrical perfections of the gardens and the white tusk balustrade at their edge. This lends the apartments a strange, enchanted air of detachment from the real world. I dare say the clear mountain air contributes to this effect of isolated purity, but there is something most especially about that lack of sight of the mundane disorder of the land-scape of men which gives the place its singular spirit.

"Will I be well enough for the ball at the next small moon?" the King asked the Doctor as he watched her prepare the new dressing for his ankle. In truth the old dressing looked spotless, as the King had taken to his bed with a tingly throat and sneezing fits shortly after the news of Nolieti's demise had been communicated to us in the Hidden Gardens the day before.

"I should imagine you will be able to attend, sir," the Doctor said. "But do try not to sneeze over everybody."

"I am the King, Vosill," the King told her, sniffing into a fresh hand-kerchief. "I shall sneeze over whom I please."

"Then you will spread the ill humour to others, they will incubate it while you grow well again, they will perhaps subsequently inadver-tently sneeze in your presence and consequently reinfect you, who will play host to it again while they recover, and so on."

"Don't lecture me, Doctor. I'm in no mood for it." The King looked round at the slumped pile of pillows propping him up, opened his mouth to call a servant but then started to sneeze, his blond locks bouncing as his head went back and forth. The Doctor stood up from her chair and, while he was still sneezing, pulled the King upright and rearranged his pillows. The King looked at her in some surprise.

"You are stronger than you look, are you not, Doctor?"

"Yes, sir," the Doctor said with a modest smile as she went back to undoing the dressing on the King's ankle. "And yet still weaker than I would be." She was dressed as she had been the day before. Her long red hair was more carefully prepared than was usual, combed and plaited and hanging down her long dark jacket almost to her slim waist. She looked at me and I became aware that I was staring. I looked down at my feet.

Poking out from under the great bed's valance was a corner of cream-coloured clothing that looked oddly familiar. I wondered at this for a moment or two until, with a pang of jealousy for the right of Kings, I realised it was part of a shepherdess's costume. I pushed it further under the valance with my shoe.

The King settled himself back amongst his pillows. "What is the news on that boy who ran away? The one who killed my chief questioner?"

"They caught him this morning," the Doctor said, busying herself with the old dressing. "However, I do not think he committed the murder."

"Really?" the King said.

Personally, Master, I did not think he sounded as if he particularly cared one way or the other what the Doctor thought on this matter, but this was the cue for the Doctor to explain in some detail—especially to a man, however exalted, who had a cold and had just eaten a light breakfast—exactly why she had convinced herself that Unoure had not killed Nolieti. I have to say that the consensus amongst the other apprentices, assistants and pages, arrived at in the kitchen parlour of the palace the previous evening, was that the only perplexing aspect about the whole business was how Unoure had been able to put off the dark deed for so long.

"Well," the King said, "I dare say Quettil's fellow will get the truth out of him."

"The truth, sir? Or what is required to satisfy the prejudices of those already convinced they know the truth?"

"What?" the King said, dabbing at his reddened nose.

"This barbaric custom of torture, sir. It produces not the truth but rather whatever those commanding the questioner wish to hear, for the agonies involved are so unbearable that those subject to them will confess to anything—or more precisely, will confess to what they think their tormentors wish them to confess to—in the hope of causing the suffering to cease."

The King looked at the Doctor with an expression of confusion and disbelief. "People are beasts, Vosill. Lying beasts. The only way to get the truth out of them sometimes is to wring it from them." The King snorted mightily. "My father taught me that."

The Doctor looked at the King for a long moment, then started to undo the old dressing. "Indeed. Well, I'm sure he could not possibly have been wrong, sir," she said. She supported the King's foot with one hand and unwound the white dressing with the other. She started sniffing too.

The King kept on sniffing and snorting and staring at the Doctor. "Doctor Vosill?" he asked eventually as the last of the dressing floated free from his ankle and the Doctor gave it to me to put away.

"Sir?" she asked, wiping her eyes on her cuff and looking away from Quience.

"Madam, have I upset you?"

"No," the Doctor said quickly. "No, sir." She made as though to start applying the new dressing, then put it aside and made an exasperated clicking noise with her mouth. She busied herself with the inspection of the small wound healing on the King's ankle and then ordered me to fetch water and soap, which I had already provided and set by the bed. She seemed annoyed that I had done this, but quickly ensured the wound was clean, washed and dried the King's foot and began to secure the new dressing.

The King appeared discomfited during all this. When the Doctor was finished he looked at her and said, "You will be looking forward to the ball yourself, Doctor?"

She smiled briefly at him. "Of course, your majesty."

We packed our things away. As we were about to take our leave, the King reached out and took the Doctor's hand. There was a troubled, uncertain look I did not think I had seen before in his eyes. He said, "Women bear pain better than men, they say, Doctor." His eyes seemed to search hers. "It is ourselves we hurt most when we question."

The Doctor looked down at her hand, held within the King's. "Women bear pain better because we must give birth, sir," she said in a low voice. "Such pain is generally regarded as being unavoidable, but is alleviated to whatever extent it can be by those of my calling." She looked up into his eyes. "And we only become beasts—we become worse than beasts—when we torment others, sir."

She took her hand carefully from his, picked up her bag and with a small bow to the King, turned and headed for the doors. I hesitated, half expecting the King to call her back, but he did not. He just sat there in his vast bed, looking hurt, and sniffing. I bowed to the King and followed the Doctor.

Unoure never was put to the question. A few hours after he was captured and brought back to the palace, while the Doctor and I were attending the King and while Ralinge was still preparing the chamber for his inquisition, a guard looked in on the cell where the youth was being held. Somehow, Unoure had slit his own throat with a small knife. His arms and legs were tightly chained behind him and he had been stripped naked before being placed in the cell. The knife had been wedged hilt-first into a crack in the stone walls of the cell at about waist height. Unoure had been able to kneel before it at the extremity of the reach the chains securing him would allow and slice his neck across its blade, before collapsing and bleeding to death.

I understand that the two Guard Commanders were furious. The guards who had been charged with Unoure's custody were lucky they were neither punished nor put to the question themselves. It was eventually agreed that Unoure must have placed the knife there before his attack on Nolieti, in case he was captured and brought back to the palace.

Our shared station might dictate both that we knew little and that our opinions were worth less, but none of us who had had occasion to experience the full extent of Unoure's intelligence, forethought and cunning found this explanation even remotely convincing.

Quettil: Good Duke, how very pleasant it is to see you. Is this not a fine view?

Walen: Hmm. I find you well, Quettil?

Q: In most rude health. You?

W: Tolerable.

Q: I thought you might want to sit down. See? I have arranged for chairs.

W: Thank you, no. Let us go over here . . .

Q: Oh. Well, very well . . . Well, here we are. And afforded an even finer view. However, I cannot imagine you wished to meet me up here to admire my own estates.

W: Hmm.

Q: Allow me to hazard a guess. You have some misgivings about . . . what was his name? Nolieti? Nolieti's death? Or rather about his and his apprentice's?

W: No. I believe that matter is closed. I attach no great significance to the death of a pair of torturers. Theirs is a despicable if necessary craft.

Q: Despicable? Oh no. No indeed. Why, I would call it a form of art at its most elevated. My man, Ralinge, is a veritable master. I have only avoided singing his praises to Quience because I'm afraid he might take him from me, and that would be most upsetting. I should feel deprived.

W: No, my concern is with one whose profession is concerned with the alleviation of pain, not the causing of it.

Q: Really? Ah, you mean that woman who calls herself a doctor? Yes, what does the King see in her? Can't he just fuck her and have done with it?

W: Perhaps he has, more likely he has not. She looks at him in a way that leads me to believe she would like to be tumbled . . . but I care not either way. The point is that he seems convinced of her efficacy as a physician.

Q: And . . . what? There is someone you would rather see in her place?

W: Yes. Anybody. I believe she is a spy, or a witch, or something between the two.

Q: I see. Have you told the King?

W: Of course not.

Q: Ah-ha. Well, my own physician is of much the same opinion as yourself, if that is any comfort. Which I warn you it ought not to be, really, given that my physician is a self-important fool and no better than any of the rest of these blood-letters and saw-bones at curing anything.

W: Yes, quite. I am sure, nevertheless, that your physician is as competent a doctor as can be found, and so I am glad that he shares my opinion of the woman Vosill. That may well prove useful if eventually we have to convince the King of her unsuitability. I can tell you that Guard Commander Adlain feels that she is a threat too, though he agrees with me that it is not yet possible to move against her. That is why I wanted to talk to you. May I rely on your discretion? I wish to speak of something that would have to be done without the King's knowledge, even though it would be done solely to protect him.

Q: Hmm? Yes, of course, good Duke. Go on. Nothing will go beyond these walls. Well, balustrades.

W: I have your word?

Q: Of course, of course.

W: Adlain and I had an agreement with Nolieti that should it prove necessary, the woman could be taken and put to the question . . . without reference to the King.

Q: Ah, I see.

W: This plan was ready to be put into effect while we travelled from Haspide to here. But now we are here, and Nolieti is dead. I would ask you to be willing and ready to put a similar plan into effect. If your fellow Ralinge is as efficient as you say then he ought to have no difficulty extracting the truth from the woman.

Q: Certainly, to date, I can think of no woman who has been able to resist his advances in that respect.

W: Well then, will you let some part of the Palace Guard arrange for her apprehension, or at least allow it to take place without their interference?

Q: . . . I see. And what would be my interest in doing so?

W: Your interest? Why, the safety of the King, sir!

Q: Which is of course my first concern, as it is so clearly and creditably yours, dear Duke. Yet without some obviously deleterious action by the woman, it might rather look as though one was acting on no more than your own dislike of her, however well informed.

W: My likes and dislikes are predicated entirely on what is good for the royal house and I would hope that my service over the past many years, indeed decades, has proved that. You care less than nothing for the woman. Are you saying you would object?

Q: You have to see this from my stand-point, dear Walen. While you are all here the responsibility for your safety is formally mine. On this occasion, only a few days after the arrival of the Court at Yvenir, one of its officers was killed unlawfully and his murderer escaped the questioning and punishment that should rightfully have been his. That displeased me greatly, sir, and it was only because the matter was concluded almost as soon as it began, and appeared to be entirely internal to the royal court that I felt no more insulted. Even so, I think Polchiek does not realise how close he came to being brought down a rung or two. And I might add that my Guard Commander still worries that something is being hidden, that the apprentice's death was somehow arranged by somebody who might have benefited from his silence. But in any event, if, after such a murder and suicide, a favourite of the King were to disappear, then it would mean that I would have no choice but to discipline Polchiek with the utmost severity. My honour could be preserved by nothing less, and arguably would still suffer. I would need the most decidedly persuasive proof that the woman meant the King some harm before I could possibly countenance any such action.

W: Hmm. I fancy the only proof you would accept would be the King's corpse, and that alone might prove satisfactory to you.

Q: Duke Walen, I would hope that your wit might devise a way to discover the woman's fraudulent nature long before that could possibly occur.

W: Indeed. And I have just such a commission in hand.

Q: There, you see? And what is your plan?

W: Close to fruition, I hope.

Q: You will not tell me?

W: It is unfortunate that it seems neither of us can indulge the other, Quettil.

Q: Yes, isn't it?

W: I have no more to say, I think.

Q: Very well. Oh, Duke?

W: Sir?

Q: I take it I can rely on the woman *not* still somehow disappearing while the court rests at Yvenir, can I? If she did, I might have to think most carefully about whether to reveal to the King what you have revealed to me.

W: You gave me your word.

Q: Why, that I did, dear Walen. But I'm sure you would agree that my first loyalty is to the King, not to you. If I judged that the King was being deceived for no persuasive reason, it would be my duty to inform him.

W: I am sorry I have troubled you, sir. It would appear that we have both wasted our time this morning.

Q: Good day, Walen.

This too I found later, not in the Doctor's journal but in some other papers (and have edited it slightly to present a more continuous narrative). The common participant of these two passages is Walen, but—especially given all that happened later—I simply do not know what to make of it. I record. I do not judge. I do not even offer speculation.

12
THE BODYGUARD

The Royal Park of Croughen Hills had been a private game reserve of the royal house of Tassasen for several centuries. UrLeyn had parcelled large parts of it out to various of the nobles who had supported his cause in the war of succession, but reserved the right of the Protector and his court to go hunting in the forests.

The four mounts and their riders circled the tall clump of brush and tangled creeper bush where they reckoned their prey had gone to ground.

RuLeuin took out his sword and leaned down from the saddle, poking at the mass of vegetation. "Are you sure he went in here, brother?"

"Quite certain," UrLeyn said, dipping his face towards his mount's neck and squinting at an opening into the bushes. He lowered himself still further, letting go of the reins with one hand to peer into the undergrowth. DeWar, riding at his side, reached out to hold the reins of UrLeyn's mount. RuLeuin, on the far side of the bushes, also leant down upon the neck of his mount.

"How is the boy today, UrLeyn?" YetAmidous said, voice booming. His big face was red and bright with sweat.

"Oh, he's well," UrLeyn said, levering himself upright again. "Better with every day. Still not strong, though." He glanced round, looking back up the slope beneath the trees. "We need some beaters here . . ."

"Get your dark man to beat for us," YetAmidous said to UrLeyn, referring to DeWar. "You'll get down and beat for us, won't you, DeWar?"

DeWar smiled thinly. "I only beat out human prey, General YetAmidous."

"Human prey, eh?" YetAmidous said with a hearty laugh. "Those were the days, what?" He slapped his saddle. DeWar's thin smile lasted a little longer.

In the last years of the old Kingdom, when King Beddun had been at his most carelessly cruel, prisoners—or poachers unlucky enough to be caught plying their trade in the forest—had provided most of the prey for hunts. That tradition of savagery had been outlawed, but there was one memento of the time present, DeWar thought, in the shape of the old King Beddun's antique hunting crossbow, which UrLeyn carried slung over his back.

UrLeyn, DeWar, YetAmidous and RuLeuin had become separated from the main part of the hunt, which could be heard on the far side of the hill. "Sound your horn, will you, Yet?" UrLeyn said. "Let's get some of the others here."

"Right you are." YetAmidous brought his horn to his lips and let a great blare of sound escape. It almost coincided, DeWar noticed, with the sound of horns coming from the other side of the hill, so probably was not heard. He chose not to say anything. YetAmidous shook some spit from the horn's mouthpiece and looked pleased with himself.

"Is Ralboute joining us, Protector?" he asked. "I thought he was supposed to."

"A message came this morning," UrLeyn said, standing up in the saddle to stare into the clump of bushes. He shielded his eyes as a beam of sunlight fell across his face. "He has been detained at—" He looked at DeWar.

"I believe it is the city of Vynde, sir."

"—Vynde. The city of Vynde is proving more resilient than expected."

RuLeuin stood in the saddle too and directed his gaze at the same place as his brother. "There was talk that we lost a couple of the siege mortars," he said.

"It is only a rumour as yet," UrLeyn said. "Simalg has rushed ahead as usual and out-distanced his supporting forces. Communication has been erratic. With Simalg, you never know. He may have advanced too fast for his guns, or otherwise misplaced them. Let's not assume the worst."

"I have heard other grumbles, still, Protector," YetAmidous said, undoing the top of a wineskin and taking a quick gulp. "Perhaps we should go to Ladenscion ourselves and take matters in hand." YetAmidous' brows compressed. "I tell you, Protector, I *miss* making war. And I'd warrant you for one would not misplace siege guns."

"Yes," RuLeuin said. "You ought to take charge of the war yourself, brother."

"I have thought about it," UrLeyn said. He unsheathed his own sword and whacked at the tops of some bushes. "I have been concerned to appear less of a warlord and more of a statesman, and anyway did not reckon the rebellion in Ladenscion merited the full weight of our forces, but I may change my mind if I think the situation demands it. I shall wait for Ralboute's return, or for a message from him. Yet, blow that horn again, would you? I don't think they heard the first time." UrLeyn put away his sword and took off his green hunting cap. He wiped his brow.

"Ha!" YetAmidous said. He lifted the hunting horn, took a gargantuan breath that raised his formidable body off the saddle of his mount and turned his expression into a deep frown, then put the instrument to his lips and blew with all his might, his face going scarlet with the effort.

The note was fit to split ears. Almost immediately there was a rustle and a commotion on the down-slope side of the clump of bushes. DeWar was closest. He caught a glimpse of a big, thick-set, grey-brown shape dart away at a furious pace towards another conglomeration of vegetation.

"Ha!" YetAmidous bellowed. "Flushed the fucker!"

"DeWar!" UrLeyn shouted. "Did you see him?"

"There, sir."

"Ru! Yet! This way!" UrLeyn wheeled his mount and charged off in the same direction.

DeWar preferred to ride right at UrLeyn's side whenever he could, but in the dense thickets of the Park woods it was often impossible, and he would have to follow the Protector's mount through the under-growth, over fallen tree trunks and under hanging boughs as best he could, ducking and leaning and sometimes hanging half out of the saddle to avoid the snagging branches.

Taking the direction that DeWar had indicated, UrLeyn set off at a gallop down a shallow slope, his mount thundering along the hint of path amongst the crowding bushes. DeWar followed, trying to keep in view the bobbing green shape that was UrLeyn's cap.

The incline was covered by undergrowth and overhung by the crisscrossed trunks of trees which had started to fall but been caught by their healthier fellows. A confusion of lushly green limbs and twisted branches made the going difficult. The footing for the mounts was treacherous. The deep litter of rotting leaves, twigs, fruits and seed cases could hide a multitude of holes, burrow entrances, rocks and partially decayed logs, any one of which could break a mount's leg or trip it and bring it tumbling to the ground.

UrLeyn was going too fast. DeWar was never so fearful for his own life or for his master's than when he tried to keep up with him on some mad dash during a hunt. He did his best, all the same, attempting to steer his mount down the trail of broken branches and trampled litter that UrLeyn had taken. Behind him, he could hear the mounts of YetAmidous and RuLeuin also crashing in pursuit.

The animal they were hunting was an ort, a powerful, thick-set scavenger a third the size of a mount. They were usually regarded as belligerent and stupid, but DeWar thought the reputation undeserved. Orts ran until they were cornered and only then did they fight, using their small sharp horns and their even sharper teeth, and they tried to avoid the clear areas under the high canopies where galloping was easy and the ground relatively free of brush and other obstructions. Instead they made for places like this, where a jumble of living and dead trees and their associated debris made both observation and chase difficult.

The trail led down a steepening slope towards a stream. UrLeyn whooped and shouted and disappeared further ahead. DeWar cursed and urged his mount to go faster. It shook its head and snorted, refusing. DeWar tried to stop himself watching where his mount was putting its feet—best to leave that to the animal. He would be better occupied ducking to avoid the overhanging boughs and branches that threatened to knock him senseless or gouge out his eyes. From far away he heard the sound of the rest of the hunt: men shouting, horns blaring, hounds yapping, prey screaming. From the noise, the others must have cornered a large group. The single beast UrLeyn was chasing had succeeded in escaping without any hounds in pursuit. It was a big animal, and hunting it without hounds was a brave or foolish thing to do. DeWar took one hand briefly off the reins and wiped his face with one sleeve. The day was hot and the air under the great trees still and sticky. Sweat still trickled down his face, stinging in his eyes and producing a salty taste in his mouth.

Behind him, a sharp report was the noise of a gun going off. Probably an ort being dispatched. Or a musketeer losing half his face. Guns small enough to be carried by a man, or even on the back of a mount, were unreliable, inaccurate and often more dangerous for the firer than the fired-at. Gentlemen did not use them, and crossbows were superior in most respects. Still, the smiths and armourers laboured to produce better examples of muskets with each passing season, and UrLeyn had used the weapons to good effect against cavalry charges during the war of succession. DeWar worried that one day within his lifetime guns would become reliable enough—and more importantly sufficiently accurate—to provide a bodyguard with his worst nightmares, but for now that day still seemed a fair way off.

A scream came from somewhere off to the left, down the small valley of the stream. It might have been human or ort. It sent a shiver through DeWar despite the heat.

He had lost sight of UrLeyn. Branches and leaves swayed and thrashed ahead to his left. With a cold feeling in his guts DeWar wondered if the scream he had heard had been from the Protector. He swallowed hard, wiping his face again and attempting to wave away insects buzzing angrily round his head. A branch caught him on the face, stinging his right cheek. What if UrLeyn had fallen from his mount? He might have been gored, or had his throat bitten out. Last year, near here, one of the younger nobles had somersaulted off his falling mount and been impaled through the back and belly on a jagged remnant of tree trunk. His screams had sounded like that scream, hadn't they?

He tried to urge his mount to go faster. A branch snagged on the crossbow slung over his back, almost yanking him out of his saddle. DeWar hauled on the reins and the animal below him shrieked as the metal bit cut into its mouth. He twisted in the saddle and tried unsuccessfully to untangle himself. Up slope, he could see RuLeuin and YetAmidous approaching. He swore, pulled his dagger and hacked at the offending branch. It parted from the tree, remaining lodged in the crossbow but letting him go. He kicked his spurs into the mount's side and it started off down the slope again.

He burst out of the undergrowth, down a suddenly steep earth bank and into a clearing by the stream-side. UrLeyn's mount stood riderless by a tree, panting. DeWar looked wildly around for the Protector, then saw him standing a little way off, near where the stream appeared from a jumble of fallen rocks, his crossbow at his shoulder, aiming at the big ort, which was whining and squealing as it tried to jump up the slippy, moss-covered rocks barring its way up and out of the clearing.

The ort leapt halfway up the boulder slope, seemed to be about to find further purchase on the rocks and complete its escape, then with a grunt it lost its footing and fell, bouncing off a lower rock and landing heavily on its back by the side of the stream. It struggled to its feet, shaking itself. UrLeyn advanced a couple of steps closer to the animal, crossbow aimed. DeWar unslung his own bow as he dismounted. He wanted to shout to UrLeyn, to tell him to get back on his mount and leave the animal to him, but he was afraid of distracting the other man while the ort was so close. The ort turned its attention away from the rocks. It growled at UrLeyn, who was now five or six strides away. Its only way out now was past the man.

Now, thought DeWar. Shoot. Loose. Fire. Now. He was another ten or so strides behind UrLeyn. He took a few slow steps to the right, along the bottom edge of the earth bank, widening the angle he could see between UrLeyn and the ort. He tried to ready his own crossbow for firing without looking at it, frightened to take his eyes off the Protector and the prey he had cornered. Something was stuck in the crossbow. He could feel it. The branch it had snagged on earlier. His hand closed around leaves and twigs, trying to pull them free. Failing.

Snarling, the ort backed away from the slowly advancing UrLeyn. The animal's rump bumped into one of the mossy boulders it had tried to scale. It angled its head downwards fractionally. Its slightly curved horns were only just longer than a man's hand, but each came to a point sharp enough to disembowel a mount. UrLeyn was wearing a light hide jerkin and trousers. DeWar had suggested heavier clothing or some chain mail in addition that morning, before they had set off, but the Protector was having none of it. The day was going to be too hot as it was.

The ort lowered its rear quarters. With a clarity which seemed almost unnatural, DeWar could see the muscles in the ort's quarters bunching, tensing. He pulled at the foliage stuck in his crossbow, waggling it. The dagger. He might have to forget about the crossbow and try throwing the dagger. It did not throw well, but it was the only other choice he had. The branch started to tear free from the crossbow.

"Brother?" a voice boomed out above him. DeWar whirled to see RuLeuin high above him, his mount's front hooves near the edge of the earth bank. UrLeyn's brother, his face caught in a stray beam of sunlight, was shading his eyes with one hand and looking across the clearing at the far bank. Then his gaze dropped to the clearing and UrLeyn. "Oh," he said quietly.

DeWar looked quickly back. The ort had not moved. It was still growling softly, still tensed. Saliva dripped from one edge of its mouth. DeWar heard his mount give a single small whimper.

UrLeyn made a tiny movement, there was a barely heard click, then the man seemed to freeze.

"Shit," he said softly.

Crossbows could kill from hundreds of strides away. A quarrel from one could pierce a metal breastplate, at close range. There was rarely time to stop, tension and load a bow during the heat of a hunt. One rode with the bow wound up and ready to fire, and many kept it loaded, too. Crossbows hanging from saddles had shot more than one hunter in the foot, or worse, and those over a man's back could be even more deadly, if they snagged on a branch in a thicket. And so a hunting crossbow had a safety latch. One had to remember to undo it before the weapon would fire. In the excitement of the chase, it was not unusual for a hunter to forget to do so. And UrLeyn's crossbow, which had been King Beddun's, was an old one. The latch release had been added later, not designed in, and was positioned badly, towards the rear of the weapon and so not easy to slip. UrLeyn would have to move one hand from its position to make the adjustment. The king UrLeyn had executed might have his revenge from beyond the grave.

DeWar held his breath. The branch which had tangled in his own bow fell to the ground. Still not taking his eyes off the ort, DeWar watched UrLeyn slowly move one hand to the safety latch on his crossbow. The weapon, its weight supported by one hand, shook. The ort growled louder and shifted its position slightly, side-stepping closer to the stream, narrowing DeWar's angle of fire so much that one side of its head was now hidden by UrLeyn's body. Above him, DeWar could hear RuLeuin's mount breathing. DeWar felt for his bow's safety latch as he brought it up to his shoulder and took another step to the right to open the angle again.

"What? What's this? Where . . . ?" another voice said from above, to the accompaniment of swishing leaves and stamping hooves. YetAmidous.

UrLeyn gently unclipped the safety on the crossbow and started to move his hand back towards the trigger again. The ort charged.

UrLeyn's crossbow started to drop, hinging down as the Protector tried to track the animal racing towards him. He began to leap at the same time, moving to the right, obscuring the clear shot DeWar had had of the ort. DeWar released the trigger on the bow just in time, an instant before the bolt would have flown towards the Protector. Suddenly UrLeyn's hunting cap leaped from his head and went tumbling away towards the stream. DeWar registered this without thinking what had caused it. He started to run towards UrLeyn, leaning forward, pushing off with one foot then the other, holding the bow in front of his belly, pointing to one side. UrLeyn was slipping, the foot he had put his weight on beginning to flick out from underneath him.

Two steps, three. Something whirred past DeWar's head and left a curl of wind to stroke his cheek. An instant later there was a splash in the stream, the water kicking high into the air.

Four steps. Still picking up speed, each stride more like a leap. The Protector's crossbow made a cracking, twanging noise. The bow pushed back in UrLeyn's hands. The bolt appeared in the left haunch of the charging ort, making the animal scream, leap into the air and twist its hips, but when it landed again, two strides from the stumbling, falling UrLeyn, it lowered its horned head and charged straight at him.

Five, six steps. UrLeyn hit the ground. The ort's snout thudded into his left hip. It reared back and darted forward again, head lower this time, aiming for the fallen man's midriff as he started to raise one hand in an attempt to fend the animal off.

Seven. DeWar brought the crossbow round as he ran, still at waist height. He took a half-stride to steady it as best he could then pulled the trigger.

The quarrel hit the ort just above the left eye. The animal quivered and stopped in its tracks. The feathered bolt protruded from its skull like a third horn. DeWar was four then three steps away, throwing the crossbow aside as his left hand crossed to his right hip and the handle of the long dagger. UrLeyn kicked, pivoting his lower body away from the ort, which was looking down at the ground less than a pace away from him, snorting and shaking its head while its front legs buckled and it settled to the ground.

DeWar drew the dagger and leapt over UrLeyn as the older man rolled away from the ort, landing between the two. The ort snorted and puffed and shook its head and looked up with what DeWar would always swear was a surprised expression as he plunged the dagger into its neck near its left ear and in one swift movement opened its throat to the air. The animal made a whooshing noise and collapsed to the ground, head tucked in to its chest, its dark blood spreading around it. DeWar kept the dagger pointing towards it as he knelt there, feeling behind him with his free hand to make sure where UrLeyn was.

"Are you all right, sir?" he asked, without looking round. The ort jerked, seemed to be trying to get to its feet, then rolled over on its side, legs trembling. The blood continued to gush from its neck. Then the animal stopped shaking, the blood began to seep rather than pulse, and slowly the beast's legs folded in to its body as, finally, it died.

UrLeyn pulled himself up on to his knees by DeWar. He put one hand on the other man's shoulder. The Protector's grip felt shaky. "I am . . . chastened, I think would be the right word, DeWar. Thank you. Providence. Big bugger, isn't he?"

"Big enough, sir," DeWar said, deciding the motionless animal was little enough of a threat to let him risk glancing behind, to where YetAmidous and RuLeuin were making their way down a shallow-sloped part of the earth bank. Their mounts stood on the bank, looking down at UrLeyn and his own mount. The two men approached at a run. YetAmidous still held his discharged crossbow. DeWar looked back at the ort, then stood, sheathed the long dagger and helped UrLeyn to his feet. The Protector's arm trembled and he did not let go of DeWar's arm once he had stood up.

"Oh, sir!" YetAmidous cried, clutching his crossbow to his chest. His broad, round face looked grey. "Are you unharmed? I thought I— Providence, I thought I'd . . ."

RuLeuin came dashing up, nearly tripping on DeWar's crossbow where it lay on the ground. "Brother!" He threw his arms wide and almost knocked his brother over as he hugged him, pulling UrLeyn's hand away from DeWar.

On the slope above, the sounds of the main part of the hunt were coming closer.

DeWar glanced back at the ort. It looked very dead.

* * *

"And who fired first?" Perrund asked quietly and without moving. Her head was tipped, lowered over the "Secret Keep" board, studying her next move. They were sitting in the visiting chamber of the harem, towards ninth bell. There had been a particularly noisy after-hunt feast that evening, though UrLeyn had retired early.

"It was YetAmidous," DeWar said, no more loudly. "His was the shot that lifted the Protector's cap off his head. The cap was found downstream. The bolt was embedded inside a log by the stream. A finger-breadth lower . . ."

"Indeed. And so it was RuLeuin's that just missed you."

"And just missed UrLeyn, too, though I think it was his waist it missed by a hand's breadth or so, not his head by a finger's."

"Could each bolt plausibly have been meant for the ort?"

". . . Yes. Neither man is regarded as a marksman. If YetAmidous really was aiming for UrLeyn's head then I imagine that most of the people in the court who consider themselves authorities on this sort of matter would judge it as a surprisingly accurate shot, given the circumstances. And YetAmidous did seem genuinely shocked that he'd missed the Protector by so small a margin. And RuLeuin is his brother, for all Providence." DeWar sighed heavily, then yawned and rubbed his eyes. "And YetAmidous, as well as being a poor shot, is just not the type to be an assassin."

"Hmm," Perrund said in a particular tone.

"What?" Only as he said this did DeWar realise how well he felt he had come to know the woman. Just the way she had made that single sound had meant much to him.

"I have a friend who spends quite a lot of time in YetAmidous' company," Perrund said softly. "She has said that he delights in card games played for money. He takes even greater delight in making it seem that he is ignorant of the subtleties of the games and pretending that he is a poor player. He appears to forget the rules, has to ask what to do at certain points, inquires as to the meaning of terms the other players use, and so on. Often he will deliberately lose a series of small bets. In fact he is only waiting until an especially large wager is at stake, whereupon he almost invariably wins, much to his own apparent surprise. She has seen this happen time after time. His friends are wise to him now, and are amused as well as wary, but many a young and smirking nobleman who thought himself in the presence of a bumbling fool ripe for the picking has been lucky to leave YetAmidous' house with a coin to call his own."

DeWar realised that he was biting his lip as he stared at the game board. "So the man is a skilled dissembler, not a buffoon. That is worrying." He looked up at Perrund, though she did not meet his gaze. He found himself inspecting the blond mass of her gathered-up hair, marvelling at its sheen and perfect fairness. "Your friend would not have any further observations or opinions on the gentleman, would she?"

Still not looking up, Perrund took a long deep breath. He watched her shoulders in the red gown, glanced down to the swell of material over her breasts. "Once, perhaps twice," she said, "when YetAmidous has been very drunk, she has thought he revealed . . . a certain jealous contempt for the Protector. And I think he has little regard for you." She looked up suddenly.

DeWar felt himself rock back slightly, as though afflicted by the force of the gaze from those blue-flecked gold eyes. "Though none of this is to say that he is not still a good and loyal follower of the Protector," Perrund said. "If one is determined to find fault then looking hard enough will produce reason to distrust everybody." She looked down again.

"Of course," DeWar said, and felt his face grow warm. "Still, I would rather know such things than not."

Perrund moved one piece, then another. "There," she said.

DeWar continued with his analysis of the game.

13

THE DOCTOR

Master, the masked ball took place six days later. The King still had a slight cold, but the Doctor had given him a preparation made from flowers and mountain herbs which dried up his "membranes" (by which I think she meant his nose) for the duration of the dance. She advised him to avoid alcohol and to drink copious amounts of water, or better still fruit juice. However, I believe that during the ball he was quickly persuaded, principally by himself, that the definition of fruit juice might include wine and so drank a deal of that during the ball.

The Grand Ballroom of Yvenage is a dramatic circular space half of whose circumference is taken up with floor to ceiling windows. In the year since the court had last visited Yvenir, the windows had been refashioned throughout their lower quarter. The great pastel-green plaster panels had been replaced with a grid of wood holding smaller panes of thin, colourless glass. The glass was almost crystal in its perfection, affording a barely distorted view of the moonlit landscape of forested hills across the valley. The effect was extraordinarily eye-catching and it seemed, from the expressions of wonder I heard uttered and the extravagance of the estimates made within my earshot concerning the cost of such a project, that people could hardly have been more impressed had the new windows been made of diamond.

The orchestra sat on a low circular stage set in the centre of the room, each player facing inwards to watch their conductor, who swivelled towards each section of the musicians in turn. The dancers swirled round this focus like fallen leaves caught within a spiralling wind, the intricate sets and patterns of the dances providing an order within that apparent chaos.

The Doctor was one of the more striking women present. Partly the effect was achieved through her height. There were taller women there, yet still she seemed to shine out amongst them. She possessed a bearing that was in all senses naturally elevated. She wore a gown that was plain by comparison with most. It was a dark and lustrous green, to set off the wide, netted fan of her carefully arrayed red hair. Her gown was unfashionably narrow.

Master, I confess I felt excited and honoured to be there. The Doctor having no other escort, it fell to me to accompany her to the ball, and so I was able to think with some pleasure of my fellow apprentices and assistants, most of whom were banished downstairs. Only the senior pages were permitted to attend, and the few of those not expected to act purely as servants were all too aware of their inability to shine in a company containing so many junior noblemen. The Doctor, in contrast, treated me as her equal, and made not one demand on me as an apprentice the whole ball long.

The mask I had chosen was a plain one of flesh-coloured paper painted so that one half looked happy, with a big smile at the lips and a raised brow, while the other side looked sad, with downcast mouth and a small tear at the eye. The Doctor's was a half-face made of light, highly polished silver treated with some sort of lacquer. It was, I thought, the best and perhaps the most disconcerting mask that I saw all that night, for it reflected the observer's gaze right back at them and so disguised the wearer—for whatever that was worth, given the Doctor's unmistakable form—better than the most cunning creation of feathers, filigreed gold or sparkling gems.

Beneath the mirror-like mask, the Doctor's lips looked full and tender. She had coloured them with the red oil-cream that many of the ladies at court use for such occasions. I had never seen her adorn herself so before. How moist and succulent that mouth looked!

We sat at a great table in one of the ballroom's anterooms, surrounded by fine ladies of the court and their escorts and looked down upon by huge paintings of nobles, their animals and estates. Servants with drinks trays circulated everywhere. I couldn't recall having seen a ball so well staffed before, though it did seem to me that some of the servants looked a bit rough and ready, handling their trays with a degree of awkwardness. The Doctor did not choose to stay in the ballroom itself between dances and seemed reluctant to take part at all. I formed the impression she was only there because the King expected her to be, and while she might have enjoyed the dances, she was afraid of making some error of etiquette.

I myself also felt nervous as well as excited. Such grand balls are opportunities for much pomp and ceremony, attracting from all around scores of great families, Dukes and Duchesses, rulers of allied principalities and their entourages and generally producing a kind of concentration of people of power and circumstance one sees seldom enough even in the capital. Little wonder that these are occasions when allegiances, plans, alliances and enmities are formed, both on the political and national scale of things and at the personal level.

It was impossible not to feel affected by the urgency and momentousness of the atmosphere and my poor emotions felt tattered and frazzled before the ball was properly begun.

At least we ought to remain safely on the periphery. With so many Princes, Dukes, Barons, Ambassadors and the like demanding his time—many of whom he would not see from one year to the next, save for this single event—the King was unlikely to concern himself with the Doctor and myself, who were at his beck and call during every day of the year.

I sat there, immersed in the hum of conversation and listening to the distant sound of a dance tune, and I wondered what plots and schemes were being hatched, what promises and enemies were being made, what desires stoked, what hopes squashed.

A group of people were passing us, heading for the ballroom. The small figure of a man at their head turned towards us. His mask was an old one made of blue-black feathers. "Ah, the lady doctor, unless I am grievously mistaken," came the harsh, cracked voice of Duke Walen. He stopped. His wife—his second, much younger than he, and small and voluptuous—hung on his arm, her golden mask dripping with gems. Various junior members of the Walen family and their retainers arranged themselves in a half-circle around us. I stood, as did the Doctor.

"Duke Walen, I assume," she said, bowing carefully. "How are you?"

"Very well. I would ask you how you are, however I assume that physicians look after themselves better than anybody else, so I shall ask how you think the King is. How is he?" The Duke seemed to be slurring his words.

"The King is generally well. His ankle still needs treatment and he has the remains of a slight—"

"Good, good." Walen looked round at the doors leading into the ballroom. "And how do you like our ball?"

"It is most impressive."

"Tell me. Do they have balls in this place Drezen, where you come from?"

"They do, sir."

"And are they as fine as this? Or are they better and more glorious and put our sad and feeble efforts into the shade? Does Drezen entirely out-do us in every matter as it does, by your claims, in medicine?"

"I think the dances we hold in Drezen are rather less splendid than this, sir."

"*Are* they? But how can this be? I had become quite convinced through your many comments and observations that your homeland was in advance of ours in every respect. Why, you talked of it in such glowing terms that sometimes I thought you were describing a fairy-tale land!"

"I think the Duke will find that Drezen is quite as real as Haspidus."

"Faith! I am almost disappointed. Well, there we are." He turned to go, then stopped again. "We shall see you dancing later, shan't we?"

"I imagine so, sir."

"And will you perhaps undertake to demonstrate for us a dance from Drezen, and teach it to us?"

"A dance, sir?"

"Yes. I cannot imagine that Drezeners share all our dances and possess none that we would not recognise. That is not feasible, surely?" The Duke's small, slightly hunched figure turned jerkily from one side to the other, seeking endorsement.

"Oh yes," his wife purred from behind her gold and gem-stone mask. "I should think that in Drezen they have the most advanced and interesting dances."

"I regret that I am no dance instructor," the Doctor said. "I wish now that I had been more assiduous in learning how to comport myself at a ball. Sadly, my youth was spent in more academic circles. It is only since I have had the good fortune to arrive in Haspidus that I—"

"But no!" the Duke cried. "My dear woman, you cannot be claiming that there is some aspect of civilised behaviour in which you have nothing to teach us! Why, this is unheard of! Oh, my dear lady, my faith is shaken. I beg you to reconsider. Search your doctorly memories! At least attempt to drag up for us some recollection of a physician's cotillion, a surgeon's ballet, at the very least a nurses' horn-pipe or a patients' jig."

The Doctor appeared unruffled. If she was sweating behind her mask, as I was behind mine, she gave no sign of it. In a calm and even voice she said, "The Duke flatters me in his estimation of the breadth of my knowledge. I shall of course obey his instruction but I—"

"I'm sure you can, I'm sure," the Duke said. "And pray, what part of Drezen was it you said that you are from?"

The Doctor drew herself up a little more. "From Pressel, on the island of Napthilia, sir."

"Ah yes, yes. Napthilia. Napthilia. Indeed. You must miss it terribly, I imagine."

"A little, sir."

"Having no one of your own kind to talk to in your native language, unable to catch up on the latest news, lacking compatriots to reminisce with. A sad business, being an exile."

"It has its compensations, sir."

"Yes. Good. Very well. Think on, about those dances. We shall see you later, perhaps, high-kicking, whirling and whooping, eh?"

"Perhaps," the Doctor said. I for one was glad I could not see her expression behind the mask. Of course, being a half-face mask, her lips were visible. I began to worry how much aspersion a pair of full red lips could convey.

"Just so," Walen said. "Until then, madam." He nodded.

The Doctor bowed subtly. Duke Walen turned and led his party towards the ballroom.

We sat down. I took off my mask and wiped my face. "I think the Duke was a little the worse for wine, mistress," I said.

The mirror-mask faced me. My own visage looked back, distorted and flushed. Those two red lips gave a small smile. Her eyes remained unreadable behind the mask. "Yes. Do you think he will mind that I cannot provide him with a Drezeni dance? I really am unable to recall any."

"I think the Duke was being rather rude to you, mistress. The wine was doing most of the talking. He sought only to—well, I am sure as a gentleman he would not seek to humiliate you—but he was perhaps having a little sport with you. The detail of the matter was not important. He will probably forget most of what has passed here."

"I hope so. Do you think I am a poor dancer, Oelph?"

"Oh no, mistress! I have not seen you put a step wrong so far!"

"That is my only goal. Shall we . . . ?"

A young man in a hide and gem-stone mask and wearing the dress uniform of a captain in the King's Own Frontier Guards appeared at our side. He bowed deeply. "Master Oelph? Madam Doctor Vosill?" he asked.

There was a pause. The Doctor looked at me. "Yes!" I blurted.

"The King commands me to invite you to dance with the royal party during the next figure. It starts directly."

"Oh, shit," I heard myself say.

"We are delighted to accept the King's kind invitation," the Doctor said, rising smoothly and nodding to the officer. She held her arm out towards me. I took it in mine.

"Please follow me," the captain said.

We found ourselves arranged in a figure of sixteen with King Quience, a small, buxom young princess from one of the Sequestered Kingdoms in the mountains beyond the land of Tassasen, a tall brother-and-sister prince and princess from Outer Trosile, Duke Quettil and his sister Lady Ghehere, the Duke and Duchess of Keitz (uncle and aunt to Guard Commander Adlain), their startlingly proportioned daughter and her fiancé, Prince Hilis of Faross, the Guard Commander Adlain himself and Lady Ulier, and, lastly, a young lady I was introduced to and had seen about court but whose name escaped me then and now, and her escort, the brother of Lady Ulier, the young Duke Ulresile we had first encountered at the King's table in the Hidden Gardens.

I noticed that the youthful Duke made sure that he positioned himself in our half of the figure, so ensuring that he would have two opportunities to dance with the Doctor rather than one.

The introductions were made and the dance was named by a very impressively dressed Wiester, wearing a plain black mask. We took our places in two lines, male facing female. The King took a last drink from a goblet, replaced it on a tray, waved away the servant carrying it and nodded to Wiester, who in turn nodded to the conductor of the orchestra.

The music began. My heart was beating hard and fast. I was reasonably familiar with the figure we were engaged upon, but still concerned that I might make a mistake. I was just as concerned that the Doctor might commit a serious misstep. I did not think she had danced so formally complicated a figure before.

"You are enjoying the ball, madam?" Duke Quettil asked as he and the Doctor advanced upon each other, bowed, held hands, circled and stepped. I was similarly engaged with the lady Ghehere, who gave every impression through her carriage and bearing that she had no interest whatsoever in conversing with the assistant to a woman who claimed the honourable but un-noble title of doctor, and so I was at least able both to dance without treading on her toes and to attend to what passed between my mistress and the Duke.

"Very much, Duke Quettil."

"I was surprised when the King insisted that you be invited to join us, but then he is most . . . most merry this evening. Don't you think?"

"He does appear to be enjoying himself."

"Not too much, in your opinion?"

"It is not my place to judge the King in any aspect, sir, save that of his health."

"Quite. I was granted the privilege of choosing the figure. Is it to your taste?"

"Entirely so, Duke."

"It is perhaps a little complex."

"Perhaps."

"So much to remember that is not entirely natural, so many opportunities to make a mistake."

"Dear Duke," the Doctor said with some concern. "I hope this is not some subtly disguised warning."

I happened to be circling my immediate partner with my hands clasped behind my back and was facing the Duke Quettil at this point. I got the impression that he was momentarily taken aback, unsure quite what to say for the moment before the Doctor went on, "You are not preparing to step on my toes, are you?"

The Duke gave a small, high laugh, and with that the timeous demands of the dance took both the Doctor and myself away from the centre of the figure. While our other four-set took the centre, we stood alongside each other, our hands clasped or on hips as appropriate, marking time with one foot then the other.

"All right so far, Oelph?" the Doctor said. I thought she sounded slightly breathless, and even as though she was enjoying herself.

"Aye, so far, mistress. The Duke seemed—"

"Were you teaching Quettil extra steps there, Doctor?" Adlain asked from her other side.

"I'm sure that there is nothing I could teach the Duke, Guard Commander."

"I'm equally sure he feels just the same way, madam, and yet he appeared to lose his way for a moment in that last turn."

"It is a complicated figure, as he himself pointed out to me."

"Yet one he chose."

"Indeed he did. Does Count Walen dance it as well, do you think?"

Adlain was silent for a moment. "I fancy he might, or at least fancy that he fancies he might." I saw him glance at the Doctor. His half-mask allowed him to show a smile. "However I myself find it takes all my concentration just minding my own steps without attempting to scrutinise somebody else's. Ah, excuse me . . ."

Another set. "Good Doctor," young Duke Ulresile said, meeting her in the centre. His companion, the young lady whose name I forget, seemed no more inclined to talk to me than Lady Ghehere.

"Duke," the Doctor replied.

"You look most striking."

"Thank you."

"That mask, is it Brotechian?"

"No, sir, it is silver."

"Ah. Indeed. But does it originate in Brotechen?"

"No, in Haspide. I had a jeweller fashion it."

"Ah! It is your own design! How fascinating!"

"My toe, sir."

"What? Oh! Oh, I'm sorry."

"And your mask, Duke?"

"What? Oh, ah, some old family thing. Do you like it? Does it please you? There is a companion one for a lady. I would be honoured if you would accept it with my compliments."

"I could not possibly, sir. I'm sure your family would object. Thank you, nevertheless."

"But it is nothing! That is, it is very—it is, I should say, regarded as most elegant and graceful, the one for a lady, I mean, but it is entirely mine to gift. It would be an honour!"

The Doctor paused, as though considering this offer. Then she said, "And an even greater one for me, sir. However, I already possess the mask which you see and have admired, and I find I can only wear one at a time."

"But . . ."

However, with that it was time for the two to separate, and the Doctor returned to my side.

"Are you getting all this, Oelph?" she asked, as we caught our breath and executed the marking-time steps.

"Mistress?"

"Your partners appear to become mute in your presence and yet you had the look of somebody concentrating on a conversation."

"I did, mistress?" I asked, feeling my face redden under my mask.

"You did, Oelph."

"I beg your pardon, mistress."

"Oh, it's quite all right, Oelph. I don't mind. Listen away, with my blessing."

The music changed again, and it was time for the two rows of dancers to form a circle and then reconstitute themselves in an alternate order. In the circle, the Doctor held my hand firmly but gently. Her hand, which I'd swear squeezed mine just before she let go, felt warm and dry, and the skin smooth.

Before too long I was dancing in the middle of the great ballroom of our Kingdom's second palace—and arguably its first in opulence—with a smiling, giggling, porcelain-skinned princess from the Half-Hidden Kingdoms in the high, snow-besieged mountains that climb most-way into the sky beyond the savage anarchy of Tassasen.

Her cloud-white skin was tattooed on eyelid and temple, and pierced with jewelled studs at her nostrils and the septum between nose and upper lip. She was short but curvaceous, dressed in a highly ornamented and colourful version of the booted, straight-skirted fashion of her people. She spoke little Imperial and no Haspidian, and her knowledge of the dance steps was somewhat fragmentary. Still she contrived to be an enchanting dancing partner, and I confess that I caught little of what passed between the Doctor and the King, noting only that the Doctor looked very tall and graceful and correct while the King seemed most animated and merry, even if his steps were not as fluent as they would normally have been (the Doctor had strapped his ankle up especially tightly that afternoon, knowing that he would be certain to take part in the dancing). Both wore smiles beneath their half-masks.

The music swelled and rolled over us, the grand people and beautiful masks and costumes surged and eddied about us, and we, resplendent in our finery, were the bright focus of it all. The Doctor moved and swayed at my side and occasionally I caught a hint of her perfume, which was one that I was never able to identify and cannot ever recall seeing her apply. It was an astonishing scent. It reminded me at once of burned leaves and sea spray, of newly turned earth and of seasonal flowers in bloom. There was, too, something tenebrous and intense and sensual about the scent, something sweet and sharp at the same time, at once lithe and full-bodied and utterly enigmatic.

In later years, when the Doctor was long gone from us and even her most manifest features were becoming difficult to recall with perfect clarity, I would, in diverse moments of private intimacy, catch a hint of that same odour, but the encounter would always prove fleeting.

I freely confess that on such occasions the recollection of that long-ago night, the magnificent ballroom, the splendid profusion of the dancers and the breath-arresting presence of the Doctor seemed like a capstan of ache and longing attached by the ropes of memory to my heart, squeezing and tightening and compressing it until it seemed inevitable that it must be burst asunder.

Engulfed in that riotous storm of the senses, by eye and ear and nose beset, I was at once terrified and exhilarated, and experienced that strange, half-elatory, half-fatalistic alloy of emotions that leads one to feel that if one died at that precise moment, suddenly and painlessly (indeed *ceased to be* rather than went through the process of dying at all), then it would somehow be a blessed and culminatory thing.

"The King seems happy, mistress," I observed as we stood side by side again.

"Yes. But he is starting to limp," the Doctor said, and sent the briefest of frowns in Duke Quettil's direction. "This was an unwise choice of dance for a man with an ankle which is still recovering." I watched the King, but of course he was not dancing at that point. However, I could not help but notice that rather than make the fill-in steps, he was standing still, weight on his good leg, clapping his hands in time instead. "How is your Princess?" the Doctor asked me with a smile.

"Her name is Skoon, I think," I said, frowning. "Or that may be the name of her homeland. Or her father. I'm not sure."

"She was introduced as Princess of Wadderan, I believe," the Doctor told me. "I doubt that Skuin is her name. That is the name of the type of dress she is wearing, a skuin-trel. I imagine she thought you were pointing at that when asking for a name. However, given that she is a female of the Wadderani royal family, her name is probably Gul-something or other."

"Oh. You know of her people?" This confused me, for the Sequestered or Half-Hidden Kingdoms are some of the most remote and thoroughly land-locked places in the known world.

"I have read about them," the Doctor said urbanely, before being pulled into the centre to dance with the tall Trosilian Prince. I was paired with his sister. A lanky, generally ungainly and rather plain woman, she nevertheless danced well enough and seemed quite as merry as the King. She was happy to engage me in conversation, though she did seem under the impression that I was a nobleman of some distinction, an illusion which I was probably rather too slow to dispel.

"Vosill, you look wonderful," I heard the King tell the Doctor. I saw her head dip a little and she murmured something back to him which I could not hear. I experienced a pang of jealousy that turned for an instant to wild fear when I realised who it was I was feeling jealous of. Providence, our own dear King!

The dance went on. We met with the Duke and Duchess of Keitz, then formed a circle once more—the Doctor's hand was as firm and warm and dry as before—and then took up again with our earlier eightsome. I was breathing hard by this time and did not wonder that people the age of Duke Walen usually sat out this sort of dance. Especially when one was masked, it was a long, hot and tiring business.

Duke Quettil danced with the Doctor in frosty silence. Young Ulresile fairly ran into the middle of our group to meet the Doctor and continued in his attempt to press some portion of his family's equity upon her, while she parried each suggestion as neatly as it was made awkwardly.

Finally (and thankfully, for my feet were becoming quite sore in my new dress shoes and I was in some need of relieving myself) we shared a set with Lady Ulier and Guard Commander Adlain.

"Tell me, Doctor," Adlain said as they danced together. "What is a . . . gahan?"

"I'm not sure. Do you mean a *gaan?*"

"Of course, you pronounce it so much better than I. Yes. A gaan."

"It is the title of an officer in the Drezeni civil command. In Haspidus, or in Imperial terms, it would roughly correspond to a town master or burghead, though without the military authority and with an additional expectation that the man or woman would be capable of representing Drezen at junior consular level when abroad."

"Most illuminating."

"Why do you ask, sir?"

"Oh, I read a report recently from one of our ambassadors . . . from Cuskery, I think, which mentioned the word as though it was some sort of rank but without including any explanation. I intended to ask one of our diplomatic people but it must have slipped my mind. Seeing you and thinking of Drezen obviously secured it again."

"I see," the Doctor said. There was more passed between them, but then Lady Ulier, Duke Ulresile's sister, spoke to me.

"My brother seemed most fixed upon your lady physician," she said. Lady Ulier was a few years older than either myself or her brother, with the same narrow-pinched and sallow look as he, though her dark eyes were bright and her brown hair lustrous. Her voice was somewhat strident and abrasive even when pitched low, however.

"Yes," I said. I could think of little else.

"Yes. I imagine he seeks a physician for our family, which is of course of the finest quality. Our own midwife grows old. Perhaps the lady physician will provide a suitable replacement when the King grows tired of her, should we think her suitable and sufficiently trustworthy."

"With the greatest respect, ma'am, I think that would demean her talents."

The lady looked down her long nose at me. "Do you, indeed! Well, I think not. And you perjure yourself, sir, for the greatest respect you could have accorded me would have been to have said nothing to contradict what I had just said."

"I beg your pardon, ma'am. It was simply that I could not bear to see so noble and fair a lady so deceived regarding the abilities of Doctor Vosill."

"Yes. And you are . . . ?"

"Oelph, my lady. It is my honour to have been the Doctor's assistant throughout the time she has treated our good King."

"And your family?"

"Is no more, my lady. My parents were of the Koetic persuasion and perished when the Imperial regiment of our late King sacked the city of Derla. I was a baby in swaddling at the time. An officer took pity on me when he might as well have thrown me on to a fire and brought me back to Haspidus. I was raised amongst the orphans of officers, a loyal and faithful servant of the crown."

The lady looked at me with some horror. In a strangled voice she said, "And you wish to teach *me* the proprieties of who should serve our family?" She laughed in such a way that the shriek produced surely convinced most of those surrounding us that I had just stamped upon her toe, then for the rest of the set she kept her nose angled as though trying to balance a marble-fruit upon its tip.

The music had stopped. We all bowed to each other and the King, hobbling a little, was surrounded by dukes and princes all of whom seemed desperately anxious to talk to him. The little Wadderan princess, whose name I had established was Gul-Aplit, gave me a polite wave as a forbidding-looking chaperone appeared at her side and escorted her away. "Are you all right, Oelph?" the Doctor asked.

"I am very well, mistress," I told her. "A little warm."

"Let's get something to drink and then step outside. What do you say?"

"I'd say that was a very good idea, mistress, if not two."

We collected two tall goblets of some form of aromatic punch which we were assured by the servants was weak in alcohol and then, with our masks off at last—and following a brief period to obey the call of nature—we made our way out on to the balcony which ran round the outside of the ballroom, joining a good hundred or so others taking the fragrant night air.

It was a dark night and would be long. Seigen had almost joined Xamis at sundown that evening and for a good quarter of the wholeday there would be only the moons to light the sky. Foy and Iparine were our lanterns that evening, their bluey-grey luminescence filled out along the balcony's tiles and the terraces of garden, fountain and hedge by glowing paper lamps, cressets of oilwood and scented pole-torches.

Duke and Duchess Ormin and their party approached us on the balcony, their way lit for them by dwarves carrying short poles, on the tip of which were large spheres of clear glass containing what looked like millions of soft and tiny sparks. As these curious apparitions came closer we saw that the globes contained hundreds and hundreds of glow-flies, all milling and darting about in their strange confinement. They spread little light, but much amazement and delight. The Duke exchanged nods with the Doctor, though the Duchess did not deign to acknowledge us.

"Did I hear you telling the very young but very grand Lady Ulier your life history, Oelph?" the Doctor asked, sipping at her goblet as we strolled.

"I mentioned something about my upbringing, mistress. It may have been a mistake. She cannot think better of either of us for it."

"From the impression, not to mention the looks I got, I do not think she could think much less of me, but I'm sorry if she finds your orphanhood in some way reprehensible."

"That and the fact that my parents were Koetics."

"Well, one must allow for the prejudices of nobles. Your forebears professed themselves not only republican, but so god-fearing they had neither dread nor respect left for any worldly authority."

"Theirs was a sadly mistaken creed, mistress, and I am not proud to be associated with it, though I honour my parents' memory as any child must."

The Doctor looked at me. "You do not resent what happened to them?"

"To the extent that I resent their suppression as a people who preached forgiveness rather than violence, I condemn the Empire. For the fact that I was recognised as an innocent and rescued, I thank Providence that I was discovered by a Haspidian officer who acted under the more humane orders of our good King's father.

"But I never knew my parents, mistress, and I have never met anybody who knew them, and their faith is meaningless to me. And the Empire, whose very existence might have fuelled an urge for vengeance on my part, is gone, brought down by the fire which fell from the sky. One unchallengeably mighty force brought down by an even greater one." I looked at her then, and felt, from the expression in her eyes, that we were talking and not just behaving as equals. "Resentment, mistress? What is the point of feeling that?"

She took my hand in hers for a moment then, and squeezed it rather as she had during the dance, and after that she put her arm through mine, an action that had fallen into disuse and even disrepute within polite society and which occasioned not a few looks. To my own surprise I felt honoured rather than embarrassed. It was a gesture of friendliness rather than anything else, but it was a gesture of closeness and comfort, and I felt just then that I was the most favoured man in all the palace, regardless of birth, title, rank or circumstance.

"Ah! I am murdered! Murdered! Help me! Help me! Murdered!"

The voice rang out across the balcony. Everybody stopped as though frozen into statues, then looked round at a tall door leading from one of the smaller rooms next to the ballroom as it opened further and a half-clothed figure fell slowly out of it into the light, gripping the pale gold curtains that fluted back inside, where thin, girlish screams began to sound.

The man, dressed only in a white shirt, gradually rolled over so that his face pointed towards the moons. The pure white shirt seemed to glow in the moonlight. High on his chest near one shoulder there was a bright, vividly red mark, like a freshly picked blossom. The man's collapse to the stones of the balcony was accomplished with a sort of idle grace, until his violent grip on the curtains and his weight overcame their supports and they gave way.

With that, he slumped quickly to the ground and the curtains came billowing, folding down upon him, like syrup on to the body of a struggling insect, entirely covering his round shape so that, while the screams from the room still sounded and everybody still stood where they were, staring, it was almost as though there was no body there at all.

The Doctor moved first, dropping her goblet on to the balcony with a crash and running towards the tall, slowly swinging door.

It was a moment or two longer before I could break the spell that had descended upon me, but eventually I was able to follow the Doctor—through a crowd of servants most of whom suddenly and to my confusion seemed to be carrying swords—to where the Doctor was already kneeling, throwing back the folds of curtain, burrowing down to where the twitching, bleeding form of Duke Walen lay dying.

14
THE BODYGUARD

"Loose!"

The small catapult bucked, the arm—indeed not much bigger than a man's outstretched arm—flicked forward and thudded against the hide cushion on the weapon's tall cross-beam. The stone burred away through the air, arcing over the lower terrace and down towards the garden below. The projectile hit alongside one of DeWar's cities, embedding itself in the carefully raked soil and kicking up a big puff of red-brown dust that hung for a while in the air, slowly drifting off to the one side and settling gradually back to the ground.

"Oh, bad luck!"

"Very close!"

"Next time."

"Very nearly, General Lattens," DeWar said. He had been sitting on the balustrade, arms crossed, one leg dangling. He jumped off on to the black and white tiles of the balcony and squatted by his own miniature catapult. He pulled quickly and powerfully on the round wheel which ratcheted the creaking, groaning wooden arm back until it settled about three-quarters of the way towards the horizontal rear cross-member. The arm bowed fractionally with the strain of the twisted hide at its base trying to force it forward again.

Lattens, meanwhile, got up on to the same stone rail DeWar had been sitting on. His nurse held on tightly to the back of his jacket to prevent him from falling. Lattens raised his toy telescope to his eye to survey the damage done in the garden below.

"A little to the left, next time, my lad," UrLeyn told his son. The Protector, his brother RuLeuin, Doctor BreDelle, BiLeth, Commander ZeSpiole and the concubine Perrund sat attended by various servants on an awninged platform raised to about the same height as the balustrade and overlooking the scene.

Lattens stamped his foot on the stonework. His nurse held him tighter.

Perrund, veiled in gauzy red, turned to the Protector. "Sir, I'm sure the nurse holds him well enough, but it makes my bones ache seeing him up there. Would you humour one of your older ladies' timid foolishness by calling for a step-ladder? It would let him see over the rail without having to climb on to it."

Foreign minister BiLeth frowned and made a *tss*king noise.

UrLeyn pursed his lips. "Hmm. Good idea," he said. He beckoned a servant.

The entire terrace of the garden two storeys below had been divided into two and modelled to resemble a landscape in miniature, with hills, mountains, forests, a large walled capital city, a dozen or so smaller cities, twice as many towns, many roads and bridges and three or four rivers flowing into a couple of small, about bath-sized lakes on each side and then on into a large body of water which represented an inland sea.

The sea was in the shape of two rough circles which just met in the middle, so that there was a short, narrow channel connecting the two great lakes. Various of each territory's towns and cities lay on the shores of the two smaller lakes, with even more on the coasts of the two lobes of the sea, though in each case one territory had many more settlements round one part of the sea than the other, DeWar's territory having the most round the lobe of water nearer to the balcony and the two catapults.

DeWar secured the triggering post on his catapult and carefully unhitched the winding mechanism, then selected a stone from the pile between the two model weapons and, once Lattens had climbed down from the balustrade, loaded the stone into the cup at the end of the machine's arm. He repositioned the catapult according to chalk marks on the black tiles, stood, eyes narrowed, to survey his target area, squatted to adjust the catapult's position once more, then took the stone out of the cup and reconnected the winding mechanism to let out a little of the strain before re-latching the triggering post.

"Oh, come *on*, DeWar!" Lattens said, jumping up and down and shaking his telescope. He was dressed as a noble general, and the servant who was tensioning and repositioning his catapult was in the uniform of a Ducal bombardier.

DeWar closed one eye and made a fearful grimace as he turned to the boy. "Har," he said, in a voice a rather unsubtle actor might employ when asked to impersonate a worthy rustic, "beggin' the young massur's pardin to be sure, sor, but I has got to be doin' me adjussmints, don't ye know, har!"

"Providence, the fellow's a fool indeed," BiLeth muttered. However, UrLeyn laughed, and BiLeth found it in him to affect a smile.

Lattens squealed with delight at this nonsense and put his hands to his mouth, nearly sticking his telescope into his eye.

DeWar made a few final adjustments to his catapult, then, with a look round to make sure Lattens was well out of the way, said, "Fire, me boys!" and flicked the triggering latch away.

The rock whistled into the blue sky. Lattens howled with excitement and ran to the balustrade. DeWar's rock landed almost in the centre of one of the smaller lakes in Lattens' territory. The boy shrieked.

"Oh no!"

DeWar had already landed a hefty projectile in the other small lake on Lattens' side, swamping all the towns and the single city on its shores. Lattens had hit one of DeWar's lakes too, but not the other. The rock sent up a great tall fountain of water. The waves from the impact rippled quickly out, heading for the shore. "Aargh!" Lattens cried. The waves made landfall, causing the water first to retreat from the miniature beaches and ports and then rear up and wash against the flimsily made buildings of the lake-side towns, washing them all away.

"Oh, unlucky, young sir, unlucky," Doctor BreDelle said, then in a low voice to UrLeyn added, "Sir, I think the boy grows over-excited."

"Fine shot, DeWar!" UrLeyn called, clapping. "Oh, let him be excited, Doctor," he said to BreDelle in a lower voice. "He has spent long enough swaddled in his bed. It's good to see a bit of colour in his cheeks again."

"As you wish, sir, but he is still not fully recovered."

"Mr. DeWar would make a fine bombardier," Commander ZeSpiole said.

UrLeyn laughed. "We could use him in Ladenscion."

"We could dispatch him forthwith," agreed BiLeth.

"Things go better there, don't they, brother?" RuLeuin said, letting a servant refill his glass. He glanced at BiLeth, who assumed a grave expression.

UrLeyn snorted. "Better than when they were going badly," he agreed. "But still not well enough." He looked to his brother, then back at his son, who was anxiously supervising the loading of his own catapult. "The boy grows better. If that keeps up I may take it as my signal to assume command of the war myself."

"At last!" RuLeuin said. "Oh, I'm sure that would be the best thing, brother. You are our best general, still. The war in Ladenscion needs you. I hope I may accompany you there. May I? I have a fine company of cavalry now. You must come and see them train some day."

"Thank you, brother," UrLeyn said, smoothing a hand over his short grey beard. "However, I am undecided. I may ask you to stay on here in Crough and be my regent, in equal partnership with YetAmidous and ZeSpiole. Would you rather that?"

"Oh, sir!" RuLeuin reached out and touched the Protector's arm. "That would be a singular honour!"

"No, it would be a treble honour, brother," UrLeyn told him with a tired smile. "ZeSpiole? What do you say?"

"I heard what you said, sir, but I can scarcely believe it. Would you honour me so?"

"I would. If I depart for the borderlands. It is still not certain yet. BiLeth, you will advise my trio of proxies as well as you have me on matters foreign?"

BiLeth, whose face had taken on a frozen expression when he had heard what the Protector was proposing, let his features relax some-what. "Of course, sir."

"And General YetAmidous is agreeable?" RuLeuin asked.

"He will stay if I ask him to, or like you he will gladly come to Ladenscion with me. I could use each of you in both places, but that cannot be."

"Sir, excuse my interruption," the lady Perrund said. "The ladder."

A wooden library step-ladder was carried forward by two servants and deposited on the balcony's tiled surface near the viewing platform.

"What? Ah, yes. Lattens!" UrLeyn called to his son, who was still fussing over the degree of tension in the catapult and the size of rock to throw. "Here. This might be a better observation point for you! Position it as you see fit."

Lattens looked uncertain for a moment, then appeared to take to the idea. "Ah-ha! A *siege* engine!" He wagged the telescope at DeWar, who scowled at the ladder as the servants brought it forward, closer to the edge of the terrace. "I have the measure of you now, bad baron!" Lattens cried. DeWar growled and retreated with comedic fearfulness from the steps as they approached.

Lattens climbed up the steps to the top, so that his feet were about level with the head of his nurse, who had remained on the balcony but followed him round as he'd ascended, watching anxiously. DeWar sidled up to the steps as well, glowering up at the boy.

"That will do nicely, bombardier," Lattens yelled. "Fire when ready!"

The rock hurtled up and out and for a moment seemed to hang above the coast-line of the part of the inland sea which held most of DeWar's remaining cities. "Oh no!" Lattens cried.

The rules were that each player could drop only one stone into the inland sea. Lattens and DeWar each had, accordingly, one very large stone apiece to be used for this very purpose in the hope of swamping a handful of his enemy's cities with one strike. The stone Lattens had caused to be lobbed on this occasion was a medium-sized projectile. If it landed in the sea, especially in one of the shallower areas near the coast, it might do very little damage on its own while at the same time preventing the boy from landing his one big rock where it might cause the most destruction.

The rock whacked into a coastal city, causing a small splash from the harbour but sending up a greater cloud of dust and scattering splintered wood and bits of delicate clay buildings across the landscape and splashing out across the water.

"Yes, boy!" UrLeyn said, jumping to his feet.

RuLeuin rose too. "Well done!"

"Fine shot!" called BreDelle. BiLeth clapped decorously.

ZeSpiole thumped his seat-arm. "Magnificent!"

DeWar clenched his fists and let out a roar of anguish.

"Hurrah!" Lattens yelled and whirled his arms about. He overbalanced and began to fall off the steps. Perrund watched DeWar dart forward, then check himself as the nurse caught the boy. Lattens frowned down at his nurse, then struggled in her arms until she put him back where he had been standing.

"Mind yourself, boy!" UrLeyn called, laughing.

"I'm sorry, sir," Perrund said. Her hand was at her throat, just beneath the red veil, where her heart seemed to have lodged. "I thought he'd be safer—"

"Oh, he's fine!" UrLeyn told her with a sort of jovial exasperation. "Never you fear." He turned back. "*Damn* fine shot, lad!" he shouted. "More of those, if you please, then the great-grand-dad rock in the centre of his sea!"

"Ladenscion is finished!" Lattens cried, shaking his fist at DeWar and holding on to the projecting spire of the steps with his other hand. "Providence protects us!"

"Oh, it's Ladenscion now, not the Empire?" UrLeyn laughed.

"Brother," RuLeuin said, "I cannot think which would be the greater honour, to be at your side or to help rule in your place. Be assured I shall do whatever you ask of me to the best of my abilities."

"I'm sure you will," UrLeyn said.

"As your brother says, sir," Commander ZeSpiole said, leaning forward to catch the Protector's eye.

"Well, it may not come to that," UrLeyn said. "We may have news by the next rider that the barons are desperate to sue for peace. But I am glad you both accept my proposal."

"Gladly, brother!"

"Humbly, sir."

"Good, so we are all agreed."

DeWar's next shot thudded into farmland, causing him to caper and make cursing sounds. Lattens laughed and followed that with a shot which destroyed a town. DeWar's next demolished a bridge. Lattens replied with a couple of off-target rocks but then hit a city while DeWar's matching shots hit nothing but earth.

Lattens decided to use his biggest rock and attempt to obliterate most of DeWar's remaining cities in one go.

"That's the boy!" his father called. "Strike now!"

With much groaning and creaking from the coiled twists of stretched hide—and a few groans and whimpers from DeWar, standing watching—the arm of Lattens' catapult was tightened to its maximum extension and sat arched with stored power.

"Are you sure that's not too much?" UrLeyn shouted. "You'll hit your own sea!"

"No, sir! I'll put other rocks on as well as the big one!"

"Very well then," the Protector told his son. "Mind you don't break the weapon, though."

"Father!" the boy called. "May I load it myself? Oh, please?"

The servant dressed like a bombardier was about to pick up the heaviest rock from Lattens' pile of ammunition. He hesitated. DeWar lost his comical expression. Perrund took a deep breath.

"Sir," she said, but was interrupted.

"I cannot allow the boy to lift such a large rock, sir," Doctor BreDelle said, leaning close to the Protector. "It will put too great a strain on his system. His frame is weakened by the long time spent in bed."

UrLeyn looked at ZeSpiole. "I'm more worried about the catapult loosing while he's loading it, sir," the Guard Commander said.

"Generals do not load their own weapons, sir," UrLeyn told the boy sternly.

"I know that, Father, but *please?* This is not a real war, it is only pretend."

"Well, shall I give you a hand then?" UrLeyn called.

"No!" Lattens yelled, stamping his foot and tossing his red-blond curls. "No thank you, sir!"

UrLeyn sat back with a gesture of resignation and a small smile. "The lad knows his own mind. He is mine, all right." He waved to his son. "Very well, General Lattens! Load as you will and may Providence guide the projectiles."

Lattens chose a couple of smaller rocks and loaded them one at a time into the waiting cup of the catapult, panting as he lifted them up. Then he squatted, took a firm grip of the biggest stone and with a grunt lifted it to his chest. He turned and staggered towards his catapult.

DeWar took a half-step closer to the machine. Lattens did not seem to notice. He grunted again as he hoisted the rock up to his neck level and shuffled closer to the tensed arm of the waiting machine.

DeWar seemed to slide rather than step another stride closer to the catapult, almost to within grabbing distance of the boy, while his gaze concentrated both on the firing latch and on Lattens' feet and legs as they edged nearer to it.

The boy teetered as he leant over the catapult's cup. He was breathing hard, the sweat running down his brow.

"Steady, lad," Perrund heard the Protector whisper. His hands clutched at the arms of his chair, the knuckles pale with their own loaded tension.

DeWar was closer now, within reach of the boy.

Lattens grunted and rolled the rock into the cup. It crunched on top of the two already occupying the scoop. The whole catapult seemed to quiver, and DeWar tensed, as though about to pounce on the child and tear him away, but then the boy took a step back, wiped his sweating face and turned to smile at his father, who nodded and sat back in his seat, sighing with relief. He looked at RuLeuin and the others. "There now," he said, and swallowed.

"Mr. Bombardier," Lattens said, with a flourish towards the catapult. The servant nodded and took up his position by the machine.

DeWar had drifted back towards his own catapult.

"Wait!" Lattens called, and ran up the library step-ladder again. His nurse resumed her place beneath. Lattens took out his sword, raised it and then dropped it. "Now!"

The catapult made a terrific snapping noise, the one large rock and the two smaller ones sailed into the air in significantly different directions and everybody sat or leant forward to see where they would land.

The big rock missed its target, splashing into the shallows near one of DeWar's coastal cities and showering it with mud but otherwise doing little damage. One of the smaller stones hit some of DeWar's farmland and the other demolished one of Lattens' own towns.

"Oh."

"Oh dear."

"Bad luck, young master."

"For shame!"

Lattens said nothing. He stood, looking utterly crestfallen, at the top of the ladder, his little wooden sword hanging loosely in his hand. He looked back at his father with sad, dejected eyes.

His father frowned, then winked at him. The boy's expression did not change. Silence hung under the platform's awning.

DeWar jumped up on the balustrade and crouched there, knuckles dragging on the stonework. "Ha!" he said, then jumped down. "Missed!" He had already tensioned his own catapult, the arm bowed back to about the two-thirds position. "Victory is mine! Hee-hee!" He chose the biggest stone from his own supply, wound some more tension into the machine and put the rock in the scoop. He looked up at Lattens with a fierce, mischievous grin, which faltered only momentarily when he saw the look on the child's face. He rubbed his hands and wagged one finger at the boy. "Now we see who's boss, my young pretender-general!"

He adjusted the catapult slightly and then pulled the lanyard. The catapult juddered and the great rock whooshed up into the sky. DeWar leapt back on to the stone railing again.

The giant stone was a sailing black shape against the sky and clouds for a long moment, then it rushed back to earth and dropped with a titanic splash into the sea.

The water threw itself up into the air in a great explosive tower of white foam, then slumped back down and rushed out in all directions in a mighty circular wave.

"What?" DeWar screeched from the balustrade, putting his hands to the sides of his head and grabbing two handfuls of hair. "No! No! Nooooo!"

"Ha *ha!*" Lattens yelled, pulled his general's hat off his head and threw it in the air. "Ha ha ha!"

The rock had fallen not into the lobe of the sea which was rimmed mostly by Lattens' towns and cities but that which held almost all DeWar's intact settlements. The great wave rushed out from where it had landed, a good couple of strides or so from the straits separating the two lobes of the sea. One by one it swamped the cities and towns by the water, flooding one or two of Lattens' but destroying a great deal more of DeWar's.

"Hurrah!" RuLeuin yelled, and threw his own hat into the air. Perrund smiled broadly at DeWar from behind the veil. UrLeyn nodded and grinned and clapped. Lattens gave a deep bow and made a rude, tongue-wagging gesture at DeWar, who had rolled off the stone railing and was curled up on the tiles by the side of the balustrade, thumping one clenched fist weakly off the tiled surface.

"No more!" he moaned. "I give in! He's too good for me! Providence defends the Protector and all his generals! I am an unworthy wretch ever to have set myself against them! Take pity on me and let me surrender like the abject cur that I am!"

"I win!" Lattens said, and with a grin at his nurse he twirled on the platform and let himself fall backwards into the woman's arms. She grunted with the impact, but caught the boy and held him.

"Here, lad! Here!" His father stood and went to the front of the platform, holding out his arms. "Bring that brave young warrior to me!"

The nurse duly delivered Lattens into his father's embrace while the others gathered round, applauding and laughing and clapping backs and offering congratulations.

"A fine campaign, young man!"

"Quite splendid!"

"Providence in your pocket!"

"Well, well done!"

"—and then we could play the game at night, Father, when it's a dark night and make flame-balls and light them and set the cities on fire! Couldn't we?"

DeWar stood and brushed himself down. Perrund looked at him over her veil and he grinned and even blushed a little.

15
THE DOCTOR

ell?" the King asked.

The Doctor leaned closer and peered at the wound. Duke Walen's body lay on a long table in the withdrawing room where he had been murdered. The small feast that had occupied the table when we had brought the body in had been set on the floor to one side. The table cloth had been wrapped over the Duke's body so that his legs and belly and his head had been covered, leaving only his chest exposed. He had been pronounced dead by the Doctor, though not until after she had done the most extraordinary thing.

The Doctor had seemed to kiss the old man while he lay bleeding and shaking on the balcony. She had knelt by his side and blown her own breath into him, puffing out first her cheeks and then his, so that his chest rose and fell. She was at the same time attempting to staunch the flow of blood that had issued from the wound in his chest, using a piece of material torn from her own dress. This then became my duty, using a clean kerchief while she concentrated on blowing into Duke Walen's mouth.

After a while, when she had been unable to feel any pulse for some long time, she had shaken her head and sat back, exhausted, on the floor.

A ring of servants, all with swords or long knives, had been established round the scene. When the Doctor and I looked up it was to see Duke Quettil, the two Guard Commanders, Adlain and Polchiek, and the King looking down at us. Behind us, in the darkened room, a girl was weeping quietly.

"Bring him inside. Light all the candles," Duke Quettil told the armed servants. He looked at the King, who nodded.

"Well, Doctor?" the King said again.

"A dagger wound, I think," the Doctor said. "A very thin, sharp blade. Steeply angled. It must have penetrated the heart. Much of the bleeding was internal, which is why it's still seeping out. If I'm to be sure of all this, I will need to open the corpse."

"I think we know the main thing, which is that he is dead," Adlain said. From beyond a line of servants by the windows, a woman's screams could be heard. I imagined it was the Duke's wife.

"Who was in the room?" Quettil asked his Guard Commander.

"These two," Polchiek said, nodding at a young man and woman, both hardly any older than myself, both quite handsome and with their dress in some disarray. Each was held from behind by two of the armed servants. It was only now starting to occur to me that there had been a particular explanation for the great numbers of servants at the ball, and for the fact that many of them looked somewhat coarser than one expected of servants. They were really guards. That was why they had all suddenly produced weapons at the first hint of mischief.

The young woman's face was red and swollen with crying, and held a look of blank terror. A wail from beyond the windows drew her attention and she stared in that direction. The face of the young man at her side looked almost as bloodless as the body of Duke Walen.

"And who are you?" Adlain asked the young couple.

"Uo-Uo-Uoljeval, sir," the young man said, swallowing heavily. "A squire in the em-employ of Duke Walen, sir."

Adlain looked at the young woman, who was staring straight ahead. "And you, madam?"

The young woman shivered and looked not at Adlain but at the Doctor. Still she did not say anything.

Eventually the young man said, "Droythir, sir. Her name is Droythir. Of Mizui. A chambermaid to Lady Gilseon. My betrothed."

"Sir, can't we let the Duchess in now?" the Doctor asked the King. He shook his head and held up one hand.

Guard Commander Adlain jerked his head back as though pointing at the girl with his chin and demanded, "And what were you doing in here, madam?"

The young woman stared at him as though he'd spoken in some utterly unknown language. It crossed my mind that she was indeed a foreigner. Then the young man started to weep and said, "It was only for his pleasure, sirs, please!"

Through his tears he looked in turn at each of the faces watching him. "Sirs, he said he liked such sport, and would reward us. We knew nothing, nothing until we heard him cry out. He was there. There, behind there, watching us from behind the screen there. He knocked it over when he—when he—" The young man looked round as best he could at a screen lying on the floor near one corner of the room, by a door, and started to breathe very quickly.

"Calm *down*," Adlain snapped. The young man closed his eyes and slumped in the grip of the two guards. They looked at each other, then at Adlain and Polchiek, who was also, I thought, distinctly pale and haggard.

"And there was a dark bird," the young woman said suddenly, in a strange, hollow voice. Her eyes stared straight ahead out of her pale, sweat-sheened face.

"What?" Polchiek said.

"A dark bird," she said, looking straight at the Doctor. "It was very dark because the gentleman wished only for one candle to light us, but I saw it. A dark bird, or a nightwing."

The Doctor looked puzzled. "A dark bird?" she said, frowning.

"I think we have learned all we can from you, madam," Quettil said to the Doctor. "You may go."

"No," the King said to her. "Stay, Doctor."

Quettil's jaw worked.

"Were you doing what I think you were doing?" the King asked the young woman. He glanced at the Doctor. The orchestra faltered in the ballroom.

The young woman turned her empty-looking face slowly towards the King. "Sir," she said, and I knew she did not realise who she was talking to. "Yes, sir. On the couch there." She pointed to a couch in the centre of the room. A candelabrum holding one extinguished candle lay knocked over nearby.

"And Duke Walen was watching from behind the screen," Adlain said.

"It was his pleasure, sir." The young woman looked down at the man kneeling weeping by her side. "We saw no harm in it."

"Well, there was harm, madam," Quettil said quietly, his voice hardly more than a breath.

"We'd been doing it a while, sirs," the young woman said, her empty, staring eyes directed towards the Doctor. "There was a noise. I thought it was somebody trying the window doors again, sir, but then the old gentleman cried out and the screen came tumbling down and I saw the nightwing."

"You saw the Duke?" Polchiek asked her.

She swivelled her head towards him. "Yes, sir."

"You saw nobody else?"

"Just the gentleman, sir," she said, looking back to the Doctor. "In his shirt. He had his hand up here." She shrugged on one side only, and looked down to her left at the top of her chest near her shoulder. "He was crying out that he'd been murdered."

"The door behind him," Adlain said. "There, behind where the screen was. Was the door open?"

"No, sir."

"You are sure."

"Yes, sir."

Quettil leaned towards the King. "My man Ralinge will make sure this is the truth," he murmured. The Doctor heard this and glared at the Duke. The King only frowned.

"Is the door locked?" Adlain asked Polchiek.

Polchiek frowned. "It should be," he said, "and the key should be in the lock." He crossed the room to the door, found that there was no key, looked to the floor for a few moments, then pulled and pushed at the door. He felt inside a fat pouch at his waist, pulled out a ring bristling with long keys and eventually found one which he tried in the door's lock. The lock clicked, the door opened inwards and a couple of armed guards dressed as servants looked quizzically in, straightening when they saw their Commander, who spoke briefly to them and closed and locked the door again. He returned to the group round the table. "The guards have been there since a little after the alarm was raised," he told Adlain. His big, clumsy-looking fingers fumbled with the ring of keys, trying to fit it back into the pouch at his waist.

"How many keys to that door are there?" Adlain asked.

"This one, one for the palace seneschal and the one which ought to be in the door, on this side," Polchiek told him.

"Droythir, where was this dark bird you saw?" the Doctor asked.

"Where the gentleman was, ma'am." Suddenly her face seemed to collapse and a look of uncertainty and sadness wrote itself across her features. "Perhaps it was just a shadow, ma'am. The candle, and the screen falling." She looked down. "A shadow," she murmured to herself.

"Let the Duchess in," the King said, as one of the guards dressed as a servant approached Quettil and muttered into his ear.

"The Duchess has fainted and been taken to her room, sir," Quettil told the King. "However, I am told there is a young page who may have something to tell us."

"Well then, bring him in," the King said, sounding annoyed. Droythir and Uoljeval were pulled back towards the centre of the room by those holding them. The young man staggered to his feet, still weeping quietly. The girl stared ahead, silent.

Feulecharo approached from the doors, looking smaller than I had ever seen him look, his face almost translucent, his eyes bulging.

"Feulecharo?" Adlain said. He looked round the others. "Page to the late Duke," he said by way of explanation to those who needed it.

Feulecharo cleared his throat. He looked nervously round us all, then saw the Doctor and gave me a small smile. "Your majesty," he said, bowing to the King. "Duke Quettil, sirs, madam. I know something—very little, but something—of what happened here."

"You do?" Quettil said, his eyes narrowing. The King shifted from one leg to the other, winced, then nodded in appreciation as the Doctor brought up a chair for him to sit in.

Feulecharo nodded towards the far corner of the room. "I was in the corridor, behind that door, sirs, earlier."

"Doing what, might one ask?" Quettil said.

Feulecharo swallowed. He glanced at Droythir and Uoljeval, who had been brought forward again to the side of the table, their arms still held behind them. "I had been asked by the Duchess to . . ." Feulecharo licked his lips. "To follow the Duke and see what he was doing."

"And you followed him here?" Adlain said. He knew Feulecharo a little, and sounded purposeful but not unkind.

"Yes, sir. With the two young people." Feulecharo glanced at Droythir and Uoljeval, neither of whom responded. "The Duchess thought perhaps there was some arrangement between the young lady and the Duke. I watched them enter this withdrawing room, and found my way to the corridor outside. I thought I might hear something, or see something through the keyhole, but it was blocked."

"By a key?" Adlain asked.

"I think not, sir. Rather by the little shutter on the far side. However," Feulecharo said, "I had with me a small metal mirror and thought to see something under the bottom of the door."

"And did you?" Quettil asked.

"Only a single light, like a candle flame, Duke Quettil. I could hear the young man and woman making the sounds of love, and sense some movement, but that was all."

"And when the Duke was stabbed?" Polchiek asked.

Feulecharo took a deep breath. "Just before that, sir, I think, I was hit on the back of the head, and rendered unconscious. I imagine for just a few minutes." He turned and held his hair up at the back, exposing a scab of glistening, half-dried blood and a large lump.

The King looked at the Doctor, who went forward and looked at the wound. "Oelph," she said. "Some water, please. And a napkin or something similar. Is that a bottle of spirit wine there on the floor? That, too."

Feulecharo sat in a seat while his wound was cleaned and inspected. Adlain looked closely at the injury. "That certainly looks to me like it might knock a fellow out for a moment or two," he said. "You would agree, Doctor?"

"Yes," she said.

"And when you woke up, what was there to be seen then?" Polchiek asked Feulecharo.

"Sir, I could hear the commotion in the room and people crying out. There was nobody else in the corridor where I was. I was very dizzy and went to the privy to be sick, then I went to find the Duchess, and that was when I heard that the Duke had been murdered."

Adlain and Polchiek exchanged looks. "You did not sense anybody behind you when you were hit?" Adlain asked.

"No, sir," Feulecharo said, wincing as the Doctor dabbed some spirit wine on his wound. "I was concentrating too sorely on the mirror."

"This mirror . . ." Polchiek began.

"It is here, sir. I had the presence of mind to retrieve it before I made my way to the privy." Feulecharo dug into a pocket and pulled out a coin-sized piece of highly polished metal. He handed it to Polchiek, who passed it round the other men.

"Is the Duchess Walen a particularly jealous woman, would you say, Feulecharo?" Adlain asked, turning the small mirror over in his fingers.

"Not especially so, sir," Feulecharo said. He sounded awkward, though that may just have been because the Doctor was holding his head forward while she completed the cleaning of his wound.

"You have told us everything of the truth, have you not, Feulecharo?" the King asked gravely.

Feulecharo looked at him as best he could with his head still bent forward by the Doctor. "Oh, yes, your majesty."

"When you were hit, Feulecharo," the Doctor said, letting go of his head, "did you fall against the door, or to the floor?"

Quettil made a tutting noise. Feulecharo thought for a moment. "I woke up resting against the door, ma'am," he said, then looked at Adlain and the others.

"So if somebody had opened the door into the room," the Doctor said, "you would have fallen in too."

"I suppose I would have, ma'am. I would have required being put back into the same position after it had been closed again."

"You are hiding nothing from us, young man?" Quettil asked.

Feulecharo seemed to be about to speak, but then hesitated. I had thought him more intelligent than that, but perhaps the blow to his head had addled his brains.

"What?" the King said sternly.

"Your majesty, sirs," Feulecharo said in a dry, strained-sounding voice. "The Duchess thought the Duke might be seeing the young lady here. That was what exercised her jealousy. She would not have minded so much, perhaps not have minded at all if she had known it was only to . . . to watch others." Feulecharo looked round the men in the room, avoiding my eyes and the Doctor's. "Why, she would have laughed to have known what was going on in here, sirs. No more. And there is nobody she would trust more than me. I know her, sirs. She would not cause such a thing to be done." He licked his lips and swallowed hard again, then looked despondently at the mound of table cloth covering the body of the Duke.

Quettil opened his mouth to say something, but the King, watching Adlain and Polchiek, said, "Thank you, Feulecharo."

"I think Feulecharo should stay here, sir," Adlain said to the King. "Guard Commander Polchiek might send men to his quarters to search for a weapon, or the missing key for the door." The King nodded, and Polchiek spoke to some of the servant-guards. "Perhaps," Adlain added, "the Guard Commander would open the door again and we'll see if young Feulecharo left any blood there."

The guards went off to search Feulecharo's room. Polchiek and Adlain returned to the door.

The King looked at the Doctor and smiled. "Thank you for all your help, Vosill," he said, with a nod. "That will be all."

"Sir," the Doctor said.

* * *

I heard later that they looked all through the Duchess' apartment as well as Feulecharo's. Nothing was found. Some blood was discovered on the outer surface of the door into the corridor, and on the floor beneath. A good part of the rest of the palace was searched soon afterwards for the murder weapon, but it was never discovered. The missing key turned up, innocently enough as far as could be told, in the key cabinet of the palace seneschal.

Master, I knew Feulecharo and did not think him capable of the killing of the Duke. The King may have been overly lenient in not allowing the two lovers Droythir and Uoljeval to be put to the question by Ralinge (though I believe both were shown the chamber and had the instruments of excruciation explained to them), but I do not believe any further truthful information would or could have been extracted from them.

Polchiek might have preferred that a scapegoat was found, and Quettil fumed and raged in private for moons afterwards, they say, but apart from taking one of Polchiek's two small estates away from him, he could do no more. Polchiek had filled the ball with extra guards and by all accounts done all he could to ensure that nothing untoward occurred.

Feulecharo was lucky, I think, that he was the third son of one of Walen's more wealthy barons. Had he been of more lowly birth, instead of just two sickly brothers away from a not inconsiderable title, he might have found himself enjoying the hospitality of Master Ralinge himself. As it was, it was generally accepted that his good family name made it almost unthinkable that he could have had anything more to do with the murder of the Duke than he had claimed.

16
THE BODYGUARD

I wish I could go too, Mr. DeWar. Can't you ask my father? He thinks you're clever."

DeWar looked embarrassed. Perrund smiled indulgently at him. From his pulpit the chief eunuch Stike looked down, fat and frowning. DeWar wore riding boots. He carried a hat, and a heavy black cape lay folded over the couch at his side next to a pair of saddle bags. The Protector had decided it was time to take personal command of the faltering war in Ladenscion.

"You're better off here, Lattens," DeWar told the boy, and reached out to ruffle his red-blond hair. "You have to get well. Being ill is like being attacked, you see? Your body is like a great fortress that has been besieged by invaders. You've repelled them, you've seen them off, but you have to be good, and marshal your forces and rebuild the walls, refurbish your catapults, clean your cannons, restock your armouries. Do you see? Only if your father feels that great fortress is going to be all right can he leave it to go and fight the war. So that is your duty. To keep getting better. To get well.

"Of course your father would rather stay here with you if he could, but he's like a father to all his men, too, you see? They need his help and guidance. So he has to go to them. You must stay, and help your father win the war by getting better, by repairing the great fortress. It is your duty, as a soldier. Do you think you can do that?"

Lattens looked down at the cushions he sat upon. Perrund patted his curls back into place again. He played with a loose thread of gold at the corner of a cushion. "Yes," he said in a small voice, not looking up. "But I really would like to go with you and Father, really I would." He looked up at DeWar. "Are you sure I can't come?"

"I'm afraid so," DeWar said quietly.

The boy sighed heavily and looked down again. DeWar smiled at Perrund, who was looking at Lattens.

"Oh," Perrund said. "Come, sir. Is this the General Lattens who won so well at catapults? You must do your duty, General. Your father will be back before too long. And Mr. DeWar." She smiled at DeWar.

"For all we know," DeWar said, "the war may be ended by the time we get there. That is sometimes the way with wars." He fiddled with his big, waxed hat, then set it aside on his dark cape. He cleared his throat. "Did I tell you about when Sechroom and Hiliti parted? When Sechroom went off to become a missionary?"

Lattens seemed not to hear for a moment, but then he rolled over on his side and stopped humming and said, "No, I don't think so."

"Well, one day the two friends had to part. Sechroom had made up her mind that she would become a soldier-missionary, taking the message of Lavishia to far-off lands and teaching the peoples there the error of their ways. Hiliti had tried to talk his friend out of this, still believing that it was the wrong thing to do, but Sechroom was adamant."

"What?"

"Determined."

"Oh."

"One day," DeWar continued, "not long before Sechroom was due to leave, they went to one of their special places, which was on an island. This island was a very wild place where people went to get away from all the riches of Lavishia. There were no streams of wine and sugar water, no ready-cooked game birds hanging in the house-trees, no perfume fountains, no piles of sweet-rocks, no—"

"People wanted to get away from sweet-rocks?" Lattens asked incredulously.

"Yes, and from being able to fly, and from having hot water gush from wash basins and from having servants pander to their every whim, too. People are strange like that, Lattens. Give them every comfort and they start to pine for the rougher life."

Lattens frowned mightily at this, but did not protest further. It was obvious he thought that the people of Lavishia, or perhaps just all adults, must be quite mad.

"Sechroom and Hiliti," DeWar said, "went to the island as a sort of holiday from all the luxuries they were used to. They left all their servants behind and they even left behind the magic amulets and jewels that protected them from harm and which let them call on the local gods, and the two of them were left to fend for themselves in the wilderness. They could still find fruit to eat and water to drink, and they were able to make a shelter from the giant leaves of trees. They had with them bows and arrows and a pair of blow-pipes which fired poisoned darts, too. They had made these before they had come on the holiday and were quite proud of them. They used the bows and blow-pipes to go hunting for some of the animals on the island, though the animals were not the cooperative sort of animals they were used to, and they didn't want to be killed and cooked and eaten, so they were quite good at keeping out of the way of two people who were really very inexperienced hunters.

"One day, when Sechroom and Hiliti had been out trying to find some animals to shoot their poison darts at, but without success, they were returning to their leaf-shelter, arguing and becoming annoyed with each other. They were both bored and hungry and that was probably one of the reasons that they were each so upset with the other and blaming the other for spoiling the hunt. Sechroom thought that Hiliti was too aggressive and wanted to kill the animals just for the sake of it, for Hiliti was proud of his skills as a bowman and a blow-piper and at hand-to-hand fighting, while Hiliti secretly thought that Sechroom, who didn't like to kill things, had deliberately made noises so that the animals they were stalking would realise they were there and run away.

"Their route took them back over a steep-sided stream where there was a natural bridge made by a fallen tree. It had been raining quite a lot that day—that was another reason they were miserable and arguing so much—and the stream below the tree-bridge was in spate."

"What's that?"

"It means the stream was swollen, full of water. So they started to cross the tree bridge. Now, Hiliti thought about saying that they should cross one at a time, but by then they had started out across the tree, with him going first, and he thought if he turned round and told Sechroom to go back and wait, Sechroom would just get even angrier than she was already, so he didn't say anything.

"Well, the tree-bridge gave way. It had been lying there rotting away for many years no doubt, and the banks on either side had been partially washed away by all the rain, so when the two of them put their weight on it, it obviously decided that it was time to give up the struggle and just succumb—ah, that means give in—to gravity, and fall into the stream.

"So down it tumbled, breaking in the middle and bringing down other bits of branches and a few rocks and a load of earth and so on from either side just for good measure."

"Oh no!" Lattens said, hand to his mouth. "What happened to Sechroom and Hiliti?"

"They fell down along with the tree. Hiliti was the luckier, because the bit of the tree he was on took its time collapsing, and he was able to hang on to it as it went down and throw himself on to the bank before the trunk hit the water. He still ended up tumbling into the stream, but he was all right."

"But what about Sechroom?"

"Sechroom wasn't so lucky. The part of the tree trunk she was on must have rolled as it fell, or she did, because she ended up underneath it, trapped beneath the water."

"Did she drown?" Lattens looked very concerned now, both his hands at his mouth. He started to suck one thumb.

Perrund put her arm round him and brought his hands away from his mouth. "Now come, don't forget this is just before Sechroom goes off to become a soldier-missionary."

"Yes, but what happened?" Lattens asked anxiously.

"Yes," Perrund said. "And why didn't the tree trunk float?"

"Most of its length was still on the steep bank," DeWar told her. "The bit sticking into the water trapping Sechroom wasn't enough to float. Anyway, Hiliti could see one of his cousin's boots sticking up out of the water on the far side of the tree and waving around. Hiliti swam and pulled himself through the water and over the rocks and the broken branches to get to Sechroom, who he realised was trapped under the water. He dived down. There was just enough light for him to see Sechroom struggling desperately, trying to push the tree trunk off her leg, but making no impression on it, because it was very big and heavy. Even as Hiliti watched, he saw a last few bubbles of air float out of Sechroom's mouth and be swept away in the strong current. Hiliti came back up to the surface, took a deep lungful of air and then went back down again and put his mouth over his cousin's and blew the air into Sechroom's mouth, so that she could live a little longer.

"Hiliti tried to push the tree trunk off Sechroom too, but it was too heavy. He thought that perhaps if he could find a strong enough, and a long enough lever, then perhaps he could take the weight off Sechroom's leg, but that would take a while. Meantime, Sechroom must be almost out of breath again. Hiliti took another gulp of air and dived back down. Again, the bubbles came out of Sechroom's mouth and again Hiliti gave his friend his own air.

"By now Hiliti could see that this could not go on much longer. The water was cold enough to be sapping his warmth and strength away, and he was becoming exhausted and starting to gasp for air himself.

"Then he thought of the blow-pipe. His own had been washed away by the stream when he'd fallen in, but he had seen Sechroom's when he'd first dived down, still slung over her back and partly trapped under her. Hiliti dived down, blew more air into Sechroom's mouth, then took hold of Sechroom's blow-pipe and pulled and twisted with all his might until it slithered out from underneath her. He had to return to the surface to gasp for air, but then he went back down and pointed to the pipe, and Sechroom took it into her mouth.

"But the situation was not yet saved. Sechroom had to spit the pipe out again, because there was too much water still inside it. Hiliti took the pipe to the surface, let the water out, held his hand over the end this time, and went back down.

"Finally, Sechroom could breathe. Hiliti waited a few breaths to make sure Sechroom was going to be all right for the moment, then he got out of the stream and looked for a lever. Eventually he found a branch straight and stout enough to do the job, he hoped, and he waded back into the river and went under, setting the branch under the fallen tree trunk and over the top of a rock.

"Well, at last it worked. The lever almost snapped, and when the tree trunk moved it hurt Sechroom's broken leg, but she was freed, and she floated to the surface, and Hiliti was able to lift her out of the stream and get her to the shore. The blow-pipe floated away downstream.

"It was just as big a struggle for Hiliti to get Sechroom to the top of the bank, because of course Sechroom was almost helpless with her badly broken leg."

"Did a surgeon have to cut her leg off?" Lattens asked, squirming on the couch, his eyes wide.

"What? Oh, no. No. Anyway, eventually Hiliti got Sechroom to the top of the bank. He was so exhausted he had to leave his friend there and return to their camp by himself, but there was a . . . a signal fire near the camp which he was able to light and that drew the attention of people who came and rescued them."

"So Sechroom was all right?" Lattens asked.

DeWar nodded. "She was indeed. Hiliti was regarded as a hero by all, and after Sechroom's leg was mended, but before she left to become a missionary, she went back to the island where it had happened and searched the length of the stream down from the collapsed tree-bridge until she found the two blow-pipes, lodged amongst rocks in different parts of the stream. She cut a piece off the end of the one that had been hers, and which had saved her life, and she presented it on a little ribbon to Hiliti at a party which their friends held to wish Sechroom well, on the evening of her leaving to become a missionary. It was the sign that what had happened by the other river, when Hiliti had let Sechroom fall into the water by the side of the waterfall—remember?—it was a sign, they both knew, that that didn't matter any more, that Sechroom had forgiven Hiliti. The little wooden ring was a bit too big to be worn as a ring, which was unfortunate, but Hiliti told Sechroom he would treasure it for ever, and he did, and he does, and as far as anybody knows, it is with him to this day."

"Where abouts did Sechroom go?" Lattens asked.

"Who knows?" DeWar said, spreading his hands. "Perhaps she came here. She and Hiliti knew of . . . of the Empire, and Haspidus. They talked about it, argued over it. She may have been here, for all anyone knows."

"Did Sechroom ever return to see her friend?" Perrund asked, taking Lattens on to her lap. He wriggled out again.

DeWar shook his head. "No," he said. "A few years after Sechroom left, so did Hiliti, and he lost touch completely with Lavishia and all the people he knew there. Sechroom could have returned there by now, but Hiliti will never know. He exiled himself from the luxuries of Lavishia for ever. Sechroom and Hiliti will never meet again."

"How sad," Perrund said. Her voice was low, and her expression sombre. "Never to see one's friends and family again."

"Well," DeWar began, but then looked up to see one of the Protector's aides signalling him from the doorway. He ruffled Lattens' hair and stood slowly up, lifting his hat, bags and cloak. "I'm afraid I don't have any more time, young general. You must say goodbye to your father now. Look."

UrLeyn, dressed in a very fine riding outfit, strode into the room. "Where's that boy of mine?" he shouted.

"Father!" Lattens ran to him and threw himself up into his arms.

"Oof! My, what a weight you're getting!" UrLeyn looked over to DeWar and Perrund, and winked. He sat down with the boy on a couch near the doors and they huddled together.

Perrund stood up, by DeWar's side. "Well, sir. You must promise me faithfully you'll take good care of both the Protector and yourself," she told him, raising her face to him. Her eyes looked bright. "I shall be most cross should any harm befall either of you, and brave though you may be, you are not so brave, I hope, as to risk my ire."

"I shall do all I can to make sure we both return safely," DeWar told her. He rearranged his cloak, hat and bags, putting one on one arm, the other two on the other, before putting the saddle bags over his shoulder and the hat over his head to hang down against his back on its cord.

Perrund watched this shuffle of impedimenta with a sort of sad amusement. She put her good hand on his, stilling him. "Take care," she said softly. Then she turned and went to sit where she could see UrLeyn and he could see her.

DeWar looked at her for a moment as she sat there, straight-backed in her long red gown, her face calm and beautiful, then he turned away too, and walked to the doors.

17
THE DOCTOR

Master, a killer for Duke Walen was of course eventually procured. It could not be otherwise. The murder of one so prominent cannot simply be left unavenged. As surely as the heir to a vacant title of note must be found, such an event leaves a hole in the fabric of society which has to be repaired with the life of another. It is a vacuum into which some soul must be sucked, and the soul in this case was a poor mad fellow from the city of Mizui who with every appearance of happiness and even fulfilment willingly threw himself into that void.

His name was Berridge, a one-time tinder-box maker of some age who was well known as a mad fellow in the city. He lived under the city's bridge with a handful of other desperates, begging for money in the streets and scavenging the market for discarded or rotten food. When the death of Duke Walen was made public knowledge in Mizui on the day following the masked ball, Berridge presented himself at the sheriff's office and made a full confession.

This was not a cause for any great surprise on the sheriff's part, as Berridge routinely claimed responsibility for any murder in or near the city for which there was no obvious culprit, and indeed for some where the murderer could not have been more obvious. His protestations of guilt in court, despite the fact that a husband of known viciousness had been discovered comatose with drink in the same locked room as the body of his butchered wife with the knife still clutched in his bloody hand, were the cause of much hilarity amongst that part of the populace which treats the King's courts as a form of free theatre.

Normally, Berridge would have been thrown out of the door and into the dust of the street without the sheriff giving the matter a second thought. On this occasion, however, due to the gravity of the offence and the fact that Duke Quettil had only that morning impressed upon the sheriff the extremity of his annoyance at a second unsanctioned murder taking place within his jurisdiction within so short a time, the sheriff thought the better of treating the madman's claims to such automatic dismissal.

To his immense surprise and satisfaction, Berridge was incarcerated in the town jail. The sheriff had a note sent to Duke Quettil informing him of this swift action, though he did think to include mention of such confessions being an habitual feature of Berridge's behaviour and that it was correspondingly unlikely that Berridge was really the culprit.

Guard Commander Polchiek sent word to the sheriff to keep Berridge in jail for the time being. When a half-moon had passed and no progress had been made discovering the murderer, the Duke instructed the sheriff to make further investigations into Berridge's claim.

Sufficient time had passed for neither Berridge nor any of his under-bridge-dwelling companions to have any recollection whatsoever of the movements of any of them on the day and evening of the masked ball, save that Berridge insisted he had left the city, climbed the hill to the palace, entered the private chambers of the Duke and murdered him in his bed (this quickly changed the better to fit the facts when Berridge heard that the Duke had been killed in a room just off the ballroom, while awake).

In the continuing absence of any more likely suspect, Berridge was sent to the palace, where Master Ralinge put him to the question. What good this was supposed to do other than to prove that Duke Quettil was serious about the matter and his appointees thorough in their investigations is debatable. Berridge presented no satisfying challenge at all to the Duke's chief torturer and from what I heard suffered relatively little, though still enough to unhinge his feeble brain still further.

By the time he appeared before the Duke himself to be tried for the Duke's murder, Berridge was a thin, bald, shaking wreck whose eyes roved about with seemingly complete independence from each other. He mumbled constantly yet spoke almost no intelligible words and had confessed not only to the murder of Duke Walen but also to that of King Beddun of Tassasen, Emperor Puiside and King Quience's father King Drasine, as well as claiming to be responsible for the fiery sky rocks which had killed whole nations of people and ushered in the present post-Imperial age.

Berridge was burned at the stake in the city's square. The Duke's heir, his brother, set the fire himself, though not before having the sad wretch strangled first, to spare him the pain of the fire.

The rest of our stay in the Yvenage Hills passed relatively uneventfully. There was an air of unsettled concern and even suspicion about the palace for some time, but that gradually dissipated. There were no more unexplained deaths or shocking murders. The King's ankle healed. He went hunting and fell off his mount again, though without incurring any injuries beyond scratches. His health seemed to improve generally, perhaps under the influence of the clear mountain air.

The Doctor found she had little to do. She walked and rode in the hills, sometimes with me at her side, sometimes, at her own insistence, alone. She spent some considerable time in Mizui city, treating orphans and other unfortunates at the Paupers' Hospital, comparing notes with the local mid-wives and discussing remedies and potions with the local apothecaries. As our time at Yvenir went on, a number of casualties from the war in Ladenscion arrived in the city, and the Doctor treated a few of those as best she could. She had little success at first in trying to meet with the doctors of the town, until with the King's permission she invited them to his counsel chamber, and had him briefly meet with them before he went off to hunt.

She accomplished less than she'd hoped to, I think, in terms of changing some of their ways, which she found even more old fashioned and indeed potentially dangerous to their patients than those of their colleagues in Haspide.

Despite the King's obvious health, he and the Doctor still seemed to find excuses to meet. The King worried that he might run to fat, as his father had done in later years, and so consulted the Doctor on his diet. This seemed bizarre to those of us for whom growing fat was a sure sign that one was well fed, lightly worked and had achieved a maturity beyond the average, but then perhaps this showed that there was a degree of truth to the rumours that the Doctor had put some strange ideas into the King's head.

Tongues also wagged concerning the fact the Doctor and the King spent so much time together. As far as I know nothing of an intimate nature took place between them during all this time. I had been present at the Doctor's side on every occasion she had attended the King, save for a couple of instances when I was too ill to leave my bed, when I diligently undertook to discover through my fellow assistants, as well as through certain servants, what had transpired between the Doctor and the King.

I am satisfied that I missed nothing and have reported everything that could possibly be of note to my Master thus far.

The King commanded the Doctor's presence most evenings, and if he had no obvious ailments, he would make a show of flexing his shoulders and would claim with a small frown that there might be a stiffness in one or other of them. The Doctor seemed perfectly willing to act the masseuse, and would happily work her various oils into the golden-brown skin of the King's back, kneading and working her palms and knuckles down his spine, across the shoulders and over the nape of his neck. Sometimes at such times they would talk quietly, more often they would be silent, save for the King's sporadic grunts as the Doctor loosened particularly tense knots of muscles. I too kept silent, of course, unwilling to break the spell that seemed to prevail on such candle-lit occasions, and afflicted with an odd, sweet melancholy while I watched in envy as those strong, slender fingers, glistening with perfumed oils, worked on the King's yielding flesh.

"You look tired this evening, Doctor," the King said as she massaged his upper back. He lay stripped to the waist on his wide, canopied bed.

"Do I, sir?"

"Yes. What have you been up to?" The King looked round at her. "You haven't taken a lover, have you, Vosill?"

The Doctor blushed, which was not something she did often. I think that every time I witnessed such an event we were in the presence of the King. "I have not, sir," she said.

The King settled his chin back on his hands. "Perhaps you should, Doctor. You're a handsome woman. I can't think that you would have other than a fair choice, if you so wished."

"Your majesty flatters me."

"No, I'm simply speaking the truth, as I'm sure you know."

"I bow to your opinion, sir."

The King looked round, straight at me. "Isn't she, ah . . . ?"

"Oelph," I said, gulping. "Sir."

"Well, Oelph," the King said, raising his eyebrows. "Don't you think so? Isn't the good doctor a pleasing prospect? Don't you think she would gladden the eye of any normal man?"

I swallowed. I looked at the Doctor, who glanced at me with a look that might have been forbidding or even pleading.

"I'm sure, sir," I began, "that my mistress is most personable, your majesty, sir," I mumbled, feeling myself blush now.

"Personable? Is that all?" The King laughed, still looking at me. "But don't you think she is attractive, Oelph? Attractive, comely, handsome, beautiful?"

"I'm sure she is all those things, sir," I said, looking down at my feet.

"There you are, Doctor," the King said, settling his chin on his hands once more. "Even your young assistant agrees with me. He thinks you're attractive. So, Doctor, are you going to take a lover or not?"

"I think not, sir. A lover would take up time I might need to devote to your good self."

"Oh, I'm so well and fit these days I'm sure I could spare you for the time it takes for a quick tumble or two each evening."

"Your majesty's generosity overwhelms me," the Doctor said dryly.

"There you go again, you see, Vosill? That damned sarcasm. My father always said that when a woman started being sarcastic to her betters it was a sure sign she wasn't being serviced properly."

"What a fount of priceless wisdom he was to be sure, sir."

"He certainly was," the King agreed. "I think he'd have said you needed a good tumbling. For your own good. Ouch," he said as the Doctor leant heavily on his spine with the heel of one hand. "Steady, Doctor. Yes. You might even call it medicinal, or at least, ah, what's that other word?"

"Irrelevant? Nosy? Impertinent?"

"Therapeutic. That's the word. Therapeutic."

"Ah, that word."

"I know," the King said. "What if I *commanded* you to take a lover, Vosill, for your own good?"

"Your majesty's concern for my health is most cheering."

"Would you obey your King, Vosill? Would you take a lover if I told you to?"

"I would be concerned what proof of my obeying such an instruction would be required to satisfy my King, sir."

"Oh, I'd take your word on it, Vosill. And besides, I'm sure any man who did bed you would be bound to brag about it."

"Really, sir?"

"Yes. Unless he possessed a particularly jealous and unforgiving wife. But would you do as I told you?"

The Doctor looked thoughtful. "I take it I would be able to make the choice myself, sir."

"Oh, of course, Doctor. I am not determined to pimp for you."

"Then, yes, sir. Of course. With alacrity."

"Good! Now then, I wonder if I should so command you."

I had by this time raised my gaze from my feet, although my face still felt flushed. The Doctor looked over at me and I smiled uncertainly. She grinned.

"What if you did, sir," she asked. "And I refused?"

"Refused to obey a direct order from your King?" the King asked with what sounded like genuine horror.

"Well, while I am entirely in your service and remain devoted to your every good, sir, I am not, I believe, in a technical sense, one of your subjects. I am a foreign national. Indeed, I am not a subject at all. I am a citizen of the archipelagic republic of Drezen and while I am content and indeed honoured to serve you under and within the jurisdiction of your laws, I do not believe that I am bound to obey your every whim as might somebody born within the borders of Haspidus or who was born to parents who were subjects of your realm."

The King thought about this for a good few moments. "Did you once tell me you considered learning the law rather than medicine, Doctor?"

"I believe I did, sir."

"I thought so. Well, if you were one of my subjects and you disobeyed me in such a matter, I would have you locked up until you changed your mind, and if you did not change your mind that would be unfortunate for you, because trivial though the issue itself might be, the King's will must always be obeyed, and that is a matter of the utmost gravity and importance."

"However, I am not a subject of yours, sir. How then would you deal with my mooted intransigence?"

"I suppose I would have to order you to leave my Kingdom, Doctor. You would have to return to Drezen, or go elsewhere."

"That would sadden me greatly, sir."

"As it would me. But you can see that I would have no choice."

"Of course, sir. So I had better hope that you do not so instruct me. Otherwise I had better prepare either to surrender myself to a man, or for exile."

"Indeed."

"A hard choice for one who is, as you have observed with such penetrating accuracy, sir, so opinionated and stubborn as I."

"I am glad you are finally treating the subject with the gravity it merits, Doctor."

"Indeed. And what of yourself, sir, if I may enquire?"

"What?" the King said, his head coming up off his hands.

"Your majesty's intentions in the matter of a wife are of as enormous consequence as my choice of a lover would be trifling. I only wondered how much thought you had given to the matter, as we are on the subject."

"I think we are swiftly leaving the subject I thought we were on."

"I beg your majesty's pardon. But do you intend to marry soon, sir?"

"I think that is none of your business, Doctor. That is the business of the court, my advisors, the fathers of eligible princesses or other ladies of rank to whom it would be sensible and advantageous for me to be attached to, and myself."

"Yet as you yourself pointed out, sir, one's health and demeanour can be profoundly affected by a lack of . . . sensual release. What might make sense for the political fortune of a state might be catastrophic for the individual well-being of a King, if, say, he married an ugly princess."

The King looked round at the Doctor with an expression of amusement. "Doctor," he said. "I shall marry whomever I feel I ought to marry for the good of my country and my heirs. If that requires marrying an ugly woman then so be it." His eyes seemed to twinkle. "I am the King, Vosill. The position carries with it certain privileges you may have heard about. Within quite generous limits, I may have the pleasure of whom I please, and I will not suffer that to change just because I take a wife. I may marry the least prepossessing princess in all the world, yet I'll warrant that I'll notice no difference whatsoever in the frequency and quality of my 'sensual release.' " He smiled broadly at her.

The Doctor looked awkward. "But if you are to have heirs, sir," she began.

"Then I shall get sufficiently but not incapably drunk, make sure the curtains are tightly closed and that the candles have been snuffed out, and then I shall think of somebody else until the proceedings reach a satisfactory conclusion, my dear doctor," the King said, a look of satisfaction on his face as he returned his chin to his hands again. "As long as the wench is fertile I ought not to have to suffer that too often, wouldn't you say?"

"I'm sure that I could not say, sir."

"Then take my word on it, and that of the girls who have borne me children—and mostly boys, too, I might add."

"Very well, sir."

"Anyway, I do not order you to take a lover."

"I am very grateful, sir."

"Oh, it's not for your benefit, Vosill. It's just that I have too much sympathy for any fellow you might take to your bed. I don't doubt the principal part of the occasion would be pleasurable enough, but then—Providence protect the unfortunate wretch—he'd have to suffer your confounded conversation afterwards. Ouch!"

I think, then, that there is only one more incident of note to relate concerning our time in Yvenir palace. It was one I only learned of later, some time after our return to Haspide, when news of it was considerably overshadowed by events.

Master, the Doctor, as I said, often went for rides and walks in the hills by herself, sometimes departing at Xamis dawn and staying away until its dusk. This seemed just as eccentric behaviour to me as it did to anybody else, and even when the Doctor had the good sense to ask for my company, I remained perplexed at her motives. Walks were the most strange. She would walk for hour after hour, like some peasant. She took with her small and not so small books which she had purchased at great expense in Haspide and which were filled with drawings, paintings and descriptions of the flora and fauna native to the area, and would watch intently as birds and small animals crossed our path, observing them with an intensity which seemed unnatural given that she was not interested in hunting them.

Rides were less enervating, though I think she only resorted to a mount when the journey she proposed to make was too long to consider undertaking on foot (she would never stay out overnight).

For all my mystification at these excursions and my annoyance at being forced to walk all day, I came to enjoy them. I was expected to be at the Doctor's side, both by her and by my Master, and so felt no guilt that I was doing other than my duty.

We tramped or rode in silence, or spoke of inconsequential things, or about medicine or philosophy or history or a hundred other matters, we stopped to eat or observe an animal or a fine view, we consulted books and tried to decide whether the animals we were looking at were those described, or if the book's author had been overly fanciful, we attempted to decipher the rough maps that the Doctor had copied from those in the library, we stopped woodsmen and bondagers to ask the way, we collected feathers, flowers, small stones and shells and eggshells, and returned eventually to the palace precincts having done nothing of any real consequence, yet with my heart full of joy and my head swimming with a sort of wild delight.

I soon came to wish that she would take me on all her excursions, and only when we returned to Haspide did I wish bitterly that I had done something I had thought about doing often when we were at Yvenir and the Doctor was making her solo expeditions. What I wished I had done was follow her. I wish that I had trailed her, tracked her, secretly kept watch on her.

What I heard, moons later in Haspide, was that two of my fellow palace juniors did chance upon the Doctor while she was alone. They were Auomst and Puomiel, pages to Baron Sermil and Prince Khres respectively, and fellows I knew only distantly and in truth without liking at all. They had reputations as bullies, cheats and rakes, and certainly both boasted of the heads they had broken, the servants they had swindled at cards and the successes they had had with town girls. Puomiel was rumoured to have left one junior page at the brink of death the year before after the young fellow had protested to his master that the elder page was extorting money from him. It had not even been a fair fight. The lad had been jumped from behind and coshed senseless. Brazenly, Puomiel did not even deny this—not to us, anyway—thinking it would make us fear him more. Auomst was marginally the less unpleasant of the two, but by general agreement only because he lacked the imagination.

Their story was that they had been out in the woods, some good distance from the palace, near dusk one particularly warm evening. They were making their way back towards Yvenir with some game in their bags, happy at their poaching and looking forward to their evening meal. They chanced upon a royal xule, a rare enough animal in any event, but this one, they swore, was pure white. It moved through the forest like a swift, pale ghost, and they, dropping their bags and readying their bows, followed it as quietly as they were able.

Neither could really have thought what they were going to do if they did find themselves in a position to bring the beast down. They could not have told anybody they had killed the animal, for the hunting of the xule is a royal prerogative, and the size of the thing would have prevented them carrying it to a dishonest butcher, supposing one brave enough to risk the royal wrath could have been found. But they moved off after it nevertheless, carried along by some instinct to hunt that is perhaps bred into us.

They did not catch the xule. It startled suddenly as it neared a small tree-surrounded lake high in the hills and took off at a run, putting itself beyond even the most hopeful of bow shots within a few heart-beats.

The two pages, just achieving the summit of a small ridge in time to see this happen through a screen of small bushes, were disheartened at losing the animal. That dissatisfaction was almost instantly relieved by what they saw next.

A startlingly beautiful and perfectly naked woman waded out of the lake and stared in the direction the white xule had taken when it fled.

Here then was the cause of the animal taking off at such a rate, and here too, perhaps, was something even more fit to be hunted down and enjoyed. The woman was tall and dark haired. Her legs were long, her belly was a little too flat to be truly beautiful, but her breasts, while not especially large, looked firm and high. Neither Auomst or Puomiel recognised her at first. But it was the Doctor. She turned away from where the xule had dashed away through the trees and reentered the water, swimming with the ease of a fish straight towards the two young men.

She came ashore just beneath where they lay. It was here, they realised, that she had left her clothes. She stepped out of the water and began to dry herself with her hands, facing out towards the water, her back to them.

They each looked at the other. They did not need to speak. Here was a woman, by herself. She had no escort, no companion, and she was, as far as they both knew, without a husband or a champion at the court. Again, neither stopped to think that in fact she did have a champion at the court, and he was without equal or better. This pale body exposed before them excited them even more than the one they had just lost sight of, and an instinct even deeper than that of hunting flooded their hearts, taking them over and extinguishing all rational thought.

It was dark beneath the circling trees and the birds were calling all around, alerted by the flight of the xule, and so providing sufficient noise to mask even a clumsy approach.

They might knock her out, or surprise her and blindfold her. She might never even see them, in other words, and they might be able to ravish her without risk of discovery and punishment. That they had been led here by the xule seemed like a sign from the forest gods of old. They had been delivered here by a creature close to myth. The opportunity was too good to ignore.

Puomiel took out a pouch of coin he had in the past used as a cosh. Auomst nodded.

They slipped out of the bushes and made their way stealthily down through the shadows between a few small intervening trees.

The woman was singing softly to herself. She completed drying herself with a small kerchief which she then wrung out. She stooped to pick up her shirt, her buttocks like two pale moons. Still facing away from the two men, who were now only a few steps behind her, she held the shift over her head and then let it fall down over her. For a few moments she was and would be blind, pulling the garment down over herself. Auomst and Puomiel both knew this was the moment. They sprang forward. They sensed the woman stiffen, as, perhaps, she heard them at last. Her head might have started to turn, still caught inside the folds of the shirt.

* * *

They woke with aching heads in the darkness of a night full save for Foy and Jairly, shining down like two grey reproachful eyes upon the calm, still waters of the hidden lake.

The Doctor was gone. They each had bumps the size of eggs on the backs of their heads. Their bows had been taken and, most oddly of all, the blades of their knives had been twisted, bent right round and made a knot of.

None of us could understand that at all. Ferice, the armourer's assistant, swore that treating metal like that was next to impossible. He tried to bend knives similar to Auomst and Puomiel's in a like manner and found that they broke almost immediately. The only way to make them behave in such a fashion was to heat them to a yellow-white heat and then manipulate them, and that was hard enough. He added that he had received a boxing about the ears from the armourer for such assiduous experimentation, to teach him not to waste valuable weapons.

I was suspected, though I did not know it at the time. Auomst and Puomiel assumed that I had been with the Doctor, either guarding her with her knowledge, or spying on her without it. Only the testimony of Feulecharo, whom Jollisce and I had been helping to sort through some of Duke Walen's possessions at the time, saved me from a coshing.

When eventually I did discover what had happened I did not know what to think, save that I wished that I had been there, either to guard or to spy. I would have fought both of those miserable ruffians to the death to protect the Doctor's honour, but at the same time I would have gladly surrendered my own for a single furtive glimpse of her such as they had been afforded.

18
THE BODYGUARD

The city of Niarje is conventionally supposed to lie six days' ride from Crough, the capital of Tassasen. The Protector and his company of fresh troops arrived there in four, and were appropriately tired after their long days in the saddle. It was decided they would rest in the city while they waited for the heavy artillery pieces and siege engines to catch up with them, and for fresh word from the war in Ladenscion to arrive. That word soon appeared in the form of coded messages from Duke Ralboute, and was not good.

The barons' forces were proving far better trained, more comprehensively equipped and reliably supplied than had been anticipated. Cities would not quickly be starved into submission. Fresh defences encircled almost all of them. The troops manning those defences were not the usual rabble but rather gave every indication of having been drilled to the highest standard. Partisan forces harried the Protectorate's supply lines, sacking camps, ambushing wagon trains, taking weapons meant to be directed at them for their own use and forcing troops needed at the front to attach themselves to each of the supply caravans. General Ralboute had himself nearly been killed or captured in a daring night raid which had issued from the besieged city of Zhirt. Only luck and some desperate hand-to-hand fighting had prevented disaster. The general himself had had to draw sword and was within one defending aide of having to join the fray.

We are told that one of the situations a soldier craves to engineer for his enemy, and dreads being caught in himself, is that of the pincer movement. So it can only be imagined what UrLeyn felt when he was caught in just such a plight in Niarje, not by the attack of enemy troops, but by information. The intelligence that the war in Ladenscion was going so ill arrived just half a day before news came from the opposite direction that was, if anything, even worse, and also concerned illness.

UrLeyn seemed to shrink in on himself. His hand holding the letter fell, and the letter itself fluttered to the ground.

He sat down heavily in his seat at the head of the dining table in the old Ducal mansion in the centre of Niarje. DeWar, standing just behind UrLeyn's seat, stooped and picked up the letter. He set it, folded closed, by UrLeyn's plate.

"Sir?" asked Doctor BreDelle. The Protector's other companions, all army officers, looked on, concerned.

"The boy," UrLeyn said quietly to the doctor. "I knew I should not have left him, or should have had you stay with him, Doctor . . ."

BreDelle stared at him for a moment. "How poorly is he?"

"At death's door," UrLeyn said, looking down at the letter. He handed the letter to the doctor, who read it.

"Another seizure," he said. BreDelle dabbed at his mouth with his napkin. "Shall I return to Crough, sir? I can start at first light."

The Protector stared down the table at nothing for a moment. Then he seemed to rouse himself. "Yes, Doctor. And I shall come too." The

Protector looked apologetically at the other officers. "Gentlemen," he said, raising his voice and straightening his back. "I must ask you to continue on to Ladenscion without me, for the moment. My son is unwell. I hoped that I would contribute to our eventual victory as soon as you will, but I fear that even if I were to continue, my heart, and my attention, would still be drawn back to Crough. I regret that the glory will be yours, unless you contrive to extend the war. I will join you as soon as I can. Please forgive me, and indulge the fatherly weakness of a man who, at my age, should really be a grandfather."

"Sir, of course!"

"I'm sure we all understand, sir."

"We will do all we can to make you proud of us, sir."

The protestations of support and understanding went on. DeWar looked round the young, eager, earnest faces of the junior noblemen gathered round the banqueting table with a feeling of dread and foreboding.

"Perund? Is that you?"

"It is, young sir. I thought I'd come and sit by you."

"Perrund, I can't see."

"It is very dark. The doctor thinks you will better recover kept away from the light."

"I know, but still I cannot see. Hold my hand, will you?"

"You must not worry. Illness seems so terrible when you are young, but these things pass."

"Will it?"

"Of course."

"Will I be able to see again?"

"Of course you will. Have no fear."

"But I am frightened."

"Your uncle has written to your father, telling him of your condition. I imagine he will be coming home soon, in fact I'm sure of it. He will give you some of his strength. He will drive away all fear. You'll see."

"Oh no! But he should be at the war. I am bringing him home when he should be at the war, to win it for us."

"Calm yourself, calm yourself. We could not keep your illness from him. What would he have thought of us? He will want to be sure that you are well. He will want to see you. I imagine he will bring Doctor BreDelle with him, too."

"And Mr. DeWar?"

"And Mr. DeWar. Where your father goes, he follows."

"I can't remember what happened. What day is it?"

"It is the third of the old moon."

"What happened? Did I start to shake as I did at the shadow-players' show?"

"Yes. Your teacher said he thought you were trying to get out of learning mathematics when you fell off your seat. He ran to get the nurse and then Doctor AeSimil was sent for. He is doctor to your uncle RuLeuin and General YetAmidous and very good. Very nearly as good as Doctor BreDelle. He says you will be better, in good time."

"Does he?"

"He does. And he seems a most honest and trustworthy soul."

"Is he better than Doctor BreDelle?"

"Oh, Doctor BreDelle must be better, because he is your father's doctor, and your father deserves to have the best, for the good of all of us."

"Do you really think he will come back?"

"I am sure of it."

"Will you tell me a story?"

"A story? I'm not sure I know any."

"But everybody knows stories. Didn't you used to be told stories when you were little? . . . Perund?"

"Yes. Yes, I'm sure I was. Yes, I have a story."

"Oh good . . . Perund?"

"Yes. Well. Let me see. Once upon a time . . . once upon a time there was a little girl."

"Yes?"

"Yes. She was rather an ugly child, and her parents did not like or care for her at all."

"What was her name?"

"Her name? Her name was . . . Dawn."

"Dawn. That's a pretty name."

"Yes. Unfortunately she was not very pretty, as I have said. She lived in a town she hated with parents she loathed. They made her do all sorts of things they thought she ought to do, which she hated, and they kept her locked up a lot of the time. They forced her to wear rags and sacking, they refused to buy her shoes for her feet or ribbons for her hair and they did not let her play with the other children. They never told her any stories at all."

"Poor Dawn!"

"Yes, she was a poor thing, wasn't she? She would cry herself to sleep most nights, and pray to the old gods or appeal to Providence to deliver her from such unhappiness. She wished that she could escape from her parents, but because they kept her locked up she could not. But then one day the fair came to town, with players and stages and tents and jugglers and acrobats and fire-breathers and knife-throwers and strong men and dwarves and people on stilts and all their servants and performing animals. Dawn was fascinated by the fair and wanted to see it and be made happy by it, for she felt that she had no life at all where she was, but her parents hid her away. They did not want her to have fun watching all the wonderful acts and shows, and they were worried that if people saw that they had such an ugly child they would make fun of them and perhaps even tempt her to leave to become an exhibit in their freaks of nature show."

"Was she really that ugly?"

"Perhaps not quite that ugly, but still they didn't want her to be seen, so they hid her away in a secret place they had fashioned in their house. Poor Dawn cried and cried and cried. But what her parents did not know was that the people of the fair always sent some of their performers round the houses in the town, to do little acts of kindness, or to help out with chopping kindling, or to clean up a yard, so that people would feel beholden to them and go and see the fair. They did this in Dawn's town, and of course her parents, being very mean, could not pass up the opportunity to have some work done for free.

"They invited the performers into their house and had them tidy it all up, though of course it was quite tidy already because Dawn had done most of the work. While they were cleaning the house, and even leaving little presents behind, for these were very kind and generous

performers—a clown, I think, and a fire-breather and a knife-thrower—they heard poor Dawn crying in her secret prison, and they released her and made her happy by their antics, and were very kind to her. She felt appreciated and loved for the first time, and tears of joy rolled down her face. Her bad parents had hidden themselves in the cellar, and later on they ran away, embarrassed at having been so cruel to Dawn.

"The performers from the fair gave Dawn her life back. She even started to feel not so ugly, and was able to dress better than her parents had let her dress, and feel clean and good. Perhaps, she thought, she was not destined to be ugly and unhappy all her life, as she had imagined. Perhaps she was beautiful and her life would be full of happiness. Somehow just being with the performers made her feel pretty, and she started to realise that they had made her beautiful, that she had only been ugly because people had told her she was ugly and now she was not. It was like magic.

"Dawn decided that she wanted to join the fair and go with the performers, but they told her sadly that they could not let her do that because if they did then people might think that they were the sort of people who took little girls away from their families, and their good name would suffer. They told her she ought to stay and look for her parents. She saw the sense of what they were telling her, and because she felt strong and capable and alive and beautiful, she was able to wave goodbye to the fair when it left and all the kind performers went away to take their happiness and kindness to another town. And do you know what?"

"What?"

"She did find her parents, and they were nice and good to her for ever afterwards. She found a handsome young fellow, too, and married him and had lots of babies and they lived happily ever after. And, as well as all that, one day, she did catch up with the fair, and was able to join it and be part of it and try to think of a way to repay the performers for their earlier kindness.

"And that is the story of Dawn, an ugly, unhappy child who became beautiful and happy."

"Hmm. That is quite a good story. I wonder if Mr. DeWar has any

more stories about Lavishia. They are a bit strange, but I think he means well. I think I ought to sleep now. I—oh!"

"Ah, I'm sorry."

"What was that? Water? On my hand . . ."

"It was just a happy tear. It is such a happy story. It makes me cry. Oh, what are you—?"

"Yes, it tastes of salt."

"Oh, you are a charmer, young Master Lattens, to lick a lady's tears up so! Let go my hand. I must . . . There. That's better. You sleep now. Your father will be here soon, I'm sure. I'll send in the nurse to make sure you're tucked in properly. Oh, do you need this? Is this your comforter?"

"Yes. Thank you, Perrund. Good night."

"Good night."

The palace concubine Yalde brought fruit and wine to the bath, where YetAmidous, RuLeuin and ZeSpiole floated in the milky waters. Terim and Herae, also concubines of Yalde's rank, sat naked by the pool side, Terim with her long legs dangling in the water while Herae brushed her long black hair.

Yalde placed the tray with the fruit bowl and the decanter near YetAmidous' elbow, then stepped out of the loose gown she had worn to visit the servants' quarters and slipped into the water. The eyes of the other two men followed her movements but she ignored them. She floated at YetAmidous' side and poured wine for him.

"So our little time of power may be drawing to an unexpectedly early close," ZeSpiole said. He brought one hand out of the water and stroked the tawny calf of Terim's leg. She looked down and smiled at him, though he did not see. Both Terim and Herae were from Ungrian, and spoke only their own tongue and Imperial. The men talked in Tassaseni.

"That might not be so bad," RuLeuin said. "The Protector told BiLeth to report to me while he's away and I'm growing tired of having to listen to that idiot pontificate on diplomatic niceties. Part of me hopes UrLeyn does come back."

"You think he will come back?" YetAmidous asked, looking from

RuLeuin to ZeSpiole. He accepted the goblet of wine from Yalde and slurped at it, spilling some into the translucent waters around his wide chest.

"I fear he will," ZeSpiole said.

"Fear?" RuLeuin said. "But—"

"Oh, not because I am so attached to a temporary third of the shadow of his power," ZeSpiole said. "But because I think it the wrong thing for him to do for Tassasen."

"The troops will go on without him, most of them, won't they?" RuLeuin said.

"It would be better if he did bring some of them back with him," YetAmidous told the Guard Commander. "There may be three of us to share his authority but there are precious few troops at our command, and when all fine words are finished with it's soldiers and swords that make power. I have barely enough men to make the city walls look lived in."

"The Protector has always said that a populace which in general assents to its ruling—and to its rulers—needs few sheriffs and no troops," ZeSpiole said.

"Easily said when you have several barracks full of soldiers to agree with you," YetAmidous said. "But you will observe that it is we who are allowed the privilege of testing our master's theory in this regard, not he."

"Oh, the people are happy enough," ZeSpiole said. "For the moment."

RuLeuin glanced at him. "Your spies are sure of that then?"

"One does not spy on one's own people," ZeSpiole informed him. "One has, rather, conduits of communication which lead to the common man. My guards mix with all sorts. They share their houses, their streets, their taverns, and their views."

"And they hear no grumblings?" YetAmidous asked sceptically, pushing his goblet towards Yalde to be refilled.

"Oh, they hear constant grumblings. The day they stop hearing grumblings I shall be sure that revolt is imminent. But people grumble about this tax or that, or that the Protector keeps such a large harem when many an honest working fellow can hardly find a wife, or they grumble about the luxurious life led by some of the Grand Aedile's generals," ZeSpiole said, accepting a piece of fruit from Terim with a broad smile.

RuLeuin smiled too.

YetAmidous drank greedily. "We are to be reassured, then, that we are in no immediate danger from the general populace," he said. "But what of our other frontiers? They are reduced to the minimum or less. Where are the reinforcements if some other place makes war on us?"

"The problem in Ladenscion will not last for ever," RuLeuin said, though he looked troubled. "The troops will come home. With the new men and machines now in Niarje, Simalg and Ralboute should be able to bring it to a swift conclusion."

"We were told that at the start," YetAmidous reminded the other man. "We should all have gone then, all of us. We should have crushed the barons with every force at our command." The general made a fist and brought it down on the surface of the water with a splash. Yalde wiped soapy water from her eyes. YetAmidous drank, then spat the wine out. "There's water in here!" he told Yalde, and tipped the wine over her head. He laughed, followed by the other men. The wine stung her eyes a little, but she bowed her head. YetAmidous pushed her head under the water, then let her bob up once more. "Here." He pushed the goblet into her hands again. She wiped it with a napkin and refilled it from the decanter.

"That might be obvious to all of us now," ZeSpiole said. "But it was not then, to any of us. We all agreed that Simalg and Ralboute's men would be more than ample for the job."

"Well, they haven't been," YetAmidous said, then tested the wine by sloshing it round his mouth. "The Protector should not have entrusted so important a mission to those fops. Noble men, indeed! They are no better than us. He is too impressed by their high birth. They make war like children, like women. They spend too much time talking with these barons when they should be fighting them. Even when they do fight, they fight as though they're frightened of getting their swords bloody. Too much finesse, not enough muscle. All is ruse and subtlety. I have no time for such nonsense. These barons are best met head on."

"Your directness has always been your most engaging feature, YetAmidous," RuLeuin told him. "I think my brother, if he ever had a concern over the style of your generalship, only worried that your assaults tended to be rather expensive in men."

"Oh, what expense is that?" YetAmidous said, waving his free hand. "Too many of them are idle wretches from the gutter who'd have met an early death anyway. They expect to return with treasure. Usually all they bring back is the diseases they picked up from the whores. Death in battle, a place in history, remembering in a victory song . . . better than most of the scum deserve. They're a crude tool and they're best used crudely, with none of this effeminate feinting and playing around. Better to attack straight and get it over with. These so-noble dandies dishonour the whole business of war." YetAmidous looked at the two girls sitting at the pool side, then briefly at Yalde. "I wonder sometimes," he said quietly to the two men, "whether there is not some other motive in the Dukes' inability to finish this war."

"What?" RuLeuin said, frowning.

"I had assumed, with the Protector, that they were trying as hard as they could," ZeSpiole said. "What do you mean, General?"

"I mean that perhaps we are all being treated like fools, sir. That Duke Ralboute and Duke Simalg are closer to the Barons of Ladenscion than they are to us."

"Apart from physically, obviously," RuLeuin said, smiling but looking awkward.

"Eh? Aye. Too damn close. Don't you see?" he asked, levering his bulk away from the side of the bath. "They go off to this war, they pull in more and more troops, they delay and delay and stumble and lose men and machines and come whining to us to help them out, taking troops from the capital and our other frontiers, leaving the way open to any bastard who might want to march in from outside. Who knows what mischief they might have got up to if the Protector had put himself in their midst? The boy about to die might save his father's life, if he really is his father."

"General," RuLeuin said, "have a care. The boy may not be about to die. I have no doubt that in any event I am truly his uncle through my brother, and the Generals Ralboute and Simalg have always shown themselves to be good and true officers of the Protectorate. They joined our cause long before it was sure to succeed and could be said to have risked more than any of us in supporting it, for they started out with much power and prestige which they entirely risked by throwing their lot in with us." RuLeuin looked to ZeSpiole for support.

ZeSpiole had busied himself with a segment of fruit, burying most of his lower face in it. He looked up at the other two men and expressed surprise with his brows.

YetAmidous waved his hand in dismissal. "All very fine, but the fact remains they have not done as well as they were supposed to in Ladenscion. They said they would triumph there in a few moons. UrLeyn thought they would too. Even I thought that the job ought not to be beyond them, if they applied themselves and threw their troops to the front. But they have done badly. They have failed so far. Cities have not been taken, siege engines and cannon have been lost. Their progress has been halted by every stream, every hill, every damn hedge and flower. I am simply asking why? Why are they doing so badly? What can be the explanation, if it is not deliberate? Might it not be some conspiracy? Might there not be some collusion between the two sides of the war, to drag us and our men in deeper and tempt the Protector himself forward to take part, and then kill him?"

RuLeuin glanced at ZeSpiole again. "No," he told YetAmidous. "I think that is not the case, and nothing is accomplished by talking like that. Give me some wine," he said to Herae.

ZeSpiole grinned at YetAmidous. "I must say, Yet," he said. "Your talent for suspicion is almost on a par with DeWar's."

"DeWar!" YetAmidous snorted. "I've never trusted him, either."

"Oh, this is getting preposterous!" RuLeuin said. He drained his goblet and sank under the water, resurfacing to shake his head and blow out his cheeks.

"What can DeWar be up to, do you think, Yet?" ZeSpiole asked, with a smile. "He certainly cannot wish our Protector dead, for he has saved him from almost certain death on several occasions, the last time being when each of us came closer to sending the Protector into the arms of Providence than any assassin ever has. You yourself came within a knuckle of sticking a quarrel straight through UrLeyn's head."

"I was aiming for that ort," YetAmidous said, scowling. "And I almost got the thing, too." He thrust his goblet out to Yalde again.

"I'm sure you were," ZeSpiole said. "My own shot was more off target. But you have not said what you suspect DeWar of."

"I just don't trust him, that's all," YetAmidous said, sounding surly now.

"I would be more concerned that he does not trust you, Yet, old friend," ZeSpiole said, staring into YetAmidous' eyes.

"What?" YetAmidous spluttered.

"Well, he may have the feeling that you were trying to kill the Protector that day, on the hunt, by the stream," ZeSpiole said in a quiet, concerned voice. "He might be watching you, you know. I would worry about that if I were in your position. He is a sly, cunning hound, that one. His approach is silent and his teeth are sharp as razors. I should not care to be the subject of his suspicions, I'll tell you that. Why, I'd be sorely frightened that I might wake up dead one morning."

"What?" YetAmidous roared. He threw down the goblet. It splashed into the milky water. He stood up, shaking with fury.

ZeSpiole looked over at RuLeuin, whose expression was anxious. ZeSpiole put his head back and burst out laughing. "Oh, Yet! You are so easy to rile! I'm jesting with you, man. You could have killed UrLeyn a hundred times by now. I know DeWar. He doesn't think you're an assassin, you big oaf! Here. Have a fruit." ZeSpiole lifted a buncher and threw it across the bath at the other man, who caught it and then, after a moment's confusion, laughed too, sinking back into the swirling water and laughing uproariously.

"Ha! Of course! Ah, you tease me like a hussy, ZeSpiole. Yalde!" he said. "This water's freezing. Get the servants to bring some more hot. And bring more wine! Where's my goblet? What have you done with it?"

The goblet, sunk in the bath in front of YetAmidous, had left a red stain in the milky water, like blood.

19
THE DOCTOR

The summer passed. It was a relatively mild season throughout the land, but especially so in the Yvenir hills, where the breezes were either pleasantly cool or tolerably warm. Much of the time passed with Seigen joining Xamis below the horizon each night, trailing after it at first, while we performed the first part of the Circuition, dancing almost in step with its senior during those eventful and perplexing early moons at Yvenir, then preceding it by gradually greater and greater increments for the rest of our stay, which, happily, was devoid of significant incident.

When time came to pack up what needed to be packed up and store what required storing, Seigen was anticipating the rise of the greater sun by a good bell or so, providing the hills with a long leading-dawn full of sharp, extended shadows when the day seemed only half begun and birds chorused and some birds did not and the tiny points that were the wandering stars could sometimes still be seen in the violet sky if the moons were absent or low.

Our return to Haspide was accomplished with all the usual pomp and ceremony. There were feasts and ceremonies and investitures and triumphal parades through newly built gates and dignified processions under specially commissioned arches and long speeches by self-important officials and elaborate gift-givings and formal conferments of old and new awards and titles and decorations and any manner of other business, all of it wearying but all of it, I was assured by the Doctor (somewhat to my surprise), necessary in the sense that this sort of participatory ritual and use of shared symbols helped to cement our society together. If anything, the Doctor said, Drezen could have done with more of this sort of thing.

En route back to Haspide, in the midst of all this ceremonial—much of it, I'd still insist, mere flummery—the King set up numerous city councils, instituted more craft and professional guilds and granted various counties and towns the privileged status of burgh. This did not meet with the universal approval of the Dukes and other nobles of the provinces concerned, but the King seemed more energetic in finding ways to sweeten the medicine for those who might lose out in this reshuffling of responsibilities and control than he had on the way to Yvenir, and no less cheerfully determined to have his way, not just because he was the King but because he knew he was right and before too long people would come to see things his way anyway.

"But there is no *need* for this, sir!"

"Ah, but there will be."

"Sir, can we be so sure of that?"

"We can be as sure of it as we can that the suns will rise after they have set, Ulresile."

"Indeed, sir. Yet we wait until the suns do appear before we rise. What you propose is to prepare for the day while it is still the middle of the night."

"Some things must be anticipated further in advance than others," the King told the younger man with a look of jovial resignation.

Young Duke Ulresile had opted to accompany the court back to Haspide. He had developed his powers of speech and opinion considerably over the summer since we had first encountered him in the hidden garden behind Yvenir palace. Perhaps he was simply growing up particularly quickly, but I think it was more likely that his new-found garrulousness was largely the effect of living in the same place as the royal court for a season.

We were camped on the Toforbian Plain, about halfway between Yvenir and Haspide. Ormin, Ulresile and the new Duke Walen—together with chamberlain Wiester and a fuss of servants—stood with the King in a fabric-walled courtyard open to the sky outside the royal pavilion while the Doctor bandaged the King's hands. Tall flagpoles bent in a warm, harvest-scented breeze and the royal standards flapped at each corner of the six-sided space, their shadows moving sinuously over the carpets and rugs which had been spread over the carefully levelled ground.

Our monarch was due to indulge in a formal stave-fight with the old city-god of Toforbis, which would be represented as an extravagantly hued multipede and played by a hundred men under a long, hooped canopy. The spectacle was that of watching a man fight with the awning of a tent, even if the awning was animated, elongated, painted with scales and sported a giant head in the shape of a giant toothed bird, but it was one of the rituals that had to be endured for the sake of local custom and to keep the regional dignitaries happy.

Duke Ulresile watched the Doctor's hands as she wound the bandages round and round the King's fingers and palms. "But sir," he said, "why anticipate this quite so far in advance? Might it not be seen as folly to—?"

"Because to wait would be the greater folly," the King said patiently. "If one plans an attack at dawn one does not wait until dawn itself before rousing one's troops. One starts to get them organised in the middle of the night."

"Duke Walen, you feel as I do, don't you?" Ulresile said, sounding exasperated.

"I feel there is no point disputing with a King, even when he makes what seems like an error to us lesser mortals," the new Duke Walen said.

The new Duke was, by all accounts, a worthy successor to his late brother, who had died without issue and so ensured that his title went to a sibling the strength of whose resentment at being born, by his reckoning, a year too late had only ever been matched by his estimation of his own worth. He seemed to be a sullen sort of fellow, and gave the impression of being, if anything, rather older than the old Duke.

"What about you, Ormin?" the King asked. "Do you think I anticipate matters too much?"

"Perhaps a little, sir," Ormin said with a pained expression. "But it is difficult to gauge these matters with any accuracy. I suspect one only finds out if one has done the right thing after some considerable time has passed. Sometimes it is only one's children who discover what the rights and wrongs of it all were. Bit liking planting trees, really." He uttered this last sentence with a look of mild surprise at his own words.

Ulresile frowned at him. "Trees grow, Duke. We are having the forest cut down around us."

"Yes, but with the wood you can build houses, bridges, ships," the King said, smiling. "And trees do grow back again. Unlike heads, say."

Ulresile's lips went tight.

"I think that perhaps what the Duke means," Ormin said, "is that we may be proceeding a little too quickly with these . . . alterations. We run the risk of removing or at least curtailing too much of the power of the existing noble structure before there is another framework properly in place to carry the load. I confess that I for one am worried that the burghers in some of the towns in my own province have not entirely grasped the idea of taking responsibility for the transfer of land ownership, for example."

"And yet they must have been trading grains and animals, or the produce of their own trade or craft for generations," the King said, holding up his left hand, which the Doctor had just completed bandaging. He inspected it closely, as though looking for a flaw. "It would seem strange that just because their seigneur has decided who farmed what or who lived where in the past they cannot grasp the idea of being able to make their own decisions in the matter. Indeed you might even find that they have been doing so already, but in what you might call an informal way, without your knowledge."

"No, they are simple people, sir," Ulresile said. "One day they may be ready for such responsibility, but not yet."

"Do you know," the King said earnestly, "I don't think I was ready for the responsibility that I had to shoulder when my father died?"

"Oh, now, sir," Ormin said. "You are too modest. Of course you were ready, and have been entirely proved to be so by all manner of subsequent events. Indeed you proved so with great expedition."

"No, I don't think I was," the King said. "Certainly I didn't feel I was, and I'd bet that if you had taken a poll of all the dukes and other nobles in the court at the time—and they had been allowed to say what they really thought, not what I or my father wished to hear—they would have said to a man that I wasn't ready for that responsibility. What's more, I would have agreed with them. Yet my father died, I was forced to the throne, and although I knew I was not ready, I coped. I learned. I became a King by having to behave as one, not simply because I was my father's son and had been told long in advance that I would become so."

Ormin nodded at this.

"I'm sure we take your majesty's point," Ulresile said as Wiester and a couple of servants helped the King on with heavy ceremonial robes. The Doctor stood back to let them slide the King's arms through the sleeves before completing the tying of the bandages on his right hand.

"I think we must be brave, my friends," Duke Ormin said to Walen and Ulresile. "The King is right. We live in a new age and we must have the courage to behave in new ways. The laws of Providence may be eternal, but their application in the world must change as the times do. The King is right to commend the common sense of the farmers and the craftsmen. They have great practical experience in many things. We ought not to under-estimate their abilities simply because they are not high-born."

"Quite," the King said, drawing himself up and putting his head back to have his hair combed before it was gathered into a knot.

Ulresile looked at Ormin as though he was going to spit. "Practical experience is all very well when a man makes tables or has to control a haul pulling a plough," he said. "But we are concerning ourselves with the governance of our provinces, and in that it is ourselves who have the whole part of the experience."

The Doctor admired her handiwork on the King's bandaged hands, then stood back. The breeze brought a distinct smell of flowers and grain-dust billowing in across the bowed fabric walls of our temporary courtyard.

The King let Wiester slide his thick stave-gloves on to his hands and then lace them up. Another servant placed stout-looking but richly decorated boots in front of the King and carefully guided his feet into them. "Then, my dear Ulresile," he said, "you must teach the burghers of the towns what you know, or they will make mistakes and we shall all be the poorer, for I hope we can all expect a better crop of taxes from such improvements." The King looked to be about to sneeze, I thought.

"I'm sure the ducal estates' share of any increase will not be unappreciated, should it materialise," Duke Ormin said, with the look of one experiencing an attack of wind. "As indeed I am sure it will. Yes, I am."

The King looked at him quickly, with the heavy-lidded gaze of one about to sneeze. "Then you would be prepared to put the reforms into effect first in your province, Ormin?"

Ormin blinked, then smiled. He bowed. "It would be an honour, sir."

The King took a deep breath, then shook his head and clapped his hands together as best he could. He cast a victorious look at Ulresile, who was staring at Ormin with a look of horror and disgust.

The Doctor knelt at her bag. I thought she was going to help me put the various bits and pieces away, but instead she took out a clean square of cloth and rose to stand before the King just as he sneezed mightily, jerking his hair out of the grip of the flunky combing it and sending the comb catapulting forward on to a brightly coloured rug.

"Sir, if I may," the Doctor said. The King nodded. Wiester looked discomfited. He was only now getting out his kerchief.

The Doctor gently held the cloth up to the King's nose, letting him sniff into it. She folded the cloth and then with another corner dabbed softly at his eyes, which had moistened. "Thank you, Doctor," he said. "And what do you think of our reforms?"

"I, sir?" the Doctor said, looking surprised. "It is no business of mine."

"Now, Vosill," the King said. "You have an opinion about everything else. I assumed you would be more in favour than anybody here. Come, you must be happy with this. It's something like what you have in your precious Drezen, isn't it? You've talked about such things at inordinate length before now." He frowned. Duke Ulresile did not look happy. I saw him glance at Walen, who too appeared troubled. Duke Ormin appeared not to be listening, though his face bore a surprised expression.

The Doctor folded the cloth away slowly. "I have talked about many things to contrast the place I chose to leave with the place I chose to come to," she said, with a deliberateness equal to that she gave the folding away of that cloth.

"I'm sure nothing we could do would be good enough for the lady's high standards," Duke Ulresile said, with what sounded like bitterness, perhaps even contempt. "She has made that clear enough."

The Doctor gave a brief, small smile like a wince, and said to the King, "Sir, may I be excused now?"

"Of course, Vosill," the King said, with a look of surprise and concern. She turned to leave, and he held up his gloved hands as a servant brought forward the silver and gold inlaid staff he would fight the false monster with. In the distance, horns sounded and a cheer went up. "Thank you," he said to her. She turned back briefly to him, bowed quickly and then walked away. I followed.

My Master knows already what took place when the surprise that the old Duke Walen had spent most of a year preparing was finally visited upon the Doctor, but I shall say something of the event, in the hope of completing the picture he will already have.

The court had been back at Haspide for only two days. I had not yet finished unpacking all the Doctor's belongings. There was to be a diplomatic reception in the main hall, and the Doctor's presence had been requested. Neither she nor I knew who had made this request. She went out early that morning, saying that she was going to visit one of the hospitals she had paid regular visits to before we had left on the outer part of the Circuition earlier that year. I was instructed to stay behind and continue with the process of getting her apartments in order again. I understand that my Master had one of his people follow the Doctor, and discovered that she did indeed go to the Women's Hospital and attend some of the sick and confined there. I spent the time removing racks of glassware and vials from straw-packed cases and making a list of the fresh ingredients we would need over the next half-year for the Doctor's potions and remedies.

She returned to her apartments at about a half past the morning's third bell, bathed and changed into more formal wear, and then took me with her to the great hall.

I cannot recall there being any great air of expectation in the place, but then it was a crowded scene, with hundreds of courtiers, foreign diplomats, consular people, nobles and traders and others milling about, all no doubt concerned with their own business and quite convinced that it was more important than anybody else's and merited, if it would help them, the particular attention of the King. Certainly the Doctor seemed to have no premonition that anything strange or untoward was about to happen. If she seemed distracted it was because she wanted to get on with the matter of getting her apartments, her study and workshop and her chemical machinery back together. As we made our way to the hall, she had me note down several ingredients and raw materials she suddenly realised she would be needing in the near future.

"Ah, my dear Doctor," Duke Ormin said, pressing his way through an exotically garbed knot of incomprehensibly jabbering foreigners. "I'm told there's somebody here to see you, ma'am."

"Is there?" the Doctor asked.

"Yes," Ormin said. He stood straight for a change, and looked out over the heads of the crowd. "Our new Duke Walen and, ah, Guard Commander Adlain said something." He squinted into the distance. "Didn't catch it all and they seemed . . . Ah, there they are. Over there." The Duke waved, then looked at the Doctor. "Were you expecting anybody?"

"Expecting anybody?" the Doctor repeated as the Duke led us to one corner of the hall.

"Yes. I just . . . well, I don't know . . ."

We approached the Guard Commander. I missed whatever the Doctor and Duke Ormin said next because I was watching the Guard Commander talk to a couple of his guard captains, two intimidatingly large, stern-faced men armed with double swords. As he saw us approach, the Guard Commander nodded to the two men. They stepped away to stand a few paces off.

"Doctor," Guard Commander Adlain said in an open, friendly manner, putting his arm to one side of the Doctor as though to grasp her far shoulder, so that she had to turn to one side. "Good day. How are you? Unpacked? Are you happily re-ensconced?"

"I am well, sir. We are not yet quite fully settled in. And you?"

"Oh, I'm . . ." The Guard Commander looked behind him, then a look of some surprise came upon his face. "Ah. Here's Ulresile. And who can this be?"

He and the Doctor both turned round to face Duke Ulresile and a tall, bronzed-looking man of middle age dressed in strange, loose-fitting clothes and a small tricorn hat. Duke Ulresile was smiling with a curious eagerness. Behind him stood the new Duke Walen, his head down and his dark eyes looking half closed.

The bronzed stranger had rather a prominent nose, and perched upon it was an odd framework of metal with two coin-sized pieces of glass set in it, one in front of each eye. He took this off with one hand as though it was a hat (that was left on) and made a deep bow. I half expected his hat to fall off, but it appeared to be held in place by three jewel-headed pins.

When he straightened, the fellow spoke at the Doctor in a language quite unlike anything I had ever heard before, full of strange gutturals and odd tonal shifts.

She looked at him blankly. His friendly expression seemed to waver. Duke Walen's eyes narrowed. Ulresile's smile broadened and he took in a breath.

Then the Doctor grinned, and reached out and took the stranger's hands in hers. She laughed and shook her head and out of her mouth rattled a stream of sound that sounded very like the sort of sound the stranger had produced. In amongst all this expeditious blabbering I caught the words "Drezen" (though it sounded more like "Drechtsen"), "Pressel," "Vosill" and, several times, something that sounded like Koo-doon. The pair of them stood beaming huge smiles at each other and talking in a continuous stream of sound, all the time laughing and nodding and shaking their heads. I watched the smile on Duke

Ulresile's face fade slowly, withering like a cut flower. The sullen, hooded expression on the new Duke Walen's face did not alter. The Guard Commander Adlain looked on with a fascinated expression, his gaze flitting to Ulresile now and again, a tiny smile playing around his lips.

"Oelph," I heard the Doctor say, and she turned to me. "Oelph," she said again, holding one hand out to me. She was still grinning broadly. "This is gaan Kuduhn, from Drezen! Gaan Kuduhn," she said to the foreigner. "Blabber blabber Oelph," (well it sounded so to me) she said to him. I recalled that the Doctor had told me that a gaan was some sort of part-time diplomatic rank.

The tall, bronzed man took the wire contraption off his nose again and bowed to me. "I ham press to meet yore, Welph," he said slowly in something resembling Haspidian.

"How do you do, Mr. Kuduhn," I said, also bowing.

She introduced Duke Ormin too. The gaan had already met Walen, Ulresile and the Guard Commander.

"The gaan is from an island in the same group as my own," the Doctor said. She looked quite flushed and excited. "He was invited here from Cuskery by the old Duke Walen to discuss trade. He took a quite different route to mine but it seems to have taken him just as long. He has been away from Drezen almost as long as I have so he has little fresh news, but it is just so good to hear Drezeni spoken again!" She turned her smile to him again as she said, "I think I shall see if I can persuade him to stay and found a proper embassy." She started blabbering to him again.

Ulresile and Walen looked at each other. Guard Commander Adlain looked up at the ceiling of the great hall for a moment, then he made a small tutting noise. "Well, gentlemen," he said to the three Dukes. "I think we are somewhat surplus to requirements here, don't you?"

Duke Ormin gave a distracted, "Hmm." The other two men glared on at the Doctor and the gaan Kuduhn with what looked like disappointment, though in the new Duke Walen's case this required no alteration to his normal expression.

"Fascinating though I'm sure this exchange is in its native language, I have other business to attend to," Adlain said. "If you'll excuse me . . ." He nodded to the Dukes and walked off, nodding to the two bulky guard captains, who followed in his wake.

"Duke Walen, Duke Ulresile," the Doctor said, still smiling. "Thank you so much. I am most flattered you thought to introduce me to the gaan with such dispatch."

The new Duke Walen remained silent. Ulresile seemed to swallow something bitter. "Our pleasure, madam."

"Is the gaan required for an audience with the King?" she asked.

"No, he is not required for an audience with the King," Ulresile said.

"Then may I take him from you for a while? I'd so much like to talk with him."

Ulresile tipped his head and gave a small twist of a smile. "Please. Be our guest."

Master, I spent a bell and a half with the Doctor and her new-found friend in an alcove off the Song Court Gallery and learned nothing except that Drezeni talk like the world is due to end at any moment and sometimes take their wine with water and a little sugar. The gaan Kuduhn did have an audience with the King later that day, and asked the Doctor to interpret for him, as his Imperial was little better than his Haspidian. She agreed happily.

That afternoon, I was sent by myself to the apothecary Shavine to buy chemicals and other supplies for the Doctor's workshop. The Doctor looked quite radiant when I left, dressing and preparing with great care for her meeting with the gaan Kuduhn and the King. When I inquired, I was told that I would not be needed again until the evening.

It was a fine, warm day. I took the long way to the apothecary's, walking down by the docks and recalling the stormy night half a year earlier when I had come here in search of the children who had been sent for ice. I recalled the child in the cramped, filthy room in the tenement in the poor quarter and the terrible fever that had killed her despite all the Doctor could do.

The docks smelled of fish and tar and the sea.

Clutching a hamper of glazed clay jars and glass tubes all wrapped in straw, I stopped off at a tavern. I tried some wine with water and sugar, but it was not to my taste. For some time I just sat and stared at the street through the open window. I returned to the palace around the fourth bell of the evening.

The door to the Doctor's apartments hung open. This was not like her. I hesitated to proceed further, suddenly filled with a sense of dread. I entered and found a pair of short dress boots and a small formal waist-cape lying on the floor of the sitting room. I put my hamper of chemicals and ingredients down on the table and went through to the workshop, where I could hear a voice.

The Doctor sat with her feet up on the workshop bench, her naked heels resting on a sheaf of papers, her legs exposed to the knee and the neck of her gown unbuttoned over her chest. Her long copper-red hair hung down loose behind her. One of the room's roof-hung censers swung in slow loops above her head, leaving a smoky, herb-scented trail. Her battered old knife lay on the bench by her elbow. She held a goblet. Her face looked red about the eyes. I got the impression she had been talking to herself. She turned to me and fixed me with a watery look.

"Ah, Oelph," she said.

"Mistress? Are you all right?"

"Oh, not really, Oelph." She picked up a jug. "Want a drink?"

I looked around. "Shall I just close the apartment door?"

She appeared to consider this. "Yes," she said. "Closing doors seems to be the order of the day. Why not? Then come back and have a drink. It's sad to drink alone."

I went and closed the door, found a goblet and brought another chair into the workshop to sit with her. She poured some liquor into my goblet.

I looked into the vessel. The liquid did not smell. "What is this, mistress?"

"Alcohol," she said. "Very pure." She sniffed at it. "Though it still has an intriguing bouquet."

"Mistress, is this the distillation you have the royal apothecary make for us?"

"The same," she said, drinking from her goblet.

I sipped at it, then coughed and tried not to splutter it back out again. "It's strong, isn't it?" I said hoarsely.

"It needs to be," the Doctor said in a morose tone.

"What is wrong, mistress?"

She looked at me. After a moment or two she said, "I am a very foolish woman, Oelph."

"Mistress, you are the cleverest and most wise woman I have ever met, indeed you are one of the cleverest and most wise people I have ever met."

"You are too kind, Oelph," she said, staring into her goblet. "But I am still foolish. Nobody is smart in every way. It's as though we all have to have something we're stupid about. I have just been very stupid with the King."

"With the King, mistress?" I asked, worried.

"Yes, Oelph. With the King."

"Mistress, I am sure the King is most considerate and understanding and will not hold whatever you have done against you. Indeed perhaps the offence, if offence there was, seems greater to you than it does to him."

"Oh, it wasn't much of an offence, Oelph, it was just . . . stupidity."

"I find that hard to believe, mistress."

"Me too. I find it hard to believe. But I did it."

I took the merest sip from my goblet. "Can you tell me what happened, mistress?"

She looked unsteadily at me again. "Will you keep what I tell you . . ." she began, and I confess that my heart seemed to sink into my boots at these words. But I was saved from a further extension of my perjury and betrayal, or from a wantonly rash admission of my own, by her next words. "Oh, no," she said, shaking her head and rubbing her face with her free hand. "No, it doesn't matter. People will hear if the King wants them to. It doesn't matter anyway. Who cares?"

I said nothing. She bit her lower lip, then took another drink. She smiled sadly at me as she said, "I told the King how I feel about him, Oelph," she said, and sighed. She gave a shrug as though to say, Well, there you are.

I looked down at the floor. "And how is that, mistress?" I asked quietly.

"I think you might be able to guess, Oelph," she said.

I found that I too was biting my lip now. I took a drink, for something to do. "I'm sure we both love the King, mistress."

"Everybody loves the King," she said bitterly. "Or says that they do. It is what one is supposed to feel, what one is obliged to feel. I felt something else. Something it was very stupid and unprofessional of me to admit to, but I did. After the audience with gaan Kuduhn—you know I do believe that old bastard Walen thought he was setting me up?" she said, as though interrupting herself. I choked on my drink. I was unused to hearing the Doctor swear. It distressed me. "Yes," she said. "I think he thought that I wasn't . . . that I was . . . well, anyway, it was after the audience with the gaan. We were alone. Just him and me. A stiff neck. I don't know," she said miserably. "Maybe I was excited at having met somebody from home."

Suddenly she sobbed, and I looked up to see her bending forward so that her head was lowered towards her knees. She put the goblet down with a thud on the workbench and held her head in her hands. "Oh, Oelph," she whispered. "I have done such terrible things."

I stared at her, wondering what in Providence she could be talking about. She sniffed, wiped her eyes and nose with her sleeve, then put her hand out to the goblet again. It hesitated by the old dagger lying nearby, then grasped the goblet and brought it towards her lips. "I can't believe I did that, Oelph. I can't believe that I told him. And do you know what he told me?" she asked, with a hopeless, wavering smile. I shook my head.

"He told me that of course he knew. Did I think he was stupid? And oh, he was flattered, but it would be even more unwise for him to respond to me than it had been for me to make the declaration in the first place. Besides, he only liked, he only felt comfortable with pretty, dainty, delicate women who had no brains. That was what he liked. Not wit, not intelligence, certainly not learning." She snorted. "Vacuity. That's what he wants. A pretty face fronting an empty head! Ha!" She threw back the last of her drink, then refilled the goblet, spilling some of the liquor on her gown and the floor.

"You fucking cretin, Vosill," she muttered to herself.

My blood ran cold at her words. I wanted to hug her, to hold her, to take her in my arms . . . and at the same time I wanted to be anywhere else but there, then.

"He wants stupidity, well . . . Oh, do you see the irony of it, Oelph?" she said. "The only moronic thing I've done since I landed was to tell him I loved him. It was utterly, completely, definitively and absolutely imbecilic, and yet it still isn't enough. He wants consistent dim-wittedness." She stared into her goblet. "Can't say I blame him." She drank. She coughed, and had to put the goblet down on the bench. The goblet's base settled on her old dagger, so that the vessel over-balanced and fell with a crash to the floor, breaking and splashing the alcohol across the boards. She brought her feet down from the bench and put them under the chair she sat on, her head in her hands again as she curled up and started to weep.

"Oh, Oelph," she cried. "What have I done?" She rocked to and fro on the seat, her face buried in her hands, her long fingers like a cage around her tangle of red hair. "What have I done? What have I done?"

I felt terrified. I did not know what to do. I had been feeling so mature, so grown up, so capable and in control over these last couple of seasons, but now I felt like a child again, quite perfectly unsure what to do when confronted with the pain and distress of an adult.

I hesitated, a terrible feeling growing in me that whatever I did next it would be the wrong thing, the wrong thing entirely, and I would suffer for it for ever more and worse still so might she, but eventually, while she rocked back and forth and moaned piteously to herself, I put my goblet down at my feet and got out of my seat and went to squat by her. I reached out one hand and placed it gently on her shoulder. She did not react. I let my hand go back and forth with her rocking, then slid my arm further round her shoulders. Somehow, touching her like that, she suddenly seemed smaller than I had always thought her.

Still she did not seem to think I had committed any terrible transgression by touching her so, and, finding my courage and taking it by the scruff of its neck, I moved closer to her and put both my arms around her, holding her, slowly stopping her rocking, feeling the warmth of her body and tasting the sweet air of her breath. She let me hold her.

I was doing what I had imagined doing only moments earlier, doing something I had imagined doing for the last year, something I thought would never, could never happen, something I had dreamed about night after night after night for season upon season, and something that I had hoped, and still hoped somehow might lead to an even more intimate embrace, no matter that that had seemed almost absurdly unlikely, and indeed still did.

I felt her grip on her head loosen. She brought her arms out and put them round me. Embraced by her. My head seemed to swim. Her face, hot and wet from her tears, was next to mine now. I shook with terror, wondering if I dare turn my face towards hers, bring my mouth close to her lips.

"Oh, Oelph," she said into my shoulder. "It is not fair to use you so."

"You may use me as you wish, mistress," I said, gulping on the words. I could smell some delicate perfume rising from her warm body, its tender scent not swamped by the fumes of the alcohol, and infinitely more heady. "Is it . . . ?" I began, then had to stop to swallow on a dry mouth. "Is it so terrible to take the risk of telling somebody the feelings you have for them, even if you suspect they feel nothing similar for you? Is it wrong, mistress?"

She pushed herself gently away from me. Her face, tear-streaked, puffy-eyed and red, was still calmly beautiful. Her eyes seemed to search mine. "It is never wrong, Oelph," she said softly. She reached down and took both my hands in hers. "But I am no more blind than the King. Nor any more able to offer requital."

I wondered stupidly what she meant for a moment before realising, and feeling a terrible sadness fall slowly on my soul, as though a great shroud had been dropped inside me, settling with a sorrowful, implacable inevitability over all my hopes and dreams, obliterating them for ever.

She put one hand to my cheek, and her fingers were still warm and dry and tender and firm at once, and her skin, I swear, smelled sweet. "You are very precious to me, dear Oelph."

I heard those words and my heart sank farther, and steeper.

"Am I, mistress?"

"Of course." She drew away from me and looked down at the smashed goblet. "Of course you are." She settled back in her seat and took a deep breath, pushing a hand through her hair, smoothing down her gown and attempting to button its yoke. Her fingers would not do as she willed. I longed, from far away, to help her, or rather not to help her with that task, but eventually she gave up anyway, and just pulled the long collar to. She looked up into my face, drying her cheeks with her fingers. "I think I need to sleep, Oelph. Will you excuse me, please?"

I lifted my goblet from the floor and put it on the workbench. "Of course, mistress. Is there anything I can do?"

"No." She shook her head. "No, there is nothing you can do." She looked away.

20
THE BODYGUARD

"I told the boy a story of my own."

"You did?"

"Yes. It was a pack of lies."

"Well, all stories are lies, in a way."

"This was worse. This was a true story turned into a lie."

"You must have felt there was a reason to do that."

"Yes, I did."

"What was the reason you felt that way?"

"Because I wanted to tell the story, but I could not tell it truly to a child. It is the only story I know worth telling, the story I think most about, the story that I live again and again in my dreams, the story that feels as if it needs to be told, and yet a child could not understand it, or if they could, it would be an inhuman thing to tell them it."

"Hmm. It doesn't sound like a story you have ever told me."

"Shall I tell it to you now?"

"It sounds like a painful story to tell."

"It is. Perhaps it is painful to hear, too."

"Do you want to tell it to me?"

"I don't know."

The Protector returned to his palace. His son still lived, though his grip on life seemed tenuous and frail. Doctor BreDelle took over from Doctor AeSimil but he was no more able to determine what was wrong with the boy than he was able to treat him successfully. Lattens drifted in and out of consciousness, sometimes unable to recognise his father or his nurse, on other occasions sitting up in bed and pronouncing himself feeling much better and almost recovered. These periods of lucidity and apparent recovery grew further and further apart, however, and the boy spent more and more time curled up in his bed, asleep or in a halfway stage between sleep and wakefulness, eyes closed, limbs twitching, muttering to himself, turning and moving and jerking as though in a fit. He ate almost nothing, and would drink only water or very diluted fruit juice.

DeWar still worried that Lattens might be being poisoned in some subtle way. He arranged with the Protector and the superintendent of an orphans' home that a set of twins be brought to the palace to act as tasters for the boy. The two identical boys were a year younger than Lattens. They were slightly built and a poor start in life had left them with delicate constitutions which made them prone to any passing illness. Nevertheless, they thrived while Lattens weakened, happily finishing off each of the meals he barely tasted, so that by the proportion consumed it might have seemed to a casual observer that it was he who tasted the food for them.

For a few days after their even more hurried return to Crough, UrLeyn and those in his immediate party had out-distanced the news from Ladenscion, and there was a frustrating lack of new intelligence from the war. UrLeyn stamped about the palace, unable to settle to anything, and found little solace even in the harem. The younger girls in particular only made him annoyed with their simpering attempts at sympathy, and he spent more time with Perrund than with all of them, just sitting talking on most occasions.

A hunt was arranged, but the Protector called it off just before it started, worried that the chase might take him too far away from the palace and the sick bed of his son. He attempted to apply himself to the many other affairs of state, but could find little patience for courtiers, provincial representatives or foreign dignitaries. He spent longer in the palace library, reading old accounts of history and the lives of ancient heroes.

When news did eventually arrive from Ladenscion it was equivocal. Another city had been taken but yet more men and war machines had been lost. A few of the barons had indicated that they wanted to discuss terms that would let them remain loyal to Tassasen in theory and through token tribute, but retain the independence they had achieved through their rebellion. As generals Ralboute and Simalg understood that this was not a course the Protector wished to pursue, more troops were called for. It was to be hoped that as this news had undoubtedly crossed with the fresh soldiers already on their way to the war, this last request was redundant. This intelligence had been delivered in a coded letter and there seemed little to debate or discuss as a result of it, but UrLeyn convened a full war cabinet in the map-hall nevertheless. DeWar was invited to attend but commanded not to speak.

"Perhaps the best thing would be for you to take yourself away, brother."

"Take myself away? What? Go on an improving tour? Visit some old aunt in the countryside? What do you think you mean, 'take myself away'?"

"I mean that perhaps the best thing would be for you to be somewhere else," RuLeuin said, frowning.

"The best thing, brother," UrLeyn said, "would be for my son to make a full and swift recovery, the war in Ladenscion to end immediately in total victory, and my advisors and family to stop suggesting idiocies."

DeWar hoped RuLeuin would hear the annoyance in his brother's voice and take the hint, but he kept on. "Well then," he said, "the better thing, I should have said, rather than the best, might be to go to Ladenscion, perhaps. To take on all the responsibilities of the war's command and so to have less room in your mind for the worry the boy's illness must be causing you."

DeWar, sitting just behind UrLeyn at the head of the map table, could see some of the others looking at RuLeuin with expressions of disapproval and even mild scorn.

UrLeyn shook his head angrily. "Great Providence, brother, what do you think I am? Were either of us raised to be so lacking in feeling? Can you simply turn off your emotions? I cannot, and I would treat with the gravest suspicion anybody who claimed they could. They would not be a man, they would be a machine. An animal. Providence, even animals have emotions." UrLeyn glanced round the others gathered about the table, as though daring any of them to assert such coldness for themselves. "I can't leave the boy like this. I did try to, as you may recall, and I was called back. Would you have me go and then be worrying about him every day and night? Would you have me there in Ladenscion while my heart was here, taking command but unable to give it my full attention?"

RuLeuin finally seemed to see the wisdom in remaining silent. He pressed his lips together and studied the table top in front of him.

"We are here to discuss what to do about this damned war," UrLeyn said, gesturing at the map of Tassasen's borders spread out in the centre of the great table. "The condition of my son keeps me here in Crough but other than that it has no bearing on our meeting. I'll thank you not to mention it again." He glared at RuLeuin, who still stared tight-lipped at the table. "Now, has anyone anything to say which might actually prove useful?"

"What is to be said, sir?" ZeSpiole said. "We are told little in this latest news. The war continues. The barons wish to keep what they hold. We are too far from it to be able to contribute much. Unless it is to agree to what the barons propose."

"That is scarcely more helpful," UrLeyn told the Guard Commander impatiently.

"We can send more troops," YetAmidous said. "But I wouldn't

advise it. We have few enough left to defend the capital as it is, and the other provinces have been stripped bare already."

"It is true, sir," said VilTere, a young provincial commander called to the capital with a company of light cannon. VilTere's father had been an old comrade of UrLeyn's during the war of succession and the Protector had invited him to the meeting. "If we take too many men to punish the barons we might be seen to encourage others to emulate them by leaving our provinces devoid of policing."

"If we punish the barons severely enough," UrLeyn said, "we might be able to convince these 'others' of the folly of such a course."

"Indeed, sir," the provincial commander said. "But first we must do so, and then they must hear about it."

"They'll hear about it," UrLeyn said darkly. "I have lost all patience with this war. I will accept nothing else than complete victory. No further negotiations will be entered into. I am sending word to Simalg and Ralboute that they must do all they can to capture the barons, and when they do they are to send them here like common thieves, though better guarded. They will be dealt with most severely."

BiLeth looked stricken. UrLeyn noticed. "Yes, BiLeth?" he snapped.

The foreign minister looked even more discomfited. "I . . ." he began. "I, well . . ."

"What, man?" UrLeyn shouted. The tall foreign minister jumped in his seat, his long, thin grey hair flouncing briefly.

"Are you . . . is the Protector quite . . . it's just that, sir . . ."

"Great Providence, BiLeth!" UrLeyn roared. "You're not going to *disagree* with me, are you? Finally found a sliver of backbone, have we? Where in the skies of hell did that fall from?"

BiLeth looked grey. "I do beg the Protector's pardon. I would simply beg to ask him reconsider treating the barons in quite such a fashion," he said, a desperate, anguished look on his narrow face.

"How the fuck should I treat the bastards?" UrLeyn asked, his voice low but seething with derision. "They make war on us, they make fools of us, they make widows of our women-folk." UrLeyn slammed a fist on to the table, making the map of the borderlands flap in the breeze. "How in the name of all the old gods am I *supposed* to treat the sons of bitches?"

BiLeth looked as if he was about to cry. Even DeWar felt slightly sorry for him. "But sir," the foreign minister said in a small voice, "several of the barons are related to the Haspidian royal family. There are matters of diplomatic etiquette when dealing with nobility, even if they are rebellious. If we can but prise one away from the others and treat with him well, then perhaps we can bring him to our side. I understand—"

"You understand very little, it would seem, sir," UrLeyn told him in a voice dripping with scorn. BiLeth seemed to shrink in his seat. "I'll have no more talk of etiquette," he said, spitting out the word. "It has become clear that these scum have been teasing us," UrLeyn told BiLeth and the others. "They play the seductress, these proud barons. They act the coquette. They hint that they might succumb to us if we treat them just a little better, that they will be ours if only we flatter them a little more, if only we can find it in our hearts and our pockets to provide them with a few more gifts, a few more tokens of our esteem, why then they will open their gates, then they will help us with their less cooperative friends and all their resistance so far will prove to have been for show, a pretty fight they have been putting up for the sake of their maidenly honour." UrLeyn hit the table again. "Well, *no!* We have been led along for the last time. The next leading will be done by an executioner, when he pulls on the chain of one of these proud barons and brings him to the public square to be tormented like a common murderer and then put up to burn. We'll see how the rest of them respond to that!"

YetAmidous slapped the table with the flat of his hand and stood up out of his seat. "Well said, sir! That's the spirit!"

ZeSpiole watched BiLeth shrink further in his seat, and exchanged looks with RuLeuin, who looked down. ZeSpiole pursed his lips and studied the map on the table. The others gathered round the table— lesser generals, advisors and aides—busied themselves in a variety of other ways, but none looked directly at the Protector or said anything in contradiction.

UrLeyn gazed round at their faces with a look of mocking admonition. "What, is there nobody else to take my foreign minister's side?" he asked, waving one hand at the subsiding form that was BiLeth. "Is he to remain alone and unseconded in his campaign?"

Nobody said anything. "ZeSpiole?" UrLeyn said.

The Guard Commander looked up. "Sir?"

"Do you think I am right? Should I refuse to entertain any further advances from our rebellious barons?"

ZeSpiole took a deep breath. "I think we might profitably threaten the barons with what you have mentioned, sir."

"And, if we take one, carry it out, yes?"

ZeSpiole studied the great fan of window on the wall opposite, where glass and semi-precious stones shone with sunlight. "I can appreciate the prospect of seeing one of the barons so humbled, sir. And as you say, there are enough widows in this city who would cheer his screams sufficient to drown them out."

"You see no intemperateness in such a course, sir?" UrLeyn asked reasonably. "No rashness, no cruel impetuousness which might rebound on us?"

"That would be a possibility, perhaps," ZeSpiole said, with a flicker of uncertainty.

"A 'possibility,' 'perhaps'?" UrLeyn said in a voice that mocked the Guard Commander's. "But we must do better than that, Commander! This is an important matter. One that needs our gravest consideration. We cannot make light of it, can we? Or perhaps not. Perhaps you disagree. Do you disagree, Commander?"

"I agree that we must think hard about what we are going to do, sir," ZeSpiole said, his voice and manner serious.

"Good, Commander," UrLeyn said with what appeared to be sincerity. "I am glad we have extracted a hint of decision from you." He looked round everybody else. "Are there any other views I should hear from any of you?" Heads went down all around the table.

DeWar began to be thankful that the Protector had not thought to turn round and ask him his opinion. Indeed he still worried that he might. He suspected nothing he could say would make the General happy.

"Sir?" said VilTere. All eyes turned to the young provincial commander. DeWar hoped he wasn't going to say something stupid.

UrLeyn glared. "What, sir?"

"Sir, I was, sadly, too young to be a soldier during the war of succession, but I have heard from many a commander whose opinion I respect and who served under you that your judgment has always proved sure and your decisions far-sighted. They told me that even when they doubted your decree, they trusted you, and that trust was vindicated. They would not be where they are, and we would not be here today"—at this the young commander looked round the others— "were it otherwise."

The other faces round the table searched UrLeyn's for a response before they reacted.

UrLeyn nodded slowly. "Perhaps I should take it ill," he said, "that it is our most junior and most recently arrived recruit who holds the highest opinion of my faculties."

DeWar thought he detected a sense of cautious relief around the table.

"I'm sure we all feel the same way, sir," said ZeSpiole with an indulgent smile to VilTere and a cautious one to UrLeyn.

"Very well," UrLeyn said. "We shall consider what fresh troops we might be able to send to Ladenscion and we shall tell Ralboute and Simalg to prosecute the war against the barons without respite or negotiation. Gentlemen." With that, and a perfunctory nod, UrLeyn rose and marched away. DeWar followed.

"Then let me tell you something closer to the truth."

"Only closer?"

"Sometimes the truth is too much to bear."

"I have a strong constitution."

"Yes, but I meant that sometimes it is too much for the teller, not the told."

"Ah. Well then, tell me what you can."

"Oh, there is not so much, now I approach it. And it is a common story. All too common. The less I tell you of it the more you could be hearing it from a hundred, a thousand, ten thousand mouths or more."

"I have a feeling it is not a happy story."

"Indeed. Anything but. It is just that of women, especially young women, caught up in a war."

"Ah."

"You see? A story that scarcely needs to be told. The ingredients imply the finished article, and the method of its making, do they not? It is men who fight wars, wars are fought taking villages, towns and cities, where women tend the hearths, and when the place that they live is taken, so are they. Their honour becomes one of the spoils, their bodies too invaded. That territory taken. So my story is no different from that of tens of thousands of women, regardless of their nation or their tribe. And yet for me it is everything. For me it is the most important thing that ever happened to me. For me it was the end of my life, and what you see before you is like a ghost, a spirit, a mere shade, unsubstantial."

"Please, Perrund." He reached out his hands towards her in a gesture that required no response and did not seek to end in a touch. It was instead a movement of sympathy, even supplication. "If this hurts you so, you don't need to continue for me."

"Ah, but does it hurt you, DeWar?" she asked, and there was a sharp edge of bitterness and accusation in her voice. "Does it make you embarrassed? I know you have a regard for me, DeWar. We are friends." These two sentences were uttered too quickly for him to be able to react. "Are you upset on my behalf, or your own? Most men would rather not hear what their fellows have done, what people who may indeed be very like them are capable of. Do you prefer not to think about such things, DeWar? Do you think that you are so different? Or do you become secretly excited at the idea?"

"Lady, I gain no benefit or pleasure at all from the subject."

"Are you sure, DeWar? And if you are, do you really think you speak for the majority of your sex? For are women not supposed to resist even those they would happily surrender to, so that when they resist a more brutal violation how can the man be sure that any struggle, any protestation is not merely for show?"

"You must believe that we are not all the same. And even if all men might be said to have . . . base urges, we do not all give in to them, or pay them any respect, even in secret. I cannot tell you how sorry I am to hear what happened to you . . ."

"But you have not heard, DeWar. You have not heard at all. I have implied that I was raped. That did not kill me. That alone might have killed the girl I was and replaced her with a woman, with a bitter one, with an angry one, or one who wished to take her own life, or attempt to take the life of those who violated her, or one who simply became mad.

"I think I might have become angry and bitter and I would have hated all men, but I think I would have survived and might have been persuaded, by the good men I knew in my own family and in my own town, and perhaps by one good man in particular who must now for ever remain in my dreams, that all was not lost and the world was not quite so terrible a place.

"But I never had that opportunity to recover, DeWar. I was pushed so far down in my despair I could not even tell in which direction the way back up lay. What happened to me was the least of it, DeWar. I watched my father and my brothers butchered, after they had been forced to watch my mother and my sisters being fucked time after time by a fine and numerous company of high-ranking men. Oh! You look down! Does my language upset you? Are you offended? Have I violated your ears with my intemperate, soldiers' words?"

"Perrund, you must believe that I am sorry for what happened to you . . ."

"But why should you be sorry? It was not your fault. You were not there. You assure me that you disapprove, so why should you be sorry?"

"I would be bitter in your place."

"In my place? How could that be, DeWar? You are a man. In the same place you would be, if not one of the violators, one of those who looked away, or remonstrated with their comrades afterwards."

"If I was the age you were then, and a pretty youth—"

"Ah, so you can share what happened to me. I see. That is good. I am comforted."

"Perrund, say anything you want to me. Blame me if it will help, but please believe I . . ."

"Believe you what, DeWar? I believe you feel sorry for me, but your sympathy stings like salty tears in a wound because I am a proud ghost, you see. Oh yes, a proud ghost. I am an enraged shade, and a guilty one, because I have come to admit to myself that I resent what was done to my family because it hurt me, because I was raised to expect everything to be done for me.

"I loved my parents and my sisters in my own way, but it was not a selfless love. I loved them because they loved me and made me feel special. I was their baby, their chosen beloved. Through their devotion and protection I learned none of the lessons that children usually learn, about the way the world really works and the way that children are used within it, until that single day, that one morning when every fond illusion I held was torn from me and the brutal truth forced into me.

"I had come to expect the best of everything, I had come to believe that the world would always treat me as I had been treated in the past and that those I loved would be there to love me in return. My fury at what happened to my family is partly caused by that expectation, that happy assumption, being defiled and obliterated. That is my guilt."

"Perrund, you must know that should not be a cause for guilt. What you feel is what any decent child feels when they realise the selfishness they have felt when they were younger still. A selfishness that is only natural to children, especially those who have been loved so intensely. The realisation occurs, it is felt briefly and then it is rightly set aside. You have not been able to set yours aside because of what those men did to you, but—"

"Oh, stop, stop! Do you think I do not know all this? I know it, but I am a *ghost*, DeWar! I know, but I cannot feel, I cannot learn, I cannot change. I am stuck, I am pinned to that time by that event. I am condemned."

"There is nothing I can do or say that can alter what happened to you, Perrund. I can only listen, only do what you will let me do."

"Oh, do I persecute you? Do I make you a victim now, DeWar?"

"No, Perrund."

"No, Perrund. No, Perrund. Ah, DeWar, the luxury of being able to say No."

He went, half kneeling, half on his haunches by her then, putting himself very near to her but still not touching her, his knee near hers, his shoulder by her hip, his hands within grasp of hers. He was close enough to smell her perfume, close enough to feel the heat from her body, close enough to feel the hot breath that laboured from her nose and her half-open mouth, close enough for one hot tear to hit her clenched fist and spatter even tinier droplets on to his cheek. He kept his head bowed, and crossed his hands on his raised knee.

The bodyguard DeWar and the court concubine Perrund were in one of the palace's more secret places. It was an old hiding hole in one of the lower levels, a space the size of a cupboard which led off one of the public rooms in the original noble house which had formed the basis of the greater building.

Retained more for sentimental than practical reasons by the first monarch of Tassasen and through a kind of indifference by subsequent rulers, the rooms which had seemed so grand to that first king had long since been judged too small and mean of proportion by future generations and were nowadays used only for storage.

The tiny room had been used to spy on people. It was a listening post. Unlike the alcove DeWar had burst from to attack the Sea Company assassin, it was not built for a guard but for a noble, so that he could sit there, with only a small hole in the stonework between him and the public room—that hole perhaps hidden by a tapestry or painting—and listen to what his guests were saying about him.

Perrund and DeWar had come here after she had asked him to show her some of the parts of the palace he had discovered on the wanderings which she knew he took. Shown this tiny room, it had suddenly reminded her of the secret compartment in their house in which her parents had concealed her when the town was sacked during the war of succession.

"If I knew who those men were, DeWar, would you be my champion? Would you avenge my honour?" she asked him.

He looked up into her eyes. They looked extraordinarily bright in the dim light of the hidden room. "Yes," he said. "If you knew who they were. If you could be sure. Would you ask me to?"

She shook her head angrily. She wiped away her tears with her hand. "No. The ones I could identify are dead now, anyway."

"Who were they?"

"King's men," Perrund said, looking up and away from DeWar, as though telling the small hole where the ancient noble had thought to eavesdrop on his guests. "The old King's men. One of his baron commanders and his friends. They had been in charge of the siege and the taking of the town. Apparently we were favoured. Whoever was their spy had told them my father's house held the town's most comely maidens. They came to us first, and my father tried to offer them money to leave us alone. They took that badly. A merchant offering a noble man money!" She looked down at her lap, where her good hand, still damp with tears, lay beside her wasted hand in its sling. "I knew all their names, eventually. All the noble ones, at any rate. They died during the rest of the course of the war. I tried to tell myself that I felt good when I heard about the first few dying, but I did not. I could not. I felt nothing. That was when I knew I was dead inside. They had planted death in me."

DeWar waited a long time before he said, softly, "And yet you live, and you saved the life of the one who ended the war and brought about a better law. There is no right of—"

"Ah, DeWar, there is always the right of the strong to take the weak and the rich to take the poor and the powerful to take those who have no power. UrLeyn may have written down our laws and changed a few of them, but the laws that still bind us to the animals cut the deepest. Men compete for power, they strut and parade and they impress their fellows with their possessions and they take the women they can. None of that has changed. They may use weapons other than their hands and teeth, they may use other men and they may express their dominance in money, not other symbols of power and glamour, but . . ."

"And yet," DeWar insisted, "still you are alive. And there are people who have the highest regard for you and feel their lives have been the better for having known you. Did you not say you had found a type of peace and contentment here, in the palace?"

"In the harem of the chief," she said, though with something more like measured disdain than the fury that had been in her voice earlier. "As a cripple kept on out of sympathy in the collection of mates for the foremost male of the pack."

"Oh, come. We may act like animals, men especially. But we are not animals. If we were there would not be the shame in acting so. We act otherwise, too, and set a better marker. Where is love in what you say of where you are now? Do you not feel even slightly loved, Perrund?"

She reached out quickly and put her hand on his cheek, letting it rest there, as easily and naturally as though they were brother and sister or a husband and wife, long married.

"As you say, DeWar, our shame comes from the comparison. We know we might be generous and compassionate and good, and could behave so, yet something else in our nature makes us otherwise." She smiled a small, empty smile. "Yes, I feel something I recognise as love. Something I remember, something I may discuss and mull and theorise over." She shook her head. "But it is not something I know. I am like a blind woman talking about how a tree must look, or a cloud. Love is something I have a dim memory of, the way someone who went blind in their early childhood might recall the sun, or the face of their mother. I know affection from my fellow whore-wives, DeWar, and I sense regard from you and feel some in return. I have a duty to the Protector, just as he feels he has a duty to me. As far as that goes, I am content. But love? That is for the living, and I am dead."

She stood, before he could say more. "Now, please, take me back to the harem."

21
THE DOCTOR

I do not believe the Doctor thought there was anything amiss. I know I did not suspect anything. The gaan Kuduhn seemed to have disappeared as quickly as he had arrived, taking ship for far Chuenruel the day after we'd met him, which left the Doctor a little sad. There had, when I thought about it later, been hints that the palace was preparing for a large contingent of new guests—a degree more activity in certain corridors than one might have expected, doors being used that were not normally open, rooms being aired—but none of it was particularly obvious, and the web of rumour that connected all the servants, assistants, apprentices and pages had not yet woken up to what was going on.

It was the second day of the second moon. My mistress was visiting the old Untouchable Quarter, where once the lowest classes, foreigners, bondagers and quarantiners were forced to dwell. It was still a far from salubrious area, but no longer walled and patrolled. It was there that the Master Chemicalist and Metaliciser (or so he styled himself) Chelgre had his workshop.

The Doctor had risen very late that morning and seemed much the worse for wear for about a bell or so. She sighed heavily and frequently, she said little to me but rather muttered to herself, she appeared a trifle unsteady on her feet and her face was pale. However, she shook off the effects of her hangover with astonishing rapidity, and while she remained subdued for the rest of the morning and the afternoon, she seemed otherwise back to normal after her late breakfast, just before we set off for the Untouchable Quarter.

Of what had been said the night before, not a further word was spoken. I think both of us were a little embarrassed at what we had admitted and implied to each other, and so achieved an unspoken but fully mutual agreement to keep our own counsel on the subject.

Master Chelgre was his usual strange and singular self. He was of course well known around the Court, both for his wild-haired and ragged appearance and his abilities with cannons and their dark powder. I need say no more for the purposes of this report. Besides, the Doctor and Chelgre talked of nothing that I could understand.

We returned by the fifth bell of the afternoon, on foot but escorted by a couple of barrow boys pushing a small cart loaded with straw-wrapped clays containing yet more chemicals and ingredients for what I was starting to suspect would be a long season of experiments and potions.

At the time, I recall feeling mildly resentful of this, for I did not doubt that I would be heavily involved in whatever the Doctor had in mind, and that my efforts would be in addition to those domestic tasks she had come to rely on me performing as a matter of course. To me, I strongly suspected, would fall most of the weighing and measuring and grinding and combining and diluting and washing and scouring and polishing and so on which this new batch of observations would require. There would be proportionately less time for me to spend with my fellows, playing cards and flirting with the kitchen girls, and, without being shy about it, that sort of thing had become relatively important to me in the past year.

Even so, I suppose, it could be said that in some cellar of my soul I was secretly pleased to be so relied upon by the Doctor and was looking forward to being crucially involved with her efforts. These would, after all, mean us being together, working as a team, working as equals, closeted in her study and workshop, passing many happily intense evenings and nights together, striving for a shared goal. Could I not hope that a greater regard might blossom in such intimate circumstances, now that she knew it was in my thoughts? The Doctor had been decisively rejected by the one she loved, or at least the one she believed she loved, while the manner in which she had declined the connotation of my interest in her seemed to me to be more to do with modesty than hostility or even indifference.

Yet I did feel a degree of petulance towards the ingredients being wheeled up the street in front of us that evening. How I regretted that feeling, so soon afterwards. How unsure that future I had envisaged for myself and her really was.

A warm wind seemed to blow us up the Market Square towards the Blister Gate, where long shadows advanced to meet us. We entered the palace. The Doctor paid the barrow boys off and a handful of servants were summoned to help me carry the clays, crates and boxes up to our apartments. I laboured under a rotund clay I knew was full of acid, chafing at the thought of having to share the same cramped set of rooms with it and its fellows. The Doctor was talking about having a work-bench-level hearth and chimney constructed to allow the noxious fumes to escape better, but I suspected that even so the next few moons would see me with running eyes and an aching nose, not to mention hands pimpled with tiny burns and clothes perforated with pin-head holes.

We achieved the Doctor's apartments just as Xamis was setting. The casks, clays and so on were distributed about the rooms, the servants were thanked and given a few coins, and the Doctor and I lit the lamps and set to unpacking all the inedible and poisonous provisions we had purchased from Master Chelgre.

A knock came at the door just after seventh bell. I answered it to find a servant I did not recognise. He was taller and a little older than me.

"Oelph?" he said, grinning. "Here. A note from the GC." He shoved a sealed piece of paper addressed to Doctor Vosill into my hand.

"The who?" I asked, but he had already turned and was sauntering off down the corridor. I shrugged.

The Doctor read the note. "I am to attend the Guard Commander and Duke Ormin in the Suitor's Wing," she said, sighing and pushing her fingers through her hair. She looked round the half-unpacked cases. "Would you mind doing the rest of this, Oelph?"

"Of course not, mistress."

"I think it's obvious where everything goes. Like with like. If there is anything unfamiliar, just leave it on the floor. I'll try not to be too long."

"Very well, mistress."

The Doctor buttoned her shirt up to the neck, sniffed at one of her armpits (just the sort of thing she did which I found unladylike and even distressing, but which I look back on now with an ache of long-ing), then shrugged, threw on a short jacket, and made for the door. She opened it, then came back, looked round the mess of straw, box-planks, twine and sacking that lay strewn across the floor, picked up her old dagger which she had been using to cut (or rather saw) the twine around the boxes and crates, and went off, whistling. The door closed.

I do not know what made me look at the note which had sum-moned her. She had left it lying on top of an opened crate, and as I pulled the straw out of another box nearby, the fold of creamy paper kept attracting my eye. Eventually, after a glance at the door, I lifted the note and sat down to read it. It said little more than what the Doctor had told me. I read it again.

D. Vosill kindly to meet D. Ormin and G.C. Adlain in the Suitor's Wing on receipt privately. P.G.t.K. Adlain.

Providence Guard the King, indeed. I looked at the last word for a few moments. The name at the end of the note was Adlain, but it did not look like his writing, which I knew. Of course the note had probably been dictated, or composed and written by Epline, Adlain's page, on his master's instructions. But I thought I knew his writing, too, and this was not it. I cannot claim that I thought any further or at any greater depth.

I could claim a host of reasons for what I did next, but the truth is that I do not know, unless instinct itself can be cited. Even to call it instinct may be to dignify the urge. At the time it felt more like a whim, or even a sort of trivial duty. I cannot even claim that I felt fearful, or had a premonition. I simply did it.

I had been prepared to follow the Doctor from the start of my mission. I had expected to be told to shadow her one day, to follow her into the city on one of the occasions she did not take me along with her, yet never had my Master requested such a thing. I had assumed that he retained other people, more experienced and adept at such behaviour, and less likely to be recognisable to the Doctor, for such work. So, in putting out the lamps, locking the door behind me and following her, I was in a sense doing something I had long thought I would one day find myself doing. I left the note lying where I had picked it up.

The palace seemed quiet. I supposed most people were preparing for dinner. I ascended to the roof-floor. The servants who had their rooms up here would all be busy just now, and probably nobody would see me as I flitted by. Also, this way to the old Suitor's Wing was shorter. For somebody who was not thinking about what he was doing, I was thinking remarkably clearly.

I descended to the dark confines of the Little Court by the servants' stairs and skirted the corner of the old North Wing (now in the southern part of the palace) by the light of Foy, Iparine and Jairly. Lamps burned in the distant windows of the main part of the palace, pointing my way for a few steps before the light was eclipsed by the shuttered façade of the old North Wing. Like the Suitor's Wing, this would not normally be used at this time of year unless there was a great state occasion. The Suitor's Wing looked shuttered and dark, too, save for one sliver of light showing at the edge of the main doorway. I kept to the two-thirds darkness at the foot of the old North Wing's wall as I approached, and felt exposed beneath the single intrusive eye of Jairly.

With the King in residence, there were supposed to be regular guard patrols, even here where there would not normally be anybody. I had seen no hint of any guards so far, and had no idea how often they made their rounds, or indeed if they really did bother with this part of the palace, but even knowing that men of the palace guard might appear made me more nervous than I felt I really ought to be. What had I to hide? Was I not a good and faithful servant, and devoted to the King? Yet, here I was, quite consciously skulking.

I would have to cross another courtyard in the light of the three moons if I were to use the main entrance of the Suitor's Wing, but even without thinking about it I knew I did not want to use that front entrance. Then I found what I recalled ought to be here—a way which led beneath the North Wing to a smaller galleried courtyard within. There were gates at the far end, just visible in the gloom of the tunnel, but they were open. The narrow courtyard was silent and ghostly. The painted gallery posts looked like stiff white sentries watching me. I took the small tunnel on the far side of the court, also gated but not locked, and one left turn later found myself at the rear of the Suitor's Wing, in the shadow of all three moons, with the building's wooden-shuttered façade tall and blank and dark above me.

I stood there, wondering how I was going to get in, then walked along until I found a doorway. The door would be locked, I thought, but then when I tried it, it was not. Now why should that be? I pulled the slab of wood slowly to me, expecting it to creak, but it did not.

The darkness inside was complete. The door closed behind me with a soft thud. I had to feel my way along the corridor inside, one hand on the wall to my right, my other hand out in front of my face. These would be the servants' quarters. The floor under my feet was naked stone. I passed several doors. They were all locked, save for one which gave access to a large, empty cupboard with a faint acrid, acidic smell which made me suspect it had once contained soap. I banged my hand on one of its shelves and almost swore out loud.

Back in the corridor again, I came to a wooden stairway. I crept upwards and came to a door. From the bottom of the door there was the very faintest suggestion of light, hinted at only when I did not look directly at it. I twisted the handle carefully and pulled the door towards me, for less than a hand's width.

Down a broad, carpeted corridor lined with paintings I could see that the source of the light was a room at the far end, near the main doorway. I heard a cry and what might have been the sound of a scuffle, and then another cry. Footsteps sounded in the distance, and the light in the doorway changed an instant before a figure appeared there. It was a man. That was about all I could ever be sure of. The fellow came running down the corridor, straight towards me.

It took me a moment to realise that he might actually be heading for the door I was hiding behind. In that time he covered about half the length of the corridor. There was something wild and desperate about him that put a terror into me.

I turned and jumped down the dark stairs, landing heavily and hurting my left ankle. I stumbled towards where I thought the unlocked cupboard door ought to be. My hands flailed around the wall for a moment until I found the door, then I pulled it open and threw myself inside just as a bang and a thin wash of light announced that the man had thrown open the door at the top of the stairs. Heavy footsteps clattered down.

I leant back against the shelves. I put my hand out towards the swinging shadow of the cupboard door to pull it back, but it was out of my reach. The man must have run into it, for there was a loud bang and a yelp of pain and anger. The cupboard door slammed shut and I was left in darkness. Another, heavier door slammed somewhere outside and a key rattled in a lock.

I pushed the cupboard door open. A small amount of light was still falling down the stairway. I heard some noise from the top of the stairs but it sounded distant. It might have been a door closing. I went back to the top of the steps and looked out through the half-open door. Down the broad corridor, the light changed again in the doorway near the main entrance at the far end. I got ready to run again, but nobody appeared. Instead there was a stifled cry. A woman's cry. A terrible fear shook me then, and I started to walk down the corridor.

I had gone perhaps five or six steps when the main doors at the far end of the hall were thrown open and a troop of guards rushed in, swords drawn. Two of them stopped and looked at me, while the rest made straight for the door where the light was coming from.

"You! Here!" one of the guards shouted, pointing his sword at me.

Shouts, and a woman's frightened voice, came from the lit room. I walked on trembling legs down the hall towards the guards. I was grabbed by the collar and forced into the room, where the Doctor was being held by two tall guardsmen, her arms pinned, forced back against a wall. She was shouting at the men.

Duke Ormin lay motionless on his back on the floor, in a huge pool of dark blood. His throat had been cut. A thin, flattened metal shaft protruded from above his heart. The flat metal shaft was the handle of a thin knife made all of metal. I recognised it. It was one of the Doctor's scalpels.

I think I lost the power of speech for a while. I lost the power of hearing too, I believe. The Doctor was still shouting at the men. Then she saw me and shouted at me, but I could not make out what it was she was shouting. I would have fallen to the floor had I not been supported by the scruff of the neck by the two guards holding me. One of the guardsmen knelt by the body on the floor. He had to kneel at the head of the Duke to avoid the still spreading pool of darkness on the wooden floor. He opened one of Duke Ormin's eyes.

A piece of my brain still functioning told me that if he was checking for signs of life this was a foolish thing to do, given the amount of blood that had flowed over the floor, and the quite stationary shaft of the scalpel protruding from the Duke's chest.

The guardsman said something. I have a feeling it was "Dead" or something similar, but I cannot recall.

Then there were more guards in the room, until it became quite crowded and I could not see the Doctor.

We were taken away. I did not hear things properly again, or find my own voice until we arrived at our destination, back at the main palace, in the torture chamber, where Duke Quettil's chief questioner, Master Ralinge, was waiting for us.

Master, I knew then that you must forsake me. Perhaps I was not supposed to be forsaken, according to the original plan, for that note, purportedly from you, did use the word "privately" which implied that the Doctor was to go alone, and not take me along with her, so I could believe that I had been supposed to remain innocent of whatever the Doctor was accused of. But I had followed her, and I had not thought to tell anybody else of my fears.

I also had not thought to stand my ground when the man who must have been the real murderer of Duke Ormin came thundering down the hall towards me. No, instead I had taken flight, jumping down the stairs and hiding in a cupboard. Even when the fellow had banged into the cupboard door, I had stayed back against the shelves of the cupboard, hoping he would not look inside and discover me. So I was complicit with my own downfall, I realised, as I was brought struggling into the chamber where last the Doctor and I had been that night when we had been summoned by Master Nolieti.

The Doctor, for those moments, was magnificent.

She walked erect, her back straight, her head raised. I had to be dragged, because my legs had entirely stopped working. I think, for myself, that had I had the wit I would have shouted and screamed and struggled, but I was too stunned. There was a look on the Doctor's proud face of resignation and defeat, but not of panic or fear. I was not so deceived as to imagine for a moment that I appeared to be anything other than the way I felt, which was shaking and quivering with abject terror, my limbs reduced to jelly.

Do I shame myself to say that I had soiled my breeches? I think I do not. Master Ralinge was an acknowledged virtuoso of pain.

The torture chamber.

It seemed very well lit, I thought. The walls were studded with torches and candles. Master Ralinge must prefer being able to see what he was doing. Nolieti had favoured a darker and more menacing atmosphere.

I was already preparing myself to denounce the Doctor and all her works. I looked at the rack, the cage, the bath, the brazier, the bed, the pokers and pincers and all the rest of the equipment, and my love, my devotion, my honour itself turned to water and drained out through my heels. Whatever it was required of me to say, I would say, to save myself.

The Doctor was doomed, of that I was certain. Nothing I could do or say would save her. Her actions had been arranged to fit this accusation. The suspicious note, the odd locale, the route left open for the real murderer, the timely appearance of the guard, so mob-handed, even the fact that Master Ralinge looked so bright-eyed and happy to see us and had arranged and lit all his candles and stoked his brazier . . . all spoke of arrangement, of collusion. The Doctor had been forced to this by people capable of wielding great power, and therefore there was absolutely nothing I could possibly do that would save her from her fate or in any way mitigate her punishment.

Those of you who read this and think, Well, I would have done whatever I could to have reduced her torment, I beg you think again, for you have not been marched into a torture chamber to see the instruments there waiting for you. When you see those, you think only of a way to stop them being used against you.

The Doctor was taken, without a struggle, to a floor sink, where she was forced to kneel while her hair was cut off and her head shaved. That seemed to upset her, for she started to shout and scream. Master Ralinge did the cutting and shaving himself, in a loving, careful way. He bunched in his fist, brought to his nose and slowly sniffed each bundle of hair he removed from the Doctor's head. I meanwhile was strapped upright to an iron frame.

I cannot recall what the Doctor screamed or what Master Ralinge said. I know they exchanged words, that is all. The master torturer's motley collection of mismatched teeth gleamed in the candle light.

Ralinge ran his hand over the Doctor's head, and at one place, over her left ear, his hands stopped and he looked more closely, muttering in his soft voice something which I could not make out, then he ordered her stripped and placed on an iron bed by the brazier. As the Doctor was man-handled by the two guards who had brought her to this awful place, the torturer slowly undid and pulled off his thick leather apron, and then began to unbutton his trousers in a deliberate, reverential manner. He watched the two guards—four eventually, for the Doctor put up a remarkably powerful fight—as they stripped my mistress naked.

And so I saw what I had always hoped to see, and was able to view what I had envisaged during many hundreds of shameful soporific imaginings.

The Doctor, nude.

And it meant nothing. She was struggling, pulling and heaving and trying to punch and kick and bite, her skin mottled with exertion, her face hot with tears and reddened with fear and fury. This was no soft dream of lust. Here was no emollient vision of loveliness. Here was a woman about to be violated in the most base and disgusting ways possible, and then tortured, and then, eventually, killed. She knew this as well as I, and as well as Ralinge and his pair of assistants did, and as well as the guards who attended us.

What was my most fervent hope at that point?

It was that they did not know of my devotion to her. If they thought me indifferent, I might only hear her screams. If they thought for a moment, for the merest heart-beat, that I loved her, then the very rules of their profession would require that my eyelids be cut out and I would be forced to watch her every torment.

Her clothes were thrown away, landing in a heap in one corner by a bench. Something clinked. Master Ralinge looked at the Doctor as she was secured, quite naked, to the iron bed frame. He looked down at his manhood, stroking it, then he dismissed the guards. They looked both disappointed and relieved. One of Ralinge's assistants locked the chamber door behind them. There was upon Ralinge's face a bright and shining, almost luminescent smile as he moved towards her.

The Doctor's dark clothes settled where they had fallen.

My eyes filled with tears, thinking of how she had thought to check her progress as she had left her apartments, being so careful as to go back and pick up that stupid, blunt and useless dagger that she carried with her whenever she remembered. What good could that do her now?

Master Ralinge said the first words that I could recall in detail since the Doctor had read out the note in her apartments, half a bell—and an entire age—earlier.

"First things first, madam," he said. He climbed up on to the bed the Doctor had been strapped to, his swollen manhood held poised within one fist.

The Doctor looked into his eyes quite calmly. She made a clicking noise with her mouth and her face took on a look of disappointment.

"Ah," she said, matter-of-factly. "So you are serious." And she smiled. Smiled!

Then she said something that sounded like an instruction in a language I did not know. It was not the language she had used with the gaan Kuduhn, a day earlier. It was a different kind of language. A language from somewhere, I thought, even as I heard it and closed my eyes—for I could not bear to see what was going to happen next—beyond even far Drezen. A language from nowhere.

And, well, what happened next?

How many times I have tried to explain it, how many times I have attempted to make sense of it. Not so much for others, but for myself.

My eyes—as I hope will seem understandable given the feelings I have attempted to imply through this journal—were closed at the time. I simply did not see what happened during the next few heart-beats.

I heard a whirring noise. A noise like a waterfall, a noise like a sudden wind, like an arrow as it passes nearby one's ear. Then a long gasp which I realised later must in reality have been two gasps, but in any case a long exhalation of sound, and then a thud, a punch-like concussion of what, in retrospect, was air and flesh and bone and . . . what? More bone? Metal? Wood?

Metal, I think.

Who knows?

I felt a strange, dizzying sensation. I may have been senseless, for a while. I do not know.

When I woke, if I woke, it was to something that was impossible.

The Doctor stood over me, clad in her long white shirt. She was bald, of course, having been shaved. She looked utterly different. Alien.

She was undoing my bonds.

Her expression seemed cool and assured. Her face and scalp were freckled with red.

There was red on the ceiling above the iron bed where she had been secured. More blood was scattered almost everywhere I looked, some of it still dripping from the nearby bench. I looked at the floor. Master Ralinge lay there. Or most of him did. His body, up to his lower neck, lay on the stones, still twitching. Where the rest was . . . well, there were quite sufficient pieces of red, pink and grey distributed around the chamber for one to re-create something like what must have happened to his upper neck and head.

Simply, it was as though a bomb had exploded inside it. I could see half a dozen teeth of various sizes and colours scattered about the floor, like shrapnel.

Ralinge's assistants lay nearby in a single great spreading pool of blood, their heads almost severed from their bodies. Only a strip of skin still connected the head of one to his shoulders. His face was turned towards me and his eyes were still open.

I swear, they blinked, once. Then they slowly closed.

The Doctor released me.

Something moved at the hem of her loose shirt. Then the movement stopped.

She looked so steady and so certain. And yet she looked so dead, so utterly overpowered. She turned her head to one side and said something in a tone I swear to this day was resigned and defeated, even bitter. Something buzzed through the air.

"We must imprison ourselves to save ourselves, Oelph," she told me. She put her hand on my mouth. "If that is possible."

Warm and dry and strong.

We were in a cell. A cell set within the walls of the torture chamber and separated from it by a grid of iron bars. Why she put us in here, I had no idea. The Doctor had dressed herself. I had hurriedly undressed while she looked away, cleaned myself as best I could, then dressed again. Meanwhile she had gathered up the long red hair Ralinge had shaved from her head. She looked at it regretfully as she stepped over the master torturer's body, then threw the gleaming red bundles on to the brazier, where they crackled and spat and smoked and flamed and gave off a sickening smell.

She had quietly unlocked the door of the chamber itself, before putting us both in this small cell, locking the door from outside and throwing the keys on to the nearest bench. Then she had sat calmly down on the dirty straw floor and put her arms round her knees and stared blankly out at the carnage in the chamber outside.

I squatted down beside her, my knee close to where her old dagger protruded from the top of her boot. The air smelled of shit and burned hair and something sharp that I decided must be blood. I felt sick for a little while. I tried to concentrate on something trivial, and was inordinately grateful to find something. The Doctor's old battered dagger had lost the last of its little white beads round the top rim of its pommel, under the smoky stone. It looked neater, more symmetrical now, I thought. I took a deep breath through my mouth, to escape the smells of the torture chamber, then cleared my throat. "What . . . what happened, mistress?" I asked.

"You must report what you feel you have to, Oelph." Her voice sounded tired and hollow. "I shall say that the three of them fell out over me, and killed each other. But it doesn't really matter." She looked at me. Her eyes seemed to drill into me. I had to look away. "What did you see, Oelph?" she asked.

"My eyes were closed, mistress. Truly. I heard . . . a few noises. Wind. A buzz. A thud. I think I was out of my senses for a short while."

She nodded, and smiled thinly. "Well, that's handy."

"Should we not have attempted to run away, mistress?"

"I don't think we'd get very far, Oelph," she said. "There is another way, but we must be patient. The matter is in hand."

"If you say so, mistress," I said. Suddenly my eyes filled with tears. The Doctor turned to me and smiled. She looked very strange and child-like with no hair. She put her arm out and hugged me to her. I rested my head on her shoulder. She rested her head on mine, and rocked me to and fro, like a mother with her child.

We were still like that when the chamber door burst open and the guards rushed in. They stopped and stared at the three bodies lying on the floor, then hurried on towards us. I shrank back, convinced that our torment would shortly be resumed. The guards looked relieved to see us, which I found surprising. One sergeant picked up the keys from the bench where the Doctor had thrown them and released us and told us that we were needed at once, for the King was dying.

22
THE BODYGUARD

S till the Protector's son hung on to life. The convulsions and his lack of appetite had left Lattens so weak he could barely lift his head to drink. For a few mornings he seemed to be getting better, but then he relapsed and seemed once again at the very door of death.

UrLeyn was distraught. The servants reported that he raged round his apartments, tearing sheets and pulling down tapestries and smashing ornaments and furniture and slicing ancient portraits with a knife. The servants started to clean up the destruction when he went to visit Lattens on his sick bed, but when he returned UrLeyn threw the servants out, and from then on he would let nobody into his rooms.

The palace seemed a terrible, bleak place to be, the atmosphere contaminated by the powerless fury and despair of the man at its heart. UrLeyn remained in his wrecked apartments during this time, only leaving to visit his son every morning and afternoon, and the harem each evening, where he lay, usually with Perrund, collapsed in her lap or bosom while she stroked his head until he fell asleep. But such peace never lasted long, and he would soon twitch in his sleep and cry out and then wake, and subsequently rise and return to his own rooms, old and haggard-looking and sunk in despair.

The bodyguard DeWar slept in a cot along the corridor from the door to UrLeyn's rooms. For most of the day he would pace up and down the same corridor, fretting and waiting for UrLeyn to make one of his rare appearances.

The Protector's brother RuLeuin tried to see UrLeyn. He waited patiently in the corridor with DeWar, then when UrLeyn appeared from his apartments and walked quickly in the direction of his son's room, RuLeuin joined DeWar at UrLeyn's side and tried to talk to his brother, but UrLeyn ignored him, and told DeWar not to let RuLeuin or anybody else approach him until he ordered so. YetAmidous, ZeSpiole and even Doctor BreDelle were all told this by the bodyguard.

YetAmidous did not believe what he was being told. He thought DeWar was trying to keep them all away from the General.

He too waited in the corridor one day, defying DeWar to force him to leave. When the door to UrLeyn's apartments opened, YetAmidous pushed past DeWar's outstretched arm and walked towards the Protector, saying, "General! I must talk to you!"

But UrLeyn just looked at him from the doorway, then without a word closed the door from the inside before YetAmidous could get there. The key turned in the lock. YetAmidous was left to fume in the doorway, then he turned and walked away, ignoring DeWar.

"Will you really see no one, sir?" DeWar asked him as they strode to Lattens' room one day.

He thought UrLeyn would not answer, but then he said, "No."

"They need to talk to you about the war, sir."

"Do they?"

"Yes, sir."

"How goes the war?"

"Not well, sir."

"Well, not well. What does it matter? Tell them to do whatever has to be done. I do not care to concern myself with it any more."

"With respect, sir—"

"Your respect for me will be expressed from now on by speaking only when you are spoken to, DeWar."

"Sir—"

"Sir!" UrLeyn said, whirling to face the younger man and forcing him to retreat until his back was hard against a wall. "You will remain silent until I ask you to speak, or I will have you removed from this building. Do you understand? You may answer yes or no."

"Yes, sir."

"Very well. You are my bodyguard. You may guard my body. No more. Come."

The war was indeed going badly. It was common knowledge in the palace that no more cities had been taken, and indeed that one had been retaken by the barons' forces. If the message to try to capture the barons themselves had got through, it was either not being acted upon or was impossible to accomplish. Troops disappeared into the lands of Ladenscion and only the walking wounded seemed to return, with tales of confusion and horror. The citizens of Crough began to wonder when the men who had been sent to the conflict might return, and started to complain about the extra taxes which had been levied to pay for the war.

The generals at the war itself called for more troops, but there were scarcely any troops left to send. The palace guard had been halved, with one half being formed into a company of pikemen and sent off to the war. Even the eunuchs of the harem guard had been pressed into service. The generals and others who were attempting to administer the land and run the war while UrLeyn closeted himself away did not know what to do. It was rumoured that Guard Commander ZeSpiole had suggested that the only thing to do might be to bring all the troops home, to burn all that could be burned of Ladenscion and leave it to the damned barons. It was also rumoured that when ZeSpiole suggested this, at the table where UrLeyn had held his last council of war half a moon earlier, General YetAmidous had let out a terrible roar and, leaping to his feet and drawing his sword, swore he would cut out the tongue of the next man to betray UrLeyn's wishes and suggest such cowardice.

DeWar came to the harem's outer room one morning, and requested that the lady Perrund attend him.

"Mr. DeWar," she said, sitting on a couch. He sat down on another couch across a small table from her.

He gestured at a wooden box and a game board, lying on the table. "I thought we might play a game of 'Leader's Dispute.' Would you humour me?"

"Gladly," Perrund said. They unfolded the board and set out the pieces.

"What is the news?" she asked, as they commenced playing.

"Of the boy, no change," DeWar said, sighing. "The nurse says he slept a little better last night, but he barely recognises his father and when he talks he makes no sense. From the war, there is news of change, but all of it's ill. I fear the whole thing has gone wrong. The latest reports were confused, but it sounds as though Simalg and Ralboute are both retreating. If it is only a retreat there may still be some hope, but the nature of the reports themselves makes me think it may in reality be a rout, or well on the way to becoming one."

Perrund stared at the man wide-eyed. "Providence, can it really be that bad?"

"I'm afraid it can."

"Is Tassasen itself in danger?"

"I would hope not. The barons ought not to have the military wherewithal to invade us, and there should be sufficient troops intact to mount an adequate defence if they did, but . . ."

"Oh, DeWar, it sounds hopeless." She looked into his eyes. "Does UrLeyn know?"

DeWar shook his head. "He will not be told. But YetAmidous and RuLeuin are talking about waiting outside Lattens' room this afternoon and demanding that he listen to them."

"Do you think he will?"

"I think he might. I also think he might run away from them, or order the guards to throw them out, or run them through, or strike at them himself." DeWar picked up his Protector piece and turned it round in his fingers before replacing it on the board. "I don't know what he'll do. I hope he will listen to them. I hope he will begin to act normally again and start to rule, as he ought. He cannot go on like this much longer without those in the war cabinet starting to think that they'd be better off without him." He looked into Perrund's widened eyes. "I cannot talk to him," he told her. She thought he sounded like a small, hurt boy. "I am literally forbidden to. If I thought I could say something to him, I would, but he has threatened that if I try to speak to him without his express permission he will have me removed from my position, and I think I believe him. So if I am to continue trying to protect him, I must remain silent. Yet he must be told what a pass things have come to. If YetAmidous and RuLeuin do not succeed this afternoon—"

"Will I, tonight?" Perrund said, her voice sharp.

DeWar looked down for a moment, then he met her gaze again. "I am sorry to have to ask you, Perrund. I can only ask. I would not even think of doing so if the situation were anything less than desperate. But desperate it is."

"He may not choose to listen to a crippled concubine, DeWar."

"At the moment, Perrund, there is nobody else. Will you make the attempt?"

"Of course. What ought I to say?"

"What I have told you. That the war is on the verge of being lost. Ralboute and Simalg are retreating, that we can only hope that they are doing so in good order but the hints we have indicate otherwise. Tell him that his war cabinet is at odds with itself, that its members cannot decide what to do, and the only thing they may eventually agree on is that a leader who will not lead is less than worthless. He must regain their trust and respect before it is too late. The city, the country itself is starting to turn against him. There is discontent and wild talk of harbingers of catastrophe, and the beginning of a dangerous nostalgia for what people call 'the old days.' Tell him as much as he can bear of that, my lady, or as much as you dare, but be careful. He has raised his hand to his servants before now, and I will not be there to protect you, or him from himself."

Perrund gazed levelly at him. "This is a heavy duty, DeWar."

"It is. And I am sorry to have to offer it to you, but the moment has become critical. If there is anything at all I can do to help you in this, you have only to ask and it will be done if I can possibly do it."

Perrund took a deep breath. She looked at the game board. With a faltering smile she waved her hand at the pieces between them and said, "Well, you could move."

His small, sad smile matched hers.

23

THE DOCTOR

The Doctor and I stood on the quayside. About us was all the usual tumult of the docks, and, in addition, the local confusion which normally attends upon a great ship preparing to depart on a long voyage. The galleon *Plough of the Seas* was due to sail with the next doubled tide in less than half a bell, and the last supplies were being hoisted and carried aboard, while everywhere about us, amongst the coils of rope, the barrels of tar, the piled rolls of wicker fenders and flatly emptied carts were played out tearful scenes of farewell. Ours, of course, was one.

"Mistress, can you not stay? Please?" I begged her. The tears rolled miserably down my cheeks for all to see.

The Doctor's face was tired, resigned and calm. Her eyes had a frac-

tured, far-away look about them, like ice or broken glass glimpsed in
the dark recesses of a distant room. Her hat was pulled tight over her
brindled scalp. I thought she had never looked so beautiful. The day
was blustery, the wind was warm and the two suns shone down from
either side of the sky, opposing and unequal points of view. I was
Seigen to her Xamis, the desperate light of my desire to have her stay
entirely washed out by the bounteous blaze of her will to leave.

She took my hands in hers. The broken-looking eyes gazed tenderly
upon me for the last time. I tried to blink my tears out of the way,
resolved that if I would never see her again, at least my last sight of her
would be vivid and sharp. "I can't, Oelph, I'm sorry."

"Can't I come with you then, mistress?" I said, even more miserably.
This was my last and most dismal play. It had been the one thing I had
been determined not to say, because it was so obvious and so pathetic
and so doomed. I had known she would be leaving for a half-moon or so,
and in those few handfuls of days I had tried everything I could think of
to make her want to stay, even while knowing that her going was
inevitable and that none of my arguments could carry any weight with
her, not measured against what she saw as her failure. During all that
time I wanted to say, Then if you must go, please take me!

But it was too sad a thing to say, too predictable. Of course that is
what I would say, and of course she would turn me down. I was a
youth, still, and she a woman of maturity and wisdom. What would I
do, if I went with her, but remind her of what she had lost, of how she
had failed? She would look at me and see the King and never forgive me
for not being him, for reminding her that she had lost his love even if
she had saved his life.

I knew she would reject me if I said it, so I had made an absolutely
firm decision not to ask her. It would be the one piece of my self-respect
I would retain. But some inflamed part of my mind said, She might say
Yes! She might have been waiting for you to ask! Perhaps (this seduc-
tive, insane, deluded, sweet voice within me said) she really does love
you, and would want nothing more than to take you with her, back to
Drezen. Perhaps she feels that it is not for her to ask you, because it
would be taking you away from everything and everyone you have ever
known, perhaps for ever, perhaps never to return.

And so, like a fool, I did ask her, and she only squeezed my hands and shook her head. "I would let you if it was possible, Oelph," she said quietly. "It is so sweet of you to want to accompany me. I shall cherish always the memory of that kindness. But I cannot ask you to come with me."

"I would go anywhere with you, mistress!" I cried, my eyes now full of tears. I would have thrown myself at her feet and hugged her legs if I had been able to see properly. Instead I hung my head and blubbered like a child. "Please, mistress, please, mistress," I wept, no longer even able to say what it was I wanted, her to stay or me to go.

"Oh, Oelph, I was trying so hard not to cry," she said, then gathered me in her arms and folded me to her.

At last to be held in her arms, pressed against her, and be allowed to put my arms round her, feeling her warmth and her strength, encompassing her firm softness, drawing in that fresh perfume from her skin. She put her chin on my shoulder, just as mine rested on hers. Between my sobs, I could feel her shake, crying too, now. I had last been this close to her, side by side, my head on her shoulder, her head on mine, in the torture chamber of the palace, half a moon earlier, when the guards had tumbled in with the news that we were needed because the King was dying.

The King was indeed dying. A terrible sickness had fallen upon him from nowhere, causing him to collapse during a dinner being held for the suddenly, and secretly, arrived Duke Quettil. King Quience had been in the middle of a sentence, when he stopped speaking, stared straight ahead and started to shake. His eyes had revolved back into his head and he had slumped down in his seat, unconscious, the wine goblet dropping from his hand.

Skelim, Quettil's doctor, was there. He had had to remove the King's tongue from his throat, or he would have choked to death immediately. Instead he lay there on the floor, senseless and shaking spasmodically while everybody rushed around. Duke Quettil attempted to take charge, apparently ordering that guards be posted everywhere. Duke Ulresile contented himself with staring, while the new Duke Walen sat in his seat, whimpering. Guard Commander Adlain posted a guard at the King's table to make sure nobody touched the King's plate or the decanter he'd been drinking from, in case somebody had poisoned him.

During all this commotion, a servant arrived with the news that Duke Ormin had been murdered.

My thoughts, oddly, have turned to that footman whenever I have tried to envisage the scene. A servant rarely gets to deliver genuinely shocking news to those of exalted rank, and to be entrusted with something as momentous as the intelligence that one of the King's favourites has taken the life of a Duke must seem like something of a privilege. To discover that it is of relatively little consequence compared to the events unfolding before you must be galling.

I was, subsequently, more than usually diligent in quizzing, as subtly as I could, the servants who were in the dining chamber that evening, and they reported that, even at the time, they noticed that certain of the dining guests did not react as one might have expected to the news, presumably just because of the distraction of the King's sudden predicament. It was almost, they hazarded, as though the Guard Commander and the Dukes Ulresile and Quettil had been expecting the news.

Doctor Skelim ordered that the King be taken directly to his bed. Once there he was undressed. Skelim inspected the King's body for any marks that might indicate he had been shot with a poisoned dart or infected with something through a cut. There were none.

The King's blood pulse was slow and becoming slower, only increasing briefly when small fits passed through him. Doctor Skelim reported that unless something could be done, the King's heart was sure to stop within the bell. He confessed himself at a loss to determine what had befallen the King. The doctor's bag was delivered from his room by a breathless servant, but the few tonics and stimulants he was able to administer (little better than smelling salts by the sound of them, especially given that Quience could not be induced to swallow anything) had no effect whatsoever.

The doctor considered bleeding the King, in effect the only thing he could think of which he had not tried, but bleeding somebody with a weakening heartbeat had proved worse than useless in the past, and on this occasion, thankfully, the urge not to make matters worse overcame the need to be seen to be doing something. The doctor ordered some exotic infusions to be prepared, but held out little hope that they would be any more effective than the compounds he had already administered.

It was you, master, who said that Doctor Vosill would have to be summoned. I am told that Duke Ulresile and Duke Quettil took you aside and that there was a furious argument. Duke Ulresile flew from the room in a blinding rage and later took a sword to one of his servants such that the poor fellow lost one eye and a pair of fingers. I find it admirable that you stood your ground. A contingent of the palace guards was sent to the questioning chamber with orders to take the Doctor from there by force if necessary.

I am told that my mistress walked calmly in to the terrified confusion that was the King's chamber, where nobles, servants and, it seemed, half the palace were assembled, crying and wailing.

She had sent me, with a pair of guards, to her chamber for her medicine bag. We surprised one of Duke Quettil's servants and another palace guard there. Both looked anxious and guilty at being caught in the Doctor's rooms. Duke Quettil's man held a piece of paper I recognised.

I have never, I think, been so proud of myself for anything I have done in my life as for what I did next, for I was still half terrified that my ordeal had merely been postponed rather than cancelled. I was shaking and sweating with the shock of what I had witnessed, I was mortified at the callow and cowardly way I had felt in the torture chamber, ashamed of how my body had betrayed me, and my mind was still spinning.

What I did was take the note from Quettil's servant.

"That is the property of my *mistress!*" I hissed, and stepped forward, a look of fury on my face. I grabbed the note from the fellow's fingers. He looked blankly at me, then at the note, which I stuffed quickly into my shirt. He opened his mouth to speak. I turned, still quivering with rage, to the two guards who had been sent with me. "Escort this person from these apartments immediately!" I said.

This was, of course, a gamble on my part. In all the excitement, it had been quite unclear whether the Doctor and I were still technically prisoners or not, and therefore the two guards might rightly have concluded that they were my jailers, not my bodyguards, which was the way I was treating them. I would modestly claim that they were able to recognise something transparently honest and true about my righteous indignation and so decided to do as I commanded.

The Duke's man looked terrified, but did as he was told. I buttoned up my jacket to further secure the note, found the Doctor's bag and hurried to the King's chamber with my escorts.

The Doctor had turned the King on to his side. She knelt by his bed, stroking his head in a distracted way, fending off questions from Doctor Skelim. (A reaction to something in his food, probably, she told him. Extreme, but not poison.)

You stood, master, arms crossed, near the Doctor. Duke Quettil lurked in a corner, glaring at her.

She took a small stoppered glass vial from the bag, holding it up to the light and shaking it. "Oelph, this is the salts solution number twenty-one, herbed. Do you know it?"

I thought. "Yes, mistress."

"We'll need more, dried, within the next two bells. Can you remember how to prepare it?"

"Yes, I think so, mistress. I may need to refer to your notes."

"Just so. I'm sure your two guards will help you. Off you go, then."

I turned to go, then stopped and handed her the note which I had taken from the Duke's man. "Here is that paper, mistress," I said, then quickly turned and left before she had time to ask me what it was.

I missed the uproar when the Doctor pinched the King's nose and clamped a hand over his mouth until he turned nearly blue. You, master, held back the protestations of the others, but then grew concerned yourself, and were about to order her away at sword point when she let the King's nose go and thrust the powder which the vial had contained under his nostrils. The ruddy powder looked like dried blood, but was not. It whistled into the King as he took a huge, deep in-drawing breath.

Most of the people in the room took their own first breath for some time. For a while, nothing happened. Then, I am told, the King's eyes flickered and opened. He saw the Doctor and smiled, then coughed and wheezed and had to be helped to sit up.

He cleared his throat, fixed the Doctor with an outraged stare and said, "Vosill, what in the skies of hell have you done to your hair?"

I think the Doctor knew she would not need any more of salts solution number twenty-one, herbed. It was her way of trying to make sure that she and I were not brought to the King, made to cure him of whatever had befallen him and then promptly led away again back to the torture chamber. She wanted people to think that the course of treatment required would be longer than what amounted to little more than a quick pinch of snuff.

Nevertheless, I returned to the Doctor's apartments, with my two guards in escort, and set up the equipment necessary to produce the powder. Even with the help of the two guards—and it was a refreshing experience to be able to do the ordering around, rather than to be subject to it myself—it would be a close-run thing to produce a small amount of the substance in less than two bells. At least it would give me something to do.

I only heard later and at second hand about the outburst of Duke Quettil, in the King's chamber. The sergeant of the guards who had released us from the cell in the torture chamber spoke quietly with you, master, shortly after the King was brought back to the land of the living. I am told you looked a little shaken for a moment, but then went, grim-faced, to inform Duke Quettil of the fate of his chief questioner and his two assistants.

"Dead! *Dead?* By fuck, Adlain, can you arrange nothing right!" were the Duke's precise words, by all accounts. The King glared. The Doctor looked unperturbed. Everybody else stared. The Duke attempted to strike you, and had to be restrained by two of your men, who acted, perhaps, before they thought. The King inquired what was going on.

The Doctor, meanwhile, was looking at the piece of paper I had given her.

It was the note that purported to be from you and which had lured her to the trap that had killed Duke Ormin and was supposed to dispose of her. The King had already heard from the Doctor that Ormin was dead, and that she had been meant to appear to be the killer. He was still sitting up in bed, staring ahead and trying to digest this news. The Doctor had not yet given him the details of what had supposedly happened in the questioning chamber, but merely said that she had been released before being put to the question.

She showed him the note. He called you over and you confirmed that it was not your writing, though it might be said to be a decent attempt at it.

Duke Quettil took the opportunity to demand that somebody be brought to justice for the murder of his men, which may have been a little hasty, as it raised the question concerning what they had been doing there in the first place. The King's expression darkened as he gradually took in all that was revealed, and several times he had to tell people trying to interrupt others to stop, so that he could get clear in his still slightly befuddled head what had actually happened. Duke Quettil, reportedly breathing heavily and with staring eyes and spittle on his lips, at one point attempted to grab the Doctor's wrist and pull her away from the King, who put his arm round her shoulders and ordered you to keep the Duke distant.

I was absent for all that passed over the next half bell. What I know was passed to me by others, and so must surrender the toll which information tends to pay when it passes through the minds and memories of others. Even so, without having been there, I believe there was some quick thinking done in that chamber, principally by yourself, though Duke Quettil must, at the least, have calmed down sufficiently to consider things in a more rational manner again and accept the path you were mapping out, even if he could contribute little of the cartography himself.

The brief of it was that Duke Ulresile was to be blamed. The writing on the note was his. The palace guards swore that Ulresile had commanded them on your authority. Later that night one of Ulresile's men was brought before the King, sobbing, to confess that he had stolen the scalpel from the Doctor's apartments earlier that day and that he had killed Duke Ormin, then run away and out of a back door of the Suitor's Wing shortly before the Doctor entered by the front door. I was able to play my part, averring that the fellow could well have been the man who had rushed towards me in the dim corridor in the Suitor's Wing.

The fellow lied about the scalpel, of course. Only one of the instruments had ever gone missing and that was the one I had stolen two seasons earlier, the day we had visited the Poor Hospital. Of course, I delivered it into your hands, master, though not in the literal sense in which it was later delivered into the body of Duke Ormin.

Duke Ulresile, in the meantime, had been prevailed upon to remove himself from the palace. I think a more mature mind might have thought this through and realised that to fly so was to appear to confirm any accusations that might be levelled at him, but perhaps he did not think to compare his predicament or possible actions with one so base as poor, dead Unoure. In any event, he was funnel-fed some story about the King's displeasure being great but brief and largely a matter of a misunderstanding which Quettil and yourself, master, would need a short period to sort out, but a short period which absolutely required the young Duke's absence.

The King made it very clear that he would take any further attempt to traduce the Doctor's good name very ill indeed. You promised that everything would be done to clear up the remaining points of confusion in the matter.

Two of the King's own guards were stationed outside our apartments that night. I slept soundly in my cell until woken by a nightmare. I think the Doctor slept well. In the morning she looked well enough. She completed shaving her head, making a neater job of it than Master Ralinge.

I assisted her in this, in her bedroom while she sat on a chair with a towel round her shoulders and a basin on her knees in which warm suds and a sponge floated. We were due to attend another meeting in the King's chamber that morning, the better to give our side of the events of the previous night.

"What did happen, mistress?" I asked her.

"Where and when, Oelph?" she asked, moistening her scalp with the sponge and then scraping at it with a scalpel—of all things—before passing it to me to complete the job.

"In the questioning chamber, mistress. What happened to Ralinge and the other two?"

"They fought over who would have me first, Oelph. Don't you remember?"

"I do not, mistress," I whispered, with a look round at the door through to her workshop. It was locked, like the one beyond and the one beyond that, but still I felt frightened, as well as a sort of anguished guilt. "I saw Master Ralinge about to . . ."

"About to rape me, Oelph. Please, Oelph. Steady with that scalpel," she said, and put her hand on my wrist. She lifted my hand away a little from her naked scalp and looked round with a smile. "It would be too ironic to survive a false charge of murder and be delivered from the very brink of torture only to suffer injury by your hand."

"But mistress!" I said, and I am not ashamed to say that I wailed, for I was still convinced that we could not be surrounded by such fatally cataclysmic events and such powerfully antagonistic personages without attracting extreme harm. "There was no time for a dispute! He was about to take you! Providence, I saw him. I closed my eyes a heart-beat before . . . there was no time!"

"Dear Oelph," the Doctor said, keeping her hand on my wrist. "You must have forgotten. You were unconscious for some time. Your head rolled to one side, your body went limp. You fairly drooled, I'm afraid. The three men had a fine old argument while you were out of your senses, and then just as the pair who had killed Ralinge slashed at each other, you woke up again. Don't you remember?"

I looked into her eyes. Her expression was one I found impossible to read. I was reminded suddenly of the mirror mask she had worn at the ball in Yvenir palace. "Is that what I ought to remember, mistress?"

"Yes, Oelph, it is."

I looked down at the scalpel and the gleaming mirror-surface of its blade.

"But how did you come to be released from your bonds, mistress?"

"Why, in his haste, Master Ralinge simply did not secure one of them properly," the Doctor said, releasing her grip of my wrist and lowering her head again. "A woeful lapse of professional standards, but perhaps in a way a flattering one."

I sighed. I picked up the soapy sponge and squeezed some more of the suds on to the back of her head. "I see, mistress," I said unhappily, and scraped away the very last of the hair on her head.

I decided, as I did this, that perhaps my memory had been playing tricks on me after all, because looking down at the Doctor's legs, I could see her old dagger sticking out from the top of her boot as usual, and there, quite plainly, was the little pale stone on the top rim of the pommel I had been so convinced had been absent yesterday, in the torture chamber.

I think I knew already then there was no going back to the way things had been before. Even so, it was a shock when the Doctor paid a visit to the King by herself two days later and came back to tell me that she had asked to be released from the post of his personal physician. I stood and stared at her, still standing in the midst of unpacked crates and boxes of supplies and ingredients which she had continued to collect from the apothecaries and chemicalists of the city.

"Released, mistress?" I asked, stupidly.

She nodded. I thought her eyes looked as if she had been crying. "Yes, Oelph. I think it is for the best. I have been too long away from Drezen. And the King seems generally well."

"But he was at death's door not two nights ago!" I shouted, unwilling to believe what I was hearing and what it meant.

She gave me one of her small smiles. "I think that will not occur again."

"But you said it was caused by some—what did you call it?—some allotropic galvanic of salt! Dammit all, woman, that could—!"

"Oelph!"

I think it was the only time either of us spoke to each other in quite such tones. I shrank from my fury like a punctured bladder. I looked down at the floor. "Sorry, mistress."

"I am quite sure," she told me firmly, "that will not occur again."

"Yes, mistress," I mumbled.

"You might as well pack this lot back up again."

A bell later I was in the depths of my misery, repacking boxes, crates and sacks on the Doctor's orders, when you came to call, master.

"I would speak to you in private, madam," you said to the Doctor.

She looked at me. I stood there, hot and sweating, dotted with little lengths of straw from the packing cases.

She said, "I think Oelph can stay, don't you, Guard Commander?"

You looked at her for a few moments, I recall, then your stern expression melted like snow. "Yes," you said, and sat down with a sigh in a chair which temporarily had no cases or their contents balanced upon it. "Yes, I dare say he can." You smiled at the Doctor. She was just in the act of tying a towel round her head, having finished one of her baths. She always tied a towel round her hair after her bath, and I remember thinking, stupidly, Why is she doing that? She has no hair to dry. She wore a thick and voluminous shift which made her denuded head look very small, until she tied the towel round it. She picked a couple of boxes off a couch and sat.

You took a moment to seat yourself just as you wanted, moving your sword so that it was comfortable, placing your booted feet just so. Then you said, "I am told you have asked the King to release you from your post."

"That is correct, Guard Commander."

You nodded for a moment. "That is probably for the best."

"Oh, I'm sure it is, Guard Commander. Oelph, don't just stand there," she said, turning to look at me. "Continue with your work, please."

"Yes, mistress," I mumbled.

"I would dearly love to know quite what happened in the chamber that evening."

"I am sure you already do, Guard Commander."

"And I am equally sure I do not, madam," you said, with a resigned sigh in your voice. "A more superstitious man would think it must have been sorcery."

"But you are not so deceived."

"Indeed not. Ignorant, but not deceived. I think I can say that if I had no other explanation I would be sorrier the longer the matter went unexplained and you were still here, but as you say you are going . . ."

"Yes. Back to Drezen. I have already inquired about a ship . . . Oelph?"

I had let drop a flask of distilled water. It had not broken, but the noise had been loud. "Sorry, mistress," I said, trying not to burst out crying. A ship!

"Do you feel your time here has been a success, Doctor?"

"I think so. The King is in better health than when I arrived. For that alone, if I can take any of the credit, I hope I may feel . . . fulfilled."

"Still, it will be good to get back amongst your own kind, I imagine."

"Yes, I'm sure you can imagine."

"Well, I must be going," you said, standing. Then you said, "It was strange, all those deaths at Yvenir, then good Duke Ormin, and those three men."

"Strange, sir?"

"So many knives, or blades, at any rate. And yet so few found. The murder weapons, I mean."

"Yes. Strange."

You turned at the door. "That was a bad business the other night, in the questioning chamber."

The Doctor said nothing.

"I'm glad you were delivered . . . unscathed. I would give a great deal to know how it was accomplished, but I would not trade the knowledge for the result." You smiled. "I dare say I will see you again, Doctor, but if I do not, let me wish you a safe journey back to your home."

And so, a half-moon later, I stood on the quayside with the Doctor, hugging her and being hugged and knowing that I would do anything to make her stay or be allowed to follow her, and also that I would never see her again.

She pushed me gently away. "Oelph," she said, sniffing back her tears. "You will not forget that Doctor Hilbier is more formal in his approach than I. I have respect for him but he—"

"Mistress, I will not forget anything you have told me."

"Good. Good. Here." She reached into her jacket. She presented me with a sealed envelope. "I have arranged with the Mifeli clan that you have an account with them. This is the authority. You may use the earnings on what pleases you, though I hope you will do a little experimentation of the type I taught you—"

"Mistress!"

"—but the capital, I have instructed the Mifelis, the capital only becomes yours when you achieve the title of Doctor. I would advise you to buy a house and premises, but—"

"Mistress! An account? What? But what, where?" I said, genuinely astonished. She had already left me what she thought might come in useful to me—and what I might be able to store in a single room in the house of my new mentor, Doctor Hilbier—from her supplies of medicines and raw materials.

"It is the money the King gave me," she said. "I don't need it. It is yours. Also, there is in the envelope the key to my journal. It contains all the notes and the descriptions of my experiments. Please use it as you see fit."

"Oh, mistress!"

She took my hand in hers and squeezed. "Be a good doctor, Oelph. Be a good man. Now, quickly," she said, with a desperately sad and unconvincing laugh, "to save our tears before we both become hopelessly dehydrated, eh? Let us—"

"And if I became a doctor, mistress?" I asked, in a far more collected and cold manner than I would have imagined I was capable of at such a moment. "If I became a doctor and used some of the money to mirror your trip, and come to Drezen?"

She had started to turn away. She turned halfway back, and looked at the wooden decking of the quay. "No, Oelph. No, I . . . I don't think I'll be there." She looked up and smiled a brave smile. "Goodbye, Oelph. Fare well."

"Goodbye, mistress. Thank you."

I will love you for ever.

I thought the words, and could have said them, might have said them, perhaps nearly said them, but in the end did not say them. It may be that that was the unsaid thing even I did not know I had thought of saying that let me retain a shred of self-respect.

She walked slowly up the first half of the steep-set gangplank, then lifted her head, lengthened her stride, straightened her back and strode up and on to the great galleon, her dark hat disappearing somewhere beyond the black webbing of the ropes, all without a backward glance.

* * *

I walked slowly back up the city, my head down, my tears dripping down my nose and my heart in my boots. Several times I thought to look up and round, but each time I told myself the ship would not have sailed yet. All the time I kept hoping, hoping, hoping that I would hear the slap of running, booted feet, or the doubled thud of a pursuing sedan chair, or the rattle of a hire carriage and the snort of its team, and then her voice.

The cannon went for the bell, echoing round the city and causing birds to flap and fly all over in wheeling dark flocks, crying and calling, and still I did not look round because I judged that I was in the wrong part of the city to see the harbour and the docks, and then when I finally did look up and back I realised I had walked too far up into the city and I was almost in Market Square. I could not possibly see the galleon from here, not even its top-most sails.

I ran back down the way I had come. I thought I might be too late, but it was not too late, and by the time I could see the docks again, there was the great vessel, all bulbous and stately and moving towards the harbour entrance under the tow of two long cutters full of men heaving on stout oars. There were still many people on the dockside, waving at the passengers and crew gathered near the stern of the departing galleon. I could not see the Doctor on the ship.

I could not see her on the ship!

I ran around the dockside like a mad man, looking for her. I searched each face, studied every expression, tried to analyse each stance and gait, as though in my lovelorn lunacy I really believed that she had indeed decided to quit the ship and stay here, stay with me, this whole apparent departure just a maddeningly extended joke, and yet, on relinquishing the ship, for a jest had decided to disguise herself, just to taunt me further.

The galleon slipped out to sea almost without me noticing, letting the cutters come creasing back across the waves while she, beyond the harbour wall, let drop her creamy fields of sail and took the wind about her.

After that, the people drifted away from the quay until there were just a couple of sobbing women left, one standing clutched in about herself, her face quite covered by her hands, the other squatting, face raised to stare emptily at the skies while the tears coursed down her cheeks in silence.

... And I, staring out at the gap between the harbour light-towers towards the distant line that was the jagged far circumference of Crater Lake. And there I stood, and wandered, stunned and unsteady, shaking my head and muttering to myself, and started to leave several times but could not, and so drifted back towards the quayside, assailed by the treacherous sparkle of the water that had let her slip away from me, buffeted by the wind that was blowing her further on her journey with each beat of my heart and hers, and attended by the caustic cries of wheeling sea birds and the quiet and hopeless sobs of women.

24

THE BODYGUARD

The bodyguard DeWar woke from a dream of flying. He lay there a moment in the darkness for the few moments it took him to come fully awake, remembering where he was, who he was, what he was, and what had been happening.

The weight of the knowledge of all that had gone so wrong so recently settled on him like a dozen coats of chain mail thrown one by one upon his bed. He even gave a little groan as he rolled over in the narrow cot and lay with one arm under the back of his head, staring up into the blackness.

The war in Ladenscion had been lost. It was as simple as that. The barons had got all they had ever asked for, and more, by taking it. The

Dukes Simalg and Ralboute were on their way home with the tattered and dispirited remains of their armies.

Lattens had edged a little closer to death, whatever was wrong with him proof against every remedy the physicians could devise.

UrLeyn had sat in on one war council, just yesterday, once the full extent of the catastrophe in Ladenscion had revealed itself through the jumble of reports and coded messages, but he had stared down at the table surface throughout, uttering only monosyllables mostly. He showed a little more animation and a spark of his old self when he had roundly condemned Simalg and Ralboute for the whole débâcle, but even that tirade, towards the end, had seemed lacklustre and forced, as though he could not maintain even his anger.

It had been decided that there was little that could be done. The armies would return and the wounded would have to be cared for. A new hospital would be set up to this purpose. The army would be reduced to the minimum necessary for the defence of Tassasen. There had already been disturbances in the streets in a handful of cities when people who had in the past only grumbled over the increased taxes required for the war had rioted when they heard it had all been for nothing. Taxes would have to come down to keep the populace at peace and so a number of projects would have to be suspended or abandoned. At some point negotiations with the victorious barons would have to be entered into, to regularise matters once the situation had stabilised.

UrLeyn nodded all this through, seemingly uninterested in it all. The others could take care of it. He had left the council of war to return to his son's bedside.

UrLeyn still would not let the servants into his apartments, where he passed almost all his time. He spent a bell or two at Lattens' side each day, and visited the harem only erratically, often just talking with the older concubines and especially with the lady Perrund.

DeWar felt a damp patch on his pillow, where his cheek had lain during the night. He turned over on his side, absently touching the fold in the head bolster which he must have dribbled on to during the night. How undignified we become in our sleep, he thought, rubbing the damp triangle of material between his fingers. Perhaps he had been sucking it while he slept, he thought. Did one do that? Did people do such a thing? Perhaps children—

He leaped out of bed, pulled on his hose, teetering one-legged and cursing, fastened his sword belt across his waist and grabbed his shirt as he kicked the door open and raced through the early morning shadows of his small living room and out into the corridor, where startled servants had been snuffing the candles. He ran quickly, bare feet thudding on the wooden boards. He pulled his shirt on as best he could.

He was looking for a guard, to tell him to follow him, but there were none to be seen. Rounding a corner that would take him towards Lattens' sick room, he crashed into a servant carrying a breakfast tray, sending the girl and the tray tumbling across the floor. He shouted back an apology.

There was a guard at Lattens' door, slumped asleep on a chair. DeWar kicked the seat and shouted at the man as he burst through the door.

The nurse looked up from the window where she had been sitting reading. She looked with widened eyes at DeWar's bare chest revealed by the half-tucked shirt. Lattens lay still in his bed. A basin and a cloth lay on the table by his head. The nurse seemed to shrink back a little as DeWar strode across the room to the boy's bed. DeWar heard the guard come in behind him. He turned his head briefly and said, "Hold her," and nodded at the nurse, who flinched. The guard moved towards the woman, uncertain.

DeWar went to Lattens' side. He touched his neck and felt a weak pulse. Clutched in the boy's fist was the pale yellow scrap of material that was his comforter. DeWar prised it from his hand as gently as he could, turning to watch the nurse as he did so. The guard stood at her side, one hand clamped over her wrist.

The nurse's eyes went wide. Her free arm flailed at the guard, who kept a hold of her and eventually succeeded in grabbing it and bringing it under control. She tried to kick him but he twirled her round and forced her arm up her back until she doubled over and screamed, her face level with her knees.

DeWar inspected the sucked end of the comforter while the guard looked on, mystified, and the woman gasped and wept. DeWar sucked tentatively at the piece of material. There was a taste. It was slightly sweet and a little acrid at the same time. He spat on the floor, then knelt down on one knee so that he could look into the nurse's reddened face. He held the comforter in front of the woman.

"Is this how the boy's been poisoned, madam?" he asked softly.

The woman stared cross-eyed at the scrap of material. Tears and snot dribbled down her nose. Her jaw was clenching and unclenching. After a few moments she nodded.

"Where is the solution?"

"Uh—under the window seat," the nurse said, her voice shaking.

"Hold her there," DeWar told the guard quietly. He went to the window and threw off the cushion in the seat set into the thickness of the wall, pulled open a wooden flap and reached inside. He threw aside toys and a few clothes until he found a small opaque jar. He brought it over to the nurse.

"Is this it?"

She nodded.

"Where does it come from?"

She shook her head. He took out his long knife. She screamed, then shook and struggled in the guard's grip until he tightened it and she hung gasping again. DeWar put the knife very close to her nose. "The lady Perrund!" she screamed. "The lady Perrund!"

DeWar froze. "What?"

"The lady Perrund! She gives me the jars! I swear!"

"I am not convinced," DeWar said. He nodded to the guard, who forced the woman's arm further up her back. She shrieked in pain.

"It's true! The truth! It's the truth!" she screamed.

DeWar sat back on his heel. He looked at the guard holding the woman and shook his head once. The man relaxed his hold on the nurse again. The woman sobbed, her whole doubled-up body shaking with the effort. DeWar put the knife away and frowned. Another couple of uniformed men came thundering into the room, swords readied.

"Sir?" said one, taking in the scene.

DeWar stood. "Guard the boy," he told the pair who had just entered. "Take her to Guard Commander ZeSpiole," he instructed the man holding the nurse. "Tell him Lattens has been poisoned and she is the poisoner."

DeWar tucked his shirt in as he strode quickly towards UrLeyn's apartments. Another guard, also alerted to the commotion, came running up to him. DeWar sent him off with the man taking the nurse to ZeSpiole.

There was one guard at UrLeyn's door. DeWar drew himself up, starting to wish he had taken the time to put on all his clothes. He had to see UrLeyn no matter what orders he might have left, and this guard's help might be needed to effect entry. He assumed what he hoped was his most commanding tone. "Straighten up there!" he barked. The guard jerked upright. "Is the Protector inside?" DeWar demanded, scowling and nodding at the door.

"No, sir!" the guard shouted.

"Where is he?"

"Sir, he went to the harem, I think, sir! He said you need not be informed, sir!"

DeWar looked at the closed door for a moment. He began to turn and move away, then stopped. "When did he go there?"

"About a half-bell ago, sir!"

DeWar nodded, then moved away. At the corner, he started running. Two more guards joined him when he called them. They headed for the harem.

The double doors to the three-domed receiving room slammed back against the walls on either side. There were a couple of concubines in the softly lit hall, talking to members of their families and sharing a light breakfast with them. All fell silent when the doors crashed open. The chief eunuch Stike sat like a sleepy white mountain in his pulpit raised near the middle of the room. His face cleared of sleep and his brows met and creased as the doors swung slowly back from their twinned impact. DeWar sprinted across the room towards the doors leading to the harem proper, the two guards trailing in his wake.

"No!" bellowed the chief eunuch. He rose and started to wobble down the steps.

DeWar reached the harem doors, wrenching at them. They were locked. Stike came lurching over the floor towards him, wagging his finger. "No, Mr. DeWar!" he cried. "You do not go in there! Not ever, in any event, but especially not when the Protector himself is in there!"

DeWar looked at the two guards who had followed him. "Hold him," he told them. Stike screamed as they tried to take hold of him. The eunuch was surprisingly strong, and each of his leg-thick arms knocked over the guards once each before they could secure him. He cried out for help as DeWar tore at his white robes, looking for and finding the set of keys he knew was there. He cut the keys from the struggling giant's belt, tried one, then another, before the third key slipped in and turned and the doors opened.

"No!" wailed Stike, almost pulling himself free from the two guards. DeWar looked around quickly, but there was nobody else who could help. He pulled the key out and took the full set with him as he entered the inner harem. Behind him, the two guards struggled to contain the mighty rage of the chief eunuch.

DeWar had never been here before. He had, however, looked at the layout of the place on drawings, so knew where he was, even if he did not know where UrLeyn was.

He ran down a short corridor to another set of doors, Stike's anguished cries and entreaties still ringing in his ears. There was a round internal courtyard beyond, gently lit by a single translucent dome of plaster high above. The glowing space rose on three colonnaded levels. A small fountain played in the centre and couches and seats were scattered about its floor. Girls in various states of dress and undress stood or doubled up where they lounged, yelping and screaming when they saw DeWar. A eunuch leaving a room off to one side of the lowest colonnaded level saw him and shouted. He waved his arms and came running up to DeWar, slowing and stopping only when he saw that DeWar held a sword.

"The lady Perrund," DeWar said quickly. "The Protector."

The eunuch stared as though hypnotised at the tip of the sword, for all that it was a couple of strides away from him. He raised one shaking hand towards the pale dome above.

"They are in," he said in a quiet, shaking whisper, "the top-most level, sir, in the small court."

DeWar looked around and saw the stairs. He ran for them, then in a spiral up them, to the top. There were ten or so doors arranged all around the highest level, but across the well of the courtyard he could see a wider entrance which formed a truncated corridor with double doors at its end. He ran, breathing hard now, round the gallery to the short hallway and the twinned doors. They were locked. The second key he tried opened them.

He found himself in another domed internal courtyard. This one had but a single level, and the columns supporting the roof and the translucent plaster dome were of a more delicate turn than those in the main court. There was a fountain and a pool in the centre of this yard too, which at first sight appeared to be deserted. The fountain was in the shape of three intertwined maidens, delicately sculpted from pure white marble. DeWar sensed movement behind the pale carvings of the fountain. Behind this, on the far side of the court, beyond the columns, one door lay ajar.

The fountain splashed, tinkling. It was the only sound in the wide, circular space. Shadows moved on the polished marble of the floor, near the fountain. DeWar glanced behind him, then walked forward and round.

The lady Perrund knelt before the fountain's raised pool, washing her hands slowly and methodically. Her good hand massaged and wiped at the wasted hand, which lay floating just under the surface of the water like the limb of a drowned child.

She was dressed in a thin gown of red. It was semi-transparent, and the light from the glowing plaster dome above fell down across her dishevelled blond hair and picked out her shoulders, breasts and hips within the gauzy material. She did not look up when DeWar appeared round the side of the fountain. Instead she concentrated on washing her hands, until she was satisfied. She lifted the wasted limb out of the water and placed it gently by her side, where it hung, limp and thin and pale. She rolled the flimsy red sleeve down over it. Then she looked slowly round and up at DeWar, who had approached to within a few steps, his face pale and terrible and full of fear.

Still she did not say a word, but looked slowly round at the door which lay open behind her, opposite the double doors through which DeWar had entered.

DeWar moved quickly. He pushed the door open with the pommel of his sword and looked into the room. He stood there for some time. He backed away, until his shoulder hit one of the columns supporting the roof of the room. The sword hung loose in his hand. His head lowered until his chin rested on the white shirt over his chest.

Perrund watched him for a moment, then turned away. Still kneeling, she dried her hands as best she could on her thin gown, looking at the rim of the fountain's bowl, a hand or so in front of her eyes.

Suddenly DeWar was at her side, standing by her wasted arm, his bare feet by her calf. The sword came slowly down to rest on the marble rim of the fountain's bowl, then slid with a grating noise near to her nose. It dipped, and the blade went under her chin. The metal was cold on her skin. A gentle pressure lifted her face until she was looking up at him. The sword remained pressed against her throat, cold and thin and sharp.

"Why?" he asked her. There were, she saw, tears in his eyes.

"Revenge, DeWar," she said quietly. She had thought that if she could speak at all, her voice would quiver and shake and quickly break and leave her sobbing, but her voice was steady and unstrained.

"For what?"

"For killing me, and my family, and for raping my mother and my sisters." She thought her own voice sounded much less affected than DeWar's. She sounded reasonable, almost unconcerned, she thought.

He stood looking down at her, his face wet with tears. His chest was coming and going inside the loosely tucked and still unbuttoned shirt. The sword at her throat, she noticed, did not move.

"The King's men," he said, his voice catching. The tears continued to stream.

She wanted to shake her head, though she was worried that the slightest movement would cut her skin. But then he would be doing that soon enough anyway, if she was lucky, she thought, and so, tentatively, she did shake her head. The pressure of the sword blade across her throat did not waver, but she avoided cutting herself.

"No, DeWar. Not the King's men. His men. Him. His people. He and his cronies, those closest to him."

DeWar stared down at her. The tears were fewer now. They had made a damp patch on the white shirt, below his chin.

"It was all as I have told you, DeWar, except that it was the Protector and his friends, not one of the old nobles still loyal to the King. UrLeyn killed me, DeWar. I thought I would return the compliment." She opened her eyes wide and let her gaze fall to the blade of the sword in front of her. "May I beg you to be quick, for the friends we once were?"

"But you *saved* him!" DeWar shouted. Still the sword barely moved.

"Those were my orders, DeWar."

"Orders?" He sounded incredulous.

"When what had happened to my town and my family and to me had happened, I wandered away. I found a camp, one night, and offered myself to some soldiers, for food. They all took me too, and I did not care, because I knew then that I had become dead. But one was cruel and wanted me in a way I did not want to be taken, and I found that once one was dead it was very easy indeed to kill. I think they would have killed me in return for his death, and that would have been that, and perhaps the better for all of us, but instead their officer took me away. I was brought to a fortress over the border, in Outer Haspidus, mostly manned by Quience's men but commanded by forces loyal to the old King. I was treated kindly, and there I was introduced to the art of being a spy and an assassin." Perrund smiled.

If she had been alive, she thought, her knees, on the cold white marble tiles, would be hurting a little by now, but she was dead and so they troubled somebody else. DeWar's face was still streaked with tears. His eyes stared, seeming to bulge in their sockets. "But I was ordered to bide my time, by King Quience himself," she told him. "UrLeyn was to die, but not at the height of his fame and power. I was commanded that I must do everything I could to keep him alive until his utter ruin had been contrived."

She gave a small, shy smile and moved her head fractionally to look at her wasted arm. "I did. And in the process I became above suspicion."

There was a look of utter horror on DeWar's face. It was, she thought, like looking at the face of somebody who had died in agony and despair.

She had not seen, or wanted to see, UrLeyn's face. She had waited until, having been given the news she claimed to have been called away to receive, he had fallen into a fit of sobbing and buried his face in the pillow, then she had risen, lifted a heavy jet vase in her one good hand and brought it crashing down on the back of his skull. The sobbing had stopped. He had not moved again or made a further sound. She'd slit his throat for good measure, but she had done that while straddling his back, and still she had not seen his face.

"Quience was behind it all," DeWar said. His voice sounded strangled, as though he had a sword at his throat, not she at hers. "The war, the poisoning."

"I do not know, DeWar, but I imagine so." She looked deliberately down at the sword blade. "DeWar." She looked up into his eyes with a hurt, pleading expression. "There is no more I can tell you. The poison was delivered by innocents to the Paupers' Hospital, where I received it. Nobody I know knew what it was or what it was for. If you have the nurse as well, you have the totality of our conspiracy. There is no more to tell." She paused. "I am already dead, DeWar. Please, if you would, finish the job. I am suddenly so weary." She let the muscles supporting her head relax so that her chin rested on the blade. It, and through it DeWar, was now taking all the weight of her head and its memories.

The metal, warm now, dropped slowly away from beneath her, so that she had to stop herself falling forwards and striking the rim of the fountain pool. She looked up. DeWar, his own head hanging down, was sliding the sword back into its scabbard.

"I told him the boy was dead, DeWar!" she said angrily. "I lied to him before I crushed his filthy skull and slit his scrawny old-man's throat!" She struggled to her feet, her joints protesting. She went to DeWar and took his arm with her good hand. "Would you leave me to the guard and the questioner? Is that your judgment?"

She shook him, but he did not respond. She looked down, then grabbed at the nearest weapon, his long knife. She pulled it from its sheath. He looked alarmed and took two rapid steps backwards, away from her, but he could have stopped her taking it, and he had not.

"Then I'll do it myself!" she said, and brought the knife quickly up to her throat. His arm was a blur. She saw sparks in front of her face. Her hand began to sting almost before her eyes and mind had registered what had happened. The knife he had knocked from her hand smacked into a wall and fell with a metallic clatter to the marble floor. The sword hung in his hand again.

"No," he said, moving towards her.

EPILOGUE

I t strikes me, having written this, how little we can ever know.

The future is by its very nature unfathomable. We can predict a very little way into it indeed with any reliability, and the further we attempt to see into what has not yet happened, the more foolish we later realise we have been—with the benefit of hindsight. Even the most obviously predictable events, which seem the most likely to occur, can prove fickle. When the rocks fell from the sky back when I was a child, did millions of people the previous evening not believe that the suns would rise as usual, on schedule, the following morning? And then the rocks and the fire fell from the sky, and for whole countries the suns did not rise that day, and indeed for many millions of people they would never rise again.

The present is in some ways no more sure, for what do we really know about what is happening now? Only what is happening immediately around us. The horizon is the usual maximum extent of our ability to appreciate the moment, and the horizon is far away, so events there must be very large for us to be able to see them. Besides, in our modern world the horizon is in reality not the edge of the land or the sea, but the nearest hedge, or the inside of a city wall or the wall of the room we inhabit. The greater events in particular tend to happen somewhere else. The very instant that the rocks and the fire fell from the sky, when over half the world woke up to chaos, on the far side of the globe all was well, and it took a moon or more before the sky darkened with unusual clouds.

When a king dies, the news might take a moon to travel to the furthest corners of his kingdom. It might take years to travel to countries on the far side of the ocean, and in some places, who knows, it might slowly stop being news at all as it travels, becoming instead recent history, and so barely worth the mentioning when travellers exchange the latest developments, so that the death that shook a country and unseated a dynasty only arrives centuries later, as a short passage in a history book. So the present, I repeat, is in some ways no more knowable than the future, for it takes the passage of time for us to know what is happening at any given moment.

The past, then? Surely there we can find certainty, because once something has happened it cannot un-happen, it cannot be said to change. There may be further discoveries which throw a new light on what has happened, but the thing itself cannot alter. It must stay fixed and sure and definite and therefore introduce some certainty into our lives.

And yet how little historians agree. Read the account of a war from one side and then from the other. Read the biography of a great man written by one who has come to despise him, then read his own account. Providence, talk to two servants about the same event that same morning in the kitchen and you may well be told two quite different tales, in which the wronged becomes the wrong-doer and what seemed obvious from one telling seems suddenly quite impossible given the other.

A friend will tell a story which involves the two of you in such a way that you know it did not happen so at all, but the way he tells it is more amusing than the reality, or reflects better on the two of you, and so you say nothing, and soon others will tell the story, altered again, and before long you may find yourself telling it the way you know for a certainty it simply did not happen.

Those of us who keep journals occasionally find we have, with no malice or thought of tale or reputation enhancement whatsoever, remembered something quite erroneously. We may for a goodly part of our lives have been giving a perfectly plain account of some past occurrence, one that we are quite sure of and seem to remember very well indeed, only to come across our own written account of it, recorded at the time, and find that it did not happen the way we remembered it at all!

So we can never be sure of anything, perhaps.

And yet we must live. We must apply ourselves to the world. To do so we have to recall the past, attempt to foresee the future and cope with the demands of the present. And we struggle through, somehow, even if in the process—perhaps just to retain what we can of our sanity—we convince ourselves that the past, present and future are much more knowable than they really are or can ever be.

So, what happened?

I have spent the rest of a long life returning to the same few instants, without reward.

I think there is not a day when I do not think back to those few moments in the torture chamber of the palace of Efernze in the city of Haspide.

I was not unconscious, I am sure of that. The Doctor only convinced me that I was for a short while. Once she had gone, and I had recovered from my grief, I became more and more certain that precisely the amount of time which I thought had passed then, had passed. Ralinge was on the iron bed, poised to take her. His assistants were a few steps away, I cannot recall exactly where. I closed my eyes to spare myself the awful moment, and then the air filled with strange noises. A few moments—just a handful of heartbeats at the most, on that I would stake my life—and there they all were, the three of them, violently dead, and the Doctor already released from her bonds.

How? What could possibly move with such speed to do such things?

Or, what trick of will or mind could be employed to make them do such things to themselves? And how was she able to appear so serene in the moments immediately thereafter? The more I think back to that interlude between the deaths of the torturers and the arrival of the guards, when we sat side by side in the small barred cell, the more sure I become that she somehow knew that we would be saved, that the King would suddenly find himself at death's door and she would be summoned to save him. But how could she have been so calmly certain?

Perhaps Adlain was right, and there was sorcery at work. Perhaps the Doctor had an invisible bodyguard who could leave egg-sized bumps on the heads of knaves and slip unnoticed behind us into the dungeon to butcher the butchers and release the Doctor from her manacles. It almost seems like the only rational answer, yet it is the most fanciful of all.

Or perhaps I did sleep, swoon, or become unconscious or whatever you like to call it. Perhaps my certainty is misplaced.

What more is there to tell? Let me see.

Duke Ulresile died, in hiding, in Brotechen province, a few months after the Doctor left us. It was a simple cut from a broken plate, they say, which led to blood poisoning. Duke Quettil died soon afterwards, too, from a wasting disease which affected all the extremities and turned them necrotic. Doctor Skelim was unable to do anything.

I became a doctor.

King Quience ruled another forty years, in exceptionally good health until the very end.

He left only daughters, so now we have a queen. I find this less troubling than I would have thought.

Lately they have taken to calling the Queen's late father Quience the Good, or sometimes Quience the Great. I dare say one or other will have been settled on by the time anybody comes to read this.

I was his personal physician for the last fifteen years, and the Doctor's training and my own discoveries made me, by all accounts, the best in the land. Perhaps, indeed, one of the best in the world, for when, partly due to the ambassadorship of gaan Kuduhn, more frequent and reliable links with the archipelagic republic of Drezen were established, we discovered that while our antipodean cousins rivalled and indeed even exceeded us in many ways, they were not quite so advanced in medicine, or indeed anything else, as the Doctor had implied.

Gaan Kuduhn came to live amongst us and became something of a father to me. Later he became a good friend and spent a decade as ambassador to Haspidus. A generous, resourceful and determined man, he confessed to me once that there was only one thing he had ever set his wits to that he had failed to accomplish, and that was trying to track down the Doctor, or indeed hunt down exactly where she had come from.

We could not ask her, for she disappeared.

One night in the sea of Osk, the *Plough of the Seas* was running before the wind past a line of small, uninhabited islands, bound for Cuskery. Then the glowing green apparition that mariners call chain-fire began to play about the rigging of the ship. All were at first amazed, but then they became in fear of their lives, for not only was the chain-fire brighter and more intense than anything the sailors could recall seeing in the past, but the wind increased suddenly and threatened to tear the sails, bring down the masts or even turn the great galleon over entirely.

The chain-fire disappeared as suddenly as it had arrived, and the wind fell back to the strong and steady force it had been before. By and by, all but those on watch returned to their cabins. One of the other passengers remarked they had not been able to wake the Doctor to come to see the display in the first place, though nobody thought much of this—the Doctor had been invited to dine with the vessel's captain that evening, but had sent a note declining the invitation, citing an indisposition due to special circumstances.

By the next morning it was realised she was gone. Her door was locked from the inside and had to be forced. The scuttles were screwed open for ventilation, but were too small for her to have squeezed through. Apparently all her belongings, or at any rate the great majority of them, were still there in the cabin. They were packed up and were supposed to be sent on to Drezen, but unsurprisingly they disappeared during the passage.

Gaan Kuduhn, hearing all this, like I, nearly a year later, became fixed upon letting her family know what had happened to her and what good she had done in Haspidus, but for all his enquiries on the island of Napthilia and in the city of Pressel, including some which he made himself on a visit there, and despite the numerous occasions when he seemed on the very brink of discovering her nearest ones, he was always frustrated, and never did find anybody who had actually met or known the woman we knew as Doctor Vosill. Still, I think that was one of the few things that irked him on his death bed, and there was, in balance, an extraordinarily influential and productive life to look back on.

The old Guard Commander Adlain suffered badly towards the end of his allotment of seasons. I think what consumed him was something like the growing disease that had taken the slaver Tunch, all those years earlier.

I was able to alleviate the pain but in the end it became too much for him. My old master told me, he swore truly, that indeed, as I had always suspected, he had been the officer who had rescued me from the wreck of my home and the dead arms of my parents in the smoking ruins of the city of Derla, but that he had taken me to the orphanage in a fit of guilt, for it had been he who had killed my mother and father and burned their house. Now, he said, from the clawing depths of his agony, I would want to kill him.

I chose not to believe him, but I did what I could to hasten his end, which came, peacefully, less than a bell later. His mind must have been going, of course, for if I had believed for a moment what he had told me, I think I would have been tempted to have left him to suffer.

Also before he died Adlain begged me, knowing he was on his death bed, to tell him what had really happened in the torture chamber that evening. He tried to joke that if Quience had not turned the questioning chamber into a wine cellar shortly after the Doctor left us, he might have been tempted to have me interrogated there, just to discover the truth. I think he was joking. It saddened me to have to tell him that I had already, in my reports to him, told him everything that had occurred to the limit of my recollection and descriptive ability.

I have no idea whether he believed me or not.

* * *

And so I am old now, and will lie on my own death bed before a few more years are out. The Kingdom is at peace, we prosper, and there is even what the Doctor would, I think, have called Progress. To me fell the immense privilege of being the first Principal of the Medical University of Haspide. I also shouldered the happy duty of being the third President of the Royal College of Physicians, and later served as a city counsellor, when I was in charge of the committee overseeing the construction of the King's Charitable Hospital and the Infirmary For The Freed. I am proud that one of such lowly birth was able to serve his King and his people in so many different ways during a time of such improvement.

There are still wars, naturally, though not recently in the vicinity of Haspidus. Even yet the three so-called Empires dispute, though with little result save to leave the rest of the world free from Imperial tyranny and so able to thrive in its own various ways. Our navy seems to fight sea battles every now and again, but as they are usually far away and we are as a rule victorious it is as if they do not really count as warfare. Going further back, the barons of Ladenscion had to be taught that who helps them resist one ruler might take it ill when they attempt to forgo all rule. There was civil war in Tassasen, of course, following the death of the Regicide UrLeyn, and King YetAmidous proved a poor leader, though young King Lattens (well, he is not so young any more, I admit, but he still seems young to me) made good most of the ill, and rules well, if quietly, to this day. I am told he is something of a scholar, which is no bad thing in a king, providing it is not taken to excess.

But that was a long time ago. All of this was.

The tale of the concubine Perrund, which forms the counterpoint to my own, and which I have included here with almost no amendment save where her taste foundered occasionally on the skerries of overly ornate prose, I searched out myself, after reading a version in the form of a play which I discovered in another bibliophile's library here in Haspide.

I chose to end her tale where I did because it is after that point that the two versions diverge most violently. The first version I read, in the guise of a drama in three acts, had the bodyguard DeWar running the lady through with his sword to revenge his dead master and then returning to his home in the Half-Hidden Kingdoms, where he was revealed in his true identity as a prince who had been spurned by his father due to an unfortunate but honourable misunderstanding. A death-bed reconciliation, decorated with pretty speeches, was effected with the expiring King and DeWar reigned well thereafter. I admit I find this the more morally satisfying ending.

The version which purported to be by the lady's own hand—and which she claimed she only committed to paper to counter the sensationalised untruths of the dramatic edition—could hardly have been more different. In it, the bodyguard whose trust she had just violated and whose master she had most cruelly done to death, took her by the hand (from which she had barely finished washing their master's blood) and led her out of the harem. They told those waiting nervously outside that UrLeyn was well, but sleeping deeply, at last, as though he already knew the cause of the boy's illness had been discovered.

DeWar said he would take the concubine Perrund to Guard Commander ZeSpiole's offices to confront the nurse who had accused her. Falsely, he suspected. DeWar apologised to chief eunuch Stike and handed him back his keys. He told some of the assembled guards to remain where they were and the rest to go back to their normal posts and tasks. He led the lady Perrund away, politely but firmly.

They were seen leaving the palace by the groom who supplied them with mounts, and observed leaving the city by a variety of honest citizens.

It was about the time they were galloping through the city's northern gate that Stike tried to open the doors into the small court, on the top-most level of the harem.

The key would not fit properly into the lock, in which something appeared to be lodged.

The doors were broken down. The foreign body which had been inserted into the lock after the doors had been secured proved to be a piece of marble in the shape of a little finger, broken from one of the maidens in the fountain in the centre of the raised pool in the little court.

UrLeyn's body was discovered in the bedroom off the court. His blood saturated the sheets. His body was quite cold.

DeWar and Perrund were never caught. They made their way after unrecounted adventures to Mottelocci, in the Half-Hidden Kingdoms, where DeWar, surprisingly, was not known at all, but which he knew a great deal about, and where he rapidly established a good name for himself.

The two became merchants, and later founded a bank. Perrund wrote the account from which I have taken half my story. They married, and their sons—and allegedly their daughters too—continue to this day to run a trading enterprise that supposedly rivals that of our own Mifeli clan. The company's symbol, reportedly, is a simple torus, a ring, such as might be cut from one end of a hollow pipe. (This symbol is one half of what I suspect is not the only set of correspondences within and between these two tales, but—considering the implications of these far too bamboozling for this old head to encompass—I have left it to the reader to discover their own points of similarity, draw their own conclusions and blaze their own trails of speculation.)

At any rate, DeWar and Perrund, we are told, both died in the mountains, in an avalanche in a mountain pass, five years ago. The snow and ice of the unforgiving peaks is their only tomb, but as they died after what appears to have been a long and happy life together, I beg to repeat that I prefer the former version of their fates, even if it is not supported by any facts whatsoever.

And now I think my divided tale is finished. I am sure there is much I have not said, much that could justifiably have been added had we—had I—only known a little extra, discovered a trifle more, but, as I have indicated above, sometimes (indeed probably always) one simply has to make do with what there is.

My wife is due to return soon from the market. (Yes, I married, and I love her now as I always have, for her own sake, not for that of my lost love, even if as I will admit she does look just a little like the good Doctor.) She took two of our grandchildren with her to look for presents, and they will expect me to play with them when they come back. I do little real work now I am so old, but still there is a life to be lived.